THE EARTH-TREADER

ALISSA J. ZAVALIANOS

THE EARTH-TREADER

ALISSA J. ZAVALIANOS

This is a work of fiction. Names, characters, places, and incidents either are the product of the author's imagination or are used fictitiously. Any resemblance to actual persons, living or dead, events, or locales is entirely coincidental.

Printed in the United States of America

Cover by Kirk DouPonce
Map and interior art by Chaim Holtjer
Interior formatting by Michelle M. Bruhn
Edited by Jane Maree

ISBN 978-1-7361371-1-6 (paperback)
ISBN 978-1-7361371-0-9 (hardcover)
ISBN 978-1-7361371-2-3 (e-book)

I dedicate this novel to my loving husband.

Thank you for seeing my vision,

for keeping me grounded,

and for letting my creativity soar.

Without you, this story wouldn't have wings.

Rylla's Map
Isles of Norvic's Throne
Serpents Cave
Isles of Norvic
Rélynda's Throne
Rélynda
Kytchidell
Cliffs of Cavalcade
Ocean Basin
Gorse Woode
North Mountains
Wharfs
Ores of Moorland
Wyllunds Throne
Wylland
Goosewyn
The Owls Tree
Heather Fields
The Furrough
Ostglenden's Throne
Ostglenden
Larkug
Thrushwoode Forest
The Great Blue
Mount Egret
Eastern Ridges
Aylabi's Throne
Ivory Valley
The Grove
Rylla's Home
Aylati
The Indigo Tide
N
W
E
S
The Earthen-Crest Kingdoms

Table of Contents

Part One: Woode

Part Two: Earth

Part Three: Sand

Part Four: Stone

Earth-Lore

The Earthen-Crest kingdoms are situated in the Indigo Tide on a large land mass with the Ocean Basin to the left and a larger sea, the Great Blue, to the right. These kingdoms are broken into five provinces, four of which are connected in the shape of a goose's neck known as the mainland: Aylati, Ostglenden, Wyllund, Rélynda, and one which is located fifty miles off Wyllund's western coast in the Ocean Basin: the Isles of Norviç.

Each province possesses a certain stone, only one of its kind: Aylati, the Jade—symbolic of purity of heart and truth; Ostglenden, the Hawk's Eye—symbolic of protection; Wyllund, the Obsidian—symbolic of prophecy and wisdom, Rélynda, the Howlite—symbolic of courage; and the Isles of Norviç, the Larimar—symbolic of peace. The kings representing each province wear these respective gemstones as crests around their necks, symbolizing their roles and duties as leaders of the Earthen-Crest kingdoms.

In addition to these five stones, there are others which are good and full of light but are not rendered as sacred nor as powerful. They are for the common people and are numerous in their kinds.

There are some stones, however—dark stones—not in color but in intent, for they are corrupt and used for selfish purposes and dark deeds; these stones remain unnamed. The wielders of such stones, whose hearts have turned almost blacker than pitch, are often found practicing dark magic; through excessive use, their souls can become entwined with the stones themselves, as if a binding magic has taken place. To use them disturbs and disrupts the course of nature and the earth, creating an imbalance and a widespread Darkness. These stones are forbidden and must remain untouched, and those who possess them, beware!

Prologue

The battlefield was littered with lifeless and broken limbs and voices crying out from every direction. A long-haired man swung his sword before him, hellfire burning in his dark eyes. One by one, he felled his enemies, ignoring pleas for mercy and stabbing his sword in anything that moved. His army followed in his wake.

Wyllund's Heather Fields had never seen such bloodshed.

He was invincible—nothing standing in his way could stop him from taking the Earthen-Crest kingdoms. They would soon be under his control.

Then a blinding light stunned him in place, and he faltered in his charge. The blade of a large broadsword reflected the sun, and as the sword shifted position the wielder came into view. But there wasn't just one man; there were five.

The five men all wielded massive swords and crowns rested atop their heads while crests made of stone hung about their necks.

The blinded man clenched his teeth menacingly, laughing in their direction. "You're foolish—you're only making my job easier." He crouched, settling into a warrior's stance, sword raised over his shoulder to strike and his muscles tense for the pounce. "Once they were finished," he pointed to the fallen soldiers and their commanders, "you all were next!"

The surrounding chaos seemed to diminish all around the battlefield as both sides were desperate for a break in the fight. All eyes turned toward the six men in the middle of the field, waiting for a signal.

"Lord Brennigan, we have come to plead with you. To end this pointless war and restore our lands to peace. Call off your men," one of the kings spoke, his Larimar crest shimmering in the sun.

"Excuse me, *Your Majesty*," Lord Brennigan said in a mocking tone, "I didn't realize the Isles of Norviç had such a coward for a ruler. That's what you get for ruling with peace."

"We ask that you stand down now, Lord Brennigan," the Howlite-crested king spoke as they all stopped within sword reach of the warrior.

"And if I don't?" Lord Brennigan motioned for his soldiers to take up their arms, steeling themselves to keep fighting.

"Then you'll leave us no choice." The tallest king, a Hawk's Eye draped around his neck, nodded to the others.

Each in turn raised their sword to Lord Brennigan's throat, leaving him little room to move.

He spat. "You Earth-Treaders think you're so special, but you're all fools! Nothing can conquer my power, not even death!" Lord Brennigan ducked below their swords and took his own to swipe at the kings' ankles in a wide arc.

The tallest king was one step ahead of him and raised his hands skyward. Mounds of thick earth and rock shot forth from the ground in a circular barricade, blocking Lord Brennigan's blows.

His eyes betrayed only a moment of concern before he tried for another attack. He dodged the Howlite king's sword and retaliated with his own, slicing the king's cheek. Lord Brennigan evaded another blow and landed behind the king with the Jade crest, his sword ready to strike. He raised his sword, about to stab him when something green snagged his arm. It was a thick, leafy vine. Lord Brennigan looked to his right. There stood the Obsidian-crested king with his hand outstretched toward the earth, muttering words under his breath.

Caught off guard and unable to use his sword, more vines wound their way up his legs. He was forced to his knees, unable to move save for his left arm.

The kings closed in around him, swords at the ready.

"You'll never get rid of me," Lord Brennigan uttered through clenched teeth. "This isn't the end. I'm more powerful than you can imagine!" He reached toward his neck and used his hand to pull out a necklace from beneath his shirt. He grasped the black stone pendant infused with red, fingers clawed around it like a cage. He quickly whispered some unintelligible speech and writing appeared on the surface, scrawling across in order to disappear into the blackness once more.

The kings were taken by surprise at his speed, but another vine burst up from the ground and took hold of his hand, wrenching his grip from the stone.

"It's too late!" Lord Brennigan let out a maniacal laugh.

"For you…" The Howlite king, blood dripping from his cut, raised his sword to Lord Brennigan's throat. "Any last words?"

Lord Brennigan met the kings gaze for gaze. A smile split his features. "I will return, and by then, you will be sorry. You'll see. You *all* will see!"

At that, all five kings raised their free arms higher as their other hands held fast to their swords. The vines grew fuller and squeezed stronger, until the only thing left of Lord Brennigan was his sword.

The kings had won, but as they peered closer, the Howlite king cried out in surprise.

"His crest!" The once black stone had dissolved, fading into nothing. One by one, the other kings' crests disappeared from their necks, as if Lord Brennigan's stone was calling them to follow.

The kings searched the surrounding battlefield, but their attempts were in vain. All the stones had vanished.

Part One:

Woode

Chapter the First

Aylati

MANY YEARS LATER

"...Merry birthday, Rylla!"

The little pastel yellow cottage, situated on a plot of farmland, beamed with celebration as a chorus of two finished their song. Everyone was so filled with joy that even the houseplants and furniture seemed to be in a good mood. All was peaceful in their little village of Aylati. The chickens happily pecked at the low dusty ground, the goat bleated from its pen, and the cows chewed their cud in the nearby fields, lazily watching the sun filter through the clouds.

"It's hard to believe you're eighteen! Where has the time gone?" Rylla's father reached across the table to touch her freckled cheek, pushing strands of loose dark brown curls behind her ear. His other hand held fast to a wooden crutch. "You'll always be my little girl, though in no time you'll be catching right up to Garth and Finn."

The sentiment was bittersweet. Sweet and warm, like the hearth fire that warmed her toes in the cold months and cooked their salted meats in the warm ones; bitter however, with the empty seats at the table where her two older brothers had once sat. Years ago, they had traveled the Earthen-Crest kingdoms serving in Aylati's military, but too soon their few letters faded into silence. Rylla missed them greatly. She made it her secret goal to find them one day, especially for her mother's sake. They should have come home at least once by now.

Still, she did love this house even with its two less occupants. It was small and sturdy and brought a comforting sense of safety. The oaken paneling on the walls and the rugged floors made her feel as though she was out in nature, all the while still retaining the comforts of cushions and soft blankets of the indoors.

"I know, Da." She squeezed his calloused hand and smiled into his brown eyes—eyes that held a certain, quiet strength. "Though I'm hardly a child anymore."

"But the amount of mud you track into the house could say otherwise…riddle me that." A dainty woman a few inches taller than Rylla winked and laughed her into a warm embrace. She was a beautiful woman of refinement and poise, yet there was a gleam of mischief in her hazel eyes. She pushed the fringe of her short brown hair from her forehead. "Though it's nothing a little soap and a rag won't clean up. You keep my hands busy and my heart full, my Sweet. That won't ever change."

The three chatted away the morning, Rylla laughing at jokes from her father and humoring thoughtful analogies from her mother. They shared stories of Rylla's childhood, of Garth and Finn's schemes, and of nostalgic times when the whole family was last together.

Bittersweet. But still beautiful, and Rylla was determined to enjoy it fully. She could tell her parents were trying to do the same.

Eventually, she picked up a knife and cut into the mulberry-cream cobbler, dishing out two pieces for her parents and one for herself. Her mother made the best pastries; for as long as she could remember, these had always been her favorite. Her mother was a wizard in the kitchen; Rylla, on the other hand, hadn't quite mastered the skill, nor patience, for baking.

The morning sunlight cascaded its rays through the window wherever it pleased as Rylla heaped her spoon. It shone bright and warm upon her face as she spooned some mulberry into her mouth, closing her eyes to savor the flavor. Memories of family picnics with sandwiches, cobblers, and stream-fed water came to mind. Garth chewing so loudly one might mistake him for a sheep and Finn stuffing his face to the point of almost getting sick.

Such fond memories were those picnics in the woods. She felt a pull to go back, a call. But something else interrupted her and it sounded like her name.

"Rylla?" her mother's voice entered her thoughts.

"What? Sorry, I was just—what were you saying?"

"How's the pie?" Her mother's eyes were curious and expectant.

"It's delicious! Like how I remember it." Rylla spooned another bite into her mouth, but her gaze drifted back to the window.

"But something else is on your mind. Tell us, my Sweet," her mother prompted. Both her parents took another bite of their pies and waited.

"Whatever happened to that place we used to visit?" Rylla asked, looking outside. The tall pines swayed gently in the wind as a flock of geese sliced through the sky. Her neighbors were tending to their vegetable gardens, and in a few weeks, they'd be knocking on her cottage door and sharing their harvest. That's if the curious squirrels and rabbits didn't get to them first. "It seems I've only just remembered it."

"What place?" Her parents exchanged a glance of interest.

"Where we had all those picnics. The golden sunlight, the stream…" Rylla turned to face them.

"You mean the Grove near the foothills?" her father questioned with a smile.

"Yes! How long has it been since we've visited?" She remembered the day her family had given that special place its name. It had felt like it was theirs because of how often they visited and all the memories that were made.

"I'd say about seven years or so, before Garth and Finn left…" Her mother's expression grew somber at the mention of their leaving; it was a sore spot for them all.

Rylla's heart ached once again. She had to find some way to heal this lonely wound, but how? Even if she found the courage to leave, her parents wouldn't want her traveling the kingdoms to find Garth and Finn. Though they hadn't said as much, Rylla felt that they never wanted her to leave their sight, watching her with an extra dose of protectiveness. Plus, she had enough of her own fears to hold her back. Still, how she longed to be free.

"We haven't been back since," her mother said softly.

"I think I'd like to visit again. I can't explain it, but I feel as if I need to," Rylla said around another mouthful of pie.

Her mother pressed her lips together and her forehead creased, but when Rylla's father placed his hand atop his wife's, the lines on her skin smoothed out and she replaced her thin-lipped smile with a reassuring one.

"As long as you're back before dinner, I don't see why not," her mother began and Rylla released a relieved breath. "I would come, but it's laundry day and I need to make sure the clothes have enough time to dry on the line before it rains." Her mother finished her last bite of pie and gathered all their dishes to wash in the sink.

"How do you know it'll rain?" Rylla glanced once more at the sun-filled sky. There wasn't a cloud in sight.

"When you get to be my age, my Sweet, you just know these things." Her mother's lips quirked into a smile. "I feel it in my knees."

"You and your knees, Clara, it drives me wild." Her father chuckled as he got up, his cane clanking on the floorboards like a third leg, and hugged his wife from behind.

She laughed and playfully swatted at him.

He had been trimming the lemon trees in the orchard last summer, and Maybelle their goat had gotten loose from her pen. She was spooked at the falling branches and bucked her head into the ladder, causing both the ladder and Rylla's father to fall a good ten feet. His leg hadn't been the same since. But seeing her father continue to smile and choose laughter everyday sent surges of pride to Rylla's heart.

He was an inspiration, and right now he was being very affectionate to his wife.

Love is weird.

"I think I'll just leave you two here while I go by myself…" Rylla chuckled and ran to the loft ladder, climbing up to grab her satchel. It was splayed across her messy desk between the papers and maps scattered over the surface.

Her father was a cartographer, and Rylla wanted to learn the trade as well. On most evenings, he would take her to his work station in the basement and show her the boundary lines of the Earthen-Crest kingdoms. They poured over ancient texts and maps together, learning history and battles as well as rulers and customs. Her father had said understanding history was the key to a mapmaker's success, for one should not only draw the lines, but live them.

Together they had worked to create a brand-new map of all the Earthen-Crest kingdoms surrounded by the Indigo Tide. Rylla was an avid learner and had picked it up quickly. This map featured terrain and trails, the thrones and landmarks, and anything else her father thought was important to add. There were even rumored secret passages and caves. They had just completed it yesterday, the ley lines and a compass rose marking the finishing touches.

Not knowing why, Rylla decided to fold this map and place it in her satchel. Something about going back to the Grove felt like an adventure, and she wanted to fit the part. She felt an inexplicable pull, a luring to return to that place where her family had built so many memories, and maybe one day she'd take her map and travel beyond the Grove to find Garth and Finn herself. Though the thought both excited her and made her nervous—she'd never left home before and most likely never would if her parents had any say.

She also grabbed her drawing book and a pencil. She turned toward the door then paused and eyed her dark blue cloak—it was long, warm, and best of all, water resistant. But what she liked most was the intricate pattern of golden wings sewn into the back. They were there as a reminder that perhaps one day she would have the courage to fly, seeking the freedom she always craved. The kind she often felt while in the mountains, way up high and perched on the tip of the world like a bird. There she felt no fear. Though it'd been years since she'd actually climbed a mountain—years since she'd been in the Grove. It was time to change that. She shoved the cloak into her satchel and left her room.

Back downstairs, Rylla found her parents talking in the kitchen as she snagged an apple, some rolls, and cheese to place in her bag.

"I'm heading out," Rylla said.

"Wait! A hug for the road," her mother protested. The two of them stopped chatting and embraced Rylla wholeheartedly.

"Have fun and let us know how it looks after all these years," her father said as he wrapped Rylla in his warm embrace. She breathed in the strong scent of paper and ink from his clothes, savoring the familiar smell while her mother snuggly placed her arms around Rylla's shoulders.

"I wonder if the foxglove will still be in bloom!" Her mother daydreamed of plants more often than Rylla could count. She hugged her tighter. "Stay safe, my Sweet, and promise me you'll return soon."

"Okay, okay, you can both let go now," Rylla laughed and headed for the door. "I promise I'll be back—love you!"

"Love you too!" her parents said in unison as they both went back to work.

Rylla left the threshold of her cottage with little idea that she was about to break that promise.

⸙ ⸙ ⸙

The sun was beating so heavily upon Rylla's back that she laughed out loud at the idea of rain. As she walked along the dirt road, she smelt a whiff of something sweet, like lavender or honeysuckle, and was awarded her discoveries with flowers a few paces ahead of her. She waved hello to her neighbors who were continuing their tilling, planting, and weeding—from the looks of the plants, the corn stalks were already growing tall. Other neighbors were doing laundry like her mother, hanging wet clothes on the vacant clothes lines by their houses. A little girl noticed Rylla walking and ran in her direction.

"Rylla, Rylla, Rylla!" the girl, about seven years old with loose blonde curls, called to her.

"Why hello there, little Winnie. What are you up to today?" Rylla stopped and crouched down to her level.

"I made you something for your birthday!" Winnie held out the gift to Rylla. "Do you like it?"

Rylla took hold of the leather strap threaded with stone beads. In its center hung a large golden locket shining like the sun itself. Winnie looked at Rylla's face to gauge her reaction.

"Oh Win, this is beautiful! Thank you. In fact, I'll wear it right now." Rylla took the necklace and placed it over her head, making sure not to snag it on her dark, unruly curls.

"Oh, the yellow looks so nice!" Winnie clapped with delight. "I knew I chose the right beads." She hugged Rylla again. "My Pa said I couldn't be long, so I gotta go."

"Thank you again, Win, I'll see you later!" Rylla returned the hug and watched her skip in the direction of home.

The first time Rylla had met Winnie, she'd been a timid little girl of four, no siblings and hardly a smile. Rylla was out tending to the infamous Maybelle when a curious blonde-haired child peered through the fence. She didn't say a word, but held out a handful of sweet grass for the goat to eat. Rylla had smiled and introduced both herself and the goat, and the three became fast friends. Now Winnie was like a younger sister, and as their friendship grew, so did her smile and confidence.

As Rylla continued her journey to the Grove, she soaked in her surroundings while her feet kicked up dirt from the road. Clouds were now in the sky, looking a little ominous in the distance, but the sun still shone bright and cheery. Meadowlarks and catbirds soared overhead while rabbits dodged into nearby brush. The mouth of the forest path was steadily approaching with the tall trees giving an almost foreboding welcome. The monotony eased her mind into daydreams.

Ever since Rylla was young, her family would often take day trips into the forest, skipping rocks in the rivers and climbing the footpaths to the summit of Mount Egret. Since growing up, she'd always held a fondness for the mountains. She felt that she belonged to them and was never truly free until she was at the top. Being up high gave her a vantage point like a bird's, and she'd determined that Mount Egret was the perfect name for such a place—her reminder that if only she had wings…

Sometimes her family would even camp overnight, spinning under the stars only to fall to the ground and try to count them. The night would end in laughter and toasted bread rolls filled with peach preserves—a family favorite.

Rylla's deep love of learning always stirred a yearning in her heart for adventure and freedom, to explore and travel the Earthen-Crest kingdoms on the maps she studied with her father and to follow in her brothers' footsteps. But that yearning was suppressed by the fear of actually *going*, for that's what one would have to do to begin an adventure. What was really out there? What hidden secrets fell within the boundary lines of her maps? She was a cage unto herself. Besides, her parents wouldn't let her go very far without receiving word from Garth and Finn first.

Nowadays, the most adventure she had in a day was guessing what color eggs the hens would lay.

As Rylla continued deeper into the woods, she was startled out of her reveries by a squirrel who practically scurried over her feet and up into a tree to safety. He paused only a few inches above where Rylla's head was, his breath heaving beneath the soft downy fur of his chest.

"Oh, hello there." Rylla smiled.

Before she could study the creature further, twigs snapped behind her and she twisted about. A speckled deer and her gangly fawn were bounding in the opposite direction of the Grove, fleeing like their hooves were upon hot coals. They disappeared in a trice and a fading rustle, and Rylla turned back to the squirrel only to find him gone.

She glanced around and resumed the path once more, her mind fading back into memories.

She was four and going on an adventure in the woods with her family, when somehow, she got lost. She had seen a squirrel and decided to follow him to his home, hoping to find what he was up to. Upon arriving there, the squirrel seemed to pause outside his burrow as if waiting for her to speak.

She had just placed her hand on the tree's trunk, reaching to say 'hello' when she heard her name being called.

"Here I am!" Rylla had called back. She removed her hand from the tree and sat down until her parents arrived. But as she pulled away from the trunk, a subtle shimmer of gold glistened in the bark.

Her parents eventually found her.

Rylla watched as they emerged through some overgrown brush, eyes wide and gasps on their lips. Rylla was seated on a small patch of grass, a gentle halo of gold wrapping around her like a wispy shawl, trying to converse with the creatures. And when her parents instructed her to rejoin her family, she was reluctant to leave, and the birds and woodland creatures were sad to see her go.

"...And I think I understood him too! He said 'squee, squee...squeee,' which basically means, 'I'm hungry,' I think..." Rylla was relaying the conversation that she'd had with a plump rabbit while her father carried her through the Woode to their camp where her brothers were busy finding sticks for a fire.

"You don't say." Her parents humored her joy and laughed at her imagination. But just before they made it back to camp, her father looked Rylla straight in the eyes, making sure she was listening.

"Rylla," his voice took on a serious and concerned tone, "you can't just wander off like that. You were a ten-minute walk from Mount Egret's foothills. Too far a journey for one so small as yourself. The world isn't full of nice people, and at your age, someone needs to go with you. Do you understand?"

"I understand, Dada," Rylla quietened, eyes stinging. She understood that she was in trouble.

Rylla hadn't known anxiety then, she'd been too young, more adventurous and carefree. But it started out slow—just small shadows.

She recalled more times while in the Woode, between the ages of nine and eleven, where she had stumbled upon a family of foxes, or a lone bear cub, those timid deer, and a vole—because she was old enough to search for campfire sticks like her brothers. She felt the forest had awakened in glistening light on those lone adventures; her ears ready to listen and understand the movements of the earth, her little anxieties dissipating in the breath of the wind.

But for some reason, over time she had forgotten these furry creatures and her love of the Woode. And as she grew in age, she stopped visiting the Grove entirely—especially once her brothers left. And that's when the shadows had grown bigger. It was as if their leaving had sent her into isolation and her parents into over-protective mode. They had lost two sons at once, and because of this, Rylla hadn't tasted freedom in years, her only friends were the shadows in her mind.

But the Grove and Mount Egret were where Rylla felt most alive, most herself, most free, and to ignore it any longer seemed borderline criminal.

So, it was here that Rylla went.

The path seemed familiar enough, though it was more overgrown and covered in thistles since the last time she walked on it. She ducked and contorted her body between the branches as to avoid the prickly briars. Her attempts were futile as a few clung to the fabric of her shirt. Rylla gingerly plucked the prickers free and sent them tumbling amongst the leaves—she knew her mother would make her spend hours picking them out later so as not to disrupt the flow of laundry day.

The trees grew thinner and frailer the further she went, bark peeling off of trunks as heads of snapdragons, clematis, foxglove, and countless plants lay dead on the forest floor, detached from their stems and branches. In the distance, Rylla could make out a small clearing, just big enough to squeeze her body through without getting tangled in the thorns, if she was careful. She ducked through the brush, becoming as small as possible in order to avoid catching her clothes and hair on the sharp projections. The clearing was a lot less spacious than she remembered, and she looked around the Grove uncertainly. This was not the welcome back she had expected.

Something's not right.

An eerie silence filled the air. The ravine no longer babbled and the doves no longer cooed, for there were neither water nor birds to be found. The trees were leafless and crooked like contortionists, the air stale and neglected, and the grass was patchy and browned. The place was empty, an utter void of disappointment, save for a few mossy rocks and the remnants of what was once a fire pit—the one her family had grown so fond of using. Her stomach plummeted like a bird swooping to catch its prey.

Rylla walked to the place where her family used to pitch their tent and stopped. There she turned in a slow circle and sank to her knees, scanning the tree line for any sign of life as a lump formed at the back of her throat.

"It's a sad thing what happened to this place..."

Rylla startled back, her hand flying to her chest. Where had the voice come from? She couldn't tell if it came from within or from someone else. She searched the Grove with her gaze. "Hello?"

And in those peculiar instances where one finds oneself wishing to be heard yet unwishing for it in that same moment, the mysterious voice replied to her from the void.

Chapter the Second

A Certain Magic

"You understand me, don't you?"

Startled, Rylla scanned for the speaker wordlessly. Who would be all the way out here? How had she not seen them before?

The low voice broke through the silence and came a second time.

"I know you must, you responded!" It was persistent.

Dried twigs grated and cracked beneath something moving in the trees and undergrowth. Rylla held her breath and prayed that whatever it was would be harmless.

As the movement became louder, she pinpointed the direction it was coming from and strained to pierce the shadows beneath the dead trees. She fished in her satchel for anything substantial to defend herself, fumbling with her suddenly clammy fingers. There was only her drawing pad and pencil. She would have to use the entire satchel, contents and all, and hope it would work all the same. She stood up, ready to fight or flee, her heart beating wildly inside her chest. Maybe her parents had been right to keep her close all these years.

In that same moment, something came out of the Woode. Something that made her feel completely and utterly ridiculous.

It was only a cat.

"I'm hopeless." Rylla fell back onto the crusty earth, annoyed by her imagination as the tension seeped from her. Spurred on by her overactive thoughts, Rylla's imagination had the tendency to run wild with endless possibilities always swarming around in her mind. Because of this, she had to be careful with what she read—she'd spent too many sleepless nights thinking monsters were lurking outside in the darkness of the lemon orchard.

But the more she thought about it, the cat's appearance still didn't explain the voice.

"Why didn't you answer me?" the voice called out again as if reading her thoughts.

Rylla continued looking around to find its source, but stopped as her gaze settled on the cat. It stared back at her intently. It had a darkened pelt with mottled brown and black patches, and its eyes were a shade of dark blue, tinted with orange and turquoise flecks. She felt drawn to them, yet she held herself back uncertainly. Had the *cat* spoken?

"Did you just…?"

"I did indeed, but why did you not respond?" The cat crossed the Grove toward her with a human-like grace.

How strange.

"But, but…you're a cat!"

"Yes, I am such a thing. And you're a human but you don't see me questioning you." It wasn't until the cat ceased its strut that Rylla realized how large it was, just short of being a bear cub. The feline perched itself on a nearby rock, nonchalantly licking its paw and smoothing the fur down its legs.

"I must have fallen asleep somewhere—this can't be real..." Though Rylla had tried talking to animals as a child, she had never succeeded. Had she? How would one even begin to understand what they were saying? Talking cats did not fit into the realm of possibility.

"Or perhaps it's because you're finally of the age to acknowledge your gifts," the cat said as if it was the simplest thing in the world. Rylla stared at him as if he had five heads. "And if I recall, you used to talk with creatures of the Woode when you were younger."

"Yes, but that was just pretend. I couldn't actually *understand* them...could I?"

"I think you already know the answer to that question." The cat smiled.

Doubtful and hopeful all at once, Rylla tried for boldness.

"What's your name, cat?"

"You can call me Fang. I'm the protector of the forest, or what's left of it." He gazed around the Grove, lingering on the desolate surroundings with a hint of somber pride in his eyes. He met her gaze after a few short moments and continued. "Bound by duty and forbidden to leave, not that I would choose to do so had I the choice..." He paused and curled his long tail about his paws. "And you're Rylla, daughter of Anders and Clara Wayscot, sister to Garth and Finn. I've watched you grow up in this very Woode alongside your brothers."

"You've been here all these years?" Rylla questioned, still in shock that she was talking to a cat. Then a spark of an idea caught her. "Have you any idea where they might be?" Then perhaps she could finally feel free and the shadows of fear wouldn't seem as large.

"I have indeed; it's been my duty for as long as I can remember. One I take very seriously. And I'm sorry to say I do not know the whereabouts of your brothers, but I can assure you they are no longer in Aylati."

Rylla's heart plummeted. *So much for freedom. And if not in Aylati, where?* "If you're the protector, what happened to this place? It looked so different…once," she finished quietly, as if it were a subtle plea for restoration.

"A Darkness has awakened, one that should have been put to rest long ago."

"Darkness?" Rylla raised an eyebrow.

"I've seen you read books, Rylla. You've brought them to the Woode on many occasions: reading while your brothers played cricket or wrestled in the crabgrass. You were quite the studious child at the age of ten."

"But what do books have anything to do with—"

"I'm getting there, just humor me for a few minutes." Fang took a deep breath and pressed on. "What do you know of Earth-Lore?"

"I'm not sure I understand…"

"Think, Rylla, have you ever read anything about this type of magic?"

Rylla thought back to her bookshelf, the overcrowded shelves with little organization. She had volumes of fairy tales, of fiction and fantasy, and volumes of history from her father, some being books on Earth-Lore and magic. Those were always some of her favorites to read with him before bedtime as a child.

"You mean about the stones?" She glanced back at Fang, biting her lip.

"Yes, indeed. What do you know of them?"

"Well…legend says that five kings of old possessed certain stones that they wore around their necks to hold the Earthen-Crest kingdoms together in harmonious rule. But it's just a myth."

"Myth, you say? I think not! It's the very foundation of the kingdoms' existence!" Fang's ears flicked backwards as his tail lashed upon the rock he sat on.

Rylla stared at him wide-eyed, unsure of what to say.

"Listen closely and listen well. There is a Darkness lurking along the Eastern ridges, spreading down into the Ivory Valley toward Ostglenden. And it continues to spread. My brethren have already fled these Woodes, the water has ceased to run its courses, and the vegetation has begun its slow decay. Soon the Darkness will accomplish what it has set out to do, and that's why I've called you here."

"Why is this happening…and what part am I to play in this?" Rylla scanned her surroundings again as she spoke. She needn't ask if his statements were true, the Woode spoke for itself.

"Because you possess a certain magic and know these lands better than most."

She was dumbfounded. *What on the good-tilled soil does he mean?* Rylla tugged nervously on her hair, threading it through her fingers.

"The first thing you need to know, Rylla, is about a race of man—the Earth-Treader kin. The kings of old, those whom you've read about, were Earth-Treaders themselves. This race is not just limited to royalty."

"Earth-Treader kin? You mean those who have the ability to control the earth and other things? I expect you're going to tell me they're real too—"

"I mean exactly that; they are as real as your toes are attached to your feet!" Fang sat up even taller, eyes locking onto Rylla's. "And you're one of them."

Rylla was silent with mouth agape. She felt like she had been wearing the same facial expression for the past half hour. She must truly be crazy now.

"You can't be serious." Rylla's hands twitched in her hair, her fingers getting tangled in one of her curls.

"Yes. You have magic in your blood. Humans born with magical abilities are termed Earth-Treaders—those who can speak to nature and thus have it do their bidding. And to the creatures of the wood, my personal favorite."

"This is ridiculous, I'm a nobody…" Rylla paused to look at her hands. Hands that drew lines on her father's maps, hands that turned the pages of storybooks, hands that were weak and trembling when battling fear. These hands were nothing great. "…magic?"

"This shouldn't surprise you so much. I think you've known all along deep down, always longing for something more. All those attempts at talking to the woodland animals, the desperate seeking of solitude amongst nature, to sit and listen. You have it in you, it just needs to be exercised. See how far you've come already just by talking to me! In no time you'll have the rest of the animal kingdom's speech in your repertoire!" Fang stood on all fours to stretch his legs.

Rylla was getting lightheaded.

"But there's something else you should know. A man, by the name of Lord Brennigan, hated Earth-Treaders. He feared them and coveted their powers. Ultimately, he wanted what he could neither have nor understand.

He had a stone, an unknown one, and he started a battle to end the Earth-Treader race completely, only to fail at the hands of the five kings. At the end of his death, something curious happened to his stone and the crests."

"So, what does this mean?" she questioned, almost afraid to hear more but curious all the same. Rylla had freed her hand from her hair and was playing with the strap on her satchel.

"It means you are the best suited for this mission." Fang regained his former seated position and looked Rylla in the eyes.

"What mission…?" Rylla frowned, a crease forming between her brows. She didn't like where this was going.

"This brings me to my next point. The second thing you need to know is that in that battle, almost five-hundred years ago, all the stone crests vanished. Hidden. Gone. Do you remember what the old Earth-Lore states?" Fang looked at her intently before answering. "Each of the five provinces are in possession of a certain stone, and they are not to be confused with the common stones such as the yellow ones upon your neck. The Earth-Lore is real, Rylla, and the need for peace is of the utmost importance—now more than ever."

Fang took another breath, all solemn and determined. "You've studied maps with your father; you know these lands better than most, even though you've never traveled them yourself." He paused briefly, "And I am beseeching you with the task to recover these scattered stones and bring peace back to our kingdoms."

"What on the good-tilled earth? Fang, how am I supposed to do this when my parents hardly let me leave the house? Why me and not my father? He's more skilled with maps than I!" Rylla didn't understand and she could feel the panic rising in her chest.

"Is your father an Earth-Treader? Does he have the means to travel with two working legs or the aptitude to converse with nature, to understand its power and learn to harness it for good? If so, bring him here and I'll have this conversation with him!" Fang gave a low growl.

Rylla shrunk back, her heart in her throat.

"Forgive me, Rylla, I didn't mean to frighten." Fang's voice held an ancient weariness. He softened his features and took a few steadying breaths.

Rylla hesitated, relaxing a little under his apology. "But why now, of all times? And why not ask the Earth-Treader kings?" she whispered.

"Because you are finally of age and one of the last Earth-Treaders with a heart as pure as they come. If another were chosen, who's to say they wouldn't try to keep the stones for their own selfish purposes or turn them over to the enemy? As for the kings of old, once their stones were gone, they either lost their fortitude or eventually withered into nothingness, overcome with despair. Over time, the rulers have become more and more corrupted, straying from the intended path. Now, hopeless and crooked rulers without a trace of magic grace all five thrones, some worse than others.

"And after all these years, Lord Brennigan's stone has finally been found. By whom, I don't know, but Darkness is spreading and it's spreading fast. If you can't recover these missing crests, Lord Brennigan will, and he'll complete his rule of the kingdoms with his growing army and renewed strength. Right now, he's a wraith, a shell of himself, and we only have hope as long as he's still weak. There isn't much time, and there's even less time to debate who's most suitable for this mission."

Rylla opened her mouth to speak, but no words came out. Instead, beads of moisture formed at the corners of her eyes, blurring her vision.

"I know this is much to digest, much to believe, but in time it will be clearer. You are finally of age and your powers are ready," Fang reassured her.

"I…I don't think I can do this…" Rylla choked.

"On the contrary. I wonder, Rylla, who is holding you back more: your parents or your own fears? I'd wager the latter," Fang spoke gently, though there was a hint of challenge in his tone.

Rylla's eyes stung and a tear leaked down her cheek.

"Earthie, are you well?" His tone softened compassionately.

Rylla stared at the ground between her knees, breathing slow and trying as hard as she could to restrain her emotions. She hated crying, especially crying in front of others. Silent tears escaped, despite her struggle, and one made the long journey to the earth's surface and hit a dead patch of grass. Rylla finally opened her mouth to speak.

"What am I supposed to do?" This task seemed impossible in so many ways.

"Rylla—look!" Fang burst out.

Rylla lifted her head, searching the clearing, and finding Fang's peculiar gaze instead. He wasn't looking at her, but at the ground directly in front of her. She followed his gaze and froze, aghast. Where there was once a patch of dead grass, there now grew a cluster of lush, living grass shimmering as golden as the sun.

"What just happened?" Rylla stared at the grass, eyes still wet, but wide opened now.

"The workings of Earth-Treader magic! If you didn't believe it before, you'd best believe it now!" Fang broke into a grand smile. "This is a good sign, a good sign indeed!"

"I did this?" Rylla plucked a golden blade from the ground and held it in her hand. She twirled it around in her fingers, letting the fading sun glisten off its surface. It was beautiful, almost too perfect to be true, but somehow ethereally authentic. "My tears can grow grass?" she asked.

"Not just grass, but many other things. And not only by tears. You'll find you can manipulate the earth by simply moving your hands or speaking."

The lightheadedness from earlier wasn't from fear anymore. Instead, it was from a breathless wonder as a rush of awe sent a tingle down her arms. "But why is it gold?" Rylla continued to stare at it.

"I suppose it's your mark. I've noticed it ever since you were young, but it's not something I can explain. Earth-Treader magic affects everyone differently," Fang replied.

Rylla twirled the blade once more, and not knowing why, felt compelled to tuck it inside Winnie's locket for safe keeping. But as hard as she tried, it wouldn't open—the lock was jammed. Instead, she placed the blade of grass in the front pocket of her satchel.

Rylla cast her gaze skyward, startled by the approach of darkening storm clouds. Even though it had been a sunny morning, the bright skies were all but a distant memory. It seemed time had awoken from its brief slumber, remembering to catch the rest of the earth up to speed. It was as if the world could feel the urgency of their situation, reflected by the oncoming storm.

Fang spoke again, his words rushed. “What say you, Rylla of Aylati? Will you accept this task?”

Rylla’s heart raced at the thought. This was all happening too fast, and she was scared and uncertain. What if this was the adventure she had always longed for but was too afraid to embark on? And perhaps Fang had a point: were her parents holding her back as much as she was herself? This could mean being one step closer to seeing her brothers again. But was she ready? Could she do this? There were still so many questions. Where would she even start?

She grasped the necklace in her hands, fingering the stone beads as droplets of rain began their slow descent upon the earth. She needed direction and confidence, but she didn’t possess either. Her fingers wrapped around Winnie’s necklace and she remembered the blade of grass. A calm washed over her, a desire to persevere. Light seemed to pour forth from the stones, warming her hands in the midst of the steadily falling rain.

“Rylla, there isn’t much time,” Fang said, his furry coat getting damper by the moment. “You must make your choice.”

“I…I…” The heat rose in her hands so intensely, a feeling so strong, almost as if it were burning her skin. She let the necklace fall back to her chest as she stood up, gasping for breath. The rain was a downpour now. “I can’t do this, Fang—I’m sorry!” She felt lost, lightheaded and confused, desperate for home and the need to flee this place.

Without so much as a backward glance, Rylla fled the Grove and took to the path that led back home, tearing her shirt on the thorns and briers in the process. She ran as fast as her legs would take her, the trees whizzing by her like a blur of green and brown. She wasn’t ready for something like this; Fang had found the wrong girl.

"Don't let anyone know you're an Earth-Treader, Rylla. You'll be hunted and captured before you know it!" Fang shouted over the downpour.

But she was too busy retreating to hear Fang's warning.

Chapter the Third

Ivory Valley

Far away, in a land well-known but in a secret place far-off, dark magic brewed like the steaming bubbles in a cauldron. Lightning flashed overhead and ravens circled the skies, acting as sentries and seeking out any who would be foolish enough to encroach upon their lands. A stone tower cut through the sky like a knife, a beacon of darkness to the waking world. Surrounding the stone, twined every sort of thistle and thorn, like menacing wolves' teeth. Ground guards scattered themselves amongst the base of the tower, ready to strike if anything should seek entry as steady drums echoed all around them. A certain Darkness languished about the place, as if it were simply waiting for a signal.

Inside the tower, in the highest room so bleak and dank, there were two beings. One of them could hardly be considered a being for it was more a skeletal creature, not yet restored. It had no legs, nor did it have arms, but the skin was pulsing in those places as if trying to grow.

Covered in a dark green cloak, the other being, younger by many, many years, was playing servant, almost as if he were a marionette doll controlled by strings. But he was free to roam, given every liberty as one would if a master. And around his neck hung a crimson stone.

On the walls, hung five gilded iron frames—ones usually used for housing faces of family and friends or even scenic landscapes. But these held neither. Each frame bore a bronze plaque with an inscription at the bottom: Aylati, Ostglenden, Wyllund, Rélynda, and the Isles of Norviç—all the Earthen-Crest kingdoms. And in each frame, there was an image of a stone. They were rather difficult to see, almost as if they were tucked away in hidden places.

In the center of the room, the younger being was feeding the deformed creature, trying to coax it back to good health.

"Rotate the leg," the command came from a raspy, weak voice. "I need more meat."

"Yes, my lord," came a short reply as the younger being gently turned the turkey leg.

"I need all the strength I can get—these feeble bones…" The decrepit being began to cough.

"Yes, my lord," came the same reply.

"I knew the price I had to pay in order to use my stone…and those foolish kings thought they could kill me with vines. Bah! What fools!" It took another bite of meat and tried to get its feeble jaw working again, spluttering over another cough.

"You're the greatest, my lord," the servant said.

"Your platitudes bore me, Gryfinn, tell me something I don't already know. The daily report…" The weak voice rasped out again.

"I believe our army has grown in numbers recently, and the count of Earth-Treaders has significantly decreased, my lord."

"How so?"

"Those caught have received immediate imprisonment or death—depending on the severity of their affliction…though most have chosen not to fight, thus filling the dungeons," Gryfinn spoke with conviction, "…my lord."

"Very good, very good…they'll rot in due time." The creature began to cough, chunks of turkey flying from its mouth. It recovered quickly. "And the king?"

"Growing more powerful by the day, but so are you, my lord," Gryfinn said.

"Hrumph…" The being coughed once more. "Let him gloat a little longer, he'll soon be stopped…How about the stones?"

"Still searching, my lord. Though one looks a bit fuzzy—hard to read."

"You must keep looking! They went back to the earth where they first came." The haggard creature looked in the direction of the frames. "Ah yes, the Jade, that one's been fuzzy from the beginning…" The creature caught its breath. "But such is the fate of all these stones—hidden and locked away, buried somewhere deep in the soil of each province…find them!" the voice rasped.

"Yes, my lord," Gryfinn replied. "If I may be so bold, why did the stones flee into the earth rather than into your grasp?"

"Ah…" the decrepit voice paused. "The stone—my Bloodstone—controls the origins and whereabouts between life and death." It coughed. "When I uttered the spell, the stones fled to where they first came and I was cursed to depart from this realm for a time…such a powerful stone, I shall never part with…" The creature heaved.

"But the danger in using such a stone again—" Gryfinn was cut off.

"I know the dangers!" The voice coughed again then regained composure. "And with the others, I'll be the most powerful ruler alive!" The figure gulped in ragged breaths, coughing again, now more violently than before.

Gryfinn changed the subject.

"It's time for your cordial, my lord." He walked toward the cauldron hanging over a green-lit fire and dipped a ladle in. He spooned a dark purple liquid into a silver chalice, and he brought the mixture to his master. "Drink, my lord."

As the thick potion passed its lips, an excruciating cry rent the air. The decrepit figure writhed in agony, howling at the pain. The stone around Gryfinn's neck gleamed. Eventually the pain subsided, and the groaning grew less intense. All that was left was the creature's heavy breathing.

"The price…must be paid…" It moaned again, catching its breath.

"My lord?"

"Leave me…dispatch a new group to continue the search…"

"Yes, my lord." Gryfinn bowed and exited the dark room, taking the stairs two at a time. He paused at the iron door, fixed his cloak tight about his shoulders making sure to shield his face within the deep hood, and crept into the outdoors. Searching for these stones was becoming one of his new favorite tasks, and if he found an Earth-Treader in the process, well, it would be like killing two grouse instead of one.

⸙ ⸙ ⸙

Rylla was almost out of the Woode, the promise of home a few miles away. And though the rain was still falling hard, her running had slowed to a jog and then a walk. Eventually she stopped altogether to catch her breath and let out an exasperated cry as tears streamed down her face. This was all too much and too soon. She couldn't leave, could she? What about her parents? Not to mention her own fears and doubts. She shouted at the trees and hit one with her fist. The bark bruised into a dark mark, and the tree groaned with the storm, as if crying in pain

Rylla stumbled back a pace, her stomach roiling with fear and anger, frustration and regret. Why had she been chosen for this? And why now?

She was also thoroughly drenched. Her mother had been right about the rain after all, but it was too late now to don the cloak. She should have put it on before fleeing the forest. Lesson learned.

After letting her emotions calm, Rylla turned to the tree's wound and placed her hand on it. She had been impulsive.

"I'm sorry," she whispered through the tears. "I shouldn't have…"

The tree responded to her gentle touch and where the dark wound had been, a bright patch of golden bark shown between her fingers, shimmering in the midst of the storm. The tree swayed slightly as if saying she was forgiven as she turned in the direction of home.

Rylla would leave her *magic* here and never return. She'd learn to be content within the confines of her home. Who needed freedom anyway?

If she had but glanced backwards, she would have noticed someone stepping out of the shadows, touching the golden bark where her hand had just been, then turning to watch her go, from beneath a dark hood.

Rylla followed the path from the Woode, but now she felt more unsettled than when she had first come. As she exited the path and stepped onto the main road, something wound the taut cord in her chest even tighter.

She was being followed.

Was it Fang? He wouldn't harm someone he thought was supposed to save the kingdoms, would he? No, this felt different. Her mind reeled with possibilities.

Rylla continued down the road, rain blurring her vision and cold creeping into her bones. She picked up her speed, knowing very well that her pursuer would be doing the same. But as she continued onward, curiosity won over caution, and she glanced over her shoulder.

A hooded figure exited the same path she had just left, emerging from the shadows almost as if he weren't afraid to be seen. Perhaps they even *wanted* to be seen.

Rylla's spine stiffened and her heart rate increased, but she forced herself to keep walking, faster again. She was getting closer to home and its coveted safety, but something still didn't feel right.

Whatever this thing was or whoever it was, she couldn't very well lead it to her house. What if he was a killer and hurt her family? She'd never be able to forgive herself. No, she had to go in a different direction, to lead her pursuer away from her home. But where should she go?

Aylati was known for its farmland which meant many miles of open plains and very little opportunity to hide. But she had grown up here, she knew the land and knew where to go. To the left was Aylati's throne, the land where the king sat upon his royal seat. To go there would make blending in easier with so many people, but at this time of day and with this weather, no one would be outside. Besides, it was a two-hour walk, much too far away to find respite there.

To the right, there were some gristmills in Aylati's Ivory Valley, a place with many twists and turns, countless abandoned mill buildings, and numerous hideouts. If she took an abrupt turn to the right and sprinted in that direction, perhaps she could make it in time to disappear.

After a few more steps, Rylla made the turn and ran, fear making her fleet-footed.

She pushed herself as fast as she could, more thankful for her long legs than she'd ever been before. But they were beginning to feel like jelly, and she wasn't sure how much longer they would hold out. It was still a good distance to the mills, but maybe, just maybe, her pursuer wasn't a fast runner. Rylla glanced behind her, and her heart lurched. The stalker was trailing close, and whoever it was, they were slowly gaining. She thought she could hear words being shouted at her back, but she wasn't interested in hearing them.

Rylla picked up her speed and continued to run, raindrops smacking her in the face. It was a miracle she hadn't slipped on the wet ground. By now, her legs were on fire and her lungs on the verge of collapsing, but she could see the mill buildings coming into view, their sturdy structures a welcome relief. She crossed the last stretch of farmland before plunging headlong into their midst. She zigzagged, ducking in and out of view, trying to fake out her pursuer. In the end, she chose a familiar mill building and jumped through a broken window. Inside, she ran up the stairs, pressed firmly on a piece of wood, and watched as it gave way to a small hole used for storing extra grain. Thankfully this space was empty, and Rylla crawled in and drew the wood back in front of her. It slid into place and left a small enough crack for her to peer through.

Now she waited.

Heavy footsteps thudded outside, and they grew louder as they followed her up the stairs.

Rylla's heart dropped, beating fast in her chest. *My wet footprints! Will he find my hiding spot?* She silently prayed it would be too dark to tell.

Her pursuer was in the same room now and only a few feet away from her. It was nearing dusk but there was light enough to see some detail. Her pursuer was definitely a man, and she only hoped he wasn't the observant kind.

Rylla peered out the crack and squinted hard. She took note of his attire in the muted light. He wore distinct brown boots with gold straps and a dark cloak with golden fringe at the bottom. His hood was drawn, and when the man shifted his position, the little light filtering through the window revealed oak leaves embroidered within the folds of his cloak.

She steadied her breath, making sure to keep quiet and not give away her position, though every second seemed like an hour.

Eventually, the man turned around and left, allowing Rylla to take her first real breath. He hadn't noticed her footprints. After ten more minutes, she finally felt safe enough to emerge. She peeled back the wooden paneling and crawled out.

"There you are!" came a voice, sounding out of breath.

Her heart stopped for a moment at the voice, but it wasn't from the man. It was from a cat—not quite a kitten but significantly smaller than Fang. It was black and white with very large whiskers, and its coat was soaked through.

"Goodness, you gave me a heart attack!" Rylla whispered in case the man was outside. "Do you realize that I'm being hunted right now? Who are you?" Rylla's words tumbled over each other like she had spoken one long word, overcome with adrenaline and the pounding of blood in her ears.

"My grandfather sent me after you—told me to keep watch and be your guardian!" The cat was regaining his breath and spoke like some sort of confident warrior, but it looked too proper to be anything threatening.

Rylla would have laughed if her life wasn't in jeopardy. "Fang?" That was the only logical explanation.

"Yes, he told me to warn you that you should be careful." The cat paused for only a moment. "There are men out hunting for Earth-Treaders, and it looks like the man who chased you saw what you did to that tree. I didn't get to see his face…"

"I didn't see anyone in the Woode, I had no idea…" Rylla started pacing, trying to formulate a plan. This was exactly what she wanted to avoid. Her magic was supposed to be forgotten, not seen. "This can't be good!"

"I ran as fast as I could to warn you, but it's not safe here anymore! They'll be searching Aylati for the stone and any Earth-Treaders. Lord Brennigan has men everywhere! You can't go back home…" the cat spoke the last sentence with caution, but still it filled Rylla's heart with dread.

Could she actually do it? She would have to leave her parents, her home, and everything she'd ever known. If there was just one man hunting her now, eventually more would follow suit. And something told her this pursuer wouldn't stop until he got what he wanted.

"But where would I go? What am I supposed to do? My parents will be so worried…" Rylla wanted to warn her parents, but telling them would only endanger them more. Besides, they'd definitely try to stop her. Part of her almost wanted them to. But as much as she longed for the comfort of home, she couldn't very well return and act like life was normal, not after today, no matter how hard she fought it.

And secretly, deep down, she longed for this adventure, though she was very afraid to do it. Fang's words came echoing back to Rylla's mind.

"You've studied maps with your father, you know these lands better than most, even though you've only longed to travel them. I am beseeching you with the task to recover these scattered stones and bring peace back to our kingdoms."

She looked down at her hands, picturing again the golden threads of light, the grass, and the tree. She was afraid of her powers—uncertain. Could she actually do this? Did she have a choice? Time was precious, and she had to move quickly.

"It seems this is my only option," she whispered, fighting the urge to cry. Now that the scare of being pursued had died down, her emotions were catching up to her. Perhaps tomorrow would be different. "I don't like it and I don't know what I'm doing nor where to begin."

"And that's why you have me. My grandfather briefed me on everything. Though I am small in stature, I'm actually a lot wiser than I look!" He stood straighter and puffed out his chest in attempts at appearing larger.

"How old are you?"

"I'm almost two years old amongst my clan, but to humans, I'm about four and twenty," he spoke with pride.

"You're older than I am." Rylla felt a little better knowing she'd have a companion, but a talking cat didn't sound like the best option. At least she wouldn't be alone. "What do we do now?"

"It's best if we start tomorrow at first light. It's too risky to leave now, especially with that man out there..." The cat stood on all fours and walked toward a window. "Are there any safe places to sleep in this building?"

Rylla thought for a moment and nodded. "Follow me!"

⸙ ⸙ ⸙

A cloaked man circled around the gristmills, entering and exiting them one by one. He needed to find the girl, though he didn't know her face nor her name. But as minutes led to hours, he grew increasingly irritated and weary. She was nimble and quick-witted. How did she disappear so fast and where did she go? No sign of any life stirred save for a random cat, some birds, and two wandering sheep. He couldn't fail; he had too much at stake, too much riding on his already weary shoulders. Perhaps if he went back to his hideout to get some sleep and rest...no—his sleep was littered with nightmares. There'd be no rest. Still, he needed to get back. It was getting late. He'd renew his search come the morning.

Yes, that would have to do.

Chapter the Fourth

And So, It Begins

Early next morning, something outside awoke Rylla from her sleep. She sat up to listen more closely. Trees rustled their leaves in the wind. Straining her hearing, she could detect a faint rhythmic pounding in the distance even through the dense fog that came with the new day.

Was it drums?

She had never heard actual drums before, but in her father's history books, she read that in ages past cruel lords had used them when going to war. And because of this, drums had been banned from the kingdoms due to being a symbol of anarchy and unrest.

When she had asked her parents about drums, she was told they sounded like loud thumping, almost like a heart beating out of one's chest, and they could come in many patterns and varieties. She could feel her own heart echo the rhythmic pattern as she strained to hear more, but eventually the noise mingled in the breeze and dissipated altogether.

Could this be what Fang mentioned? Lord Brennigan's army?

With the accumulating silence and a growing awareness of her surroundings, she recalled the events from yesterday—events which led her to waking up today in a dusty cellar room in an abandoned gristmill. And beside a cat as black and white as a cow.

Cold fear pooled in her middle.

Today was the day. She'd had a restless sleep, tossing and turning different ideas in her head, trying her hardest to find a way out of this. But try as she might, it didn't change anything. She had to leave her home and her parents behind. Already they were probably worried sick over her not coming back last night. The thought did little to calm her nerves.

As she moved to a seated position, her cloak fell from her shoulders and her body felt stiff and sore from yesterday's sprint. A groan slipped from her lips.

The cat stirred, ears alert and eyes wide, afraid that something had happened while he was asleep on the job.

"Everything's fine, just in a little pain," Rylla said, rubbing the back of her head and rolling her neck from side to side. She looked at the cat. "What's your name?"

"Claw, but everyone calls me Moo, though I don't know why," Moo stated with all seriousness.

Though far from jovial, Rylla found she couldn't help but let out a small laugh. "Well, you do look like a cow, and honestly, I think the name suits you just fine. I like it." She got up and brushed the dust and dirt off her clothes. As she did, she felt a tear in her shirt from her time in the Woode. *So much for being careful.* She'd have to mend it somehow. The rain from yesterday was mostly gone from her clothes, now only slightly damp. She was alive and that's what mattered most of all.

"It's early morning, I think we're good to head out soon." Moo finished stretching and started cleaning his fur.

"How do we even start this impossible task?" Rylla questioned, wishing again that there was some other way.

"You brought your map, right?"

"I did…but how did you know? I never told Fang…"

"He tells me a lot of stories about Earth-Treaders and Earth-Lore, similar to the stories I'm sure you've grown up hearing. Apparently being an Earth-Treader means you can *feel* things. We creatures of the Earth and Woode have our own kind of magic, and my grandfather used some to inspire you, or prompt you to bring the map, knowing that you might need it." Moo began licking his paw.

"I don't get it. How did Fang get to be so powerful? How come he knows so much?" Rylla wanted all of this to make sense.

"He's not the first to guard Aylati's Woode. There were many before him who were protectors of it too, all assigned by the past kings of Aylati. It's a position I hope to earn one day! All protectors of the Woode worked for the kings, and therefore received all their information from them. If you recall, all the Earthen-Crest kings were Earth-Treaders, except nowadays with all the corruption and spreading Darkness, they've become a thing of the past—simply legends. That being so, my grandfather has eyes and ears in the Woode who report and tell him what's going on. The current king of Aylati can't be trusted, nor any of the other kings for that matter." Moo started cleaning his other paw.

Rylla was beginning to catch on, but this still didn't explain where they should go next. Or where these stones could be hidden.

She reached for her satchel and pulled out the folded map, curious to actually be using it for something other than history lessons. As she placed it on the ground, dawn's light illuminated the kingdoms as it filtered through a small cellar window. Both Moo and Rylla scanned the map.

"We have to find the stones, but we can't stay here. There's already one man after you, and I fear more are to come. Aylati's stone has to wait," Moo spoke as he stared at the map.

"Wait. Are you thinking there's a stone hidden in each of the provinces, then?" Rylla rested her hand on her chin as she studied the unrolled parchment.

"Yes, my grandfather told me a peculiar detail that these stones are drawn back to their homelands, the places where they first originated. There's a good chance that's where they are now," Moo said.

"So, if we can't search Aylati now, that means we'll have to come back later. That's promising, to say the least." Rylla felt a little lighter with that prospect. *Home.* She just had to stay alive in order to see it again.

But what was she to do when she got all the stones? Something about defeating Lord Brennigan—she knew that much. But Rylla couldn't even begin to guess where he was nor how to defeat him if five powerful kings had failed to do the same.

Rylla placed her finger on the map, tracing various routes and options, trying to see if they could contrive a better plan.

"I think this will have to do. We're closest to Ostglenden's border, so perhaps we should try searching Thrushwoode Forest first. Do you think we can make it there safely without getting caught? I don't know much about those woods aside from the types of trees and what year Ostglenden took Thrushwoode into its province."

Moo nodded. “But we have to be quick and stealthy. I suggest you follow my lead since it’s in my nature to hunt.” At this, Moo ducked down and moved agilely from side to side, proving his point.

“I see your meaning,” laughed Rylla as she refolded the map, placed it in her satchel, and made ready to do the same with her cloak. But she paused. She was dry enough now to wear it, and perhaps this would help disguise her from her pursuer. He had seen her clothes, so the dark blue cloak would make her less distinctive.

She fastened the clasp tight about her neck and fitted her arms through the loose sleeves, letting the dark blue material fall gently from her shoulders to her feet. Snug and warm. Her wet hair had now dried into a dark mass of curly frizz, so she tied it back into a low ponytail away from her face before fitting the hood over her head.

This would be her first time leaving home and in a way she never would have imagined. A mixture of fear warred with a growing excitement, though fear was definitely the greater of the two. But she’d learned to press on many times despite it—retrieving lemons from the orchard in the dark, labeling a map for a client all on her own while her father was on business, and writing letters to her brothers to eventually find them unreturned. She had no choice but to do so again.

Can’t turn back now.

Rylla walked over to the cellar door, rusted at the hinges, and paused. She twisted around to face Moo, giving voice to her question from earlier. “What am I to do with all the stones after I find them? Fang didn’t mention anything save for defeating Lord Brennigan, but how am I to do that? That seems like an exceedingly important detail.”

“That is a good question, but all my grandfather told me is that time will tell,” Moo replied.

“Time will tell? So, I’m supposed to find these stones with promises of ‘time will tell’ as my guide? That doesn’t feel very hopeful.” That wasn’t the answer she had wanted. She had half a mind to flee the gristmill and abandon the mission altogether by running in the opposite direction.

“Yes. Most reasons for a journey don’t turn up until the end of it, so perhaps you’ll figure it out along the way,” Moo continued.

At least he was honest.

“I guess I have no choice but to hold you to that,” Rylla said as she faced the door once more. She couldn’t run home even though she wanted to. She had little choice.

Rylla placed her hand on the rusted door handle and twisted; it gave way, creaking slightly as it opened to an ascending brick staircase covered in weeds and dust. The sun filtered through the clouds, casting a dappled blanket upon the earth. Rylla and Moo crept up the stairs, checking out their surroundings before making any movements.

“The coast is clear. Let’s move!” Moo whispered.

They fled the gristmill, side by side, clinging to the low-rising shrubs. Being a creature of small stature, Moo could remain hidden whereas Rylla had to work extra hard at being inconspicuous. They moved quickly and cautiously, stopping at times to reevaluate their situation and then proceeded again.

They continued in this stop and go rhythm for quite some time, and if anyone happened to look closely enough, they might notice a small girl and a black and white spotted cat sneaking across the empty field to the border of Thrushwoode Forest. But no one was looking, and the two passed safely.

Rylla gawked as they stepped foot within the forest's walls. Never had she seen such strange, towering trees. She'd only read about them in her books. From the outside, they could pass as common Aylatian Firs, but from within the forest itself, they loomed like limbless, skinned warriors. It was as if someone had come and stripped off every branch and every piece of bark, leaving the trunks a mottled brownish yellow in the process. The only indication that these were indeed trees, was the cauliflower-like canopy that protruded from the tops of them, shading the forest floor with leafy shadows and dappled sunlight. Occasional oaks and elms joined in their company.

"It will be hard to track the sun's movements with such dense covering overhead," Rylla said as she gazed upward. "We'll just have to rely heavily on the map and keep track of how fast time passes." She turned in a circle once more before she reached into her satchel and pulled out her map.

Rylla placed it on the ground so it could lay flat, allowing both her and Moo to peer at it. With the countless trees about her, there was little fear in having it blow away in the wind.

"Thrushwoode Forest," Rylla whispered aloud as she glanced around them. "We just entered through the southernmost border." She looked back down and traced her finger along a path that would lead them through the woodland to the first neighboring town. From studying these lands for years, Rylla surmised it would be about a day's journey through the forest before she reached any signs of Ostglenden's civilization.

"Moo, did Fang tell you how much time we have to find these stones?"

"No." Moo shook his head. "He just said to hurry and not waste time. I can't imagine he'd want us to tarry." Moo investigated the map a moment longer, then scanned his surroundings again.

Tracing the map's routes, Rylla estimated about three days in Ostglenden, about five in Wyllund, and about four in Rélynda. She had no idea how they'd reach the Isles of Norviç, but traveling by boat sounded frightening. They would have to find a way over there somehow, though.

Standing up, she peered deeper into the Woode and found the markings of a path. "If we head north, we'll pop out at Larkug, one of Ostglenden's villages. We should probably steer clear of people as best we can—I don't know who's safe to trust…but let's follow the path until then." Rylla folded the map up and put it back in her satchel, hoping she was right. She didn't know what kinds of things inhabited a forest such as this and would rather not care to find out.

Moo was busy sniffing various plants, obviously pleased to find some catmint. He chewed and rolled around, momentarily forgetting himself.

Rylla made a motion to head deeper into the forest, calling Moo to follow. She didn't want to waste any time, especially out here in the open.

He eventually shook his head and ran after Rylla, making up for the distance. "Sorry, I just really like that stuff," Moo said, remnants of catmint still clinging to his whiskers.

Rylla just laughed and shook her head, traversing along the path that led deeper into the shaded cover of the trees.

And so, it begins.

Chapter the Fifth

Thrushwoode Forest

"Do you think we're getting closer?" Rylla asked Moo through exhausted breaths. For the past ten minutes, they had been running quietly along the forest path, hoping to cut down on their time. Plus, Moo had challenged her to a race, and she couldn't say no. She had figured running would help to distract her from her thoughts.

"I'm not sure, but that felt great!" Moo clearly wanted to keep running but Rylla begged for some respite. "I won by the way."

"I think we better slow down and take it easy for a while. I'm still sore from yesterday." Her thoughts trailed back to the Grove and her interaction with Fang, but she stilled when something stirred in the forest, out of place from the usual rustle of noises.

"We should probably start looking for the stone—" Moo began.

"Hush, I hear something. Listen." Rylla stopped in her tracks and tried to steady her breathing and rapid heartbeat.

In the distance, twigs crunched gently. The wind alone couldn't have made that sound, could it? Something was out there and now was not the time to be breathing heavily.

They stood like statues for what seemed like ages, only moving their necks to challenge their peripherals. But the sound had ceased and Rylla began to second-guess that she had heard anything at all.

Was exhaustion already getting to her? This journey didn't look promising.

"I think it's safe to—" Rylla took a step forward as she spoke, and a loud whistle hissed through the air past her head. An arrow lodged itself in a tree a few yards away from where she stood.

"RUN!" Rylla shouted at the top of her lungs as she bolted through the forest once more, this time adrenaline fueling her weakened legs.

Moo sprang back into a sprint as if it were as natural for him as breathing. Behind them, men's voices were accompanied by the trampling of hooves. Countless arrows buzzed over their heads and shoulders as they ran, just barely missing their mark.

Rylla was growing desperate. What kind of imbeciles hunted people for sport?

She diverged from the trail and plunged deeper into the forest. Together she and Moo dodged trees and jumped over fallen logs as they desperately searched for a place to hide. It would be harder for the men to catch them now—horses would be slowed by the thick undergrowth, right?

Rylla's hope plummeted when the group of men crashed through the forest with the same vigor as before, if not more. Her simple diversion had lengthened the space between them, but that would be covered in a matter of minutes. She and Moo continued to zigzag and duck in attempts to avoid the arrows.

Would she always be running from something? It seemed she'd run more in the past twenty-four hours than she had in her entire life.

A few yards away, Moo motioned for Rylla to follow as they darted for a group of large boulders. They ran side by side for the shelter as fast as they could before more arrows had a chance to find their mark.

Just before Rylla reached the promise of safety, a force like a punch struck her upper arm. Pain exploded in streaks of red across her vision. She staggered, a cry seething from her throat as her sight blurred. A rough hand gripped her shoulder, dragging her to the earth with a strength she'd never felt before.

Pain blackened her vision further as she hit the ground, and her will to fight slipped through her fingers like grains of sand.

⁂

The warmth against her cheeks and the smell of firewood tickled Rylla awake. Slowly opening each eye, she began to register her surroundings. Where was she? The space was small and the walls were made of jagged stone, damp with moisture. The ground was a mixture of dirt and rocks, but it had a neatness about it—like it had recently been swept. The light from the fire danced along the walls, creating obscure shadows.

"Good, you're awake." Strong, but lean hands tended the wound on Rylla's left arm as she finally came to. Callouses rubbed against her reddened skin where her arm was exposed, but she didn't dare flinch as panic pricked at her nerves. She was still wearing her cloak, still in disguise, just in case.

What happened? Where's Moo...?

Moo sat in a corner giving himself a thorough cleaning, leg extended and tongue working out the bugs and dirt in his fur. His green eyes reflected the torchlight of the dim room, and once turned in her direction, they lit up.

"Rylla, you're okay!" Moo bounded toward her and sat opposite the man who was still wrapping her arm. "How are you? I saw what happened after the arrow hit and you fainted. This man saved your life!" Moo said excitedly.

"Lady, your cat sure does meow a lot." The man's voice was deep with a hard edge. She looked into his face, meeting his honeyed-brown eyes. He was both handsome and very serious, unnervingly so, and looked a few years older than herself. Something in his appearance, with his tanned skin and dark hair, reminded her of her eldest brother Garth.

"Who are you?" Rylla finally found the voice to speak.

"I should be asking you the same thing." There was a hint of challenge in his tone.

"...I asked you first," Rylla countered.

"I don't have time for this." The man began rummaging around, cleaning up bandages and rinsing out the bloody water bowl.

"What's that supposed to mean?" Rylla questioned, not quite liking his attitude. Hadn't this man chosen to help her? Though she was no stranger to fear, she had learned to stand up for herself and hold her own around men, thanks to her brothers. They had always been easier to talk to than girls her age. It was just that most girls she knew wanted to talk *about* boys, whereas she would rather talk *to* them, face to face. But this one was proving difficult to converse with.

The man finished putting away his supplies and crouched next to Rylla, double checking her wound to see if any blood was leaking through. He appeared deep in thought as if contemplating what to say.

"It's risky enough for me to have done what I did. What are you thinking traversing through Thrushwoode? And all alone? Those poachers would have had you before you knew it—they're expert trappers, and not just of game." His tone rang with anger, but was underlined with a hint of genuine concern.

"Well how was I supposed to know this forest harbored an entourage of cannibals?"

"Cannibals? Hah, oh that's rich," the man faked a laugh. He looked at Rylla's face as she cinched her brows together, frowning at him.

"You were serious? No, of course those men aren't cannibals, though they are relentless and bloodthirsty. But for power, not people. You don't want to cross them. They track anything that moves within Thrushwoode and serve as Ostglenden's protectors. Those lucky enough to survive their pursuit are either imprisoned or sent to work as soldiers for the king. They're guarding the border as we speak, to apprehend any trespassers."

"King Grievon? Why would he do such a thing? I thought him to be decent…" Rylla remembered reading about him in recent news articles—he had been known for his charity throughout Ostglenden and his protection of Thrushwoode Forest, but now? Apparently, that had changed.

"You can't always trust what you read." If it was possible, he had grown even more serious than before.

“Well, what’s he guarding the place for anyway? Seems pretty brazen of him to think the entire forest answers to his call.” Rylla clamped her fists together, the freshness of her recent wound sending jolts of pain down her arm. She clenched her teeth.

“I have a hunch as to what he’s seeking,” the man returned.

Rylla waited a moment, but he didn’t explain. That was the only answer she’d be getting.

He gave her a curious look, scrutinizing her from head to toe, searching for something. “Who are you? What are you doing out here anyway? No one in their right mind would enter Thrushwoode…”

“I’d appreciate it if you stopped staring.” Rylla attempted to sit up and applied too much pressure on her hurt arm. She winced and would have fallen on the hard ground had the man not caught her.

“You’re not going to get any better if you don’t pay attention to what you’re doing,” he warned as he gently steadied her on her feet.

“I can manage just fine on my own, thank you.” Rylla broke eye contact, feeling a little too vulnerable. Her brothers had also taught her to be independent and to feign confidence even if it was hard, but this man was challenging every resolve she had.

She shifted her focus and searched the cave for her satchel, her eyes scanning the wall of garments and essentials. Rylla’s eyes alighted upon a curious looking cloak hanging from a peg. It had gold trim at the bottom and a pattern of oak leaves sewn throughout. Where had she seen it before? A pair of brown boots with familiar golden straps were on the ground beneath, wet from recent use.

And then it hit her. These were the articles her pursuer had worn last night. She froze, and her heart throbbed against her ribcage like a bird struggling to break free from her chest.

"You'd better rest up before making any more narrow escapes. That wound will take time to properly heal." The man paused in thought. "I can't give you much but there's a small cot near the door you could use. I have some things I need to tend to, but you can rest while I'm gone." He rose to grab some tack hanging on the wall, making ready to outfit a horse.

Rylla felt like anything but resting. This was the man who chased her last night. He'd caught her even after she tried to evade his grasp. She was trapped and needed to get away. Fast.

"If you're looking for your bag, it's by the bandages near the cook fire."

How could she have been so careless? If he didn't know she was the one he was after, he would soon.

Rylla found her bag and quickly slung it over her shoulder.

"We need to leave," Rylla said, suddenly breathless.

The man's brow furrowed in confusion, his hands pausing on the stirrups.

"Thank you." She didn't know why she thanked him, but he had helped her, hadn't he? Then again, he'd also chased her, making her run in fear for her life.

She called Moo to her side and quickly approached the exit of the cave. She was moments away from stepping into the sunshine when the man's voice spoke once more.

"You really shouldn't leave with your arm in the state that it's in. And the poachers—"

"I'll be fine—goodbye!" She practically fled the cave as one would a burning house, sprinting into the Woode.

She needed to clear her head, to reset her course and make sure she didn't stray too far from the main path. But no matter how hard she tried, she couldn't get the face of her pursuer-turned-rescuer out of her mind.

Rylla and Moo had gone a considerable distance from the cave and were now surrounded by a thick cluster of trees. After rounding one of the trunks, she suddenly stopped short.

"Halt!" a voice called out to her.

Rylla's heart pounded. *Has the man from the cave discovered the truth? And so soon?*

She startled to see someone she didn't recognize—a strange, bearded man in a long cloak, eyes intense as he stepped from behind a nearby oak. His hand was on the hilt of his sword, thankfully sheathed. Her arm pulsed under his severe scrutiny, and her heart beat hard like a hammer to a nail.

"Uh…sir?" Rylla stammered. She could tell this man meant trouble, and already she was berating herself for having stopped at all.

"You're coming with me." The man stepped nearer, closing the distance between them. He was now an arm's length away.

Much too close.

As he reached out a muscular arm, Rylla deflected his grasp and ran. Moo ran beside her, his tail flailing in their haste.

But the man was faster. His hand came down hard on her shoulder, stopping her retreat. His grip was firm and sent her wounded arm into a splattering of pain.

Rylla stifled a cry.

"Now there's enough of that, you insolent girl!" The man gritted his teeth and leered at Rylla.

Was this to be her lot? Would she die here and spoil the Woode with her blood?

His grip squeezed harder. Panic seized Rylla's throat as the pain blurred her vision. She feared she'd have little choice but to comply.

"Rylla—your magic!" Moo shouted, reminding her of the very thing she'd tried to forget.

She didn't know what to do, but there were plenty of sticks on the ground. Maybe if she just threw them at the man? Would that be good enough?

Rylla ducked and twisted beneath his grasp, her arm screaming. She crouched to the earth, grabbed a handful of sticks, and sent them flying in the man's direction.

He was taken by surprise, his expression twisting from a scowl into one of shock.

Rylla moved quickly, her dexterity working to her advantage. She flung more branches, sending them speedily toward her attacker. She hardly knew what she was doing, but it was working. The sticks were flying like shafts of lighting, flashing golden as they struck the man all over.

He shielded his eyes and attempted to unsheathe his sword. "You're in for it now!" He fumed, his eyes full of fire as he stepped nearer.

But Rylla didn't give him the chance. Instead, her knee came up to meet him where it hurts. He groaned in pain, and she fled before his knees hit the ground.

Chapter the Sixth

The Woode Speaks

Rylla was back in the Woode. Arrows hissed overhead and flew past her with incredible speed, lodging themselves into trees and bushes. Trampling hoofs and savage cries reverberated in her chest as she ran away from her pursuers. Rocks and potholes littered her path, and when her ankle caught in a ditch, she almost didn't feel it. Rylla was running as fast as she could, and if she slowed her pace to catch her breath, surely she would be done for. She looked to her left and to her right, but Moo was nowhere in sight.

Where did he go?

She was alone, running through the mysterious Woode for her life. *Keep running!* Rylla tried to stay calm and focus on finding a place to hide.

An arrow sliced through the air and pierced through the brush a few yards in front of her. A cry of pain escaped the lips of a creature hidden within.

Rylla ran to the wounded animal, but stopped abruptly in her tracks as she saw a flash of white and black through the leaves.

Moo lay on his side, an arrow protruding from his back leg. The shaft was broken, and it didn't appear too deep. Still, he closed his eyes in pain as he slumped to the ground in a dead faint.

"No, no, no…Moo! Wake up! Come on—" Helplessness stole Rylla's words as tears stung her eyes. She needed to find shelter. If she didn't, infection would seep into the wound and finish him for good. But how could she get away with a group of men on her back?

This was her fear in tangible form. Another loss. She knew she shouldn't have left home.

By this time, the horses and men were much closer, and if she didn't leave now, they would surely catch her. But her legs wouldn't budge, nor would her conscience allow her to. She just sat there and waited for her fate. To flee would eventually lead to her capture anew. The hoofbeats finally slowed, trampling on the fallen leaves before her. Rylla looked up into the familiar eyes of the unnamed man who had rescued her from the poachers earlier. He had captured her again, and he was sitting atop a horse with an arrow pointing at her chest.

How can this be happening?

She cringed. "Please," she pleaded.

He let loose the arrow, and it tore at her garments and plunged straight through her heart.

Rylla flung the bed sheets off the wooden cot and onto the floor as she sat up, panting for breath and clutching her chest with her good arm. She felt for the arrow but there was nothing but her clothes bunched in their usual places.

"I'm okay. I'm alive..." Rylla closed her eyes to blink away the images. When she opened her eyes, she was relieved to see Moo at the end of her bed. He was alive as well, and by the looks of him, uninjured. This wasn't the first time she'd had nightmares, though this one seemed more vivid than anything in the past.

She scanned the room and noted a brick hearth in its center. To its right was a small kitchen with rusted pots and a shabby table, and to its left was an upholstered chair. She was close enough to see that the chair's seat and back were faded, showing signs of wear. On the floor, a dust-covered rug, frayed around its edges, covered the majority of the wooden floorboards.

Rylla's cot was tucked next to the worn chair, giving her a perfect view of the room. The space was homey, if not a little unkept.

Yesterday's adventures left Rylla tired and desperate for a place to rest, a place to slow her racing thoughts. After narrowly evading the clutches of two men, both she and Moo needed respite.

They had gotten lost briefly, but after consulting her map, Rylla regained her bearings and eventually found an old building tucked behind a tangle of moss and climbing vines. Her father had told her forests usually housed lodges for huntsmen, and she was lucky enough to find one of them, thankfully abandoned.

"What's wrong, Rylla?" During the night, Moo had moved to the end of the cot to stretch out, but now he came up to her face. "You're sweating!"

Moo darted from the bed and ran over to the kitchen. He found a dusty rag and dipped it into the small wooden bucket by the water pump. Once the cloth was fully saturated, he brought it over to Rylla.

"Thank you." She took the cloth from Moo, and he walked over to the chair. He jumped atop it to get to the window where a plant was sitting on its sill. He began sniffing it.

"I had a nightmare. That man from yesterday wounded you and I was left to defend myself from his merciless hand. I know it was just a dream, but I'm glad we left when we did." Rylla shuddered.

"Why'd we leave so quickly?" Moo questioned, rubbing his sides against the plant, tasting it with interest.

"Because that man was the same one who chased me out of Aylati's forest."

"How could you tell? Neither of us ever saw his face." Moo stopped sniffing to look at her.

"I recognized his cloak and boots. The same ones I saw the night he chased me." Rylla gave another shudder, glad to have escaped yet again.

"Odd, really. He smelled interesting, almost conflicted. And like catmint." Moo went back to sniffing the plant.

"That stuff addles the brain, Moo. You should stay away from it—especially when we need to be on high alert."

"But I can't help it!" Moo lost himself in the plant, and Rylla couldn't help but laugh.

Her laughter cut off in a gasp as pain twinged in her still-injured flesh and memories of the day before came flooding back.

The arrow. Her arm.

"I still can't believe I was shot! I thought this only happened in stories." Rylla gently ran her hand over the wound; it was sore to her touch. "I hope this isn't a sign for what the rest of our journey will be like." Part of her wanted to turn around and head home now, but that would mean facing those poachers again. Besides, she couldn't stop thinking how the hands that tended her wound belonged to the same man who had chased her into the Ivory Valley.

That nameless man with the honeyed eyes and an expression of stone.

There was something about him that she couldn't quite place, and that unnerved her all the more.

Who was he and why was he chasing her? And why had he helped her?

There was no use questioning what was better left to the unknown. She was alive and she had a mission, however reluctant she was to complete it. The fate of all the Earthen-Crest kingdoms rested in her tiny hands.

"It's too big a burden, but too important to flee now. I'm here, and this is my fate," Rylla reassured herself, trying to assuage her doubts.

"Hmm? What's that?" Moo was coming out of his stupor.

"Come on, Moo, we've got a lot of ground to cover and a short window of time! We should only be in Thrushwoode for a few more hours." *Plus, I think we're safer if we keep moving.*

Rylla got out of bed and gingerly checked the contents of her bag, ignoring the throbbing pain in her arm.

"That man was right about one thing, you know." Moo sat in front of her again.

"What's that supposed to mean?" Rylla silently berated herself for having a defensive tone, but something about this man raked her every nerve.

"You should rest. It's not safe out in the Woode. You heard him; the poachers are guarding Ostglenden's borders as we speak, and they'll find us no matter which way we cross!"

"We have to keep moving, Moo. Besides, we have to find the stone, remember? What other choice do we have?" Rylla wanted to get out of the forest as quickly as possible. To linger meant death, she was certain of it.

"Well now that you mention it, my grandfather once told me the trees serve as portals. If they ask kindly for passage, a traveler may be granted their destination. That was how the Earth-Treaders of old travelled to distant realms, even to those beyond our kingdoms."

"But trees can't speak!"

"And neither can cats."

"I see your point." Rylla scratched her head. "What do you have in mind?"

"My grandfather said that oaks possess the most wisdom and have been around the longest. They know the ins and outs of every forest. They might even know the location of the stone."

"I still can't believe how much Fang knows. I've studied history my whole life and I don't know half as much as him."

"Well, he's also been around a lot longer than you. We just celebrated his two-hundred-and-seventeenth birthday. I'm proud to be related to him." Moo puffed out his chest once more.

Rylla broke into a soft smile at the pride Moo had for his grandfather. She hoped that one day she could see them side by side, conversing about nature and the magic of Earth-Lore back in the Grove. Maybe one day too, she and her entire family could once more be together under the same starlit sky. But dwelling on wishes would do nothing for her now.

"I think we should get going." Rylla headed for the door, Moo following at her heels. "Let's see if we can find those trees."

⸙ ⸙ ⸙

Rylla and Moo had been sneaking and poking around Thrushwoode for the past few hours, their attempts at finding a useful tree futile. Most oaks were unresponsive and even the elms, their faithful kindred, wouldn't utter a sound. Most of their branches were mottled and stripped bare like the ones in the Grove.

"The Woode has shut down, and there's this…eerie stillness…" Moo paced from tree to tree, sniffing out any signs of life.

"I wonder if this is the Darkness Fang mentioned. If so, it must be spreading, but how fast?" Rylla ran her hands along the rough bark of an oak, trying to shake her growing paranoia.

"The Darkness has been lying dormant under caves and deep places ever since the curse, so the roots and rocks and plants are affected first upon its unleashing. My grandfather told me when Lord Brennigan uttered his spell five-hundred years ago, it sent a wave of magic into the earth—a poisoned sleep. When the Bloodstone was found, the poison began to spread, and the Bloodstone's dark magic not only woke Brennigan, but it also awoke in other things—trees, plants, stones—spreading Darkness and malintent throughout the realm. We have to be careful for we don't know which side the trees are on."

A cold chill filled the air and the hair on the back of Rylla's neck prickled. Someone was watching them. Rylla stepped away from the oak and stood in the center of a cluster of trees, slowly spinning to take in her surroundings. Yes, she was definitely paranoid now.

"I don't like how this feels, Moo. If the Darkness spreads faster below ground than it does above, we'll never see it coming!"

As if on cue, a gust of wind stirred the still air, pulling strands of hair from Rylla's ponytail and messing Moo's freshly licked mane. The dead leaves on the ground began to rustle and swirl, slowly at first and then swiftly into a cyclone. The whirling mass shaped into a vague figure.

"What is…that?" Rylla asked, pointing at the wind and leafy form, fear edging her words.

The wind spun faster and faster and began to move in her direction. An outstretched hand seemed to be reaching from within the turbulence, beckoning them forward.

"I don't like this, Ryl—" Moo was cut off by a hiss.

"T-r-e-sss-p-a-sss-e-r-sssssss…" A voice came from within the leaves, speaking in a slow, hissing breath.

"I don't either!" Rylla scrambled for her senses. Either she could stay where she was, frozen in fear, or she could get Moo and try to outrun whatever this thing was. She fought for the second option, grabbing Moo around his middle and hauling him in the opposite direction. Moo gave a low growl, clearly not happy to be touched, let alone picked up by a human, but there was no time to argue.

"N-o-t ssssss-o f-a-ssssss-t." Within an instant, the cyclone of leaves spread wider and encircled Rylla and Moo in an endless torrent of suffusing wind. From within the leaves, the bony figure of a woman emerged right upon them. "Ssssss-t-a-y."

Rylla and Moo fell to the ground. The wind stole her breath as the pressure from the whirling cyclone rendered her lightheaded and speechless. She clutched her chest, finding Winnie's necklace between her groping fingers—gasping, choking. Air. She needed air.

Moo lay next to her, panting with his tongue sticking halfway out of his mouth.

The leaf-woman's frail, bony hand was now only inches away from Rylla's face.

It was a curious thing, if Rylla could have dreamed up this scenario, she surely would have cowered in fear, too scared to move. But now that she was in it, she felt compelled to fight. She must keep going and press on.

It will not end this way. Her parents wouldn't lose their third child.

Summoning all her strength, Rylla clenched her fists into the pulsing earth. Warmth tingled in her fingertips and streamed up her arms as if from the earth itself, filling her with an overwhelming sense to protect—anything and everything, especially Moo. She needed to protect him like her life depended on it. Closing her eyes from the swirling debris and searching for her courage, she opened her mouth, the words pouring out from some place deep within her soul:

No surging wind
Can find its mark
Though oft it does try—
It will not destroy
Who seeks to protect
All that Darkness
Has sought to wreck

Ripples of rocks and earth spread forward from beneath her fingertips, creating a sea of gravel and green surging upwards in a shielding dome. A muted scream echoed through the forest, blocked out by the protective walls of earth. In a matter of seconds, the wind cut off completely and an eerie silence settled in its place. Moo and Rylla's panting breaths were the only sound.

Rylla slowly opened her eyes and gasped. Walls of earth towered around her, filtering in sunlight through its many cracks. A layer of dust floated in the air before settling upon the ground. "What just happened?" She croaked.

Moo tried to stand but sank down again almost instantly as he looked all around him in the same wonder. "It appears we were rescued. By you…" He tried to stand again and walked to the earthen wall. He stood on his hind legs and pushed his front paws against it. The structure gave a little and crumpled under his touch. "I think your powers are growing!"

"I didn't know I could do this…" Rylla finally stood. The dome was roomy enough for her to stand at her full height. She touched the ceiling with her hand and pulled back quickly as it too gave way and began to crumble atop her head. As it disintegrated, bits of golden rocks fell to the earth and landed near her feet.

"Moo…my arm doesn't hurt anymore." She pushed back her sleeve to reveal a large scab no longer inflamed nor searing in pain. Her head spun. "This isn't normal."

"I'm not sure anything that happened within the last few minutes could be considered as normal."

Rylla gawked again at the dome around them. How could she have formed the structure without knowing what she was doing? "I haven't been practicing any of my magic. I honestly don't even know how to! It was so strange, I just felt compelled to speak, though I can't remember what I said." She picked up the crumbled pieces of earth that had fallen. "This needs some work."

"Yes, but it's still progress! And they're Earth-spells, many Earth-Treaders use words for the earth to do their bidding. It seems you're quite the natural, though, my grandfather told me that you'll need training. Sometimes the power can be too much to control the stronger you become." Moo walked to the center of the dome, sniffing the rubble.

"Training? Where would I—"

"Wait, look at this!" Moo interrupted. He was staring intently at the ground.

The familiar wisp of a frail, bony hand disappeared beneath the surface of the earth. A small, indistinct voice came from its place. "Many th-a-nk-ssssss…"

A tiny sapling sprouted, its leaves unfurling to grasp at the sparse sunlight. It shone with a radiant golden glow, illuminating the crumbling dome with light.

"Rylla! I know what this is now!" Moo beamed. "My grandfather warned me about Woode Drifts, but I didn't remember them until seeing this."

"What are Woode Drifts?"

"Lost spirits of the Woode! They travel around in many different forms, feeding on wandering souls to satisfy their own wandering souls. When a Woode Drift ensnares another living thing, it takes that life as its own."

"So, if that hand had touched my face…?" Rylla shuddered.

"I don't know how long it takes…but if this thing had touched you, you wouldn't be alive. Instead, you restored this one back to the earth by using the earth itself, not your life. There are very few known to have this kind of power!" Moo began to clean his fur.

Rylla looked at the growing sapling, its golden leaves glistening and shimmering like rays of sunshine. In years to come, this tree would be a beacon of light amidst the shadows of Thrushwoode.

"Are you saying that all trees were once…human?" She swallowed.

"Not exactly. Many trees are simply trees, but every tree has a spirit. Everything has a spirit, and if disturbed before a natural death, a spirit *drifts* until it finds a place to settle. This makes them unruly and unpredictable—hungry even. The Darkness has caused a lot of disturbance in this Woode, and I expect there are more Woode Drifts to come if we linger too long."

"Well, then I suggest we don't linger…" Rylla ran a hand through her curls, tugging out the twigs and leaves snared in them. The sooner they found a way out of this forest, perhaps her heart would begin beating at a normal pace again.

Rylla pushed through what remained of her earthen dome, rocks and sticks tumbling to the ground by her feet. She scanned the towering trees around her, thick and strong, some skinless and others rough. They rustled their branches, creaked, and groaned—they were telling stories. Perhaps they would listen to one of her own.

If all trees had spirits, perhaps it didn't matter which kind she approached—be it oak or elm or otherwise—only that it was conscious enough to heed her call. Rylla smoothed her hands over the bark of the nearest elm, feeling the rough grains beneath her fingertips. She looked up into its green mass of leaves. "I request passage," she began. "Please."

But there was no response. If anything, the trunk had grown cold.

Behind her, Moo was sniffing out other trees, placing his paws on their trunks and brushing them with his whiskers.

"I assume my grandfather told you about Lord Brennigan, right?" Moo said behind her. "Since his reign, the Earth-Treader race has been disappearing—captured, tortured, enslaved, killed. He doesn't trust them."

"Fang told me, but I still don't understand why though." Rylla knocked gently on a nearby oak.

"Did you not see what you just did? He's worried about a power he cannot control nor understand. Power-hungry people will only be satisfied if there are no obstacles in their way. That's why he wants the stones, to obtain a power he thinks he'll be able to wield."

"How does this relate to the trees?" Rylla loved trees, but right now she wanted more than anything to see the open sky above her. To be on a mountain top with the land spreading out before her like the landmarks on a map.

"It all goes back to Lord Brennigan's fear and his death when he used his stone to cast a spell of Darkness upon the earth. This spell was so dark that it etched words into his stone—cursed words—words that once read, held enough power to bring Lord Brennigan back to life. Dark magic holds power we cannot understand in this realm, even across the boundary of life and death, but he neglects to accept the truth."

"The truth?" Rylla turned to face him.

"That Darkness can only hide for so long. Truth is revealed in light." Moo nodded in the direction of the golden sapling now glistening a little way behind them. "That tree is a sign that an Earth-Treader has begun to fight back. The golden light. It's your mark. And I believe people will look to it as a promise of hope. You're one of the last free Earth-Treaders left to fight, one with the purest of intentions and heart, and that's why it's important to grow your powers in order to defeat Lord Brennigan and his army. With a little more practice, I think that dome of yours could become a mountain."

Rylla tried to grasp what just happened and reconcile it with her fears and doubts. Her powers were growing, whether she liked it or not.

She didn't even know if this power was good or not, even if Moo kept saying she had pure intentions. But then, she could still remember the golden light that flowed from her, the power she felt, and the surprising peace and calm that came with it. This time with the Woode Drift she had felt something different, something that spoke louder than her fears: a need to keep fighting and to protect. It was violent, an urge uncontrollable. Almost as if it were coming from somewhere else, somewhere deep beneath the earth, lodged in its core.

Rylla spun around and almost stepped on Moo. "What's Ostglenden's stone known for?" she asked, a thrill tingling in her stomach and fingers.

"What?" Moo startled back to dodge her feet.

"The crest! The stone! What kind is it again and what's its power?" Rylla's heart raced.

"The Hawk's Eye, symbolic of protection, but why…?"

"I knew something felt different! Quick, Moo, I think we found the first stone!" Rylla ran back to the crumbling dome and began digging around the golden sapling. "I felt a sort of power, something I don't normally. I know it couldn't have been me—it has to be the stone!" Rylla grabbed clumps of dirt and threw them over her shoulder as Moo followed suit and began scrabbling at the hole with his front paws.

They dug all around the sapling for at least twenty minutes, numerous shallow and deep holes pockmarking the ground, when finally, Rylla jammed her finger into something solid.

"Oww!" She pulled her hand back to stare into the hole she was digging in. Something flashed, reflecting the golden sapling's glow from a smooth, shiny surface. "I think I found something!"

Moo jumped down, grabbing the object with his mouth. As he climbed out, he dropped it on the ground. A blue-green opaque gemstone shone brightly against the dirt.

The Hawk's Eye. It had to be.

Rylla picked up the stone and stared at it, cupping it in her small hand. It looked like an ocean colliding with the earth, the blue and green swirling into a cohesive mass of sparkling rock. The green reminded her of the trees back home—a green as bright and vibrant as the sun is bold, and the blue reminded her of the clear waters off Aylati's coast—a blue as serene as the waters themselves. It stole her breath and it pulsed with magic. Her fingers tingled with power and it spread up her arm like gooseflesh. If she continued to hold onto it, she was convinced her body would lose control and burst; part of her almost wanted it to. With the stone in her hand, the beating of her heart turned from one of fear into confidence and boldness. She no longer felt weak and afraid. She could do anything.

And then Fang's voice came back to her, reminding her *why* she was chosen for this mission in the first place. She was trustworthy, or at least she tried her hardest to be.

No, this stone was not hers to use. Rylla slipped the smooth rock into her satchel. She let her gaze linger on the golden sapling and the remains of her crumbling dome. Maybe she could do this after all; maybe she could start to believe. Just maybe.

Chapter the Seventh

Passage to Somewhere

The wind howled, sending the trees dancing violently. Gray clouds swirled overhead and the wind caught crumpled leaves and twigs and hurled them toward the dark mass. The flying debris scatted amongst the rocks or crashed into the windows of the stone tower, only to rattle down and be snatched once more by the turbulent wind.

The decrepit figure sat alone in the center of the highest room, watching the rise and fall of the outdoors. How much longer would its recovery take? Growing back five-hundred-year-old limbs was more gruesome than anticipated. If it had known fully the pain, if it could have but foreseen the future, would the choice have been different?

The being glanced around the room, scanning the walls with sunken eyes and resting them upon the gilded frames. From right to left, The Isles of Norviç's stone shimmered, Rélynda's sparkled, Wyllund's gleamed, Ostglenden's was empty, Aylati's…

The being whirled its head back in the direction of Ostglenden's frame, a smile parting its cracked lips. What was once a picture of a shimmering stone, there now shone a black, empty canvas.

The being stirred in the chair with restlessness and hope. A stone only disappeared from the frame if touched by human hands, thus marking it as found. Someone had found it; someone had tracked down one of the Earthen-Crest stones. Gryfinn had finally done it!

A maniacal laugh echoed throughout the empty chamber, disrupting the sleeping ravens. The creature's body was healing—slowly, but still healing—and the rest of the stones would be found in no time. Once all were captured and its body fully restored, there would be nothing standing in its way.

The creature thought back to its own stone, of its destructive power and the risks it had taken. If the decrepit being could but find all the lost crests, then the pain would be worth it in the end. Then its cursed body wouldn't have suffered in vain.

⸙ ⸙ ⸙

Rylla's patience was growing thin, and Moo's ears twitched in aggravation. They had spent countless hours trying to wake the forest—hoping, wishing, waiting. The trees refused to listen.

Rylla placed her hand on another oak, shaky and spent. She bit down the irritation at being refused once more but was surprised when the bark grew warm at her touch. A tingle of excitement shot up her arm.

"Moo! Come here!" Rylla shouted, eyes searching for the cat.

"What? Did you find a willing tree?" Moo ran over and stood beside her, sniffing.

"I don't know. I haven't asked it yet." Rylla returned her gaze to the rugged trunk, its bark like miniature mountain peaks beneath her fingers. "If you may. Grant us passage from this place," Rylla pleaded. "Please." An extra dose of politeness couldn't hurt.

The tree shook its branches, sending a waterfall of leaves cascading toward the ground. Rylla looked up and watched them fall before settling her gaze once more on the trunk. The bark grew warmer beneath her hand, and then it vibrated like a stampede of hooves. A golden root climbed the trunk and formed an arch in the bark just above Rylla's head before curving downwards once more. It was the beginnings of a doorway, but there was still no door.

Rylla removed her hand and watched as the bumpy tree bark smoothed into wooden planks within the arch. They clicked and clamped into place, creaking and groaning in the effort. An intricate brass knob with a pine cone engraved on its face popped out from the grains and gleamed brilliantly. The rustling had quieted, but the wooden door awaited them, pulsing with magic.

Rylla glanced at Moo, eyes wide and mouth open in wonder. "It's so beautiful." She reached toward the grains, the wood smooth beneath her touch. "Thank you," she said to the oak. She looked back at Moo. "Are you ready?"

Moo nodded. "Though I don't like the idea of being trapped for very long."

"Me neither." Rylla reached for the knob and paused. What was that? Voices and what sounded like horses' hooves echoed in the distance. More poachers? Woode Drifts?

"We need to leave now!" She turned the knob with a creak and peered inside. It was a sunlit space, just big enough for the two of them.

Without so much as a second thought, Rylla plunged into its safety, Moo jumping after her. Once inside, the door closed behind them, followed by the sounds of wood snapping and shifting into place.

⸙ ⸙ ⸙

The tree's bark was rough and textured, and it gleamed with a golden light. It was just a tree, but this was no ordinary woman. After rescuing her from the poachers the other day, he had kicked himself in the shins for letting her go so fast. If he hadn't been so concerned to get back to the Ivory Valley, if he had but slowed down, perhaps he would have realized these women were one in the same. *What a dolt*!

He had journeyed back to the valley only to find it more abandoned than yesterday—no sign of life at all. It wasn't until he paused and recalled the cat he had seen from the day before that he started putting the pieces together. The black and white fur, the same as the cat he had seen in the cave. At that moment, he backtracked and reentered Thrushwoode, this time more determined than ever to find her.

And he eventually did, but it was too late, for she had disappeared *into* a tree just before he could reach her. He needed to find her—she was his ticket to freedom.

He bent to observe the brilliant golden and green grass surrounding the tree's base. The other trees harbored dead grass with roots mottled and shriveled at their trunks. But this tree resembled the one she had touched back in the foothills of Mount Egret.

What was she up to? Who was this mysterious woman?

"Caz, it's 'bout time we got back on the road. We 'ave ta report back by dusk if we don't want our 'ands cuffed or our 'eads in the stocks," a distant voice with a heavy Wyllund accent called to him from somewhere in the forest.

"Hold up, just relieving myself." Caz preferred to travel alone and had originally planned to before Jovin decided to tag along. He was just grateful Jovin hadn't seen the girl or the tree; that would take too much explaining that Caz didn't want to get into. He turned and made his way back toward his friend.

Caz kept thinking about it: why would the girl willingly travel into an even greater danger? In Aylati she would've been safer—or at least uninjured. That onerous woman. If only she hadn't run away.

He knew her face now, her hair, her eyes, and he would be able to spot her cloak from anywhere with the gold wings on the back. She couldn't hide for much longer.

"All right. When yeh done, yeh rouncey's takin' a dip in the ravine," Jovin stated nonchalantly as Caz emerged from the tangle of trees.

"And you did nothing about it?" Caz couldn't help asking, knowing full well that his horse, Rembrandt, didn't listen to anyone. Not even to him most days.

"Thought yeh might need the exercise."

"How considerate…" Caz reluctantly made his way to the nearby gorge to retrieve his horse.

The chestnut brown animal had his mouth submerged in the water, guzzling the clear liquid like it was the elixir of life. He was in the stream, the water up to his ankles as his tail swished happily, oblivious to the men's banter.

"'ey, whatever 'appened ta that girl we shot?" Jovin called after Caz before picking his teeth with a twig.

Caz tensed. "*We* didn't shoot her. That was Bryant. And I don't know." This conversation needed to end. He didn't need more images of bloodshed, screams, and tears darkening his mind. The nightmares were enough.

Caz had prepared Rembrandt earlier in the day, getting ready to search for the girl back in Aylati, but his plans were interrupted by the high-speed chase. He saw his unit hounding after a girl and felt compelled to join the fray with hopes of rescuing the frightened damsel. In the end, he had been able to accomplish his goal, but at a cost. If anyone found out what he had done, he'd be dead.

It was hard enough to have averted the group's attention, but dragging her safely to his hidden cave…he didn't ever want to do that again.

"Who knew 'e was such a good shot, eh? Thought 'e couldn't even get a mallard." Jovin took a swig of water and belched. "Better get that 'orse, brothur, the 'our's almost upon us. Gotta report back."

Grateful to end the conversation, Caz retrieved Rembrandt and quickly mounted. Within minutes he was back on the path with Jovin and headed for the border. He shoved his secrets deep into the back of his mind, spinning a smooth story to deceive the headquarters. No one could ever know what he'd done.

⸙ ⸙ ⸙

Sunshine blinded Rylla's eyes as she emerged from the hollowed tree. It was a strange feeling—dizzying and tingling—being teleported through the Woode, but pleasant all the same. It felt as if she was a newborn swaddled in warm sheets, gently being lulled to sleep by the sun as she moved like she was floating upon a river of grain. It felt strangely peaceful and comforting, reminding Rylla of her warm bed. She hadn't felt claustrophobic or afraid, but that was probably because the other option was meeting more Woode Drifts and that far outweighed her fear of trusting a tree.

When it came time to emerge, the tree coughed them out like a croaking frog, tumbling them gently along the grass. Rylla laughed as she rolled into some ferns and Moo growled irritably, his hair sticking up everywhere.

"That was incredible!" Rylla said, standing up to brush the dirt from her clothes.

"I'm glad it's over. I need to stretch my limbs!" Moo walked a few paces and did just that.

Before them was a wide expanse of low-lying grass and shrubs which eventually led to taller overgrowth. Rylla turned toward the distance where high peaks of some mountain range reached toward the blue sky. Her heart soared. The sun was beginning its slow descent, stretching the shadows along the ground. Behind them was a small cluster of elm trees, one exceptionally taller than the rest. It was beautiful here, and for the first time, Rylla didn't think of home.

"Where do you suppose we are?" Rylla placed her satchel on the ground and took out her map, scanning both the parchment and her surroundings for anything she recognized. They were at the edge of a field, birds flying overhead with cornflowers and lady's mantle swaying at the wind's command.

"Who, who, who, art thou?" came a voice from above them.

Rylla and Moo shot their glances skyward and found a gigantic barred owl resting alone on the branch of the tallest elm tree. It was big enough to carry a human, maybe even two! Its feathers were a mottled brown and white and its gaze sharp. It had one piercing silver eye. Countless other owls and birds of varying species and sizes surrounded him on the branches of the nearby trees, almost as if they were sitting in parliament.

"We humbly make your acquaintance, my lord." Moo bowed his front legs to the creature in greeting.

"Moo, what are you doing?" Rylla prodded him with her foot. "Get behind me or they'll eat you!" She stared at the fleet of fowl before her. She loved birds; for the longest time they had been her favorite creatures, but now she was more concerned for Moo's life.

Moo ignored her and continued to address the Great Owl. "We are Lady Rylla of Aylati and Squire Claw of the Felines. I come from a long line of Fleebanes, my father was Hunter, and my grandfather is Fang of the Grove. We are humbly at your service."

"Taw, taw, taw, you do amuse me, small one. I knew of your father; Hunter was a friend of ours before his life departed from these kingdoms. 'Tis an amplitude of sorrows to recount his passing. Hunting accidents are no small matter. But what do I owe this pleasure of meeting his offspring? It's not every day new personage enter my domain unbidden, though welcome, but still unbidden." The owl turned his head so his large silver eye pierced Rylla and Moo individually.

"We have recently outrun Ostglenden's border patrol and are bound to travel the entirety of the kingdoms. We sought safe passage in great Thrushwoode through a hearty oak and are now inquiring about our whereabouts. Do you know the location upon which your domicile is placed?" Moo, still kneeling, addressed the owl with all politeness.

"Yes, where are we? It would help place us on my map," Rylla interjected, staring at the owl and back at her map. It wouldn't hurt to confirm their location, though she had an idea of where they were.

"Roo, roo, roo, child. An Earth-Treader!" At this the Great Owl and his company squawked, hooted, and chirped, obviously greatly moved by this realization. The owl gave a signal and the noise ceased. "I do not understand such simple speech—the young lady is still acquiring the language of the Aviaries—I shall address the young squire."

The owl fixed his eye on Moo. "As to the answers you seek from your inquiries, you grace the Heather Fields of Wyllund. They are set in the south-west of the province, just moments away from Ostglenden's northern-most border. You two, however, currently stand in the proximity of the Owl's Tree, my own kingdom." At this, the Great Owl puffed out his feathers and shook his head as if to show dominance. The rest of the birds gave slight reverent bows.

"We made it past Ostglenden? Just like that?" Rylla scanned her map again, biting her lip.

"That miserable speech of hers, it is too plain." The owl shook his head yet again.

"A million gratitudes on your behalf, my lord. We request passage to proceed on our journey," Moo said.

"Passage granted. The Owl's Tree is always acquaintance to the Earth-Treaders and friendly kin. Assistance is always bestowed to those in grave need," the owl spoke this with pride while the others bobbed their heads in agreement.

"However, take heed." The owl grew suddenly more serious. "A growing Darkness, a whispering lurks amongst the heather and the brush. The fields lie in an enchantment, and those who pass through it are not always fortunate. Tarry not and rest not but make haste lest the shadows find you. You'll find that even in town the people are lacking in hope and turning brash in their despair. Lord Brennigan's army is on the move!" the Great Owl hooted his final warning and flew from his perch, circling the sky as if on the lookout, searching.

The rest of the birds left their positions and either joined him or went on their own way.

"That was curious. How did you know what to say?" Rylla looked at Moo with wonder.

"Owls are wise sages in the animal realm. Their minds are too intelligent for common speech." Moo began to lick his paw. "Where do we go now?"

"We keep moving forward. We're ahead of schedule…" Rylla gazed toward the darkening horizon. A sudden calm flowed through her and she stood, staring out toward the mountains.

"What are you thinking?" Moo inquired.

"My brothers have traveled these lands once—maybe still." She brushed a loose curl behind her ear. "I'd like to find them." The thought of seeing Garth and Finn again sent a jolt of hope into her aching heart. It had been too long. She wanted to find them for both her sake and her parents'.

"Do you think they're here in Wyllund?"

"I don't know, they could be anywhere, even back in Ostglenden." Rylla lowered her gaze to study her father's map. "But that would be highly inconvenient seeing as we just crossed its borders." She smirked and once again the image of her rescuer's face came to mind. She recalled his calloused hands taking the time to mend her arm. Would an enemy do that?

She wasn't sure, but the man had been curt and severe. Was his heart as calloused as his hands? What did it matter anyway? She had left him far behind and he'd no longer be able to find her again.

These thoughts pooled in Rylla's mind as she scanned the map and settled her eyes on what she guessed was the closest marking to their location. They were at the cusp of the Heather Fields of Wyllund like the owl had said, and according to the map it would take a few hours' journey to get through it—if there were no complications.

"Moo, if we keep going northwest, we should come to Wyllund's small village of Goosewyn by nightfall. I remember my father telling me about that place, saying they had the best bread rolls and minced meat pies. Perhaps it's a safe bet…" Rylla paused. "But according to the owl, I'm not sure what's safe anymore."

The thought sent a shiver up her spine as she played the owl's warning over in her head. Perhaps it was all hearsay and the heather wasn't as dangerous as rumored. Rylla carefully refolded the map, placed it back in the satchel next to the stone, and took out a bun and a wedge of cheese. Talking about dinner made her remember the provisions in her bag.

"You brought food?" Moo circled Rylla's legs in eager expectation.

"I wasn't completely brainless." Rylla ripped some cheese off and threw it to Moo while she bit into the bread. "I guess I've been too distracted to notice how hungry I actually am though." *Or too worried.* "I wish I'd brought more."

"Well, if we head out now, maybe we can reach that village soon and eat those minced meat pies you mentioned!" Moo licked his lips.

"Yes, that does sound good." Rylla brushed some crumbs off her face and a drop of moisture fell on the back of her hand. "I think it's beginning to rain."

Out in the distance, rain clouds slowly clustered to form subtle masses of shadow. A haze veiled the land beneath them, indicating that a heavier rainfall would be reaching them soon.

"I don't like getting wet." Moo hissed at the oncoming storm.

"Don't assume I like it either. I'm tired of getting drenched!" Rylla fixed her hood over her head and motioned Moo to her side. "Let's get moving, then. Stick close and you might stay dryer. I want to make it to the village before dark."

Rylla and Moo took their first steps into the dense heather with the owl's warning of Darkness haunting their every step and a wall of rain approaching them like a predator.

Chapter the Eighth

In the Heather

Caz and some others stood talking near the northernmost border of Thrushwoode in Ostglenden. His cloak was pulled close and his hood up, shielding him from the heavy rainfall. It came down in sheets, filling the roads with puddles and muddy trenches. Near the horizon, a break in the thick clouds revealed a misty half-moon.

Caz looked up to see a large man in a thick overcoat and sturdy boots approaching, riding a white charger and surrounded by four bodyguards. The large man's face appeared to be carved of stone and upon his head was a bronzed crown. Caz dared not meet his gaze. Not yet.

The man dismounted; his feet hit the ground with a heavy thump and his footsteps puckered in the sodden earth with every step he took.

"The week's report?" His jet-black hair fell to his shoulders and his chin was covered with a thick Van Dyke.

Caz remained silent along with the others, as if they were all waiting for someone to speak first.

"Has no one anything to report?" The man unsheathed his sword and swung it by his hip like a jolly man his cane.

"Your Majesty, our unit can report no unusual occurrences in Thrushwoode. Ostglenden remains unchanged," a shorter man with graying hair spoke up for his men.

"And you were stationed where, may I ask?" King Grievon stopped and stared the man down.

"Along the western border near the Indigo Tide."

"Ah, yes…no unusual occurrences, like you said." King Grievon stared at the graying man a few more seconds. "At ease, take your men and get refreshment." He continued down the line and stopped at Caz, Jovin, and the others in their squad.

"And?" he prompted.

"Your Majesty, the day proceeded as normal—there's nothing to report," Caz chose his words carefully.

"And where were you stationed?"

"In the central regions, closer to the southern border near Aylati," another man named Aar'nen cut in.

Caz's heart quickened just thinking about the girl. This week his unit was stationed in southern Thrushwoode, and the fact that he had entered Aylati alone on a whim would be considered borderline treachery. He was the leader, his men followed him, and he was meant to be responsible and loyal only to King Grievon. But nothing would make him regret that rash decision, nothing would make him regret what he had stumbled upon.

"Curious, very curious. And you said nothing unusual happened today?" The king glanced at Caz, but directed his question to Jovin and Aar'nen with a challenge in his eyes.

"Well, there wasn't much ta report 'til we almost caught a wo—" Jovin was cut off.

"A woodchuck. We almost caught one for dinner, but it got away. We won't bore you with the details," Caz spoke confidently, but his heart was beating so hard that he could feel the blood rushing to his ears. He glanced at Jovin and quickly arched his brows, pleading for him to understand.

"A woodchuck, you say? How riveting." King Grievon took his sword and pressed it firmly on Caz's boot, applying enough pressure to puncture the top and nick his skin. "Now, would you like to tell me the truth?"

Caz stiffened and clenched his jaw. He locked gazes with the king even as his mind was in turmoil, trying to conjure some lie that would make him believe.

Caz never had courage enough to defy the king before, to challenge his authority. Caz's loyalty sent a wave of guilt to his gut. Because of his actions, he couldn't get the women's screams or children's cries out of his head. If he had but saved one, maybe his conscience would be clearer.

He shifted under the pressure of Grievon's sword. Any reasonable explanation to avoid getting stabbed would mean him mentioning the girl, but no matter how he tried to form the words in his mouth, he couldn't. He wouldn't.

"I see. You're growing soft. A pitiful excuse for a soldier, let alone border patrol," the king scoffed, jerking his sword out of Caz's boot. Droplets of water bounced off the metal as it came plunging deep into Caz's thigh.

Pain flared across his senses and a cry wrenched from his lips. His leg gave way, sending him to the mud. He clenched his teeth at another gasp of pain as the blade tore free with his movement. White, then red flashed across his vision, taking his breath away.

"Let's see if that'll toughen you up." The king crouched beside him, eyes narrowed and scornful. "I know more than you realize, and I won't be made the fool. Be thankful that wasn't your heart."

The king got up and glanced at Jovin. "If you continue to associate yourself with the likes of him, you're next."

He turned and walked back to his horse, gesturing to his bodyguards. "Appoint Bryant as chief officer of the second branch and dispatch him to the north. And find the girl."

"Caz, stay with me, brothur. 'ow's the pain?" Jovin knelt beside Caz and moved the folds of his cloak.

A dark stain crept at the cloth of his pants, and Caz bit back another grimace. That wasn't just mud. Warmth stung his skin, despite the freezing rain. Jovin's frown wavered in and out of focus above him as the man pressed a bundled cloth to the wound. Pain flared again at the pressure and Caz choked on a groan.

Aar'nen and the others in their branch, their faces masked with confusion and fear, lingered a little apart from Caz. He was a traitor now, he supposed. They wouldn't want to bring the same fate upon themselves. One by one, they darted into the shadows and made a run for who-knew-where, to escape his presence. Caz couldn't care less. Only a few men from other units remained a few paces off.

"He knows," Caz spoke through gasps. "He knows about her."

"The pain, brother—can yeh walk?" Jovin grabbed his shoulders.

Caz tried to focus on his friend, but the rain seemed to be blurring his vision. "We have to find her before he does..." She'd have no chance alone with the king's best men tracking her down.

"Yeh going delusional—'ang on, let me grab my medicine bag!" Jovin ran to his horse and retrieved a large, canvas sack.

"I'm not delusional, just need some stitches or..." Caz's vision began to darken as the warm blood spread along his thigh. "Don't let me fade, Jovin, don't...don't let..."

The world became night, but this time with no moonlight or rain.

⸙ ⸙ ⸙

The world dipped into rain and darkness as Rylla and Moo journeyed through the Heather Fields with only the faintest glimmer of moonlight squeezing through a gap in the clouds. The long wisps of lady's mantle, cattails, big bluestem, and every type of heather imaginable wove around them like a maze. The feathery bristles brushed Rylla's cheeks as she pressed onwards, the promise of Goosewyn's warmth and safety keeping her going.

They had been walking at a steady clip for what seemed like hours without many inconveniences, aside from being completely sodden and getting tangled in roots and thistles. Moo had a few burrs in his coat, which he failed miserably in keeping dry, and Rylla had several scratches on her face and her hair was plastered to her forehead. Only a few more miles until the village, then they could rest and get some good food.

"When we get to Goosewyn, I'm not leaving," Moo called behind him to Rylla. "Not until I get every inch of water off of me."

Rylla was thinking similar thoughts as she trudged after him. "What I wouldn't give for a fire."

Though her cloak was water-resistant, the rain had somehow drenched her pants below the knees, parts of her shirt, and her boots. Cold chilled her bones. She was shaking from head to foot, and Goosewyn couldn't come fast enough. But what she longed for most was the warmth of home—her soft bed, her library, and her parents now more than ever. She'd trade the cloak off her back and suffer more of the rain if it meant the promise of seeing their faces again.

Rylla was so lost in her thoughts that it took Moo's voice to shake her from her reveries and remind her where she was.

"I believe the weather is finally letting up a bit," he spoke.

Rylla brushed some stringy hair out of her mouth and paused. "Actually, it's stopped completely." That change occurred a little too suddenly considering it had been pouring only a few steps ago.

Odd.

"Does it feel warm to you?" Moo stopped to shake his drenched coat.

Rylla looked around her and noticed it had grown even darker. Too dark. There were silhouettes of plants and trees all about her, their shapes getting harder to discern. After a few more steps, she noticed the increase in temperature too.

"Now that you mention it…"

"And I'm feeling rather sleepy, like I want to take a nap now." Moo sat down and blinked slowly, yawning.

"Me too…something doesn't feel right." Rylla blinked through heavy eyelids at the horizon, trying to make sense of her surroundings by the light of the moon. In the distance, shifting shadows moved in zigzag patterns through the fields, heading in their direction.

A dull knot of fear cramped in her stomach, but she was too overcome with an overwhelming need to close her eyes, if only for a moment. She clutched her chest and found Winnie's necklace, clinging to something, anything that might ground her.

Something nudged her deep inside to keep fighting and fend off the desire to sleep. To endure and hold on.

"Moo, don't fall asleep, we need to keep going…I think this is what the owl was talking about—this must be the enchantment!" Rylla desperately fought to keep her eyes open. Sleep seemed like a welcome friend amidst the approaching shadows, and she felt how lovely would it be if her shadows of fear finally had some company of their own.

She glanced out to the horizon again as her knees hit the earth. The shapes and shadows were closer now, but still unidentifiable for certain. Moo's head was beginning to droop, only inches from touching the ground.

"Moo! Don't…!"

But the weight of the enchantment was too strong for his smaller frame, and Moo rested his head upon the earth, falling into a deep and dark sleep.

"No! Wake up—Moo!" Rylla cried with as much intensity she could muster and crawled over to the limp cat. "Come on, boy, come back…" Rylla cradled his still frame in her arms and watched his chest rise and fall in subtle motions. She wiped her face as tears leaked from her eyes. He would be gone in a matter of moments. And she would be too. Would this be the end?

Suddenly, the world went dark.

Rylla glanced skyward, but there was nothing but black. No trees in the distance, no heather, no moon. She was trapped in a cave of Darkness. Her worst fear: a place where the monsters of imagination could loose themselves from their cages without limitation. Her heart throbbed wildly in her chest, her breathing stifled and gasping; a twisting and smoldering panic stung her throat as tears dripped from her chin. Light. She needed light!

This was the kind of blackness she had experienced when she was ten. Hide-and-seek was supposed to be a fun game, but being trapped in a pitch-black closet with no way out was how she realized her fear of the dark. She'd never been able to forget that moment.

Now this Darkness would be the end of her.

The shadows moved in closer, suffocating the very air she breathed. She counted the minutes—no, seconds—until her inevitable death as she held fast to Moo. They had to escape, but she couldn't move, could barely even breathe. Fang's mission would be wasted on her. Her parents would lose their third child.

And then it came. A light so bright it rendered the moon and stars speechless, splintering the wall of shadows into pieces like broken china. The light burst through the shadowed wall and ruptured the very core of its Darkness. The brightness was so fierce, it made the shadows flee, taking the overwhelming sleepiness with it.

Rylla gasped and blinked, adjusting to the intense light. She could see again, could breathe again, could hope—and when she looked up, she couldn't believe what she saw.

Her brother.

Chapter the Ninth

The Furrough

Anger, hatred, fear. These emotions swirled around inside the broken soul. It was bursting at the seams, desperate for action, desperate to reclaim what was stolen—to take it back. But this wretched body, this immovable vessel of garbage…wrecked. If only, if only.

Gryfinn had returned only moments ago with nothing to report—not much was happening within the borders of Rélynda, let alone the rest of the kingdoms. Their southern units had only just breached Ostglenden's northernmost border, not quite knowing the best way to enter Thrushwoode. No stones had been found, no Earth-Treaders captured…The day had been a bland one.

"GrrrRRR-AAARGHHH!" the creature let out a savage howl, writhing in the chair and shaking the fire-lit sconces. Ravens fled in fear, erupting from their perches with a fluster of wings and feathers.

"My…lord?" Gryfinn spoke hesitantly.

"No stones have been found, you say?" The creature was seething, sweat trickling from its brow, too angered to give into a coughing fit. Its limbs were growing, slowly, but still growing. What had once been the beginnings of shoulders now led into fully formed elbows—pretty soon forearms and hands would follow.

"That's what I said, my—"

"Then how do you explain this?" The creature lifted its half-formed arm and gestured to the gilded frames, Ostglenden's blank and empty.

"I…I assure you, my lord, this can be remedied." Gryfinn pulled at his collar as he fumbled over his words. This wasn't what he had planned for, surely no one knew about the whereabouts of these stones like his master, surely this was some mistake!

"Dark magic makes no mistake, Gryfinn," the creature spat his name as if reading his thoughts. "Maybe it was my mistake taking you on…"

"No, my lord, I am worthy." Gryfinn dropped to his knees and removed his hood, running his hand over his bearded face. "Please give me more time."

"Time? There is no time! All these stones are to be mine and in my possession!" The creature was growing stronger, no longer taking breaks to hack and wheeze. Instead, it was sitting up straighter, bulkier, and menacing. "This is your last chance; find the stolen stone and whoever took it, be it an arrogant fool or some lowly peasant. And find the others. If more go missing, it'll be the end of you." The creature spat on Gryfinn. "Now get out of my face!"

"Yes, my lord." Gryfinn rose and bowed, retreating from the room with as much decorum he could muster. Once outside the door, he slid to the ground breathing hard and clutched the stone around his neck. Heat spread across his chest, mingling with the boiling in his stomach. The hatred and jealousy filled him and fueled him.

He wouldn't be second best, not again. This time he would win, and he would prove himself worthy.

⸙ ⸙ ⸙

Caz awoke to a waning sun and something wet hitting his face. His horse leaned over him, drool falling from his mouth as he tried to nudge his rider awake.

"Quit that, will you? I'm up!" Caz wiped the saliva off his chin and reached up to pet his horse.

"Rembrandt's been nudgin' yeh for the past 'alf 'our. I guess 'e finally decided ta try a new tactic." Jovin's voice carried over to where Caz was lying down.

Caz realized he was on some sort of stretcher and in a small alcove with a tarp overhead. The tarp was strung up high, tied to trees and surrounded by mounds of rocks. He didn't recognize this place and wasn't sure where they were.

"Where are we?" Caz inquired. He pushed up onto his elbows but regretted the action at once. The pain from yesterday's wound stabbed up his leg like the blade was still in his flesh. He winced and slowly tried to move his leg manually with his hands. How could he have been so careless to let this happen?

"A place I like ta call the Furrough." Jovin spread his hands wide, gesturing to their surroundings. He didn't look all that amused, but instead was growing serious.

"And where is that? I don't remember Thrushwoode—"

"Ta smithereens with Thrushwoode, brothur. We're up north near Wyllund's bordur. What were yeh thinkin' pullin' a trick like that in front o' the king? Yeh 'eard what 'e said—it's either yeh life or mine next."

"You don't understand," Caz protested.

"What don't I understand? Yeh 'ave us runnin' for our lives because of a stupid woodchuck!" Jovin shouted. He paced the length of the small enclosure, hands pulling at his hair.

"I had to come up with something, Jovin. She's not any ordinary girl."

"What's that got ta do with anythin'?" Jovin demanded, though the frown creasing his brows faded more to confusion than anger.

"Two days ago, I was in Aylati." Caz paused, watching Jovin.

The other man's eyes widened, but he didn't interrupt, so Caz pressed on.

"I'd never left Ostglenden before and Thrushwoode was close to the Eastern Ridges, so I couldn't help it. When I made it to those mountains, I descended to the foothills and found something strange. A young woman was leaning against a tree. When she removed her hand, the bark turned gold."

"Yeh can't be serious…" Jovin raised an eyebrow, arms crossed over his chest, but he cocked his head to the side, obviously willing to hear more of an explanation.

"I second guessed it too, but then I went over and took a closer look. Here—" Caz shifted his position and fished in his pocket. He withdrew his hand and held out a piece of bark as golden as the sun.

Jovin took it and studied it, turning it over between his fingers.

"I knew what I saw, Jovin, and so I followed. I tracked her into the Ivory Valley, but I'm afraid she thought I was some poacher trying to—"

"Well, yeh are," Jovin interrupted.

"That's not the point, I wasn't hunting this time." Caz ran a hand over his face, blinking away memories of fire and smoke. The images were still clear like they had happened yesterday, and his guilt weighed as heavy as iron shackles. "You know our positions. We report anything that moves within Thrushwoode, closed in by walls of trees, never to see the light. It's treacherous and dark. Horrid work. You know that yourself." Caz reasoned, "Grievon is hungry for power, and he's searching. This girl…"

"Yeh think she's what 'e's looking for?" Jovin asked, eyes still on the bark.

"Yes, since coming to Thrushwoode, the king found out about her. If the stories are true, she's an Earth-Treader. He must have a hunch about that though, and if he gets his hands on her, who knows what crazy things he'll do next." Caz closed his eyes, trying to ignore the dark possibilities that flashed through his mind.

"But why do *yeh* even care?" Jovin handed the piece of bark back.

"Because I can't let Grievon use this girl as his new play toy. He's taken too much already. From all of us." Caz pocketed the golden bark, the memory of Grievon dragging him by his hair across a dusty street flashed through his mind. He had been seven at the time, stripped from his only home. The memory was still raw, and there were plenty more—haunting memories he'd wish to forget. "I need to find her first."

Caz stood up, the effort sending streaks of pain through his lower half. It killed. The throbbing felt like thousands of needles being hammered into his flesh. He took hold of a tree branch to steady himself.

Jovin rubbed his chin. "But what made yeh rescue that girl we chased yesterday? Yeh didn't know it was the same girl then, did yeh?"

"I didn't, no. But when our unit tried taking her down, something compelled me to defend her. Maybe it was to act the hero, maybe not. I just knew I had to do something." Caz smirked but it faded quickly. "I want to spite Grievon and offer this girl my help; if she doesn't want it, then at least I gave the warning that he's after her. Then I can leave for the Isles. Start afresh, you know—new name, new life."

"Well, I very well can't go back ta Thrushwoode either—the king doesn't trust me, thanks ta yeh." Jovin gave him a sidelong glance. "I guess that means I 'ave ta tag along."

"Wait. You're coming? That easily? Something tells me there's more at stake here." Caz crooked his brow.

"Let's just say I've never liked the king. 'e took me from my 'ome in Wyllund when I was only eight an' 'ave been 'ere far too long, servin' as a field medic for *'is Majesty*," he said the name rather irreverently. "Besides, this girl reminds me of my uncle. It's been years since anyone's last seen 'im though. I guess I'd like a chance ta change my fate an' start fresh on the Isles too. But what I really want is ta make Grievon eat the gravel 'e walks on."

Caz and Jovin shook hands, and warmth filled Caz at the firm grip. They'd always gotten along well, but now there was something different between them, like brothers. They were one in the same, taken at a young age and forced to join a side they didn't believe in. But now? They had a plan. First to find the girl and warn her, offering their help if she wanted it. And second, to head to the Isles where they would start anew.

"How'd we make it here this fast, by the way?" Caz tried putting pressure on his leg. A twinge of pain shot through the wound, but it was bearable, so he pressed on. After a few strides, he was able to abandon the tree branch altogether.

"I strapped yeh onta Rembrandt's saddle an' made for the Furrough last night. It's 'bout midday now, so it took longer ta get 'ere than it seems."

"You just strapped me to my saddle, while unconscious?" Caz tried to slap the back of Jovin's head, but he ducked before he was given the chance.

"'ey, watch it! Yeh were on there pretty good, an' Rembrandt knew what 'e was doin'." Jovin held his hands up, playing the innocent.

Caz let out a laugh. "How'd you even know about this place? I've grown up in these lands, but only knew of Ostglenden's throne." He surveyed the landscape. He climbed atop some rocks, gritting his teeth as his leg twinged again, and elevated himself enough to see into the horizon. If he squinted hard enough, he could make out the pointed spires of a gray castle in the distance. "I've had the unfortunate pleasure of walking those halls years back…"

"Even though I grew up in Wyllund, I 'ad many adventures in the Furrough as a child. I'd sneak across the bordur with some friends an' we'd play blind-man's-bluff. We named this place the Furrough 'cause it looks like a giant crack in the earth, surrounded by trees an' rocks, almost imperceptible ta the eye. All this 'appened before Grievon stole my child'ood, of course. The good ol' days, I like to call 'em."

"It's a wonder I hadn't noticed it before." Caz continued to stare around the makeshift camp. "We should probably get going. We need to find that girl, and she could be anywhere." Caz sat down once more to check his wound.

The cloth was stained a dark red, almost brown, and when he removed the bandage, a raw line of flesh the length of his hand, stared back at him. Neat stitches were what kept the wound from reopening. Jovin's handiwork, do doubt. The wound didn't feel that deep which was a good sign. It would heal in a matter of days.

Jovin broke the silence. "Not everyday someone decides ta go after a girl they just met, just to be the 'ero. I bet yeh sweet on 'er." Jovin smirked and made ready to outfit his horse.

"I don't even know her name!" Caz protested, but a smile broke through his thoughtful expression.

"Can still be sweet on 'er without a name," Jovin returned.

Despite trying to ignore Jovin's taunts, the girl's face came to mind. Why had she entered Thrushwoode? And even when she learned of its dangers, she had plunged herself into it once more. She had never uttered one word of protest about the arrow wound. She was small and agile, but he was certain she was a lot stronger than she looked.

She'd also been very relieved to know her cat was okay. And then all over again, he remembered the fire in her eyes and her resolve to flee. Those frightened eyes, beautifully large and hazel.

But sweet on her? He barely knew her.

And he wasn't looking for love; the prospect had never been a priority. He just wanted a chance to change his past, to ease his guilt, and the Isles were calling his name.

Part Two:

Earth

Chapter the Tenth

Stories at Dawn

"Garth!" Rylla practically ran into his arms, not even caring to hold back the stream of tears in her eyes. "How did you…what are…how…what are you doing here?" Rylla couldn't even properly ask a question. Her relief had never felt so palpable.

"Rylla! What are *you* doing here? It's not safe, we need to leave, and quickly!" Garth pulled away, then stopped short, frowning at the limp cat on the ground.

Rylla followed his gaze and tried to break free from his grasp, but Garth wouldn't let go. His fingers tightened around her arms.

"Please, Garth, the enchantment did that to him." Rylla desperately wanted to pick Moo up, to make sure he was okay. "We need to save him!"

"It's too late, and we don't have time. We need to move!" Garth picked up the lantern he had been carrying, still shining but not as brightly as it had been when it broke through the Darkness. "The light's fading; we must leave—now!" He held fast to her arm, pulling her away from Moo's limp figure.

“We can’t just leave him, Garth! He’ll die!”

“He’s already dead!” he snapped cold-heartedly, not relenting. “We need to go!”

In the distance, swirls of Darkness began to form and advance toward them once again, this time much faster as they danced in and out of the moonlight. As they approached, the shadows seemed to hum with a powerful force as if hungry for something to devour. Garth gripped Rylla’s hand harder and began to run.

Tears stung Rylla’s eyes, this time not of joy, but her struggle was futile, so she fled after Garth. She felt as if she were being ripped in half, that part of her heart was being left behind in the heather with Moo. *I could have healed him. I should have tried.*

Garth continued to pull her away, running at breakneck speed through the remaining brush. If they continued at this pace, they should be exiting the fields in no time. They dodged roots and small streams, thorny brambles and young saplings, running and jumping off small rocks and mounds of earth. The Darkness was encroaching wraith-like, reaching out like a shadowed hand, seeking to claim what it desired. It was wispy and thick all at once, like a dense fog under too much moonlight. The lantern was a slow flicker now, and at any moment it would go out. The Darkness was catching up to them, but Garth and Rylla pressed on.

Rylla wondered if the Darkness and shadows were Woode Drifts or some other Drift longing to reclaim their souls. If Moo were here, she’d ask him. The thought of his limp form sent another twisting to her gut.

As the final stretch of heather lay before them, the Darkness seemed to pull back slightly, as if afraid to touch the boundary line of the fields. Instead, it arched up high and plunged down for an aerial attack to capture them before they escaped. But Garth was quicker. As the final light of the lantern died, he loosed a flare from his pocket, lighting it with a match, and thrust it into the void.

The light exploded and the shadows reared back with a shriek. Garth dragged Rylla across the border with a final jerk, unharmed.

They flung themselves on the ground, catching their breath as they turned to watch the Darkness writhe in fury and agony, scouring the land for anything it might find satisfactory enough to consume.

Moo.

Rylla unleashed a cry so strong and loud that she felt her heart crack anew. Her companion, her main source of information, her friend—she had left him for dead. And all she could do was watch while the Darkness finished what it had started. Deep shadows hovered above the heather, diving and plunging to the earth only to spiral once more into the air.

After a few moments, Garth finally spoke.

"Rylla, we should find some shelter." Garth picked up the strewn lantern, opening it to take something out. Whatever it was, he placed the object around his neck, tucking it under his tunic while dismantling the lantern to fit inside his bag—his hands moved swiftly like it was a routine he was well used to.

"I can't believe you made me leave him in there," Rylla whispered, her tears drying into anger.

"We had no choice. You should be thanking me, otherwise it would've been you!" Garth slung his bag over his shoulders and made to walk off in the opposite direction of the heather.

"Where are you going?" Anger boiled in Rylla's stomach, the heat rising to her chest and up her throat. *How can he just walk away?*

"To claim shelter enough for the two of us. If you value your life, I suggest you follow." Garth's voice was hardened like stone.

"What happened to you?" Rylla demanded. "You act as if you're heartless, as if you don't even care."

Garth paused, his muscles tense. "War changes you, Rylla, in ways you wouldn't understand," he said over his shoulder, his form blending into the surrounding night.

"Oh yeah? Try me!" she yelled, willing her brother to turn around.

"I can't lose another, Rylla! I can't lose—not you!" Garth snapped. His blue eyes were hard and worn—as if they had weathered countless storms. He was much older than Rylla had remembered.

She shrank back a step, startled by his outburst at seeing him so on fire. What had caused him this much pain?

But then something in him softened, as if the strains of their narrow escape were finally loosening their hold.

"Come, let's find a place to rest, and I'll tell you all about it." He filled the gap between them and reached out to push a strand of hair behind her ear. "Please, just come." Garth dropped his hand again and stepped away, turning and beginning to walk.

Rylla was rendered silent. She felt she had no choice but to leave Moo and the heather behind. Too much had happened, and her head spun with thoughts and dizziness, faint both in her heart and body. Perhaps some rest would do her good, though she doubted it would remove the deep pain of her loss.

As the Darkness moved closer to the place where Moo had been, it twisted in furious, discouraged patterns. There was no life, no body to be found, save for a large bird soaring overhead, flying as if carrying a bundle in its talons.

The Darkness lunged skyward toward the bird only to find its thin, wispy fingers clawing at empty space. The creature was out of its reach. The shadows gave a screeching, hissing cry. Nothing. It would go hungry tonight, and it had been far too long since its last meal.

Next time, surely. Next time it would feast.

⸙ ⸙ ⸙

Rylla and Garth entered Goosewyn by early dawn, the moon low in the sky. The town was asleep, the streets empty, and the market turned down. There were no signs of life save for a few pheasants pecking at day old corn and pigs rummaging for scraps in the trough. Houses of stucco and straw were tightly fitted together and conjoined in several places, some towering high to rival the surrounding trees while others were shorter and stouter in their appearance. Everything was gray and covered in layers of fine dust, but if one were to simply blow enough air or summon a strong enough gale, the true colors of the village might show underneath. It looked to be a pleasant enough place, if not a little sad and fusty. Rylla wouldn't mind seeing it full of life and in action. But right now, what she needed most was answers.

Garth led her down a narrow side street, clotheslines with damp laundry dangling high from the windows above them. The walls of the slim alleyway were mismatched stone, chipped and broken in places too numerous to count. Wooden doors intermittently broke up the stonework where little bronze characters were nailed to their surfaces, doormats and shoes laying on the ground before them. These and the clothes were the only indication of Goosewyn's inhabitants.

Garth rounded a bend with Rylla following close behind, and stopped so abruptly she almost walked into him. He stood outside one of the wooden doors with strange markings scratched into the paint—a variety of lines and dashes—and he looked both ways before knocking in a rhythmic pattern.

The door unlocked and opened a crack as if by magic or some invisible hand.

"Mari?" Garth spoke the name quietly as if he were trying to make himself known while also remaining quiet. "I'm home!" He pushed the door open the rest of the way only to find a small girl on the other side, yawning and grinning up at him.

"Hi, Daddy!" The little girl rushed into his arms, her nightgown swaying at her ankles.

"Gracelynn, you're up early!" Garth lifted the small brunette into his arms, kissing her gently on the cheek. "And where's your mother?" He locked the door behind Rylla.

Rylla's stomach dropped. Daddy? Mother? *What is going on here?*

"She's right here." A tall, slender woman who looked to be in her late twenties entered the small, sparsely decorated room, holding a sleeping baby in her arms and looking both relieved and exhausted. Another woman followed behind her, similar in appearance but younger and shorter, a bow strapped to her back. "We've been up all night wondering when you'd return." Mari rushed over to hug Garth and give him a kiss, making sure not to jostle the sleeping child awake.

"I'm fine, Mari, I promise. How's Tobie feeling? Any better?"

"His fever broke midday, and he fell asleep around dusk; he's the only one who's actually gotten any rest in the past eight hours…" Mari tucked back a strand of her light-brown hair, her warm gaze seeming to soak in Garth's appearance as she pressed against him, her slender frame fitting perfectly in his strong embrace.

"I managed to get a few winks," the other woman chimed in and hugged Garth like one would a brother. "It's easy with little Gracelynn telling you bedtime stories." The woman bent down and tickled the little girl until she laughed.

Rylla just stared, feeling like an intruder to a family reunion. Her brother was married? And a father? She was beginning to think she didn't know him at all, at least not this version of him. Jealousy pricked Rylla's heart. If she were honest, she wasn't sure she liked sharing her brother. Well perhaps sharing him wasn't so much the problem, it was more of how out of place she felt. She'd been wishing for this very moment to see her brothers, to reconnect and share stories, but this wasn't what she had imagined.

Speaking of…where was Finn? Surely, he was here too, though probably hiding and ready to pull a prank on her.

As Rylla was left to her thoughts, she glanced about the small living quarters. There were two rooms with a window in each of them. They were covered by thicker curtains than she would have expected—her brother had always loved the outdoors. Sparse furnishings took up little space—a table, chairs, a few pots and pans, and a bed were among them. She also saw very few toys for a family with two kids—a doll, some wooden blocks, and a few pine cones were scattered about the wood-paneled floor.

Rylla again thought of her home, missing the warmth of the house and her parents. How she longed to go back, to sleep in her own bed and rest for hours. But something else pricked her conscience. If she left now, Moo would have died for nothing. No, she had to press on, no matter how much sorrow and remorse she felt.

"Who's this, Garth?" the unnamed woman spoke amidst Rylla's thoughts. They had finally realized it wasn't just their family in the room.

"Yes, forgive me. This is my sister Rylla." Garth moved to introduce her to the two women. "Rylla, this is my wife Mari and our two children Gracelynn and Tobie. And this is Elowen, Mari's younger sister."

"Nice to meet you, Rylla." The shorter woman, Elowen smiled, sincerity in her words. She held her right hand out and shook Rylla's firmly. She was strikingly beautiful with plaited light-brown hair and looked to be around Rylla's age.

Rylla immediately felt her own filth and longed for a long, hot bath.

"Tobie is about three months and Gracelynn just turned two. The perfect niece and nephew, are they not?" Elowen winked at the little girl who giggled in response.

Rylla nodded and smiled at Gracelynn, but the little girl suddenly grew shy. She hid behind her mother's skirts, acting the coy child, while Tobie slept on, his tiny hands clamped into gentle fists.

"It's nice to meet you all," Rylla replied, looking at Elowen, Mari and the kids. Gracelynn had Garth's blue eyes and dark hair while Tobie looked to have his mother's rounded nose. "I had no idea you got married!" She turned to her brother, but he wasn't looking at her—he was looking at the door.

Outside, the small village was beginning to wake. Chickens squawked their morning calls only to be shushed by some unwilling slumberer. Squeaky carts rattled past, beginning their journeys into town to set up for the day's purchases. A sheep's bleating came gently from somewhere nearby, a cow's moo, and the sound of chickadees singing their ode to the sunlight.

But there was something else, something that sent chills up Rylla's spine: a pounding of drums.

It was vague and far off as if muffled in a cloud, but it persisted nonetheless. And following suit came a sharp knocking on a nearby door.

Everyone jumped at the noise, then froze, listening. An eerie stillness filled the room, as if no one dared breathe.

Rylla stared at Garth as he checked the bolt on the door and looked to make sure the curtains were still drawn. There was tension in the skin around his eyes, a tension born of exhaustion and weariness, and a new stiffness of worry in his movements. He rejoined the group and grasped his daughter's hand.

"There's a lot you still don't know," Garth addressed Rylla. "I'll tell you as much as I can, but we must be quiet and quick about it." He gestured for Rylla and his family to take seats around their small, kitchen table, placing Gracelynn on his lap while Mari still cradled their son.

Elowen stood watch near a window, her bow strung over her shoulder and a quiver of arrows on her back. She looked both elegant and dangerous with her perfect posture and hard-set eyes.

Rylla braced herself, unsure, but eager all the same.

Garth began, bluntly and serious, "I've committed treason, and I'm being hunted as we speak."

Rylla stared at him in mark horror. Treason? He was being hunted? What had he done?

“I left home about seven years ago to join a noble cause, fighting in Aylati’s military. You were only eleven, Finn sixteen, and I had just turned eighteen. I was supposed to go alone, but Finn begged and pleaded to come with me, even though he was on the younger end. Ma and Da were reluctant at first, but I promised them that I’d look after Finn, that I’d whip him into shape and keep him out of trouble, as you might remember. They finally agreed.”

Rylla nodded. How could she forget?

“We were soldiers, both fighting for the same ideals, upholding the triumphs and truths of Aylati and serving alongside those with the same mind. We sent you letters of our experiences and tried to keep you informed.” Garth looked down, as if remembering what once was. “But it didn’t last. The Aylatian military had different units spread throughout all the kingdoms, and one by one they were dropping like flies. No one knew what was happening to them.

“There was hearsay and rumors of growing tensions amongst the kingdoms, so my unit was tasked with a peace treaty to bridge gaps and mend broken alliances. However, we failed to realize that Ostglenden would be our biggest adversary.

“I was made commander of my unit, and Finn and I were stationed together. We were a small but strong team of fifteen, headed over the Eastern Ridges into Thrushwoode, only to be overtaken by stealth and force, made to grovel on our knees. We were captured by Grievon’s men, and we soon realized that Aylati’s military wasn’t the only group imprisoned. He’d already taken from the other provinces.”

Rylla's heart dropped and twisted in her gut. Her brother was supposed to be a soldier, not running for his life! How was this fair? Where was Finn?

"Thus, Finn and I became soldiers—footstools—to King Grievon, a man so fierce there seems to be none his equal. Some of the other kings, though not faultless either, have tried to oppose him only to fail. Even now they are too afraid to fight back and restore the peace; or they've just given up entirely. Grievon broke and beat us, determining our every move as if hungry to claim more and more power. Under his service, one was forbidden to do anything but work for him, to shed blood for him…"

Garth paused to rub his eyes. When he finished, his gaze met Rylla's, a new gleam in them that wasn't there before.

"But on a spy mission to Rélynda, I stumbled upon Mari. She was outside learning to shoot a bow from Elowen, and her poor aim almost took my eye out. I met these two sisters and fell in love with the very one who almost wounded me." At this Garth rested his hand on Mari's knee in a loving way; she squeezed his hand back.

Elowen gave a subtle laugh at Garth's quick wink.

Rylla smiled in spite of her growing anger. She wasn't sure how she felt about her brother's marriage, not to mention all this information, but it was evident Garth had found happiness in the midst of his pain. The thought soothed her a little.

"I determined to marry her in secret to avoid inciting the king's fury. He wants focused soldiers, not ones softened by a pretty face. But that's where the king is mistaken. Mari's love has made me stronger. Grievon's heart can't understand love; its primary motivation is one built on the foundations of fear.

"It was a miracle my actions went unnoticed for so long—for years even. During that time, we had Gracelynn, but it wasn't until three months ago when we had Tobie that I was found out. Someone told Grievon my plans, and I had no choice but to flee and go into hiding."

Rylla looked around the small room once more, eyes landing on the thick, drawn curtains and the sparse furnishings. It was all making sense.

"Grievon has been hunting me down ever since, for reasons I can only guess at. If he can't have me, he rather me dead than working against him. That's why I was near the Heather Fields; I was on watch making sure we'd be safe for the night and weren't followed. Our family has been moving around ever since I left Grievon's army and we only just settled here last month. Nowhere is safe enough to make permanent, though that is what I long most to give my family."

Garth paused and took a long gulp of water from a mug on the table. He swallowed and dragged his sleeve across his mouth.

Rylla's head spun and her heart was now in her toes. How could this have happened? She hated to admit it, but the man from the cave had been right. Grievon was a monster.

"Grievon's army is continuing to grow," Garth took up the explanation again, "and he's on the search. He's been tracking down an old race of man, a race I'm not sure he's convinced even exists: the Earth-Treaders. I've heard he's starting in Thrushwoode Forest and Larkug."

Rylla swallowed hard. This is what her pursuer-turned-rescuer must have been hinting at.

"He has yet to find any, but he's even gone so far as to put out a reward for anyone who finds an Earth-Treader, which just goes to show how desperate he is..." Garth paused only briefly. "*I've* even thought about the chances of finding one, as a means to release me from my debt and live a normal life. Perhaps then I can finally return home, and our parents can know their grandchildren."

Moo's warning about heeding caution and remaining inconspicuous echoed in Rylla's mind as her stomach churned. She wiped her clammy palms on the edge of her cloak as she fidgeted in her seat, her heart pounding—any thoughts about telling her brother of her powers completely gone out the window. Would he turn her in? She wouldn't chance it to find out.

She tried to still her heart and remain focused. "How do you know all of this if you've left his army?" Rylla asked the first of many questions that vied to spew out of her mouth at once.

"I have to be constantly vigilant, and though I have enemies, I still have some trusted friends in the king's army who keep me updated. Also, Elowen has offered to help us, being our eyes and ears when we need rest."

It seemed there was more at stake here than the reemergence of Lord Brennigan. The kingdoms were falling apart at the seams, in more ways than one. And her brother was only focusing on King Grievon—did he not know an even greater danger was lurking and growing in the Darkness? That Grievon would only be a portion of the problem?

And that she, an Earth-Treader, might be the very one everyone was after.

Rylla was about to ask another question when Garth spoke again.

"There's something else, though." He paused briefly, this time with brow furrowed. "Tremors, more like murmurs—of something. I can't quite put my finger on it, but it feels sinister. I've been to the Heather Fields many times, a place that's always felt eerie, unsettling, and dark, but yesterday I saw something I've never seen before. It was as if a new type of Darkness was there, bitterer and grander than before—the kind rumored to reside below towers of stone or places where no light dwells." Garth shuddered. "I always carry my Sunstone, especially in those fields, but I've never been more thankful for it than when I rescued you." Garth fished below his tunic to draw forth a smoothed stone the color of sand with brilliant flecks of shimmering orange inside. He took it from around his neck and placed it on the table.

"Where did you get that?" Rylla asked in awe, hand outstretched to touch the stone. As her fingers found its smooth surface, a tingling of warmth crept into her hand and up her arm, pooling in her middle.

"I gave it to him as a wedding present," Mari spoke up, still rocking the sleeping baby. "My sister and I come from a family of miners; we grew up in Kytchidell, but we've spent many years digging through Wyllund's dirt in the Ores of Moorlund: a place known for its variety of stones and secret passages. I thought it was only fitting to give my first love the first stone I'd ever found. Though Sunstones are common and can be found all throughout the kingdoms, they *are* hard to find, and I figured a love like ours is too." Mari's slightly crooked smile made her even more lovely.

"But why was it in a lantern?" Rylla questioned. "I saw what you did on the edge of the Heather Fields."

"The heat is too strong when I'm using it. I've worn it before when it was radiating light and singed a hole through my clothes, branding my skin." Garth peeled back his shirt to reveal a stone-sized scar on his chest. "I built the lantern to hold the stone while at its hottest, until it cools down enough to wear safely again. I hear Moonstones can do the same thing, but the light they give off is less intense—perhaps if it had been one of those…"

"Oh hush, I had warned you, but—" Mari chimed in.

"But I was too stubborn to listen. I've heard it countless times before," Garth chuckled as he finished her sentence, giving his wife a smirk.

"Where did you get those?" Elowen asked, disrupting their banter as she leaned over the table to stare at Rylla's neck.

With all this talk of stones, Rylla forgot about her own.

"A little girl back home made it for me," Rylla said looking down, touching the beads on the leather-strap necklace.

"Those are Yellow Jaspers! I've never seen one before." Elowen walked over and bent to study the stones. She picked them up and turned them around in her fingers. "These are native to Aylati and are known to give their wearer perseverance, similar to how the Sunstone gives off light. The provinces have so many common stones, my goal is to find them all one day."

"I don't know much about stones…" Rylla felt like a half-wit. She had a hard enough time keeping track of the five stone crests she was searching for, let alone all the common stones.

"Stick around long enough, and you'll learn more than you care for." Elowen stood up and smiled as she resumed her place by the window. She continued to watch Rylla, but this time more closely, eyeing the stones and locket attached to the end of Rylla's necklace.

After a moment's pause, conversation continued.

"Rylla, I've talked a good portion of the morning away, but I have yet to ask why you're here. What *are* you doing out here? And travelling all alone?" Garth inquired, letting the restless Gracelynn squirm off his lap.

She grabbed her doll, hidden behind a tower of blocks, and went into the bedroom, lying down with her thumb in her mouth and the treasured toy between her arms.

Again, Moo's words and Fang's warning came back to her. There was the desire to share her mission while also remaining secretive, both warring within her. And now that her only conspirator was dead, she felt lonelier than ever. But she couldn't share it, at least not yet.

She fished out her map and tried for a half truth, hoping it would be enough. "Over the years, I've been making a map of the kingdoms with Da, and we finally finished. Since I just turned eighteen, I figured I was old enough to explore on my own like you, to try out the map we had worked so hard on." The second part was definitely a lie, though it *was* nice to finally put the map to use. She swallowed and then continued. "Ever since you and Finn left, I promised myself that I'd find you both someday. And it seems I finally did! But…where's Finn? I half expected him to be here by now."

A stir of fear curled in her heart. Why *hadn't* she also run into Finn?

Garth exchanged a look with Mari, and Elowen looked out the window, avoiding eye contact.

"Garth?" Rylla implored.

Her brother cleared his throat and shifted in his seat. "Finn's been missing for some time now. Even months before I had to run away. I've searched for him, have tried to keep watch, but it's hard to do when also trying to remain hidden…" Garth rubbed a hand over his face, his expression grim. "I have no idea where he is…"

Chapter the Eleventh

Life and Death

Outside, waves crashed against the tower's bulwark and surrounding cliffs, sounding like clanging cymbals and bass drums. Clouds smeared the sky gray, dulling the morning sun, but otherwise the weather was cooperating. Ground guards patrolled the base of the tower while the ravens took advantage of the mild winds.

Inside, the stone tower pulsed with life and voices murmured all throughout the corridors.

"Bring the prisoner to me," the haggard voice was growing stronger, forearms and wrists beginning to show growth into hands.

Gryfinn had returned only moments ago with a prisoner in tow. He had found the man precariously close to the perimeter of their base, and quickly took action to stop him. Word of this incident spread to his master before Gryfinn had even stepped foot into the tower.

"Yes, my lord." Gryfinn bowed and left the room. In a matter of moments, he returned with four guards and a man bound with ropes. They flanked him on all sides, giving him little room to move. The prisoner was dressed in armor and looked about Gryfinn's age—young, bearded, and strong—with a mixture of boldness and fear behind his eyes.

"Here he is, my lord." Gryfinn shoved the prisoner to his knees. "You'll be begging for mercy in no time…" Gryfinn hissed at him, then crossed to stand beside his master.

"You've got some nerve," the being spoke. "To try to infiltrate my headquarters by yourself…" The voice was menacing and cold.

The prisoner's gaze lifted to the vile creature, his face contorting in horror. He couldn't seem to look away.

"What? Repulsed by a little growing flesh?" The creature spat, watching him. "Stare any longer and these wraithlike nubs might strangle your very throat."

The prisoner dropped his gaze instantly, his eyes cinched tight.

"Look at him. How he cowers. Pitiful." The creature cackled. "I wonder who you're working for…perhaps the king or an anarchist group hiding out in the Gorse. Your armor speaks for itself." The deformed being leaned forward. "Yet I have a feeling you won't tell me."

"I work alone," the prisoner uttered, eyes on the floor.

"You dare speak without being asked?" Gryfinn struck him on the back of his head. The man's head snapped to the side, but no sound escaped his lips.

The haggard creature let loose a cackle, no longer needing to cough or catch its breath. "Easy, Gryfinn, I'm not quite finished with him yet." The being paused and turned its attention back to the prisoner, teeth sharp and dangerous. "You were sneaking around here with a purpose, I am sure. And if you work for Grievon, then I have cause to believe you're after what I am myself. Where's my stone? Are you working with the Earth-Treaders? Tell me what you know."

"I have no idea what you're talking about," the prisoner said, eyes still on the floor.

"Maybe...but you do know something..." The being stared at the prisoner for a few seconds and then motioned for the guards to move forward.

They moved in, spears raised and angled at the prisoner's throat. The man stiffened, eyes widening.

"Let's try this again, shall we? What do you know?" the being growled.

"I..." The spearheads pressed into the prisoner's skin, pinching and drawing pinpricks of blood. "I don't know...please..."

"I'll give you one more chance. Speak now, like your very life depends upon it." The creature's eyes blazed, eager for information.

"I...there's only rumors..." The prisoner's gaze darted about the room like he was trying to remember something, anything that could spare his life.

"Yes?"

"A girl with unique abilities," the prisoner croaked out, the spears still poking his throat.

"Did you see this girl yourself?"

"Not her face...no." The prisoner's throat worked in a swallow, the movement driving the spear points a little deeper. A trickle of blood traced a red track down to his collar.

"But you have seen her...?"

"Yes..." the prisoner responded, gritting his teeth.

"Where?"

"In…Thrushwoode…"

"Thrushwoode? All the way down there? Have you any proof?" The being's eyes narrowed, lips pursed.

"She…she flung branches at me as if…they were commanded by the wind…studded with golden tips that hit my eyes. Golden tips!" The prisoner gasped for breath as the guards' spears threatened to enter his throat.

"Golden tips? Bah! Surely just arrowheads! And this is how you plead for your life? Pathetic…" The being spat on the prisoner's face. It turned to the guards. "Take him to the torture chamber for the night. Strip him of his armor and dress him in rags. I want better answers. And if he refuses to speak, I want his clothes out to dry before morning."

"No, please! She mentioned something about finding a stone…and she was with a cat." The prisoner groveled before them all, trying to dislodge the spears and plead for mercy.

The being snapped its gaze back to the prisoner's face, eyes locked on his. "A stone? What kind of stone? Have you told anyone else about this?"

"I have no clue, and no, I…I work alone…" The prisoner tried to swallow.

"Pity, I'm sure whoever you're *really* working for will miss your incompetence. Guards!" The being leaned back in its chair and played indifferent.

"No, I beg of you!" the prisoner yelled.

The guards dragged the screaming man away, his cries echoing in the stairwell and down to the dungeons.

The decrepit being stared at the door as if in deep thought, then it spoke.

"This girl has Earth-Treader written all over her. She must be stopped; she must be destroyed. And she's going after *my* stones, I'm sure of it!"

"What are you saying, my lord?"

"Your new mission, Gryfinn—find this girl and bring her to me."

"I don't even know what she looks like, my lord," Gryfinn replied cautiously.

"You expect me to care? She has a blasted cat with her, and she'll be the one looking for the stones!" the being yelled, spittle flying from its mouth. "I can't rest until I know every last Earth-Treader is imprisoned or dead. You will not fail me."

"Yes, my lord." Gryfinn bowed quickly and was about to leave the room when he was stopped by his master's voice. This time much quieter and more restrained.

"You know why I don't like them, Gryfinn? You know why I detest the very earth they walk on?" The being's voice was an anticipating whisper, as if waiting to spew the truth.

"My lord?"

The haggard creature opened its mouth to speak but all that came out was a grunt. It seemed a memory flashed through the creature's mind for a dark shadow fell over the room, a blanket of weighty silence covering things unspoken. The haggard being creased its brow, shook its head, and the dark shadows were replaced with renewed hatred.

"The only good Earth-Treader is a dead one!" the being spat, clenching its teeth. "Get out of here and get my stones. Don't forget the girl!"

The being growled loudly, and then it began to chuckle. The manic laughter continued, seeming to have no end; the being shook and rocked its seat in the process.

Gryfinn, feeling uncomfortable, bowed once more and fled the room, eager to begin his new mission.

However, he couldn't help but feel unsettled over his master's words. What had he wanted to tell him?

Gryfinn grasped his stone for strength, felt the anger, and pressed on. He would follow through.

⸙ ⸙ ⸙

Caz and Jovin had left the Furrough a few hours ago and journeyed north, the warm sun bidding them good tidings as it filtered through the leafy canopy above. According to Jovin, this forest was the boundary line between Ostglenden and Wyllund. Caz's heart sped in anticipation. He'd be leaving Ostglenden for only the third time in his life, considering the second was his revisit to Aylati's Ivory Valley. What awaited in Wyllund?

They rode at a leisurely pace, Jovin's singing echoing through the trees.

With raven 'air
Lives a woman so fair
Upon the Isle
Of Abbredun

Dark are 'er tresses
She sways in 'er dresses
An' dances the night
In Abbredun

'er beauty a dart
She smote the king's 'eart
On the glistenin' shores
Of Abbredun

When queen she is crowned
'er island is drowned
An' no longer she dances
On Abbredun

Alas, there's no more
Of the beauty she bore
As we say goodbye
To Abbredun

Jovin finished the song and hummed quietly to himself, a somber smile on his face.

"I've never heard that one before. What's it supposed to mean?" Caz glanced at him from atop his horse, his mind mulling over the lyrics.

"The *Lay of Abbredun*—a Wyllundian tale of myth an' legend, of lost love an' land. Legend says that Abbredun fell ta corruption an' sunk. It's rumored ta be the 'ome of mer-folk an' the maiden with the raven 'air is their queen." Jovin laughed. "It's not unlike Ostglenden's tale o' *Neptucadis*. Children seem ta fancy that one more, so Abbredun is oft overlooked. Yeh know 'ow children's stories go."

Caz did know. There were plenty stories he held onto and cherished, *Neptucadis* being one of his favorites—the only good thing about his childhood. Stories gave him hope when he had none.

Jovin resumed his humming, and they continued their path through the woods. Birds flitted over their heads and squirrels darted in front of them. Caz looked ahead through the trees and thought he saw a clearing on the other side. He quickened Rembrandt's pace.

He emerged from the forest first, his horse whinnying as Caz tugged on the reins to stop. Caz breathed in deeply—the taste of a new place. "My first time in Wyllund." Already if felt like a fresh start. A field of tall plants stretched before him, and in the distance, vast mountain peaks climbed the sky. "Where do you think we are?"

"Aye, brothur, these are the inf'mous 'eather Fields of Wyllund, the battlegrounds of that legendary war where Lord Brennigan tried takin' down the Earth-Treader kings of old…a sad place, really," Jovin responded from astride his own horse.

"Surely you jest." Caz surveyed the land, recalling more of the stories and legends he had heard growing up.

"I played in those 'eather Fields as a wee child, but they've always been eerie. So much bloodshed—it feels as though the souls o' the dead are still there."

"And we have to pass through them, I'm assuming." It was more of a statement than a question. Caz glanced at his friend.

"Aye, but we've got our 'orses. They'll make quick work of it." Jovin pulled up his horse near a tree and dismounted to check its hooves.

Before Caz did the same, he checked on his leg wound. He had feared riding would reopen the cut, but surprisingly Jovin's handiwork was holding up. The pain was minimal. Caz deftly dismounted Rembrandt and bent to check his hooves, then stopped short. A pile of leaves rustled by his tree. Were they moving on their own? He bent down to examine them, brow furrowed. A hint of something black and white lay underneath the covering. Could be a skunk. Cautiously, he brushed away a few leaves and the thing came into view.

"Hey, look over here!" he called to Jovin.

There amongst the tangle of leaves was a cat, black and white and limp. Caz recognized him at once. It was the same one that had been with the girl they were searching for. But if the cat was here, where was the girl? A stab of worry pierced his gut.

"It's the girl's cat," Caz explained, hesitating to touch the creature. "He doesn't seem to be breathing."

Jovin grabbed his medical bag and moved to join Caz's side.

"'e's breathin' slightly," Jovin spoke, "but only just. This isn't any normal sickness…not somethin' I'm used ta curin' anyway." He ran a hand through his hair.

"What happened to him?" Caz asked.

"A work of dark magic, a Darkness. It's a miracle 'e's still alive." Jovin moved to grab a bottle out of his bag. "Unstop this an' give it ta me when I say so."

Caz took the bottle and worked the cork loose. Garlic and wormwood stung his nose. The liquid sloshed inside—it didn't sound like much was left, whatever it was. Hopefully it would be enough for a cat.

Why was the creature here and where was the girl? This was turning out to be more of an adventure than he'd thought.

Chapter the Twelfth

The Underground

Rylla fled the house, Garth's words haunting her flight. She only recently lost Moo and now she'd lost Finn all over again. Rylla had always held onto some hope that her brothers were both safe, that perhaps there was a reason for their unresponsive letters and lack of visits. But now? She knew better. Her lungs craved oxygen—desperately, and exhaustion battled amidst too many emotions whirling through her heart, all fighting to claim control. She clung to the beads around her neck. She must press on and move past her fears. But she couldn't, not now.

Elowen found Rylla at the large well in the center of town, hood drawn and head bent. Elowen had her bow and quiver strapped over her shoulder and she stopped to lean against the well with one foot propped behind her. Without so much as looking in Rylla's direction, she spoke. "Being out in the open like this, a hunter could drop you like a hare." Though she sounded serious, her tone held hints of jest.

"I hadn't noticed." Rylla rolled her eyes beneath her hood, trying to ignore Elowen's attempts at humor.

Elowen grew silent a moment and shifted to her other foot. “You must be hurting deeply.” Elowen’s tone softened somewhat, both blunt and patient. “Garth told me about your cat.”

Rylla gritted her teeth, unresponsive. To mention Moo felt like a fresh stab to her already wounded heart. *Why is Elowen here away? Can’t she see that I want to be alone*? Rylla’s need for fresh air fanned the suppressed spark of anger in her core, and it was now climbing into a brilliant flame.

“I’m sure Finn is fine, Rylla. From what your brother told me, he’s always been independent and capable of—”

“He’s always been pigheaded and impulsive, too proud to heed instruction,” Rylla interrupted. She stood, removing her hood, and began to pace near the well.

“In my experience, those aren’t necessarily negative qualities, just bold ones,” Elowen countered, her arms crossed over her chest.

“You don’t know him like I do. Who knows what kind of trouble he got himself into!” Rylla continued to pace, brow cinched in thought as her steps echoed her racing heart. Who was this woman to suggest otherwise?

“Well…perhaps those very qualities will be what get him out of trouble—”

“You don’t know that!” Rylla snapped and turned to look hard in Elowen’s eyes, her heart beating like a trapped bird beneath her ribs.

Elowen held up her hands and seemed taken aback. A hardness edged her words. “You’re right. I don’t. You don’t need to bite my head off.”

The bird still flapped its wings beneath Rylla’s ribs, but when it settled, the rhythm of her heart returned to its normal pace. The flame had now diminished to a tiny spark once more, and a slow blush crept up her neck.

"No…I'm sorry. I'm not angry with *you*, Elowen. This is just a lot to take in at once, enough to remind me that nothing is in my control."

Rylla ran a hand over her filthy cloak and brushed off the night's dried dirt and grime. She didn't know if she could do this mission, but she had to try. She had to keep going. And if Garth couldn't find Finn, then she would do it herself. Another thing to add to her list of tasks.

"So much for first impressions, huh?" Rylla looked up and forced a smile, the effort more difficult than she anticipated.

"I've seen worse," Elowen laughed. It appeared their banter hadn't left her exhausted like it had Rylla. In fact, it seemed to bolster Elowen's spirit. "Are you ready to head back? I know Garth was worried…" She watched Rylla carefully.

As if Garth was really worried. Rylla pressed her lips together in a thin line. Ever since she'd stepped foot into his house, he was more concerned with his new family than he was with her. Had he smiled in her direction? Laughed? Made a joke? Was he even happy to see her? This new version of her brother was hard to grasp. He was nothing like she remembered. She certainly hadn't received the warm welcome she had anticipated after all these years.

War changes you, Rylla, in ways you wouldn't understand. It seemed Garth was right.

"I can't stay here. I need to keep going," Rylla responded, though she longed for a bed to sleep on and a good meal more than anything. If she were honest with herself, she longed for the past and to relive those memories with her brothers before they left. But her mission wouldn't allow her to stay.

“Where? Surely you don’t mean to travel alone, especially in these lands.”

“I’ve made it this far.” Rylla tilted her chin, determinedly, though the thought of travelling alone freaked her out more than she cared to admit.

“If your brother hadn’t rescued you…”

“I know—that was lucky,” Rylla replied.

Would there be more obstacles like those in the Heather Fields? She’d rather not think about it. Rylla fingered the stone beads around her neck. She was thankful to still be alive, to have escaped that coffin of Darkness.

“Then where are you going?” Elowen crossed her arms, brow furrowed.

“Where did your sister say she found that Sunstone?” Rylla asked. She still had four stones to find, and every moment not searching for them was a moment lost.

“The Ores of Moorlund, the most fertile soil in the west,” Elowen said. “We’ve found most of our materials there for our father’s mining company. But what has that to do with anything?”

“That’s where I’m headed.” Rylla drew out her map and unfolded its wrinkled corners. The rain from last night had found its way into her bag, wetting all its contents. Her eyes scanned the inky map, smudges here and there, and traced a path with her finger from Goosewyn to the mines. Rylla glanced at the sky and saw the sun rising in the east, just above the last pinnacle of Wyllund’s throne. To the west she glimpsed something in the distance that looked like the mines, too far away to tell, but still reachable. If she travelled in the daylight, she was sure she could make the journey in a few hours’ time. Perhaps she would even be able to find a Sunstone or Moonstone in the mines to light her path through the ores.

"Why? What are you looking for?" Elowen questioned, eyes narrowed.

Rylla couldn't very well mention her mission and the stone crests, but she also couldn't lie—she had a feeling Elowen would see right through it.

"I want to find Finn and your sister said the Ores of Moorlund had many places to hide. I figured that'd be a good place to start." It was partly truth, for in going to the mines, she did hope to find Finn. Plus, the thought of finding him gave her something to look forward to rather than the fear for all that she was leaving behind.

"If you're headed there, then I'm going with you," Elowen stated. She uncrossed her arms to tug her bow closer.

What? Elowen would even offer such a thing? "I don't think that's necessary. I'll be—"

"I know those lands better than most. I have a way of getting you there faster, since you seem to be in such a hurry…" Elowen raised her eyebrows at her. "You'll need a guide."

Rylla hesitated, but perhaps the company would be okay, and secretly, she didn't want to go alone. She just didn't know how she felt about Elowen yet, and having her tag along seemed risky. Could she be trusted? Rylla would have to find out.

"All right, but I can't tell Garth. I have a feeling he'd try to stop me." Though Rylla had felt partially unwanted, family was still family and she knew Garth would try to save her yet again, especially with Finn missing. Besides, she didn't feel quite ready to face him again, not until she had a chance to form new expectations.

"He might…but I think there's a way. Leave it to me." Elowen moved from the well and made to head in the direction of home. "Meet me at the edge of town by the garden wall leading to the north. There's a secret passage we can take to the ores." Elowen turned, arrows rattling at her sudden flurry of movement, and jogged back the way she came.

Rylla pulled her hood back over her head, adjusted her satchel, and made for the garden wall.

⸙ ⸙ ⸙

"How'd you tell Garth our plans without him coming after us himself?" Rylla questioned, watching Elowen try to pull back a wall of ivy.

"I just told him we were going to the ores and that we'd return in a few days," Elowen said, still trying to dislodge the tangle of vines. "Seemed to be at ease knowing I'd be going with you."

"But I'm not returning…at least, not yet." Rylla couldn't face this version of Garth yet. Maybe after she found Finn things would be different.

"You're not?"

"No." Rylla looked Elowen hard in the eyes, her gaze unwavering.

"Well, he doesn't have to know that…though I can't imagine where you'll go next." Elowen paused to look at Rylla before trying to get the ivy to submit to her tugging. She released an exasperated cry. "These accursed roots, will they never budge?"

They were at the garden wall in the northern part of Goosewyn, a high stonewall barrier between the village and the surrounding landscape. The stones and rocks were covered in mossy patches and the countless vines of ivy, lonicera, and clematis left little room for much else to grow.

"Here, let me help." Rylla reached to pull at the vines beside Elowen, but the leafy plants seemed to move with a will of their own, loosening their hold and falling away easily as they worked.

In a few moments, the plants were pulled aside and an oddly shaped door with a padlock appeared before them. It reminded Rylla of *The Lost Garden of Iridü*, an Aylatian tale of a lad named Salmm who finds a door to a lost garden by the help of Gringfold the sparrowhawk.

But in real life, the vines and flower petals Rylla had just touched were now tipped with gold, evidence that her magic had helped them. Hopefully Elowen wouldn't notice.

"Well, that was…thanks." Elowen looked at the wall like she was sizing up an opponent, but taken aback at their easy victory.

Rylla kept her face neutral. The furrow between Elowen's brows hinted on confusion and curiosity, a dangerous combination. Yes, Rylla would have to be very careful.

Elowen shrugged as she fished in her pocket. She pulled out a set of iron picks, sifting through them and selecting one. She inserted the curved pick with iron teeth into the lock and wiggled it around, her ear close to the contraption. The levers clicked into place and the padlock fell to the ground. Elowen lifted the latch and pushed the door open; the doorway led to a set of narrow stairs which descended into a blackening hole.

At least Salmm had opened a hidden door which led into a sunny garden. Rylla hadn't expected to find a darkened abyss on the other side of hers.

"This is the quickest and safest way to the ores, about an hour's journey," Elowen said.

Rylla peered into the darkness, fear overtaking her reasoning. It was as black as a moonless sky. *The Heather Fields. Moo. The darkened closet.*

"Is there no other way?" Rylla's throat tightened the longer she peered into the darkened path. A knot formed in her stomach, her mouth gone completely dry.

"This is the most direct route to the ores. Besides, I've spent so much of my life underground that I only know how to get to them through tunnels. This is the surest way." Elowen reached into her quiver and produced a long flare. She took a flint stone out of her pocket and lit the fire stick. The flame exploded into a brilliant red, illuminating the nearest four stairs as she stepped past Rylla to descend. "I stole this from Garth when I went back to the house." Elowen gave a wicked smile, full of mischief. "If we're lucky, he won't even know it's missing." She paused and turned around. "Are you coming?"

Rylla nodded. At least this adventure would have some light. She wouldn't be trapped in the dark, though the idea of tunneling still twisted at the knot in her stomach. She would take her misgivings and reluctance into the very abyss, caution on her side.

⸙ ⸙ ⸙

It seemed to Rylla that they'd been trudging for hours, turning left and right more times than she could count.

"We're almost there." Elowen held the fading flare before her, illuminating the tunnel in front of them. The light flickered and cast strange, ghostly shadows along the walls.

Rylla took care not to look at the taunting, writhing shapes as they danced with the red light. "How did you know this tunnel existed?" She asked, trying to focus on the flare itself. She gripped a stick in one hand, a treasure she had randomly found on the ground of the tunnel. She held onto it as a promise from the world above.

"My father dug it years ago. There's also another tunnel running north from the mines into Rélynda and the outskirts of Kytchidell. My grandfather dug that one, and it's much longer than this tunnel and a lot older. It's been years since anyone has used it, though, since parts of it caved in."

"If your family made these tunnels, why'd you have to pick the lock?" Rylla cocked an eyebrow.

"I'm notorious for misplacing things, such as keys, so I've become an excellent lockpicker because of it." Elowen laughed.

Having Elowen accompany her to the ores wasn't as bad as Rylla had anticipated, though she was still getting used to the girl's bluntness and confidence. Regardless, she was thankful Elowen knew the way and wasn't asking her questions.

But how would she search for the stone amidst her companion's prying gaze? Maybe when the time came, she would feel comfortable enough to tell her. Maybe Elowen would understand.

"Do you hear that sound?" Elowen stopped, raising the dying flare from side to side, illuminating the walls and floor.

"What sou…?" Rylla stopped in her tracks, the words fading into silence as her ears picked up on something in the distance. A faint echo of pounding, or perhaps flapping wings. "I do hear something."

"It's coming from up there, I think." Elowen took a few steps forward, then a piercing cry wrenched from her.

Rylla stumbled back, barely smothering a scream of her own.

"Something landed on my head!" Elowen cried.

Rylla grabbed the flare from her and raised it toward her head. There in Elowen's hair was a skeletal creature, its teeth bared and wings fluttering in a frenzy. It had a long, spiked spine that reached down its back and led into a razor-sharp tail. Its fangs and claws were like iron nails and its body was that of an overgrown, hairless squirrel.

"Get out! Shoo! Leave her alone!" Rylla commanded the creature, waving the flare as close as she dared to Elowen's head.

"Talking to it won't do anything!" Elowen yelled.

"I want blood, I long to feast!" The creature screeched, getting ready to plunge its fangs into the skull.

"Oh no you don't!" Rylla remembered the stick she had in her other hand and whacked the hideous creature off Elowen.

It spun through the tunnel, slamming against the wall and flopping to the ground a few feet in front of them.

"What was it? What is *that*?" Elowen gasped, pointing to the black, bony object on the ground.

"I don't know. But something tells me there's more to come!" Rylla warned. She'd never been afraid of animals, but these creatures were like winged demons.

"Oh yes, we are many, and we all will feast!" The wounded creature growled from the ground, hobbling toward the two girls.

"We need to get out of here, fast!" Rylla spoke quickly. "How much longer to the mines?"

"We're nearly there—but these monsters!" Elowen looked like she was experiencing fear for the first time, eyes wide, face pale, and arms shaking.

"I don't think we have a choice, the chance of sunlight is closer on this end now, and the flare is running out—we don't have much light left! If we stay, these monsters will get us one way or another." Rylla grabbed Elowen's hand and dragged her forward, in the direction of the approaching mass of bloodthirsty creatures.

They ran swiftly through the earthen passage, ready to meet the winged fleet. The flapping grew louder, the screeching more intense. Dark balls of fang and wing descended upon them, ready to break skin and devour. Their high-pitched cries filled the space around them like a cacophony of deafening screams.

Rylla swung her stick and the flare at the creatures, but their screams set her head whirling. There were too many of them! Elowen fitted an arrow to her bow and aimed it at the mass, but what good would an arrow do against so many? They had to fight, though. It was either get devoured by the bloodthirsty animals or fight them off with their weapons in what little light they had left.

But there *was* another way.

Rylla wished it could be different, but her instincts told her otherwise. If she were to use her magic now, they'd have a chance at survival. The need to see daylight and taste fresh air was her final resolve; she'd save them both, even if it meant revealing her identity.

She quickly tossed the flare to Elowen and dropped her stick.

The need to survive and protect became second nature as she whispered words under her breath, almost as if they were coming from somewhere deep within. This Earth-spell felt like a song sung from her very core.

Trapped in darkness
With winged beasts
We will survive

They shall not feast
Though darkness grows
So does the light
And these swift varmint
Will flee in fright

Rylla began twisting her hands in a circular motion before her. She didn't know what she was doing, but it felt natural and right. Walls of earth and dirt crumbled from the ceiling, hitting the hungry beasts and burying them into the ground. The dirt moved like a wall behind them, like a wave approaching the shore, ready to break at a moment's notice. Rylla and Elowen ran on, dodging the screeching creatures and the falling dirt, the promise of sunlight being their only hope. A few more steps and they'd be out of the tunnel and into the mine itself. After that, they'd only have to remain underground a little longer before tasting fresh air.

Rylla's foot caught on a loose rock, and she tripped into Elowen. The two women went tumbling forward, then Rylla's palms met gravel and dirt, and her head met something sharp. They had just entered the mines, and if they had looked up, they would have seen the wall of tumbling earth reaching and rolling all around them, slamming into the cave walls and blocking out any daylight. It circled the room and sent a mist of dirt into the air, blanketing over them like light snow. Eventually the soil stopped moving and the final screech was drowned out completely by the onslaught of earth.

But Rylla and Elowen were out cold and unmoving, the flare altogether dead. The tunnel was blocked, and their only road back to Goosewyn gone.

Chapter the Thirteenth

The Pride of a Cat

Moo stirred, slowly blinking as the world shifted into focus. He felt like he had just awoken from a very long and deep sleep, one that he feared had no end in sight. Going from being encased in complete blackness and then immediately thrust under the midday sun, it was difficult for his eyes to adjust. However, when he shifted his gaze, he finally managed to focus on the silhouettes of two men kneeling over him, looking both curious and relieved.

"Hello?" Moo rasped out. He paused, blinking up at the strangers—no, not quite strangers. He recognized one of them. *The man from the cave?*

"'e just meowed, so 'e must be feelin' better," the other man stated, getting up to put some sort of medical pouch into his saddlebag. He was tall, his eyes blue, and his hair blonde and straight. "'e was almost a gonner—that dark magic rendered 'im nearly dead."

"Thanks to you he's alive. I'm sure the girl's pretty worried about him. I wonder how they separated." The man from the cave said, standing up to brush the dirt from his hands.

Moo recognized his voice as much as he did his face—the deep baritone and the brown eyes.

“Perhaps he knows where she is.” The same man looked down, eyeing him curiously.

“I have no idea what’s happening,” Moo responded, finally taking in his location. He was by the Owl’s Tree on the outskirts of the Heather Fields. “How did I end up back here? Where’s Rylla?” Moo questioned, eager for answers. He got up, stretched his legs, and looked at the two men and then the trees clustered above.

“‘e sure ‘as a lot ta say, ‘eh?” the other man said as he rejoined them.

“He meowed a lot back in the cave when I rescued the girl.” The first man folded his arms over his chest and frowned down at Moo.

“Well, maybe ‘e’s scared an’ needs a good pat.” The blonde-haired man tried to reach out and pet Moo only to be swatted by his paw. “‘ey, watch it!”

“I’m guessing he didn’t appreciate that.” His friend laughed.

“I most certainly am not scared! Nor do I want to be coddled.” Moo stalked away and scanned the trees. “But perhaps I can implore for some assistance—from someone who can actually *understand* me,” he spoke louder, trying to claim the attention of the towering saplings.

On cue, the Great Owl alighted onto a nearby branch, startling the two men and eyeing Moo with his large silver eye.

“Marry! That thing’s as big as a ‘orse!” the blonde-haired man said, his eyes wide.

“It can’t be a normal owl. There’s no chance,” the man from the cave said in equal shock.

The large owl ruffled his feathers and hooted a call which brought the rest of his feathered parliament into view. One by one, more birds alighted on branches—sparrows, wrens, hawks, falcons—all clustering together to form a half moon in the trees.

"The young squire has awoken!" the Great Owl squawked. "It seems my ministrations had preserved him long enough until rescued by these two swains."

The choir of birds chirped in response.

"Now, how may I be of service?" The owl leaned his head closer.

Moo heard voices behind him and turned to see the two men speaking simultaneously.

"Unbelievable."

"What sort of aviary is this?"

Their arms crossed over their chests, brows raised in disbelief.

Moo turned his attention back to the feathered parliament. "Pray tell, my lord, what transpired and how did I end up back at your domicile, and with these two men?" Moo beseeched the great bird.

"The answers you seek are simple. While in the Heather Fields, the Darkness almost consumed your very soul. The young lady, however, was rescued by another while you were forsaken for dead." At this, the owl leaned in closer. "They thought you were lifeless in body and form and fled to safety, but my silver eye pierces through shrouds of life and death—I could sense the slowing heartbeat of your bosom and rescued you myself." The owl puffed out his chest, clearly impressed with himself.

"How was my life preserved?" Moo asked.

"I could only do so much—though I am the wisest of beings, my power is still limited. These two swains completed the task. I foresaw their approach and placed you at the base of my very perch, trusting in my supreme wisdom that they would discover your whereabouts."

"Many gratitudes, my lord." Moo bowed and glanced at the two men. They were still staring in confusion, clearly taken aback by this uncommon exchange between cat and bird. Though they wouldn't understand a word, they could surely tell some form of communication was occurring.

"And where might my friend dwell? The Lady Rylla? Do you know her whereabouts?" Moo asked.

"That I do know, the journey dangerous and reacquainting with the Darkness," the owl hooted a low tone. "She has fled to the Ores of Moorlund, on a fool's errand, I assure you."

"Then that's where I must traverse!" Moo replied at once.

"It's too dangerous a venture. The heather will surely consume you before you have any hopes of survival. You would have to run uncommonly fast, and I fear you'd tire before making it through…however, I could fly you there, of course," the barred owl spoke as if this were the only plausible option.

Moo didn't like the idea of flying in the sky for a second time, though to be fair, he had been unconscious for the first. He gazed steadily at the two men who seemed eager to get going. Their glances were now toward the sun and the distant horizon. Moo recalled their help and how they could have left him for dead. But they had chosen to rescue him.

Moo focused back on the owl and shook his head. "No offence, my lord, but something compels me to abide by these travelers, though I am a tad leery of the blonde one. I presume they seek justice and to find my friend. Be assured, I heartily thank you for your ministrations."

"Broo-hoo-hoo, the young squire has shrewdness and loyalty of heart, if not also a fear of the heights." The owl ruffled his feathers and laughed, turning his head to eye the cat more closely. "However, if you ford the heather, horseback is the surest way—you must mount a steed."

At this realization, Moo looked at the horses with a slight hesitation. He felt it a little below him to ride another creature and especially after having just avoided being petted by a human, but then again, hadn't he ridden in the talons of the Great Owl? And if that hadn't happened, wouldn't he be dead?

He couldn't leave Rylla to find the stones by herself. His grandfather had sent him on a mission of his own, and he had to complete it. There was little choice; he would have to do it.

"But how am I to steer these men in the right direction? Surely, they cannot understand our speech," Moo replied.

"Taw-taw-taw, young squire. You leave that task to me." And with that final word, the Great Owl flew into the sky as if on a mission of his own.

⸙ ⸙ ⸙

"What do yeh suppose that was 'bout?" Jovin asked as they watched the large owl fly away and disappear. "Never seen the likes of that in my life."

"Nor have I, but I think they just had some sort of meeting," Caz said turning to watch the owl vanish over the treetops. He turned to face the cat, shrugged, then moved beside his horse. He'd seen stranger things, like that time in the forest, like that golden tree.

The girl was out there, and he needed to find her and give the warning—but where was she exactly? He had half a mind to deliver her the cat himself with hopes that it would persuade her to trust him.

The sun was beating heavily now, tanning Caz's already browned skin and warming his cold fingers. No matter where he was or what he was doing, he always had poor circulation in his hands. Maybe since he was always doing something, his body only had so much energy to keep up.

He blew warm air on his fingers before readying his horse to continue their journey. He looked to Jovin. "Any idea where we should look first? You know this land better than most."

"True, but we 'ave no idea where she could be, right? Is she even in Wyllund?" Jovin asked.

"The last I saw of her disappeared through a tree. I can't imagine where she ended up…" Caz looked at the cat who was sitting where the bird left him. He looked like he was waiting for something. "But I have a feeling we're getting close."

"Well, we 'ave ta go through the 'eather Fields if we 'ead north ta the wharfs anyway." Jovin walked to his horse and made ready to ride. He checked the saddle and grabbed the reins. "Or we could 'ead back ta the Furrough an' rethink our first steps."

Caz set one foot in the stirrup, but startled as a tremendous screech rent the air, followed by the heavy flapping of wings. The barred owl returned, but this time with a large burlap sack in its talons. The owl dropped the sack on the ground before Caz's feet and flew up to its perch in the trees. The bag opened as it hit the ground and the contents spilled out.

Sticks of various shapes and sizes cascaded from the burlap folds. Caz and Jovin exchanged quizzical looks as the chorus of birds screeched and tittered from the trees above. The owl was squawking as if giving out commands, and simultaneously the other birds were responding. Cardinals, finches, hawks, wrens, sparrows, and birds of varying kinds, all swooped down upon the loose branches and began picking them up in their beaks and talons. They picked up the pieces of wood, placing them down again in a pattern on the grass. A small tufted titmouse gathered a few sticks, narrowly avoiding collision with a crow who cawed angrily in response. The smaller bird dropped its provisions and flew away to hide in the nearest elm.

"What do yeh think they're doin'?" Jovin asked Caz amidst the flutter.

"I don't…wait, hold on…I think those are words." Caz walked over to the sticks, tilting his head from side to side, trying to read the formation of the branches. They were strewn along the ground, their careful placement indicating shapes and letters.

Jovin joined him and frowned at the crude letters, trying his hand at deciphering them.

"T-H-E -O-P-E-S- O-E -M-O-C-P-L-U-N-O," Caz read aloud, scratching the back of his head.

The birds twittered in a frenzy and dropped back to the ground to make several adjustments. After they finished, they flew back to the trees and waited.

"T-H-E -O-R-E-S -O-F…The Ores of Moorlund!" Jovin guessed, the birds chirping happily above them. "Of course! 'ow could I 'ave been so blind?"

"The Ores of Moorlund? Are they far?" Caz asked eagerly.

"Just north of the 'eather Fields, 'bout a 'alf day's ride, maybe less. They 'appen ta be near the wharfs too," Jovin said, still staring at the sticks. "This is some kind o' magic for sure."

"I think her cat understands us and wants to help." Caz turned to make eye contact with the black and white animal.

It gently nodded its head and walked toward Rembrandt.

"And I think he wants to come with us." The more Caz thought about it, he wasn't sure he could have gotten the cat to go with him against his will even if he had tried. Jovin made the mistake earlier of touching him once, let alone if they tried for a second time.

Caz and Jovin moved to their horses once more and mounted. Caz twisted to glance down at the cat as it meowed plaintively.

The creature stared up at him helplessly from the ground.

"'e probably needs some 'elp, but I'm not touchin' 'im." Jovin laughed and moved his horse a few paces closer to the looming fields.

Caz dismounted again and crouched before the cat, feeling a little foolish. "I can't understand you, but I believe you can me. I mean no disrespect, but I can only get you on the horse if I pick you up…" Caz paused a moment, thinking, "Or you could just climb on my back, and I wouldn't have to touch you at all."

With that last statement, the cat nodded and jumped onto Caz's back. He winced as its claws dug through his cloak and pinched his skin. He'd have to get used to this.

"All right, I think we're good." Caz stood and mounted his horse with the cat perched precariously around his shoulders, but before he turned away, he hesitated and faced the owl who was still watching them from its perch. His mouth went dry. "Er…um…" How did one go about speaking to a bird? “Thank you.” He placed a hand over his heart and bowed his head. Was it his imagination, or did the owl seem to bob its head in response?

Caz didn’t contemplate it much longer for the cat was now clinging even harder and tighter than before. He grimaced at the pinpricks of pain. “Watch it with the claws.”

“It’ll be a long journey at this rate, ‘eh?” Jovin laughed again. “Let’s get goin’.” He urged his horse forward and plunged through the heather.

Caz kicked his horse and drove into the heather behind him, the cat’s claws still digging into his back.

Yes, a long journey indeed.

Chapter the Fourteenth

The Ores of Moorlund

Gryfinn entered the Gorse armed with a shovel and a sword by his hip, the pounding drums resounding close by. He had done his rounds near the cliffs earlier in the day and was growing restless, desperate to find what his master was looking for. He had no idea where to start searching for the girl, had no idea what she even looked like. The stone, however, seemed an easier target. He didn't have any clue where that was either, but he would check Rélynda's large forest first.

Ever since the day Gryfinn found his master's stone and spoke the ancient words of revival, he had found purpose again. He had found a chance to prove himself as a valued member, the leader he always longed to be. He took pride in his efforts, taking full credit for bringing the most powerful ruler back into existence. And because of these efforts, his master was growing and getting stronger; it was only a matter of time before the limbs would be ready to walk and wield a sword.

And his master wasn't the only thing growing; its army was growing steadily by the day: captured prisoners-turned-soldiers and those pledging their allegiance. But there was something else, something new and dark lurking deep below the tower. Rumors, murmurings of iron and the smithy. Gryfinn had heard nasty screams and grunts, noises that belonged to wild beasts, echoing upwards from the depths. But to this, Gryfinn was blind; as far as he knew, there were only Earth-Treaders in the dungeons, not ragged creatures. His master was planning something, but even he was not privy to such knowledge.

"Pretty soon, Gryfinn, my army will be ready to march on Grievon's. I'll crush him like the little roach he is, and then the kingdoms shall know true power."

It was only a matter of time until he knew what that entailed.

But even in the unknowing, Gryfinn felt he had the upper hand; until Lord Brennigan could actually walk, Gryfinn had the power to call the shots. He would do as much as he could before his master fully healed, and he would prove himself worthy in the end. He would complete what he set out to do.

Finding a clear surface devoid of shrubs and twigs, he unhooked his baldric and set it on the ground before he began digging. The rusted spade hit the earth, and he moved the displaced dirt into a separate pile. This was a tedious undertaking, one that he worried had no clear direction or end in sight. But as Gryfinn moved his hand to clutch his own stone around his neck, the crimson color pulsing to life in his fist, a renewed wave of vigor and vengeance washed over him, a desire to overcome and overtake anything and everything that stood in his way.

His master had given him this stone as a reward for the "awakening," and he was told to wear it daily. *"It will strengthen you when you feel weak and empower you to trample your foes."* His master had uttered those words more times than he could count, and so not to anger him, Gryfinn made sure to wear the crimson rock every day. And he was beginning to grow so fond of it that it was nearly impossible to part with it at all.

Simply clutching the stone brought clarity to his mind and fortitude back into his bones. He would find Rélynda's stone and bring it to his master. He would dig it up and feel its power, but above all, he would be acknowledged for his competence.

And then, yes then, he would find this supposed Earth-Treader girl.

⸙ ⸙ ⸙

"Rylla," a voice was speaking through her darkened world. "Rylla, wake up!"

A hand nudged her arm, and she opened her eyes.

Elowen's dirt-covered face leaned over hers, brow furrowed and rocks and twigs stuck in her braid. What had happened?

Rylla sat up stiffly. She coughed, then winced, as pain throbbed in the back of her head. She must have hit her head on a rock or something. She rubbed the sore spot, remembering the dark tunnel and the flying creatures.

"Where are they? All those monsters," she asked, glancing around.

"They're gone, all of them. Everything is gone!" Elowen said, eyeing the walls of earth and rubble all around them, blocking the tunnel back to Goosewyn. She turned and fixed her gaze on Rylla, dark and serious, eyes full of questions. "We're in the mines now. What happened back there?"

"I don't know—"

"Oh don't play the fool, Rylla. I know what I saw and heard—you uttered words and then the tunnel practically swallowed us whole! You didn't just come here to find your brother."

"I can explain," Rylla countered.

Elowen crossed her arms over her chest and peered into Rylla's very soul. A glint in her eyes hinted that she'd already guessed the truth.

"You know, don't you?" Rylla couldn't bear to raise her voice above a whisper.

"Well, *I* couldn't move those vines just by touching them, and now—all this!" Elowen gestured to the mounds of soil and rock scattered around their feet and the cavernous walls of the mine surrounding them. The tunnel back to Goosewyn had disappeared, and clumps of golden dirt were strewn amidst the remains, shimmering in the light. "You could have killed us both!"

"I didn't mean to, I wasn't—"

"You're one of them*,"* Elowen stated bluntly. She danced around the word *them* as one would a foreign substance. As if she wasn't quite sure what to make of it, unsure and cautious.

Rylla stared, stunned by Elowen's candor. After a few moments, she slowly nodded her head, meeting Elowen's gaze. "I'm not anymore thrilled with the idea than you seem to be."

Elowen cinched her brows together. "Such power is dangerous, Rylla. Earth-Treaders are being hunted—everywhere. No one can be trusted!"

"Not even you?" Rylla countered.

Elowen remained silent.

"I'm going to get some fresh air," Rylla croaked. "I know you're mad, but we can still make for Goosewyn by the main road instead of the tunnel.

We aren't trapped in here." In fact, the main road sounded far better anyway. Rylla stood and headed in the direction of the sunshine. Anywhere to be away from Elowen's prodding questions and fuming gaze.

Elowen blanched slightly and moved to block Rylla's path.

Frustration—and a hint of something more—welled in Rylla's tight chest. "What are you doing?" she asked. "I just want some sunlight." *And for you to get out of my way.*

Elowen shifted her feet then sighed. She turned and walked over to where the light was shining in.

"That's not necessarily sunlight." She bent down in the corner and lifted something in the air, causing the light to sway and shift the shadows. As the light moved, it danced around the large cave structure, bouncing off dirt walls, high ceilings, and pointed spires.

"Elowen, you didn't!" Rylla stared at the Sunstone in shock, putting her filthy hand over her mouth.

"I couldn't help it! I was worried the flare wouldn't be enough." Elowen defended herself, this time looking a little remorseful. "I was hoping we wouldn't have to use it."

"Garth is going to kill us." Rylla stared at the lantern in Elowen's hand, the Sunstone shining brilliantly inside. "I thought you said the tunnel led us outdoors!"

Something in Elowen seemed to harden once again. "Well, I'm not sure who'll kill us first. Garth or your walls of dirt! There *was* an exit out of this mine, but because of you, we're trapped in here. Our only way out is through the tunnel to Kytchidell," Elowen said, all bluntness. "*If* we can even get through it in the first place. Thankfully we have his Sunstone so we can at least see."

“Well, it looks like we both have our blunders then,” Rylla suggested. She tried to steady her racing heart at the thought of being trapped in this place of darkness. At least they could see, even if the source of light didn’t belong to them.

The two girls just stared at each other for a moment, covered from head to toe in dust and soil. Having Elowen join her was a mistake after all. Perhaps Rylla could have done this journey better on her own. But even still, she felt a burden was lifted; to have anyone know her secret, even someone so unwilling as her new confidant, made her load lighter to carry. She felt less alone.

If she had caused this much destruction, perhaps then she could undo it and make a way out of the mines, ensuring their escape. Maybe she could get them to see the sun. But then another thought broke through those possibilities. What if she couldn’t control her own powers and made the situation worse?

As if reading her thoughts, Elowen spoke. “Even if you do more of your…” she waved her hand in the air as if conjuring magic, “…whatever it is you do, we’d most likely end up dead like those horrid creatures if we tried to escape. It’s too risky. It’s best if we find the tunnel.”

The words stung, but part of her knew Elowen spoke some truth. Unless Rylla learned how to properly control her magic, she very well could bury them alive. It wasn’t worth the risk. She thought about the dome she made back in Thrushwoode and what Moo had said afterward.

“My grandfather told me that you’ll need training. Sometimes the power can be too much to control the stronger you become.”

That dome had basically been a flimsy shield, but if she had been more careless or even stronger, would the dome have crushed them? Her powers were growing, and she wasn't sure what to do; she'd have to be more careful. The fact that she and Elowen had narrowly escaped the waterfall of dirt was pure luck, if not a miracle.

"Now what?" Rylla questioned, hating the tension that lingered in the silence.

"I guess while we head for the other tunnel, maybe you can tell me why you wanted to come here and why you left Aylati in the first place," Elowen suggested. Her irritability had cooled, if only slightly, and she seemed ready to move on.

Rylla thought for a moment, but Elowen already knew the biggest secret. Telling her one more couldn't make matters much worse, could it? They could end up dying in these mines for all she knew, so her secrets could die with them both. Rylla took a deep breath and began her tale, weaving it from when she first met Fang and her mission to find the stones.

⸙ ⸙ ⸙

The story completed, the two girls found themselves searching for the stone instead of the tunnel. If Moo's words remained true, the stone would return to the earth where it first came, and Rylla figured inside the mine was as good a guess as any. Elowen was still visibly unsure what to make of all the new things she had learned and Rylla was still uncertain of her powers and her feelings toward their situation, but after Rylla had shown Elowen the Hawk's Eye in her satchel, it seemed they were on the same team. Or at least slowly heading in that direction. At least Elowen appeared eager to find the stone.

"I thought the five stones were only a myth," Elowen said, scanning the room they just entered. "Though I won't lie, I've tried searching for them as a child. But I didn't think I'd ever find anything!"

"I didn't think they were real either, but recent circumstances have led me to believe otherwise," Rylla replied with a short laugh. She pushed aside some loose dirt with her boot and ran her hands over stones lodged in the walls. Where to begin? The mines were huge!

"How did you find the last one again?" Elowen inquired, this time plying at a rock with her fingers.

"It's hard to explain, but it was as if I *felt* it…like it was calling to me." Rylla flushed, feeling slightly foolish.

"Interesting…I'm not all that surprised. It must be the magic in your blood," Elowen said matter-of-factly, though there seemed a hint of jealousy in her words. "Have any idea where this one might be?"

"I'm not sure. Wyllund's stone is the Obsidian, symbolic of prophecy and wisdom if I remember correctly, but I can't imagine where that would be buried. It was kind of by pure luck that I found the Hawk's Eye in the first place."

"Well, since it's known for prophecy and wisdom, and wisdom is usually discerned through the heart, then perhaps we should check in the heart of the ores," Elowen reasoned.

"That sounds like a promising start!" A thrill shot through Rylla. It sounded hopeful, so she gestured for Elowen to lead the way, ready to check another box off the impossible list of tasks.

"Okay, follow me closely, it gets a little hairy the deeper we go. Thankfully we still have a few more hours of Sunstone light left, but we should be quick." Elowen motioned for Rylla to follow as she headed deeper into the ores.

Countless twists and turns, passages up and down accompanied by small tunnels where they had to crouch and crawl, eventually led them out to a giant, cavernous room. The ceiling towered high above them, its highest point too far away to be discerned, and the floor was mostly gaping holes, dropping into an impossibly black abyss. At the center of the room there was an island of earth with its base descending into the depths. Numerous bridges of varying sizes and lengths extended toward the island, some too short to meet at both sides while some were as thin as strands of hair. And around the entire room was a narrow ledge to walk on, just wide enough for one person if their back remained pressed against the wall.

Rylla's heart raced. This was the place; she could sense it. Anticipation bubbled in her stomach. She stepped out onto the ledge behind Elowen, and a buzzing sound interrupted her excitement. She gripped the wall behind her as dizziness took her breath away, her vision blurring for a second time. Now was not the time to be feeling light-headed, not when falling would very well mean her inevitable death.

"What's that sound?" Rylla asked, rubbing her temples and trying to keep from stumbling.

"What sound? I don't hear anything." Elowen looked at Rylla, knitting her brow.

"It's so loud, how can you not hear it?" Rylla cried through her teeth, holding her head with one hand and clinging to the wall with the other.

"I don't know, maybe it's the stone!"

"I figured as much, but I can't tell which direction it's coming from." Rylla scanned her surroundings through slitted eyelids, trying to find the location of the humming. The walls gleamed with gems and stones of varying kinds. Where was the Obsidian? She knew it was a black stone, but aside from that, she was clueless.

"I guess we need to start searching through these rocks. I see a lot of dark ones, maybe we can start there." Elowen inched ahead of Rylla and clung to the wall for support. One wrong move and she would fall, but she moved confidently despite that.

"Be careful!" Rylla warned, the humming still thrumming in her ears.

"Don't worry, Rylla. I've grown up here—I know this room inside and out, though, that abyss is still a mystery. Just don't look down and don't fall." Elowen took an arrow from her quiver and began digging around a black stone she found tucked in a crevice somewhere on the wall.

Rylla inched along the wall to mimic Elowen's path, clutching her necklace for comfort while one hand was used for balance. At that moment, the humming seemed sharper and clearer, less fuzzy and more focused.

She paused to look at Elowen.

"That's not it," Rylla said. She stared around the room, gaze resting on the rocks and gleaming gems. All the stones were silent and dull, as if telling her they weren't anything special. She scanned the black abyss once more and the humming pierced her head like a spear and sent her reeling.

Her knees gave way on the narrow ledge and she whirled her arms to catch something for balance, a scream frozen in her throat. The next second, she was tumbling hard and fast through the darkness below her. She was like an arrow slicing through the air, a hawk descending swiftly upon its prey. Except she wouldn't find her mark; it would find her instead. She needed to catch onto something—anything, to stop herself.

Suddenly, a blinding light and a gust of snowy wind met her from beneath and shoved her sideways, slowing her fall. A gasp escaped her lips, though the scream was still lodged in her throat. A glowing, black orb came toward her, or rather, she flew toward it. *The Obsidian.*

Her knees hit solid earth, waking her from her stupor.

Rylla cried out in pain and grabbed her head between her hands. What just happened? She didn't fall? No, she fell where one of the first bridges began, catching herself before she could plunge into the abyss. It had only been a vision.

"Rylla!" Elowen practically sprinted to where Rylla was. "What happened? I told you not to look down! You could have fallen into the abyss!"

"I know where the stone is…" Rylla ignored Elowen and tried to steady herself despite the ringing in her ears.

"Where?" Elowen scanned the large room, then turned to Rylla again and paused.

Rylla looked downward and Elowen followed her gaze. "Rylla, where's the stone?" Elowen's tone stung with impatience.

A shiver traced Rylla's spine, but she pointed downward.

"You must be joking," Elowen guffawed.

"I'm not joking, it's down there. It's beckoning me to come." The vision of the bright light and glistening stone flashed across Rylla's vision again and she pressed her hand against her temple.

"How are we supposed to get it? We'll die if we go down there!"

"I don't know, are there stairs? Anything?" Rylla's head burned as she tried to search the darkness.

She couldn't explain what just happened, but she was more certain than ever that the stone lay underneath their feet in the darkness below. She had seen it, hadn't she? But the thought of going into the darkness made her head ache even more.

"No, there's only the pulley, but that's been inactive for as long as I can remember. We don't even have the tools in here to construct it again," Elowen responded, lips pursed and twisted sideways, clearly not liking this turn of events. "I don't want to go down there, and I don't see any reason to—the stone could still be up here, Rylla."

"I don't like it either, but I feel like we should try." *Anything to stop this accursed ringing.* Rylla hated the dark, feared it more than anything, but at this point, she hated the ringing more. Her head throbbed, each heartbeat pounding against her temples with a painful intensity. She couldn't manage a full breath between the stabbing behind her eyes.

"We can't, Rylla, there's no way down!" Elowen protested.

But Rylla didn't hear her. The ringing drowned out her voice, her vision went black, and Rylla tumbled over the edge and into the abyss.

Chapter the Fifteenth

The Obsidian's Master

"It looks like the entrance 'as been sealed off," Jovin spoke.

They had just arrived at the ores and were analyzing the large, copper-colored mountain of rock, searching for some sort of opening to the inside.

"By what? Can it be moved?" Caz cinched his brow, not quite certain what he was looking for. What kind of door would a mining mountain have? The cat finally loosened its grip enough to seat itself rather uncomfortably atop his shoulders, still remaining as far away from the horse as possible.

"By mounds an' mounds o' packed earth. It would take 'ours ta move with just our swords. There's no way she got inside this." Jovin shook his head, taking a swig of water from his canteen.

"Unless…" Caz paused, thinking.

"Unless what?"

"Unless she was already inside before the entrance got blocked off—what if she's trapped? Wouldn't we have seen her stranded outside the ores otherwise?" Caz wasn't sure he was thinking straight after having a cat dig trenches through his flesh for the past few hours, but something told him this girl was unpredictable and had done stranger things than turn tree bark into gold. Anything was possible. He had to enter the mines and track her down.

"Yeh think this woman of yers is trapped in 'ere?" Jovin quirked a brow.

"She isn't *mine*, but yes, I do." Caz didn't back down. The owl had sent them in this direction for a reason.

"Yeh 'ave ta be the 'ero, eh?" Jovin let slip a chuckle as he shook his head and ran a hand over his face. "All right…I guess we 'ave no other choice than ta dig."

At that moment, the cat jumped from Caz's shoulders and landed on the ground with a thud. It took off, sprinting around the mountain without so much as a backward glance. It seemed to be scanning the rocks as it ran, intent on its purpose.

"Hey, where are you going?" Caz shouted.

The two men exchanged confused looks before they turned their horses to follow. They galloped after the cat for a while, until it finally had slowed to a stop. In turn, the two men reined in their horses and observed their surroundings. A strip of blue gleamed in the far-off distance with a wall of mountains to their right. Even from this great distance, the subtle smell of salt danced around Caz's nose.

"That's the Ocean Basin an' the North Mountains, see," Jovin said, pointing to the landmarks.

Both men breathed the air in deeply, letting the salty scent fill their lungs while the afternoon sun shrouded them in warmth. Caz could tell that Jovin felt the pull toward the sea but Caz's eyes lingered on the mountain tops. *Will the Isles have mountains such as these?* He wanted to find out, but he had to find the girl first.

Caz turned his attention back to the cat. It paced at the base of the mines, meowing at him. Caz dismounted and walked over to the animal, squatting down to its level. What was it trying to show him?

"Looks like he found an entrance to the mines!" He peered into the black hole, chewing his lip. It was too small. There was no way he and Jovin could fit through it.

"'ey! That's great! Now we don't 'ave ta dig through that blasted wall." Jovin took another swig of water from his canteen, clearly satisfied with the turn of events.

"It's not big enough for us to fit through." Caz replied.

"Yeh can't be serious—"

"I'm always serious, take a look."

Jovin dismounted and walked over. He frowned down at the hole that was just big enough for a small mammal, not fit for the size of humans.

"Well, we're buggered for sure." Jovin chuckled as he showcased his girth, though still slim, obviously too big. "I might 'ave squeezed through that as a wee child, but I'd barely get a leg in there now."

"So I guess it's a yes to the digging," Caz replied, eager to get a move on. "Let's head back and start."

The two men mounted their horses and turned for the mouth of the ores, but Jovin raised a hand.

"'ey, brothur, 'old up. The cat's dallyin'."

Caz turned to look the cat in the eyes and studied it for a few moments. The cat didn't break eye contact but looked very intent on its purpose. Caz finally understood.

“He wants to go through the small hole.”

“But we’ll lose ‘im,” Jovin suggested. “I mean, it don’t matter ta me, but this girl ye’re after, she might care…”

“I think he knows what he’s doing. I think he intends to find her first and let her know we’re coming.” Caz felt like he was getting pretty good at reading the cat’s intentions, but then again, the cat was magical and he wasn’t. How was he to tell who was doing all the reading?

“That’s fine with me, brothur, one less thing ta worry ‘bout when flingin’ clumps o’ dirt ‘round.” Jovin chuckled to himself.

“Let’s get a move on and be quick about it.” Caz turned around once more and kicked his horse into a canter. The quicker they started digging, the quicker they could get inside and find the girl.

As the two men retraced their steps back to the entrance of the mountain, the cat disappeared through the small hole, squeezing its body until safely through.

They were close to finding the girl now, surely. Caz only hoped she’d be less upset about seeing him than he was anticipating.

⸙ ⸙ ⸙

Rylla was falling hard and fast through the darkness. She screamed as her hair whipped behind her like a cape, the gravity pulling her downwards. Her gut heaved, and she clasped one hand over her mouth as her stomach felt like it was left behind. It was almost enough to make her pass out again.

The vision. Elowen’s warning. The ringing in her ears. Everything happened too fast, and now there was no way to catch herself.

But hadn't she already experienced this? It was the vision all over again. Would the Obsidian lead her astray? Her head pounded, and as her thoughts turned into doubts, she was met with a blinding light and a gust of wind from below. The warm air enshrouded her like a cape and pushed her gently to the right. She was being buffeted in a cloud of wind and wispy snow as it propelled her sideways at a much slower pace than before. And there, in the distance, the glowing black orb approached in a shroud of misty light. *The Obsidian.*

Rylla stretched out her hand as she was guided forward by the wind's momentum. Just a few more feet and the stone would be in her grasp. But there was a curious thing. As the stone moved forward, so did something else: a hooded figure cloaked in the colors of the cave walls with arms outstretched. She caught muttered words but couldn't quite understand past the ringing in her ears. The figure stopped moving and Rylla did the same. The cloud set her down gently on her feet, the humming and ringing louder than ever.

Rylla fell to her knees, gripping her head in both her hands. She grit her teeth against the cry that built up in her throat. The pain was enough to make her rip her hair out. "Please…make it stop." Tears leaked from the corners of her eyes. If this sound continued, she was certain her head would explode.

The figure lifted gloved hands to the stone and whispered some unintelligible words. When his hands moved away, the humming ceased altogether. Rylla took a breath of relief for the first time since stepping into the cavernous room. All that was left of the pain was a pounding headache, but she could deal with that.

Then a voice broke through the silence. "Who are you and why 'ave you come?" The voice bore a slight Wyllund accent.

"I'm nobody important," Rylla gasped, still catching her breath. "I'm not from here." Could this man be trusted?

"Why would a girl be traveling these caves alone and willingly fall into this pit unless otherwise *compelled?*" The man questioned, clearly trying to get to a point.

"I think I passed out." Rylla was still trying to wrap her brain around what happened. She'd survived the fall, for one. How had that even happened?

"Ah…but you 'aven't told the 'ole truth. You were *drawn* 'ere by something, and you're not alone—your friend is left up above, wondering if you fell to your doom. Even now she is scouring the darkness for any signs of life. Let's invite 'er to the party, shall we?"

The man uttered some words and swept a hand forward. A gust of heavy wind heaved through the tunnel and shot upwards through the chasm. Rylla thought she heard a scream, and a moment later was confirmed in her imagination as the wind brought a fuming Elowen gently into the cave. She fell to her knees, trying to reclaim her breath and poise as flecks of snow danced in her hair. She looked to Rylla, eyes full of questions.

"Now, can you tell me why you really came 'ere?" the man spoke once more.

"I told you, sir, I passed out above on the ledge," Rylla responded, eyes on the floor.

"'Tis no fun when they lie," the man replied as if speaking to someone else. "No matter, I already know." He turned to face Rylla, his eyes hidden underneath his hood. "You're on a mission and desiring a way to flee this place. But you can't because you trapped yourselves in 'ere and fear is following your every move. It 'aunts your steps. You 'ave much doubt and guilt is festering like a fresh wound, and you dread you'll never be good enough. For what, I wonder?" He paused and his words sent a trickle down Rylla's spine.

"You're torn about your family: thinking about your brothers—'urt by one and worried for the other, missing your parents, and feeling replaced as a sister—the jealousy eating at your core. What a pity." He looked to Elowen and shook his head. "But there's something else, the face of a man…a lover, per'aps?"

"Stop! Enough!" Sweat trickled down the back of Rylla's neck from this man's exhaustive analysis. How did he know so much? Was this the power of the stone? "You don't know anything!"

"I don't? I wonder…Rylla of Aylati, why you've come and what compelled you to get so close to this chasm."

At the mention of her name, Rylla blanched. Her heart raced. How did he know who she was? Who was this man? Hard as she tried to hide the truth, it was no use. He already knew too much and to lie only seemed to make matters worse. If perhaps she told the truth?

"I…I saw a vision…of that stone," Rylla said, pointing to the black gem hanging from the man's neck. "I felt it calling to me." She could feel Elowen's eyes on her profile, but she wouldn't meet her gaze, not yet.

"Ah yes, like calls to like, my friend. Rylla, you are an Earth-Treader—you can 'ear thrumming magic as good as any. And you long for a teacher. Per'aps that's the real reason you've come."

The man lifted his hands to remove his hood. As the fabric peeled away the shadows, an aged man in his early seventies stood before them, graying beard and glossy, distant eyes. His expression ached with loneliness and hints of something else—something Rylla determined to figure out. She noted he made no attempt to remove his gloves.

"You've come to the right place. My name is Uwan Volmalt, and I will be your teacher."

Chapter the Sixteenth

Six is a Party

Uwan led them down a dark tunnel, winding and twisting first to the left and then to the right. Rylla felt the hairs on the back of her neck rise with each new step she took. Where was he taking them?

“I see you’ve ‘ad a run in with the winged Fleet of Vatra,” Uwan said, walking ahead of them. “The cuts on your arms and faces could be from none other.”

“The flying monsters? What were they?” Rylla asked, remembering the winged beasts, their pointed fangs and bony backs. She ran her hand over one of the cuts on her arm. The gash wasn’t too deep, but it stung.

“Were? Kabog-waiths are nasty, irksome beasts, but they cannot die,” Uwan chuckled. “Wherever they are, they’ll regroup and be back. But we’ve made a truce, you see. I don’t bother them, and they don’t bother me. You two were fortunate, though. They’ve been restless as of late. Nothing seems to quench their appetites.”

“Where did they come from?” Talking seemed to ease the fear in Rylla’s heart. She could see light ahead of them now. They were getting closer to something. Was it the outdoors? Hope blossomed in her chest.

“They’re creatures birthed from Darkness. As to their beginnings, I do not know. Only that they multiply like nuts in a squirrel’s burrow and suffer themselves to live solely on living flesh and blood.”

A shiver ran down Rylla’s spine. She glanced at Elowen, who although was still scowling, walked with unease, her bow gripped firmly in her hand.

The light was growing closer, and pretty soon it revealed a brilliantly lit room beyond. So it wasn’t the outdoors. Rylla tried to mask her disappointment, biting nervously on her lip.

“Welcome to my ‘ome!” Uwan said, spreading his arms wide.

They stepped over the threshold, the room coming into view. Rylla caught her breath. The space was illuminated by twinkling fireflies and Sunstones placed strategically throughout. The air tasted salty and circulated around them like a breeze had somehow found its way inside. There was a carved table in the corner of the room surrounded by several chair-like stones. A small fire flickered in a hollow of the wall near the entrance, with pots and pans hung above it. A large oval rug was splayed in the middle of the floor, bearing an image of dancing fairies, and curtains were hung at random intervals about the walls, framing moving landscapes underneath them: birds flying, trees swaying, and flowers blooming. This place was full of life despite it being so buried.

Five hallways extended from the main portion of the cave and Rylla craned her neck to peer down each one as far as she could.

“The guest chambers are down the first two ‘allways on your left,” Uwan explained. “The third leads to the privy. The fourth is the training arena, and the fifth is my wing." Uwan's eyes crinkled at the corners, beaming with pride as he gestured to each hallway in turn.

When he talked, he never focused on anything in particular but seemed to be gazing off into the distance. Was he blind? Judging by his glassy, blue eyes he might be, but the way he moved about the cave and described his surroundings seemed to say otherwise.

"And there you 'ave it!" Uwan finished. "I will leave you two to wash up and rest before a light snack—training begins tonight!" At that he walked away.

Uwan retreated to his own compartments, and Elowen grabbed Rylla by the arm and dragged her down the first hallway on the left, the farthest one from him. They walked a good many paces before reaching a bedroom, and upon entering, Elowen locked the door behind them. Afternoon light sparkled about the room from the countless Sunstones on the ceiling, and there were two small cots on opposite ends of the room. A circular rug lay in the middle of the floor like the main room and there was another moving landscape on the wall: deer grazing. The image was one of stained glass, and when the deer bent to drink from the stream, the glass pieces shifted to adjust to the new scene. It was a homey space and a twinge of homesickness settled in Rylla's stomach.

"What on the good-tilled earth do you think you're doing?" Elowen disrupted Rylla's observations, clearly not happy.

"I don't know! I passed out up there and somehow ended up down here. I didn't want to fall—honest!" Rylla replied. "Apparently he wants to train me. Maybe he can teach me enough so we can get out of here." Rylla looked around the room, still nursing her pounding headache and trying to calm her racing heart. How much longer would they be trapped underground for?

How far down were they exactly? Her breath came choked in her tight lungs.

"Well, I'm not sure we have any other choice. We're stuck down here with this…this blind man who *says* he can train you. What if we can't trust him? Don't you find it a little odd that he's hermited himself away, and down *here* of all places?" Elowen crossed her arms, her brows knit together.

"I know, I'm worried about the same things, but do you think he'd offer to train me if he meant ill? I want to believe he's trustworthy, for my own peace of mind, and don't forget, we still need his stone." Rylla touched the Yellow Jaspers hanging around her neck and grew still. She'd never met another Earth-Treader before, and if she were honest with herself, the idea of understanding this type of magic seemed to excite that small part of her that wanted to believe she could do this. The fear was definitely louder, but perhaps she needed to take this leap and simply trust.

She already had the Hawk's Eye and the Obsidian was only a breath away. Maybe she could work out a deal with Uwan and somehow get the stone? The idea left her mouth dry, but there weren't many options.

"Fine, but I don't like this. Not one bit." Elowen sat on one of the beds and took her bow and quiver off her back. She grabbed a stone off the floor and scraped it along the edge of an arrowhead, sharpening the point with quick, nervous movements.

"I don't either, but what other choice do we have?" Rylla responded, holding her throbbing head in her hands. "I still feel so dizzy and nauseous, perhaps if I could just take a quick nap…" She sat on the opposite cot and took her satchel off before sinking down against the pillow. "You don't mind keeping watch, do you?" She just needed to get rid of this headache and then she'd be ready to think properly.

"Are you kidding? If you're sleeping, then I'm definitely staying awake," Elowen replied.

"Great, wake me if something goes amiss." Rylla rolled to her side and fell into a deep sleep, not noticing the wandering eyes of Elowen looking at her Yellow Jaspers and then her satchel; she was forgetting she was in the very bowels of the ores and dreaming of her pursuer-turned-rescuer coming to find her.

⸙ ⸙ ⸙

"I trust you both are rested and 'ad your fill with the provisions," Uwan said. His voice echoed ahead of Rylla and Elowen as he led them down the fourth corridor, one that seemed to have no end in sight. "We'll be there in a matter of moments."

The path arched upwards, the smell of salt water and seaweed tickling their noses. A gleam of pale light shone from somewhere just out of sight.

"No offense, Uwan, but it smells like a fish market down here." Elowen adjusted her grip on her bow and covered her nose with her hand. Elowen obviously still didn't trust this man; she kept fidgeting and checking the arrows in her quiver.

"You get used to it, being so close to the Ocean Basin as we are."

They walked a few more feet and gasped as they entered another room. The space was vast and lit by the midnight sky with countless stars and the moon shining in through the glass ceiling designed to resemble the peak of a mountain. A warmth flooded Rylla's chest as she stared up at the sparkling heavens. Perhaps they weren't as deep in the ground than she had originally thought.

Jutted stones lined the high walls, reminding her of Mount Egret back home. Oh, how she longed to go back and climb its peaks. Mist from the Ocean Basin speckled the glass—they must be close indeed to the shores. Three rings were etched into the floor, the outer circle being the biggest and the inner circle being the smallest and in the center of the room. Aside from a few pillows and chairs along the wall, the room was sparsely furnished.

"I've never seen anything like this…" Rylla walked to the center circle and stared upwards. She was overcome by the beauty and the joy of finally seeing the waking world again. What kind of magic was this?

"We Earth-Treaders 'ave the ability to manipulate the earth and thus live in 'armony with it, as you know. Since secluding myself down 'ere many years ago, I figured I needed someplace to view the stars." Uwan gestured to the vast expanse above him.

He walked over to the chairs and motioned for Elowen to take a seat.

"I'd rather stand, thank you," she replied, back straight and muscles tense.

"No matter to me." Uwan took one of the chairs and pushed it toward the outer circle. He gently lowered himself in the seat and looked at Rylla in the center of the room, though his eyes didn't quite meet hers. "Now, show me what you know."

"Excuse me, sir, but I have a question first." Rylla walked toward him. "I was wondering if there was another way out of the mines, or if you could teach me enough so we could leave here." She tried to be as polite as possible, but kept her chin set boldly.

Uwan's jaw twitched and his eyes squinted slightly; it was the same look Rylla had noticed earlier, but he masked it quickly. "Of course, in due time, but first you must show me what you know."

"What do you mean?" Rylla frowned.

"Show me what you already know," Uwan repeated once more, nodding his head and pointing in the direction of the arena floor.

Rylla's palms grew clammy under the gazes of both Uwan and Elowen. She had no idea what to do—anytime she performed magic was an automatic response to her situation. She couldn't just conjure up something for show, could she? How had she done it before?

"I'm not sure I can…" Rylla began.

Then she noticed Uwan uttering strange words under his breath and whistling, clicking his tongue and nodding his head. A huge gust of wind exploded into the room, followed by screeching and a dozen razor-beaked birds.

Rylla panicked. She bolted and began running around the room, scrambling for a place to hide. She was too slow. One of the birds zipped by her ear and nicked it. She cried out and ducked away. A trickle of warmth ran down her neck and onto her shirt. Another bird zoomed past and cut her shin while another sliced the space behind her knee. She was being torn apart. Was Uwan going to let her die like this?

Rylla howled in frustration and uttered some quick words:

Birds of flight
Your razor beaks
No longer fright
Be gone!

She lifted her arm upwards like one would if wielding a shield, and a wall of earth came up with it, acting as the very thing. Some birds flew into the wall and got stuck, their beaks too sharp to let loose. She bolted in the other direction and ducked under the raging wind. The flap of wingbeats told her the few remaining birds chased at her heels.

She clapped her hands together and a dome of earth encased her. She splayed her hands in a vicious outward circle and shoved against the sides, and the dome burst out in every direction, rippling outwards like waves. The earth surged forward, and everything else ceased.

The birds were gone, and the wind no longer tousled her hair. At the center of it all, Rylla stood breathing heavily, head down and exhausted.

She slowly lifted her gaze to the walls of earth and dirt speckled with golden flecks in places where they weren't before. Parts of the glass dome above were now covered in soil, and she noted some cracks in the exterior. Elowen and Uwan were nowhere to be found.

Then a rumbling sound echoed about her, like a stone or heavy object being rolled away. A wall of packed earth moved and glided along the floor, revealing a very irritated Elowen and a passive Uwan behind it. Uwan's hand was outstretched as the mound of golden earth settled heavily on the far side wall. Everything was covered in dirt aside from the two onlookers, but Rylla couldn't say the same for herself.

"*Golden.*" It was barely a whisper, but there was awe in his voice. "I see," Uwan uttered louder as he got to his feet. He headed toward the doorway, leaving both Rylla and Elowen staring after him in shock.

"Wait! Where are you going?" Rylla called, not sure what was happening. "What about my training?"

"You're very strong, Rylla of Aylati, and you lack control. But you show promise. We will continue."

"Then why are you leaving?" she asked.

"Because we 'ave guests," Uwan replied.

"Guests?" Rylla and Elowen said at the same time, fear forming in the pit of Rylla's stomach.

"Yes, one 'as been circling the abyss for some time now, but the others have just arrived. 'ere they come now." Uwan outstretched his hands and a surging wind followed behind. The girls exchanged looks as they heard hollers and strange noises tumbling toward them through the tunnels. The noises grew louder as three figures entered the room and were set gently on their feet, a light dusting of snow encircling them. As the wind and snow settled about their frames, Rylla could make out three shapes: two men and a cat.

Surely it wasn't…She couldn't believe it.

"Moo?" Rylla ran to the cat who bounded toward her at the same time. She scooped him up into a hug and placed him gently back on all fours. Tears stung in her eyes. "How did…what happened? I thought you were dead!"

"I thought so too, but then the Great Owl rescued me, and so did these two men." Moo turned to look in their direction, and Rylla followed his gaze.

Her heart stopped. It was the man from the cave. That serious, difficult man. The man whose face often popped in and out of her thoughts, and who just last night she had dreamt had found her in this very place.

Had he followed her here on purpose? Who was he? And what were his motives for rescuing Moo? If she didn't stop her racing thoughts, she was sure to go crazy. Instead, she looked to Moo and sought the answer to at least one of her many questions. Perhaps if she had the answer, everything would make more sense.

"Moo, what's he doing here?" Rylla questioned, but he didn't have time to respond because Uwan cleared his throat.

"Ah…so nice of you to join us, Jovin. It's been too long," Uwan said as he embraced the other man.

"Uncle?"

Rylla's attention was arrested when she saw the same look gracing Uwan's face as he glanced at Jovin, the one he had given her when she first arrived. It was more than just loneliness; there was almost something…needy in his expression. What was that look? And then it hit her.

Hunger.

Chapter the Seventeenth

Introductions & Full Mouths

"Uncle? What are yeh doin' 'ere? No one's been able ta find yeh for years!" Jovin asked in obvious disbelief.

"Ah, still the same spunk I remember, but my, 'ave you grown." Uwan tilted his head as if observing Jovin's height, his eyes still not quite meeting their mark. He shifted his gaze. "And 'im?"

"My friend Caz, we've been journeyin' through these lands together. But Uncle, what 'appened to yeh? Why are yeh 'ere?" Jovin studied his uncle's face.

"Well, my boy, when they took you all those years ago, I tried to find you. But it was no use; I was captured and tortured by an old extremist group, my eyes blinded and my 'ands deformed. I learned then they were searching for Earth-Treaders, and since capturing me, they knew them to exist. I 'adn't really tried to 'ide my powers when they were attacking me…pity.

"Anyway, I escaped one night, on a whim really, and came 'ere. The journey was 'ard, not being able to see, but I made my way. I believe fate drove me to this place—I've grown quite fond of my 'ome and the power it possesses." At this, Uwan took his gloved hands and stroked the Obsidian around his neck as if compelled by a force he couldn't control. He seemed lost in thought but Rylla noticed the look of hunger glinting in his eyes.

"And it seems I'm no longer alone for fate 'as also brought me an apprentice." Uwan turned and gestured in the general direction of Rylla as all eyes turned toward her. "Rylla of Aylati."

Heat rose to her face at the mention of her own name, completely taken off guard. Her heart was thrumming in her chest but seemed to beat twice as fast when the man's eyes—*Caz's eyes*—locked on hers. His expression looked sincere, almost earnest, and Rylla shifted uncomfortably. She was covered from head to toe in dirt and keenly aware of it under his scrutiny. Not like she really cared. At least Moo was sitting by her feet.

"And this is her friend, Elowen." As Uwan introduced her, both men glanced in Elowen's direction. She was beautiful, bold, and irritable, but Rylla didn't think they noticed. After all, she wasn't the one covered in dirt. Either they were too addled by her beauty or too much of gentlemen to care. She didn't know which one was worse.

"It seems you two came at an unfortunate time, seeing as we 'ave just begun training." Uwan motioned to the room around him. "But no matter, 'ow about tonight we chat and tomorrow we train anew? Surely men such as yourselves are on some sort of mission with swords strapped to your waists and could use a little refresher. It will be quite fun." He looked to Jovin, smiling. "For tonight, a little conversation gives us time to catch up and meet your friend 'ere." Uwan spoke with a mixture of eagerness and calm, as if this was what his very soul needed but was afraid might not last.

"Sounds good ta me, Uncle. Where do yeh want us?" Jovin questioned as he looked around the room.

"Let's go to the kitchen and talk over some food and drink. I'll 'ave enough to fill your stomachs until the end of time." Uwan laughed and he motioned for everyone to follow him back through the corridor and into the kitchen once more.

Rylla bent down to whisper to Moo. "Be on your guard. There's something in Uwan's expression that makes me ill at ease. He's yearning for something, hungry for it, but I'm not sure what. Besides, we need to get his Obsidian."

"I'll keep my eyes keen and my whiskers preened," Moo replied. "It's an expression my father always used."

"Good. Thanks, Moo." Rylla stood up quickly and tried to dust off as much dirt as she could before following everyone. She accidentally caught the attention of Caz who was lingering behind. Their eyes met and her heart pounded louder all over again.

How on the good-tilled earth had he known where to find me? Clearly he was a stalker, and he was now walking toward her.

"What are you doing here? Have you no understanding that when a woman tries to run away from you, and twice for that matter, perhaps she doesn't want to be followed?" Rylla demanded, facing up to him squarely.

Caz winced briefly, rubbing the back of his head. It was almost endearing and left Rylla surprised by her own boldness. Now that she was in mixed company, she had little to fear if Caz truly did mean anything sinister.

"Perhaps I could have handled things a little better beforehand…but I had to find you." Caz looked both serious and earnest. There was no ill intention behind his eyes.

Still, she frowned at his words.

"You had to find me? Whatever for?" Of all the crazy things she'd already endured, this man puzzled her the most. Not to mention her growing irritation at her own heart. Why wouldn't it stop pounding? Was it fear? She didn't know, and this man was affecting her more than she liked. Regardless of how foolish her heart was acting or how many somersaults plagued her stomach, this man couldn't be trusted. Not by her.

Caz stepped closer. "I came to warn you—" he cut off as Elowen came back through the tunnel.

"There you are, I was beginning to worry. You've left me alone with these strangers…" Elowen's stormy brow creased deeper as her gaze fell on Caz standing only a few feet from Rylla. "Oh…I didn't realize you were getting familiar with our guests. If you'll excuse me." She inserted herself between them and practically growled in Rylla's ear. "I'd appreciate some backup, if you don't mind." She grabbed Rylla by the hand and dragged her back toward the kitchen.

Rylla couldn't tell if she was relieved or aggravated. Here was this man who held so many secrets, and Elowen had come in and disrupted him before he could finish. Had she been safe talking with him alone, though? She hardly knew him. What had he wanted to warn her about anyway? Suddenly the somersaults in her stomach turned into a sinking dread.

"What were you doing back there? Do you know that man?" Elowen whispered and looked over her shoulder at Caz following at a distance behind.

"Hardly. We met once...or twice." Rylla resisted the urge to squirm under Elowen's severe scrutiny. "I only just learned his name."

"I don't trust them, especially the blonde one. He's got to have the strongest accent out of anyone living in these kingdoms. I've never heard the likes of it before. Stick close to me, and whatever you do, don't leave me alone again." Elowen's scowl returned in full force. It was going to be a long night.

As the rest of their party gathered around Uwan's table, introductions were made in greater detail as the group conversed.

"What brings you runaway soldiers all the way out 'ere? I could guess, but that would rob you of the opportunity to speak the truth. Though I'd wager you're on a mission and you're both none too 'appy with your pasts," Uwan said as he stroked his Obsidian.

Caz blanched a bit and Jovin shifted in his seat. Rylla felt their discomfort herself, for only recently had her deepest secrets been discovered in the same way.

Jovin recovered quicker than Caz and spoke first. "Ta be honest, Uncle, yeh speak the truth yerself. We 'ave only recently escaped Grievon's army an'—"

"Do you mean the king?" Rylla cut him off. Normally she wouldn't have been so bold, but maybe they had news of Finn.

"Yeh know of another?" Jovin questioned.

"Both my brothers were captured by him, forced to do his bidding. But I don't know where Finn is. Have you heard of him? Finn Wayscot?" Rylla gripped the edge of the table, her knuckles turning white as she searched their faces. Perhaps this was why Caz had come, to bring her news of her missing brother. A surge of hope filled her chest. Perhaps she had misjudged him.

Caz cleared his throat, furrowing his brow. "I'm sorry to say, but I haven't heard his name until now. Have you, Jovin?"

His friend shook his head.

Weight crashed down on her shoulders again, the briefest flirtations with hope gone. If Rylla felt this way, how much more would her parents, especially her mother? And if Rylla didn't make it through this mission alive, she was sure her mother would die of a broken heart if she found out one of her kids was missing and another one dead. Rylla couldn't bear that thought.

"Have you any idea where he might be? Where one might hide throughout these lands?" Rylla questioned, looking at the two men before her.

"There are countless places to hide, Rylla. They can hardly take a guess at where your brother chose to go." Elowen sighed.

"Where are the places ye've checked?" Jovin questioned.

"I had hoped I might find him here." Rylla's fingers tightened their hold on the table and it wasn't until a hand rested atop hers that she realized her knuckles were practically numb.

"If you keep doing that, I think the table will begin to beg for mercy." Caz gently lifted her hand away.

Rylla stretched out her palm and messaged feeling back into her fingers, trying to ignore the way Caz's touch had made her cheeks blush. Had he done that purposefully? The thought aggravated her.

"I'm sure he'll turn up. I can assure you the chances of him being in Ostglenden are slim. Anyone who wants to be away from Grievon wouldn't dare to live in his domain." Caz shifted in his chair. He spoke as if from experience.

"An' my guess is if 'e isn't in the ores, chances are 'e's not in Wyllund either. Though one ca' never be sure just by guessin'," Jovin offered.

"I appreciate the help," her reply came out more snappish than she'd intended. For some reason, she didn't want to talk about this anymore.

The conversation continued like nothing was amiss but Rylla was aware of Caz looking in her direction on more than one occasion.

Uwan changed the topic and asked where everyone was from and it seemed that between the four of them, they each had a province covered. Though no one had a claim on the Isles.

"I'm still in shock at seeing you, Jovin—it's been too long. I can't tell you 'ow great it is to 'ave you 'ere!" The slight blur of tears glistened in Uwan's glassy eyes.

"I know, Uncle. I was tellin' Caz 'ow I 'aven't seen yeh in years an' wasn't sure where yeh ended up. It seems a stroke o' luck brought us yer way," Jovin said past a bite of food.

"A stroke of luck, ey? Do you think most encounters happen just by mere chance?" Uwan raised his brows.

"I'd wager that most do," Jovin replied.

"Intriguing, Jovin. Would anyone else like to chime in?" Uwan glanced around the room.

"I think sometimes it's a little more than luck; that perhaps a natural prompting or a pull brings one to find what they're looking for," Caz said. His gaze flicked briefly to Rylla, then dropped away again.

"Would relentless pursual count as this prompting or pull you speak of? It seems stumbling upon what you're looking for is often initiated by intention," Rylla countered, finding her voice once more. She wasn't sure why she felt the need to argue, but Caz's presence unnerved her.

"Sometimes intention is necessary, especially if it's well intended," Caz spoke, his eyes not leaving hers. He looked sincere and Rylla scowled as her heart beat wildly against her ribs. It seemed no one else was understanding the undertones of their banter.

"I agree with Caz. It seems intention an' luck can often be mixed. An' it just so 'appened that we stumbled upon yeh 'ere after I 'ad spoken of yeh earlier. We got a whiff of the sea outside, an' believe me, it was 'ard ta leave it ta come in 'ere," Jovin said.

There, that was confirmation now—Caz had intentionally tracked her to this location. He had come to warn her about something, but what?

"Ah yes, you and your love of the sea. You've got the gills of a trout on you somewhere," Uwan chuckled. "And what about you, Caz? Do you fancy the ocean as much as my nephew? It seems if given the choice, 'e'd be sailing the seas even now."

"As much as I love the ocean, I find I'm quite taken by the mountains. Being up so high, there's a vastness—a forgiving freedom—unlike anything I've ever felt before," Caz said as he took a bite into a meat pasty.

Rylla looked up quickly, staring at him. This mysterious and impossible man felt that way too? She couldn't help but study him a little closer as she took another bite of her own food. Though she had eaten a few short hours ago, she found she was still quite hungry after her Earth-spells.

"And what about you, Rylla?" Uwan directed the conversation to her.

Rylla covered her mouth, glancing at Uwan as she tried to chew faster. She felt every bit unladylike trying to converse through the chewing. A blush of embarrassment crept up her neck. Why was it that people seemed to ask questions at the most inconvenient times?

"I'm, sorry…" she managed and tried to swallow.

Caz shoved half a loaf of bread in his mouth before talking. "I for one think conversation is greatly inspired with a full mouth of food." He gave her a reassuring smile which rendered her speechless. What was he doing? *Who is this man?* Those questions would have to wait. She preferred not to have an audience.

Rylla quickly swallowed again and looked back at Uwan. "I prefer the mountains as well, and for the same reasons." She chanced a glance in Caz's direction and the corner of his mouth quirked up in a smile, then he gave her a wink. What passed between them was so quick, no one seemed to notice. Heat rose to her cheeks as she cast her gaze to the floor and noticed Moo looking up at her, a curious expression in his eyes.

"Does no one here like to dwell in caves?" Uwan bolstered loudly with some humor.

"As a matter of fact, I prefer them to both the mountains and the sea, though that doesn't mean I'd like to live in one." Elowen crossed her arms across her chest, pretending not to care.

"A woman who isn't afraid of a cave? Who prefers them ta the great outdoors? Don't know if I've ever 'eard such a thing in my life," Jovin replied, a smile on his face.

"Well perhaps you need to meet more women," Elowen challenged, staring him down.

"I think I just 'ave." Jovin chuckled.

The look of irritation that was once on Elowen's face was now infused with something else. Was that a hidden smile?

"Well, it does my 'eart good to 'ave a full table once more, and though time ticks away, my 'ope is that you'll all stay for quite some time," Uwan said, a strange hitch in his voice.

Rylla looked at Moo who seemed to shake his head. "I don't trust him, Rylla," he whispered.

"Now, it's almost daylight, and seeing as I live in a cave, I prefer to sleep during the day. I suggest you all do the same. But before we do…" Uwan snapped his fingers and tray of goblets whisked by on a silver platter before dropping onto the table. "Let's drink a toast to such good company."

Rylla grabbed a glass, watching the others do the same. Uwan gave the toast, and they all lifted their goblets high before drinking. It was a rich cherry-tasting liquid, thick like blood. Rylla only took a sip. Jovin downed his glass and Elowen and Caz drank only a little more than her. Rylla's head spun with dizziness.

"Tomorrow night we shall train, but this morning, you shall get some rest." Uwan pushed back his chair before standing, smiling as he clutched onto the Obsidian hanging around his neck. "You ladies already know your sleeping chambers, per'aps you can show the men theirs. Until the morrow!" He gave a slight bow and then retreated to his rooms.

By now the fog was so great, Rylla wasn't sure if she could keep her eyes open much longer. The others looked more comatose than herself. They all got up, rather reluctantly, and shuffled in the direction of their chambers. Elowen went into the girls' room as Rylla pointed down the hallway the men should take. As Jovin retreated to the chamber, Caz lingered yet again.

"I…I'm sorry about…your brother." He seemed to fumble with his tongue, finding it noticeably hard to speak. "I wish…I…" A brief look of regret passed his features before he spoke once more. "I hope you sleep well, Rylla." He looked at her briefly before following after Jovin.

"Thank you," she whispered, and something in her chest twinged as she realized she really meant it.

He had said her name, and for some reason that seemed to wake her up a bit, if only by a degree. She walked the corridor to her room, thinking about all that had passed between her and Caz over the past few hours. He had come as a stalker and a serious, stern man, but now it felt like there was something more. And that was more of a mystery than before.

She still had yet to learn of his errand and heed his warning, but sleep seemed too sweet and was beckoning her like the moon tugging on the tide. Perhaps in the morning she would find out more. As her head hit the pillow, she thought she heard a whispering, a nudging, a tuft of soft fur trying to urge her awake. But to no avail. Sleep came upon her as boldly as the sun claims the sky.

Chapter the Eighteenth

Training to Flee

By the time Rylla woke groggily from her sleep, the sun was setting on the horizon. She looked over to where Elowen was also stirring, though more slowly. Noises from the other room indicated that they weren't the only ones in Uwan's cave. Who else was there? Memory returned in a flash and Rylla sat up straight.

Caz was here, and for reasons she couldn't place, he had sought her out intentionally. Why had he gone to such effort? But the more she tried to find the words to ask, it seemed she wasn't quite able to get them out or form a coherent thought. What was wrong with her?

"Good, you're finally awake! I've been trying to get through to you for hours." Moo hopped onto the cot beside her. "We need to get out of here. This place is buzzing with magic." Moo leaned in closer, his gaze searching Rylla's eyes. "You don't look so good, Rylla. What happened to you?"

"I'm trying to figure that out myself," Rylla said but felt like it wasn't coming from her. It was as if she was simply a puppet, watching someone pull the strings.

"Well I suggest we get to the bottom of whatever's going on. Uwan's been up for hours, getting ready for tonight, and though I agree that you need training, I think it's best if we don't linger too long." Moo jumped off the cot, stretching his legs.

Before following, Rylla double checked her satchel and placed it under her pillow. One could never be too careful. She exited her bedroom and entered the kitchen—Caz and Jovin were already there, swords hanging by their waists and dazed looks in their eyes. Elowen followed behind Rylla with her bow and quiver strapped to her back, and before they knew it, the four of them were ushered into the training arena.

Rylla wanted to find an opportunity to talk to Caz, to ask him the meaning of his warning, but she was afraid that even if presented the opportunity, her words wouldn't come out. She was feeling groggier by the minute. And by the time they entered the arena, Uwan sectioned them off: Jovin and Caz were to practice their sword fighting on the left side of the arena while Elowen would work on target practice on the right. That left Rylla alone to work with Uwan in the middle. But she wasn't completely alone, for she had Moo.

"What is that *thing* you 'ave next to you? It's disrupting my thoughts." Uwan pointed in the direction of the cat.

"Oh, this is Moo! He's been my loyal companion on my journey," Rylla replied.

"Bah, tell 'im to sit elsewhere, 'e disturbs me," Uwan implored. "Curious 'ow I 'adn't noticed 'im before."

Rylla, not wanting to offend, walked Moo over to the outskirts of the circle, rubbing her temples.

"Rylla, something's not right here. Look at you, you're practically becoming a shell of yourself," Moo whispered.

"I fear that too. I want to trust him, and strangely, I almost do. But I know deep down something's off. I just don't have the strength to figure out why that is." Rylla rubbed her eyes, hoping to brush away the groggy feelings.

Moo nodded. "Leave it to me, I'll figure something out." He watched her with a skeptical look on his face. Rylla could tell he didn't much like Uwan, and he probably never would.

She walked back to the floor, and Uwan appeared relieved.

"Ah, much better. Now, let us begin."

The training seemed to last forever. As Rylla was instructed by Uwan, she stole frequent glances at the others. Caz and Jovin were fighting hard despite their obvious exhaustion and Elowen hit her targets one after another, missing only a few. Rylla caught Elowen glancing at the men several times, a look of scrutiny and curiosity in her gaze, and the men did the same in return. However, Caz wasn't looking at Elowen, he was looking at Rylla. Though he was far away, the look he gave her held the promise of secrets, of words she needed to know. But she still hadn't a clue why he had followed her in the first place and why he even cared to.

Already, Rylla had learned how to summon tendrils of vines and how to make a dome of earth less destructive. She had learned to summon her own wind and create a path of budding poppies. It felt good, almost freeing, like she was standing on the top of Mount Egret, close to soaring on the wings of the wind. For a brief moment, she forgot her exhaustion and was content. Maybe she didn't have to fear her magic after all, perhaps she could do this. But then her Earth-spells died, leaving Rylla even more tired than before. How much more would Uwan teach her? Would this night never end? The training lasted until the wee hours of the morning as the glass dome above showcased the first rays of morning light. The moon and its stars had already done their duty and were given leisure to rest, unlike her.

"That's enough for today," Uwan remarked loud enough for everyone in the room to hear him. "Well done, Rylla. You're learning quickly. And it seems the rest of you are refining your skills as well." He snapped his fingers again and another tray of goblets came rushing into the room. "To quench the thirst." Uwan motioned for everyone to partake and he watched them carefully. Rylla only took a small sip of the red liquid. What she really needed was water.

"Good, now off to bed once more. You all need your rest in order to train again tomorrow." Uwan smiled at them.

Rylla wanted to protest that she wasn't too tired, to linger longer in the sunshine and finally have that talk with Caz, but her tongue couldn't keep up with her brain. She looked at everyone else, but they too seemed incapable of fluent speech. What had Uwan done to them?

She glanced at the Obsidian dangling from his neck. Did the stone have something to do with the way they were all feeling? The more she wondered, the more certain she felt.

They all seemed too exhausted to argue or discuss things further, and they obediently walked down the hall and to their rooms. Moo followed concernedly at their heels, but before he could exit after them, Uwan seized him by his scruff and he was yanked skyward.

“And where do you think you’re going? Now that I’m aware of your presence, let’s be clear about one thing. Varmint sleep outdoors, not in.” Uwan tossed Moo to the side and walked through the doorway. He sealed off the entrance to the tunnel leaving Moo stranded in the training arena with the first lights of dawn.

❦ ❦ ❦

Days led to weeks the longer they were in this cave. Something wasn’t right. In fact, something was most definitely wrong. They were all puppets to this Master Uwan—that’s what everyone had started calling him, but Moo could see right through him. However, Moo wasn’t able to talk to Rylla much; he was never given an opportunity aside from when she came to train in the arena. Even then, it seemed Uwan was trying his best to keep her away from him.

Rylla had warned him about Uwan’s longings and hunger, but the more Moo observed, it seemed he ate nothing while he watched everyone stuff themselves full. Did the food and drink hold some binding magic over them? What exactly was in those goblets?

And the more Moo thought about it, the clearer it became. Uwan *was* hungry, hungry for power—his loneliness was eating him alive. What was causing this much Darkness? It must be the Obsidian; the old man couldn’t keep his gloved hands off of it.

“We need to get that stone away from him,” Moo spoke aloud as he paced the arena. It needed to happen before everyone came to train for the night. Sometime when Uwan wouldn't be awake. But how to get the stone? And how to warn Rylla?

Moo closed his eyes and sat down, trying to steady his thoughts. Perhaps he could master his grandfather's skill of persuasion and send Rylla a message. Like his grandfather encouraging Rylla to bring her map, maybe he could coax her awake and fill her mind with truths and plans of escape. He had never done that before, had never received the proper training.

"Succeed or not, the middle-ground is a hazy void filled with regret," Moo uttered with eyes still closed, remembering the wise words from one of his ancestors. This had to work.

They were going to flee this place if he had any say about it. And it would be soon.

⸙ ⸙ ⸙

Rylla tossed and turned in her sleep, the full effects of the magic not quite working as they should. She dreamt of Elowen across the room, of Jovin and Caz in the adjacent chambers down the next hall, and of Moo trapped in the arena…Her pulse quickened, and her senses became more alert. Why was Moo trapped in the arena?

Rylla flung the sheets off her cot and reached to grab the necklace around her neck. It wasn't there. Fear rose in her chest as she quickly checked underneath her pillow. Her satchel was missing too.

Her vision blurred like she had been asleep for weeks and had only just woken up, but her tongue finally felt free. Where was she? What had she just been doing? All she remembered were the ceaseless training sessions and the small conversations they'd had at dinner. Had it all been a dream?

Rylla looked at Elowen. She was still fast asleep, the only movements being her breathing. The room felt stuffy even with Uwan's makeshift wind-magic circulating throughout the room, but there was something light and clear twirling about Rylla's mind.

She closed her eyes and steadied her thoughts as a wave of clarity washed over her drowsiness. If something broke through the enchantment, perhaps she should learn how and why. As she listened, pictures of Moo popped in her head. She could see images of meat pasties and goblets of red liquid one after the other followed by visions of glossy eyes and puppet strings, of Uwan's Obsidian and the hungry look in his eyes. She could see the defeated and tired bodies of Elowen, Jovin, and Caz, and Uwan's magic in sealing off Moo from the rest of them. Lastly, she could see Uwan's heart in agony, torn and overpowered by the stone itself.

"Good ol' Moo," she whispered quietly to herself. She didn't know how, but he had freed her trapped mind and tongue.

Rylla had to get them out of here, and fast. It was hard work waking up Elowen, but a touch of Earth-Treader magic and a gentle nudging for good measure did the trick. She was furious, but she would thank Rylla later. Now it was on to the men.

As Rylla and Elowen entered their chamber, they could see two forms fast asleep on cots identical to theirs. The men lay as unmoving as statues aside from their breathing.

Rylla approached the bed closest to her and noticed Caz's arm dangling over the edge. She knelt down, picked up his hand, and closed her eyes to speak. The same words she had used to wake Elowen came pouring out like a stream of water.

Wake, wake,
The time is now
For shadows lurk
Below thy brow
Haste, haste,
Do not linger
The light is here
Upon my finger

At the final word, Rylla gently poked Caz's wrist with the tip of her finger before letting his hand go. After a few moments, he blinked his eyes open. He stared up at her with a dazed expression, and not being fully awake, he reached out his hand to touch her cheek.

"Rylla…?"

She stared into his eyes. What was she meant to do? Images of the past few weeks flooded back into her memory. How he stuffed his face full of bread to spare her the embarrassment and of their quick conversations consisting more of looks than words, for Uwan made sure to limit how often they could all talk. How Caz had caught her on multiple occasions while she was practicing new Earth-spells in the arena, how the power sent her careening too far in his direction, knocking her off balance and practically into his arms. He'd caught her gently each time and asked if she was okay, and her response had always been to get out his arms as quickly as possible. His touch had sent her heart pounding, and she couldn't tell if it was from fear or something else. His kindness had confused her, but as the weeks continued, she had come to find it was sincere.

But there were still so many questions she needed answers to. She had yet to hear his warning.

As Rylla poured over these thoughts, she remembered she was still looking into his eyes. She shouldn't stay this close to him, especially while he was half asleep. She was more confused than anything, for she still didn't know much about Caz or why he was even here in the first place. His hand upon her cheek unnerved her and made her feel the same fear as before, though now she was slightly dizzy and almost wanted to stay where she was. Maybe it wasn't fear at all. But he didn't know what he was doing, and in a matter of minutes he'd be fully aware of his surroundings to never do something like that again.

Rylla pulled away and moved on to Jovin and woke him the same way as the others.

After everyone had reclaimed their wits and their strength, Rylla told them her plan. She wanted to eventually finish that conversation with Caz, but they needed to get out of Uwan's cave first. Lingering would only get them into more trouble.

"He's been poisoning our minds with that cherry drink, controlling us from the inside out," she said. "Jovin, I know this must be hard to hear, considering he's your uncle and all, but he's not himself. His mind is being controlled by the stone he wears around his neck." She looked them each in the eye. "We need to get the Obsidian and get my satchel back. I believe Uwan took my necklace and Garth's Sunstone too…"

"He what?" Elowen protested.

"Why don't we just escape? Are those things really that important?" Caz questioned as he looked to Rylla for more information.

"Yes, I don't have time to explain now," Rylla responded.

Caz seemed to shift gears as he noticed how serious she was. "Okay, well, what do you have in mind?" he questioned.

"I, uh…we need to sneak in and steal it all back." She felt the fool, not used to being in charge. Not to mention, she hadn't quite figured out *how* they were going to accomplish this.

"An' 'ow are we gonna do that? 'e's got ears and eyes everywhere it seems," Jovin said, speaking aloud the question Rylla dreaded.

They all stared at her, waiting. A knot formed in her gut and she looked away. Rylla feared disappointing them. Everyone was counting on her in order to leave this place—it seemed only she could get them out. She met their curious gazes once more and paused, remembering that one face was still missing from their group.

Moo! How could she have forgotten? He was their answer! Uwan's magic didn't affect him. Moo was the only one who could sneak in, but if he were to get trapped somehow? He'd also need her. They'd have to go together.

"The cat and I—we have to get the stone together. Moo's the only one who can go in undetected. For some reason Uwan doesn't like his magic, and I'm the only one who can fight Earth-Treader magic with my own," Rylla answered. "We'll get all the stolen items too. It's the only way." She glanced around the group, ready for a burst of protest.

"That blasted cat, eh?" Jovin laughed to himself. "At least 'e's good for somethin'."

Elowen rolled her eyes, pretending to ignore his laughter but Rylla detected another one of those slight smiles on her lips. It seemed that Elowen didn't mind "the blonde one" so much after all.

"I don't know, Rylla, it sounds like it could be dangerous." Caz turned to face her. "You shouldn't have to do this alone." The light from the nearby candles flickered in his honey-brown eyes and his brow furrowed.

Her heart beat a little faster. How was it that the sound of her name could bring butterflies to dance in her stomach? And why was he so worried for her safety? *Foolish thoughts.* Although she had come to know Caz over the course of a few weeks, he couldn't be fully trusted no matter how much she wanted to believe his honesty. Not until she learned his reasons for everything. Until then, she had to guard herself.

"It's the only way," she replied, though she wished it weren't.

"Then we're waiting in the corridor just in case," Caz countered, a serious and protective tone in his voice.

"Yeh, we'll grab our weapons and make ready if need be," Jovin said.

"I'll just shoot him in the neck with my arrow if he does anything stupid," Elowen offered.

"'ey, that's my uncle ye're talkin' 'bout." Jovin turned to her.

"Oh, I'm sorry, I didn't realize blood was more important than sanity. You know your uncle's insane right?" Elowen crossed her arms over her chest, cocking her brows.

As the two bickered back and forth, Caz met Rylla's gaze and nodded. "We're ready."

If they wanted to get out of here, they'd have to start with the cat. Rylla set out to lead the way to Moo.

⸙ ⸙ ⸙

After trying to contact Rylla via magic, Moo had fallen asleep on the spot. It wasn't until he was awoken by the low rumbling of earth grating against stone that he realized something was moving. When he looked up, four figures loomed in the hallway, a finger pressed over Rylla's mouth as a warning to be quiet.

It worked! The communication spell had woken her and she'd come to her senses! He barely retained his excitement enough to listen to Rylla's instructions.

"And remember, we mustn't make a sound," Rylla reminded him.

"Wouldn't dream of it," Moo replied as they approached the entrance to Uwan's chambers.

"We're here if you need help." Caz gently touched her elbow and it sent a flurry of warmth to her middle. "You need only to yell." He reached for the hilt of his sword as indication that he would indeed be ready to help if needed.

"I know." She looked Caz briefly in the eyes and then glanced at everyone else. "Be back soon."

Rylla and Moo carefully walked the ominous path toward Uwan's chambers. The thought alone filled her with apprehension—she'd never wanted to venture this way, but now she must. Something else, too, nagged at the back of her mind.

If this stone was able to control Uwan, what would stop it from doing the same to her? Maybe she had to wear it for it to control her. No matter, she would put it in the satchel along with the Hawk's Eye; the two would get along swimmingly.

As they rounded a bend, they came upon a darkened room lit with flitting fireflies and Moonstones. Uwan lay asleep in the bed, his Obsidian worn loosely around his neck. It gleamed in the light but otherwise looked unaware. Rylla stood in the doorway as Moo crossed the threshold. She scanned the room for her stolen items and found them all on display on a wooden dresser opposite her. Moo was tasked with the Obsidian; she would recover the items. Rylla crossed the threshold, urgency pulsing in her temples as a thrumming magic filled her ears. It was gentle this time, as if warning her, but she pressed on, ignoring the temptation to run away. Instead, she focused on her breathing and tried to ignore the wild beating of her heart.

She tiptoed to the dresser and grabbed her satchel—it was empty. With shaky hands, she placed the map, her drawing pad and pencil, the Hawk's Eye, and Garth's Sunstone and lantern inside it. When she got to her necklace, she put it around her neck once more, thankful for its familiar weight. She paused.

The thrumming was growing louder, warning her to leave the room. Uwan tossed in his sleep, clearly not receiving the slumber he was hoping to get. Rylla hurried back to her spot in the doorway and slipped behind a wall tapestry before Uwan picked his head up and scanned the room. He must have been too tired to notice the missing items as the gentle lull of silence rocked him back to sleep. This time he was snoring.

Rylla sighed in relief, though the pounding of her heart felt like it was filling the entire room with noise.

Moo gingerly crawled out from where he'd hidden under the bed and looked up. The man was sleeping, his glassy eyes closed and his mouth open. Now was the perfect time.

Moo placed two paws on the bed and jumped his rear legs up behind him, taking extra caution not to rock the mattress. Still, the man did not move, his snores continuing to fill the room. Rylla watched anxiously from the doorway, holding her breath.

Moo stretched his neck to peer down over the sleeping man. The Obsidian hung around his neck by a leather strap and rested on the center of his chest. Perhaps Moo could snap the leather with his teeth and grab the freed stone. He bent down to begin the task, shaking slightly. He pulled the leather gently, clasping it in his teeth.

Rylla stood in the doorway, watching Moo try to break the leather. Movement caught the corner of her eye and her heart dropped to her toes. Two arms were rising upwards from the bed, very slowly, as not to shock Moo. Uwan was awake! His arms were going to crush Moo before he had a chance to get the stone, and she had to stand and watch.

No, this was why she was here; she'd have to save him—she wouldn't leave him this time. Rylla whispered underneath her breath. Two strong gusts of wind hurled forward and challenged Uwan's arms to retreat.

The wind alerted Moo and he twisted and tugged at the leather more frantically, obviously starting to panic.

"Now, Moo, grab it now!" Rylla yelled.

Her voice began the spiral of all things catastrophic. The very walls began to shake as Moo snatched the stone in his mouth. The two arms came crashing down, narrowly missing him.

Uwan, realizing his mistake, ignored Rylla's wind and shot up from bed, his own wind challenging back. It buffeted out in a snowy cyclone, pushing Rylla backwards as Moo came running after her. Caz, Jovin, and Elowen met her halfway through the corridor after hearing her yell, but Rylla didn't stop. Instead, she grabbed them and yelled again.

"Run!"

The walls around them shook as all five sprinted up the long passage to the arena. They could hear Uwan's loud footsteps pounding behind them, his wind raging like an angry storm at sea.

"Bring it back! It belongs to me!" he hollered.

They burst into the arena and Rylla glanced behind her long enough to see Uwan walking into things as he entered behind them. He was no longer gliding with his usual ease. He looked lost, infuriated, and completely broken. He tripped on a chair and his knees slammed into the ground. His snowy wind stopped as he groaned and shuddered. He was becoming a shell.

"I need it…" Tears leaked from his eyes as he implored the five companions, "…Please…please." His fury dissolved into misery.

All five stopped in their tracks and turned to face Uwan. No one dared move.

"Please…take pity," Uwan uttered once more.

Jovin bridged the gap and knelt down before his uncle, sympathy creasing his brow. "Uncle."

Uwan glanced upwards, hope shining in his broken eyes. "Jovin? Is that you?"

"Yes, Uncle, but the stone is no longer yours."

Uwan's face contorted in anger and he yelled and grabbed Jovin around the throat. Caz was there in a second and struggled to pry the old man's firm grip off his nephew. Rylla stared in horror as Caz wrenched his friend from Uwan's hold and they staggered back. Elowen had her bow aimed and ready to strike if necessary while Moo hissed menacingly.

Uwan sank back, gasping as if he just realized his actions.

"What 'ave I done…?" Uwan picked himself up and began to back away, a look of remorse in his eyes. "For…forgive me." He stumbled out of the room, crashing into walls and objects along his way back toward his chamber. Pitiful cries echoed through the halls as he vanished from sight.

Jovin started to follow him but Caz pulled him back. "Let him be. This is a lot to come back from."

Rylla approached Jovin and placed a hand on his other arm, "I'm sorry, Jovin. But I believe we did him a favor." She bit her lip, her heart aching at his pained expression.

"Is your throat okay?" Elowen asked as she walked over, her arms crossed over her chest.

"I'll be fine." His eyes met hers as he rubbed his neck, a small smile straining his lips.

"Well, I'm glad that's over. How do we get out of here? Rylla, did that monster of a man teach you something useful?" She turned to Rylla. Her bow was strung over her back, her features hardened.

"Yes, give me a few moments." Rylla wanted more than anything to taste fresh air again and be gone from this dark chamber of pain and loss. She knew it must be hard for Jovin to see someone he loved so broken, but they couldn't dwell on it here.

She whistled and pushed her hands together. Vines and tendrils of plants sprouted from the walls, responding to her call. She whistled again and the vines caught onto the glass dome—as she pulled her hands apart, the vines mimicked her actions and moved the glass aside. A torrent of fresh sea air flooded the space as a blanket of mist sank down over the lip of the ceiling window, making the room immediately feel damp.

“We’ll have to climb out.” Rylla knelt low as she held out her hand to Moo. He dropped the stone into her open palm and for the briefest of moments she felt the pang of Uwan’s struggle, a tempting desire to hold onto it, to slip it around her neck. She quickly slid it into her bag and a hollow choked in her throat. The Hawk’s Eye and Obsidian gleamed up at her as the two stones touched, sending a jolt of longing through her middle. She stared at them a few more seconds before closing her satchel and standing up.

As she moved forward, both Caz and Jovin sheathed their swords and Elowen adjusted her bow. Rylla found a foothold, and began the scramble up the wall, clinging to the stones and crevices as she climbed.

The sooner they left this foreboding place, the sooner they could start a new leg of their journey. Then perhaps Rylla would find more answers to her questions and put to rest the mystery of Caz.

And now that she was two stones down, there were only three more to go. She had to believe she could keep going.

Part Three:

Sand

Chapter the Nineteenth

Bloodstone Past

Long weeks had transpired, and the being was growing restless. It had thought the process wouldn't take as long as it had, and now the idea of sitting any longer in this foul chair racked its nerves. It was time to move. It groaned and moaned as it struggled to its feet, limbs trying to remember how to properly function. It was progress.

The being had gained some strength—enough to stand and move a few inches before crumbling to its knees.

Gryfinn burst into the room and was rendered motionless at the sight.

"My lord—are you hurt?" he asked cautiously.

The being made another attempt to stand, this time holding onto the chair for support. Its legs shook a little as it stood, but its eyes gleamed with hunger. A venomous smirk lifted a corner of its mouth. It was breathing heavily when it looked into Gryfinn's eyes.

"Bring me the Bloodstone," Lord Brennigan commanded. "It is time."

Gryfinn's fingers twitched as he walked to where the stone sat gleaming on a pedestal. Taking care not to touch the stone itself, Gryfinn picked it up by the leather strap and carefully brought it to his master.

"I've been waiting five-hundred years for this moment," Lord Brennigan said as he grabbed the leather strap from Gryfinn's hands. "Now I am finally strong enough to wear it again." As he fitted the stone over his chest, a surge of power coursed through him, sending bolts of blue and red through his veins. He cursed and yelled in agony as the stone transferred its energy into him, tearing at his existing strength. Would the stone crush him? Was this some sort of mistake?

But then it stopped; Lord Brennigan's breathing returning to normal. He had done it, the stone and him were now one.

"Lord Brennigan…lives," he uttered.

"My lo…?"

"SAY IT!" The chandeliers shook at the force of his shout and the ravens squawked in agitation. Though still weak, he was growing stronger by the moment.

"Lord Brennigan lives! My lord." Gryfinn bowed, sweat dampening his palms.

Lord Brennigan started laughing, a maniacal laugh that sent chills through the air. He took hold of the chair he'd been forced to sit on and pushed it over, then kicked it across the room.

"Burn it! I never want to see that cursed seat again!" Lord Brennigan walked to one of the windows and flung the glass open. Ocean mist infiltrated the space as the sound of waves crashing on rock reverberated nearby. Never again would he be confined to a chair. Never again would he have to sit and wait for the weak and foolish to do his bidding. Lord

Brennigan touched the Bloodstone around his neck and reveled in its power. He had come so far since he'd first found it that day, so many centuries ago.

He was ten and playing with his thirteen-year-old sister along the shores of the Indigo Tide, along the base of the gooseneck or what some might call Aylati's boot.

He belonged to a poor family, and being the youngest of three siblings, he was often pushed around or teased mercilessly. And whenever he'd see his friends outside of school, they'd rather poke fun at his tattered shoes than actually play games with him. He had grown tired of the looks and the names, but his brother was the worst.

"Hey Brenn, check this out!" Odinel, his oldest sibling of six years, walked over to join him. He was moving his hands in circular motions, causing a gale of sand to dance across the ocean waves. The sand depicted two brothers, one older and one younger, fencing—the larger of the two sand figures jabbed the smaller in the stomach and before the smaller could parry back, a giant wave came and broke the magic. Odinel laughed at the joke.

Brenn's insides roiled in anger.

"Wait, wait, how about this?" Odinel whistled and a flock of geese swarmed over Brenn, their squawking and flapping like unruly drums. It didn't take long for them to defecate above his head. "Let me fix that." Odinel scrunched his brow and waved his arms out to sea. When he swung them back in his brother's direction, a giant wave of water followed him.

Brenn looked up, eyes wide in panic. Was that wave coming toward him? He got up to run, but the wall of water plowed into him before he had the chance. It drenched him through and through, the look of anger on his face as clear as day when he came up coughing and gasping for air. He glared at Odinel. He hated this, hated him.

"Oops…" Odinel laughed as he joined some friends who were waiting for him.

"Brenn, are you all right?" his sister approached him.

"I just want to be alone."

"But you're—"

"Talih, please!"

"Fine!" Talih scowled, her lips pursed as she turned to leave.

Young Brenn was all alone. He was angry and hurt more than he wanted to admit. He watched Talih walk away, regret stinging his stomach, but he wouldn't go to her. He hugged his arms across his chest, scowling at her back. Anger bubbled in his stomach—not at her, but at…everything.

As he sat on the shore, he gazed out into the horizon. The waves crashed onto the sandy banks and then pulled back. The same repetitive motion lulled his mind into a sleepy daze as the noonday sun dried his clothes. He shook his head and made sure he was still angry; he wasn't quite ready to move on yet.

Then something caught his eye; an object was bobbing in the ocean, heading in his direction. The closer it got, the clearer it became. It was some sort of bottle. Brenn got up and ran to the water, eager to get his hands on it before it washed back out to sea. Or perhaps, if he was honest with himself, before his brother got his hands on it first.

He waded into the knee-deep water and retrieved the bottle. Waves jostled him off balance as he stumbled his way back to shore. He found some tall rocks to secret himself, keeping the bottle clutched to his chest lest anyone see it. The last thing he needed was prying eyes or to be teased for playing pirate. He held the bottle up to the sunlight and peered through the glass. It must have been in the water a long time, for the glass was blurred with a milky-green sheen, but there *was* something inside, he could tell that much.

Brenn pried the cork out and tipped the bottle upside down. Out dropped two rolled pieces of paper and a small drawstring bag. *Curious*. He decided to start with the bag first since words often bored him. He reached his hand inside the fabric, and his fingertips met something smooth and hard. When he withdrew his hand, he held a stone the size of a large chestnut. It was the most interesting stone he had ever seen.

As he turned it over in his palm, the anger and hatred he had momentarily forgotten, boiled up in his stomach again. Images of what his brother had done replayed in his mind. Red marred his sight, rimming the ocean before him in dark, bloody shades; visions of his brother dying in agony flashed before his eyes.

He dropped the stone with a gasp, backing away from it. His heart raced wildly like a horse just loosed from its pen. What just happened? What was that?

With shaky hands, he grabbed one of the rolled papers, curiosity winning over caution. It was a note. He squinted hard at the messy words, running his finger underneath each line and slowly deciphering the scrawled letters.

Dear Unlucky One,

May this serve as a warning and reminder to anyone who finds this message: this stone is not what it seems. Even now, as I write this, I am addled in the head, for my allegiance is torn. To keep or to destroy. No, no, too precious to destroy. But to make disappear? Much better. For if it falls into the right hands, who's to say some good might not be done? If it were to fall back into mine, I'd take that as a sign of fate. I'd cherish it and never let it go.

Bah! What am I saying? I can't. Its power is too strong. Only the greatest Earth-Treader or a man more powerful than I might withstand it. Alas, I am too weak. My greatest fear is for this stone to perish, but I fear it must, as we all have.

Be warned, take heed, and throw this bottle back: the origins of life and death are not to be tampered with—unless you want the Bloodstone to lead you into a life of torment and uncertain doom.

In earnest,
Aggrieved & forever loyal
King Cuthbert—
The Isle of Abbredun

Little Brenn stared at the message wide-eyed and fearful. King Cuthbert? The Isle of Abbredun? What did it mean? But even in that fear, there was an inkling of curiosity and desire. Would he be strong enough to use the stone? Would his brother? No. He couldn't let his brother ever touch the stone. It was *his.* Brenn pocketed the precious treasure and letter and picked up the bottle again to throw it back out to sea. No one would be the wiser, no one would even know. And his brother would never find out about the stone nor have the chance to hear about it.

Brenn wasn't planning on using the stone himself, he was only keeping it as his little gift from the sea. Something to lord over on his own whenever the onslaught of teasing and jokes came.

He knew something no one else did, and that thought alone would give him power. He shifted and remembered the second rolled paper that had fallen from the bottle. He picked it up and unfurled its edges. It revealed a map that looked strangely like the Earthen-Crest kingdoms, except something was different. He stared at the paper and felt the stone sized lump in his pocket, and he realized he had found a great secret—perhaps something only he alone would ever know.

Lord Brennigan continued to stare out the window as he clutched the Bloodstone in his hand. Thank the depths he'd grown from that witless child into someone who actually saw logic in using it. What a coward he'd been. True it had taken years for him to finally wear it, but once he did, it was like being acquainted with a lifelong friend. He was able to think clearer, see further, and reason without fear. His only regret was how long it had taken him to realize just how great the stone was. But even so, it fueled his anger and had empowered him to enact revenge on his brother.

He remembered the moment vividly. Cold rage in his chest, blood on his blade. Odinel falling, falling…Brennigan's lip curled and he curled his fingers tighter about the stone. His brother had deserved nothing less than what he'd received.

Lord Brennigan shook himself from his reveries and looked out to sea. He had missed his stone, and he was glad to finally have it back where it belonged: upon his neck. He turned to face Gryfinn who had been silently watching him, then glanced beyond his servant to the wall of frames. Three stones were missing.

"My lord?" Gryfinn's voice shook just slightly as he followed his master's gaze.

"You found Rélynda's stone over a week ago now. Are you here to tell me you also found Wyllund's and obtained Ostglenden's?" Lord Brennigan's eyes narrowed as he glanced back at his servant, eyes laced with warning.

"It is true, my lord, that Rélynda's stone was found, and it's locked away like you asked. But…"

"But?" Lord Brennigan sneered.

"We are still searching for the Hawk's Eye and now…" Gryfinn paused tugging awkwardly at his cloak as if he were suddenly too hot. "And now…the Obsidian…my lord."

"You blasted idiot!" Lord Brennigan shouted. "And I suppose you're going to tell me you haven't found the girl yet either, hmm?"

Gryfinn blanched.

"GrrrruAGGHH!" Lord Brennigan threw a water goblet across the room, shards of glass shattering at Gryfinn's feet. "We are down four stones, two of which have yet to be found!" He scanned the frames once more. "Only Aylati and the Isles are left, and seeing as Wyllund's has only recently been acquired, my guess is the Isles will be disappearing next!"

Lord Brennigan began pacing, his mind whirling with plans. "Go there and find the stone yourself. If the same cutpurse who stole the other stones is headed there like I think she is, then all the better. You'll be getting three stones instead of just one, which will only leave Aylati's." He paused his pacing and looked at Gryfinn. "I know this girl is trying to undermine me, Gryfinn. Earth-Treaders usually are!"

Lord Brennigan went back to pacing. "Lucky for you, our prisoner is still alive. He came clean and revealed he works for Grievon—I figured as much—but he may know more than he lets on, and I feel he'll be useful in pointing this girl out. Besides, you need all the help you can get." Lord Brennigan scowled at Gryfinn, eyes menacing and filled with power. He paused only long enough to stretch his neck, the blue veins popping through wrinkled skin.

"But there's more—these past weeks I've been running numbers, and the bodies I have in my army aren't enough, nor are they all loyal. Some of my guards have fled, afraid of my growing power. With this duplicity, the race of man can't be trusted! But I shall soon fix that." Lord Brennigan stroked his stone and stared at Gryfinn thoughtfully. "And this new prisoner talks of the king, *Grievon of Ostglenden*, and his large army which he hopes to fill with Earth-Treaders. Not to mention how he wants my stones too…It would trouble me, but I've already started to take matters into my own hands." His lips twitched into a smirk that showcased his yellowed teeth. By now, he seemed almost to be in a trance-like state, talking more to himself than Gryfinn. "In a few days, everything will be ready. A new army will rise, one that will ground Grievon's numbers to a pulp. He'll be sorry to even think he stands a fighting chance."

Lord Brennigan looked back over the land beyond the window, wistful and seething at once. What foolish king would think he could stand against a force like Brennigan's up and coming army? The frailty of man's allegiance wouldn't be his problem anymore, but this Grievon would be hard pressed to keep his soldiers from fleeing before Brennigan's forces in battle.

Even though some of Brennigan's men had slunk off in the night, he still had the Earth-Treaders rotting in his dungeons. That was enough to keep him sane. Lord Brennigan stroked his stone and his eyes met Gryfinn's again.

"What are you doing still standing there? Have I hired an addle-brained puppy? Get that prisoner, get some men, and move out. NOW!"

"Y-ye-yes, my lord," Gryfinn stuttered, scrambling for the door. As he left the room and made for the dungeons, something told him that if he failed this mission, it would be his last mistake.

Chapter the Twentieth

Across the Basin

Rylla had never seen the Ocean Basin in real life, only from pictures in books or on maps. The sight before her knocked the wind out of her lungs. It was nothing like the crystal, tranquil waters of the Indigo Tide back home—no, these waters were deep and dark and mysterious. Rylla gulped.

Though there was plenty of daylight from above, the depths below lurked as black as pitch and the idea of crossing it sent a chill down her spine.

Rylla studied her map and marveled at how far she had come. They were standing on the wharfs, at the very edge of Wyllund's western border with the North Mountains to her right, and if she were to walk a few more steps, she'd be standing over the basin itself. She wished she could climb the mountains instead of getting on a ship. How long ago was it when she had first left? Two weeks? Three? Were her parents okay?

The fact that she had to leave them without saying bye still plagued her. And now she was journeying across an ocean with two mysterious men and a sister-in-law who she still didn't quite get along with. At least there was

Moo. But what would it be like to leave the mainland? And be on a ship? Thoughts and questions jostled about in her head, and the unknown made her queasy. Better to just do it than to worry herself ill.

"Yeh both ready?" Jovin called to her and Moo from further up the dock. He was helping Elowen into the ship, or at least trying to, but Elowen slapped his hand away and climbed aboard herself. He laughed and looked at her with mirth in his eyes.

Caz was already on deck, readying the masts and preparing the large vessel for launching. It was swaying impatiently in the choppy waters as if eager to set sail.

Rylla both questioned and marveled at their stalwart commitment, especially since she only met them a few weeks ago. After leaving Uwan's cave, the men had looked to her, asking what was next and where she was going. But before Rylla could utter a word, Elowen had told them about the stones and the mission to find them.

Irritation churned in Rylla's gut as she recalled the conversation. For some reason, it felt even more ridiculous a mission when someone else was saying it, and now that they all knew, she still wasn't settled. Could the men be trusted? Would they think she was insane? Did it even matter?

Even still, they had agreed to join her—and seemed almost eager to, in fact. Before heading to the wharfs, though, the two men had quickly gone to find their horses, unexpectedly returning to report that they had been well cared for in the weeks their owners had been missing, though they hadn't seen anyone nearby. The only clue that something had indeed visited the animals was the scattered coating of feathers on the ground. Rylla didn't have to think too hard to guess who the horses' beneficiary had been.

Rylla's feet were planted firmly on the wooden boards of the wharf. She stared at the looming figure of the old ship, a rough and weathered exterior made of oak with a yellowed, horizontal stripe winding around its middle; it appeared to be as ancient and unyielding as the sea. She gazed upwards to where Caz was lowering a mast, the wind tousling his brown hair and the clothes around his broad shoulders. He must have some other motive for being here, or why else would he be heading for the Isles? He had come to deliver a warning, but was that it? She had to find out eventually, but in the meantime, he was here, and he was helping.

She glanced across the deck to Jovin and was grateful he was doing the same. Though it still didn't take away her feelings of distrust, especially in regard to Caz.

"There are many battles ahead," Moo spoke beside her.

"What?" Rylla was startled out of her thoughts.

"And I don't just mean the physical kinds, though there will be plenty of those too," Moo replied.

"What makes you say that?" Rylla gazed at the vast ocean beyond the ship, Moo's paw a gentle comfort against her leg.

"Many a journey has the power to reveal true character and desire. Wait long enough and all shall come to pass, all shall be revealed in light. Though I think he can be trusted."

"Who?" Rylla questioned.

Moo looked in Caz's direction. "I'm usually never wrong." He dropped to all fours and began to move down the dock to board the ship. "We should head out while there's still daylight."

Rylla pondered Moo's words and the depth of his impossible riddles as she followed him across the dock and to the ship. She couldn't lie, his words set her skepticism at ease. But what was he getting at?

Jovin was patiently waiting for Rylla, helping her step up the gangplank and into the monstrous vessel. The deck tilted beneath her feet and her stomach somersaulted.

She clutched the ship's railing for support. So this is what it felt like to be on water.

"Right, the journey's 'bout five 'ours if the weather's any good. 'Bout four if the wind's on our side." Jovin smiled as he untethered the ship from the dock.

The ship stirred to life and Rylla clutched the side tighter, bile stinging the back of her throat. "Let's hope for four then," she managed, and made her way toward the middle of the vessel. She sat down at the base of one of the masts, allowing the salty air to fill her lungs. This was going to be a long ride no matter what she did, but perhaps she could make it as short a torture as possible.

⸙ ⸙ ⸙

It was ironic, really, that Rylla's plan was to head to the Isles next. It made his decision that much easier since he had already planned to go there himself. They were now moving at a steady clip, the waves sweeping over the bow whenever it dipped low amidst the swell, a shimmer of gold tinging the air behind them like evening sunlight. It was lucky, the wind seemed to be on their side today.

Caz finished adjusting the sail on the mizzenmast and tied the rope into place, scanning the quarterdeck. Elowen was busy sharpening arrowheads and talking to Jovin who was steering at the helm. Caz knew the horses were tucked away in the captain's cabin, away from the sea-winds, but where was Rylla? He hadn't seen her come on.

Caz looked down and found her seated on the main deck with her back against the mainmast; she was busy looking tired, her eyes closed as Moo rested by her feet. His heart sped up. She was all alone. No more enchantments separated them from having a proper conversation—his goal in the first place. If he didn't warn her about Grievon's army now, his guilt would begin eating him alive. This was one step toward muffling the terrors of his past.

He made his way down the deck but stopped short. Rylla's eyes were closed, but more out of an intense focus than a need for sleep. She appeared to be muttering softly under her breath. What was she doing? The ship sliced through the waves, sending spray over the bow in huge explosions of white foam. The deck slanted sideways and Caz stumbled a pace, crashing to the ground beside her.

Rylla's eyes flew open and the deep crease on her brow disappeared as the wind slowed to a steady breeze. A light dusting of gold floated in the air and settled gently on the ship and on the wooden planks around them. Color rose to her cheeks, and she looked away quickly.

Now he understood the reason for the cooperative weather.

"I apologize, I hadn't meant to startle you," Caz said as he righted himself, his gaze finding a group of barrels nearby. He brought one over and sat down across from Rylla, his back now against the cylindrical crate of wood.

The cat had perked up, but now rested his head again, watching Caz from Rylla's other side. The ship rocked gently in the wind, their passage much slowed. The cat's eyes began to close once more.

"You didn't really," Rylla responded, hesitating only a moment. "I was just…"

"You gave us some tailwind, we appreciate that," Caz said, saving her the trouble of having to explain.

"I don't think my stomach appreciates this way of travel. I figured the wind could get us there faster." Her gaze lifted from the deck to meet his, her eyes full of questions.

Caz stared back and felt he was truly looking at her face for the first time. She was actually…even more beautiful than he realized. Her unruly curls looked as if they had a story of their own, and they matched the depth of her hazel eyes. He hadn't remembered the freckles or the slight bump on the bridge of her nose, but they were charming. Her cheeks held hints of sunshine as her delicate lips pulled sideways in a nervous smile.

He vaguely remembered touching one of her cheeks in a half daze and instantly felt heat rise to his face. Had that only been a dream? He sure hoped so. He ran a hand over his face to refocus his thoughts.

"What I wanted to say is, I'm sorry I startled you back in Aylati." Caz shifted his position, cocking one elbow on his drawn-up knee. He wanted to get this off his chest before anything else could interrupt him. "That wasn't my intention."

"I can't say I wasn't terrified, but I guess if you were really cruel, you could have made things worse," Rylla said slowly, as if she was searching for the right words. "Though I half feared your severe scowl would imprint permanent lines on your face. Tell me, are you always so serious when you meet new people?"

Caz was taken aback by Rylla's words. "*If you were really cruel, you could have made things worse.*" If only she knew the half of it, the guilt he carried. He had been short with her in the cave. He'd been short with everyone over the past years. Grievon's army had changed him. He looked back in her eyes and noticed the twitch at the corner of her mouth like she was trying to hold back a smile. Was she teasing him now?

"It seems all my faults are on display today." Caz chuckled lightly.

"Not all, just the few I've noticed," Rylla replied.

"Are you implying there's more?" Caz quirked a brow.

"Oh I'm sure of it! We all have our faults. Just promise me chasing and scaring women will no longer be one of yours." Rylla laughed, her smile breaking free.

"You have my word—I think I've thoroughly learned my lesson." Caz laughed in reply. "But truly, I shouldn't have been so short with you, and I never meant to cause you concern. Honest. I've never been good at pursuing women—I mean, trying not to frighten them, that is." Caz stumbled over his words to correct himself, flushing warm again. He was a total buffoon.

Rylla seemed to consider his words a moment. "Well, I *was* worried because I figured that sooner or later, you'd realize I was the same girl you both chased and rescued. And seeing you show up at Uwan's confirmed my fears—But now I find, strangely, that I'm not afraid of you anymore, merely curious."

Caz released a sigh, some of the tension seeping from him. That was a relief to hear.

"I'm still not sure why I should trust you, though. Do you have a habit of chasing women you plan on giving vague warnings to?" She furrowed her brow, a challenge in her tone.

"No, just you." He scratched the back of his neck. "And I don't deserve your trust. I'm a poacher, like the ones who were chasing you in Thrushwoode—but I'm not like them, at least not anymore." He was doing everything in his power to make that clear. "When I was 'pursuing' you back in Aylati, I had just snuck away from my unit to taste freedom, if only briefly. It wasn't until I saw you were an Earth-Treader that I felt I had to find you, to warn you that Grievon's men are hunting you as we speak."

Rylla stared at Caz in silence, seeming to digest this new information. He shifted his position and withdrew the crumbling piece of bark from his pocket. He gave it to her, his fingers gently brushing against the palm of her hand. A jolt thrummed in his chest. Instantly his mind was taken back to when he had touched her hand in Uwan's cave. He quickly withdrew his own and began fidgeting with the folds of his cloak.

"It's the bark from the tree you touched in Aylati. I took some as a way to remember it, to remind myself if I ever forgot. It's been in my pocket these past couple of weeks."

"The Grove," Rylla whispered so softly Caz almost didn't hear it. She turned the bark over in her fingers, seeming lost in thought. Then her eyes widened and her lips turned up in the corners. "You didn't hear me yelling at the tree, did you?"

Caz raised his eyebrows, then chuckled. He hadn't, but now he wished he'd been a little earlier to witness that part of the incident. "No, I didn't." He smiled, but the lightness in his chest faded as her smile faltered. What had he said wrong? He wanted more than anything to put the smile back. "What's wrong?"

"It's just…if you hadn't chased me that night, or if I knew you were harmless at the time, perhaps I could have warned my parents before I left," she said softly, her voice tinged with regret. "Or maybe I wouldn't be here at all."

"Rylla, I should have been more careful, I'm sorry." Caz's throat tightened around the words, heart heavy. Another child he had separated from her parents…another failure to add to his long list. The guilt twisted deeper. Of course she had parents who cared for her and were probably worried sick. And he had caused her to run away. All the more she should hate him for it.

"'Tis nothing for it now," Rylla released a shuddery breath and straightened, seeming to pull herself together. She stared off into the distance as the waves lapped by. Her throat worked in a swallow, tense lines still creased around her eyes, and her face had gone a shade lighter. She was seasick—of course!

Caz grimaced, wishing he could do something to help.

After a few moments she turned back to him. "How did you even know where to find me in the mines?"

Caz coughed and adjusted his position. "A large owl pointed us in the right direction." He felt foolish but told Rylla the story of how the cat seemed to communicate with the owl, about the twigs forming words, and their brief, but alarming journey through the Heather Fields. He explained how he and Jovin ended up digging through the mine entrance for hours with just their swords and how after a time of searching inside the mine, they had been summoned to Uwan's cave.

Rylla nodded like she believed him, but suddenly her eyes narrowed. "Why *are* you here? I know you're coming with us to help—but you didn't have to."

Caz met ger gaze, choosing his words carefully. "I'm tired of the life I've been leading, and I want a change of pace. Being a poacher was never my choice—I was forced into it as an orphan. And seeing you in the forest…" He paused, wondering how to keep going. He couldn't very well admit that he was drawn to her that day in Aylati, could he? That seeing her fit of passion in the Grove had ignited the same fighting spirit in himself. Or that all the wrongs he had committed as a poacher still plagued his mind in images and nightmares. Or even that he had plans to run away and start new in the Isles after giving her this warning…

He decided to soften the truth. "Seeing you in the forest inspired me to break from the mold. And offering you my help was my first priority." Caz met Rylla's gaze, trying to analyze her thoughts.

"I just don't understand why you want to give it, and so freely. Besides, you owe me nothing," Rylla countered. "If anything, I should be paying you back after you rescued me from the poachers."

"You owe *me* nothing." He leaned back on the barrel and crossed his arms over his chest. He was eager to help her. Anything to start wiping his past clean. "Helping you is the least I can do after making you leave home without saying bye to your parents. Perhaps I can even help you find your brother."

Rylla seemed to consider what he said, but she didn't speak. Instead, her face looked even paler than before.

"And I agree with you—from what I saw back there, you seem pretty capable on your own. You have a warrior's spirit," Caz hurried on. "But if Grievon were to find you or—"

"Or Lord Brennigan," Rylla interrupted, a quiver of fear etching her words.

"Lord Brennigan?" Caz was utterly bewildered by such a statement. "He died over five-hundred years ago, Rylla." Maybe she was more seasick than he thought.

Rylla turned to him, her skin pale but her eyes serious and searching.

"I beg you to listen, for this very well could include you and the fate of all our kingdoms. If you value your life, you'll hear me out," Rylla spoke with conviction, a hard edge in her voice. Caz could tell she was more than serious and that her words probably held more truth than he realized.

"Of course, forgive me." Caz swallowed hard at the look of intensity in her eyes.

"Elowen told you about the stones I'm searching for, the Earth-Treader stones used by the kings of old." She waited for Caz to nod. "Well, apparently Lord Brennigan had a stone of his own, a dark stone filled with a dark magic. The Earth-Lore and history books say he died on the battlefield in the Heather Fields, but the truth is he uttered a spell which somehow preserved his life within the stone itself. Someone recently found the stone and brought him back from the dead." Rylla paused to catch her breath. "And he's searching for each provinces' stone so he can grow more powerful. He hates Earth-Treaders—that's what Fang told me."

"Fang?" Her words sounded absolutely crazy, but strange things had been happening as of late. Perhaps Lord Brennigan really was back from the dead. Would he be after her like Grievon? Great. She was potentially being hounded by two power-hungry men. Who knew what they were capable of?

"Moo's grandfather," Rylla stated matter-of-factly, like conversing with animals was completely normal. At the mention of his name, the cat stirred and looked up. He yawned and moved to sit between Rylla and Caz.

Moo meowed at her.

"He just warned me that King Grievon's men are out searching for Earth-Treaders, me in particular, and I told him about Lord Brennigan. I'm filling Caz in on the details," Rylla said to Moo.

Moo meowed again.

Rylla looked at Caz and eyed him carefully. "I think he's taking it rather well."

"What are you doing? Are you two talking about me?" Caz looked between the two of them. He was still getting used to this whole magic business.

Moo meowed again and this time a flush darkened Rylla's pale cheeks as she looked up at Caz.

"What? What did he say?" Caz questioned.

"Nothing…just mentioned a dream he had is all." Rylla shook his question off, but Caz could tell she was lying. "Moo, why don't you go see if land is in sight yet," she suggested.

Without saying anything more, Moo stretched and made for the quarterdeck. Silence settled between Caz and Rylla aside from the gentle lull of the wind and the rocking of the ship on the waves.

Caz watched Rylla out of the corner of his eye; she was growing paler and her gaze was a little dazed. Maybe he should let her get back to harnessing the wind and getting them to their location faster. It was selfish of him to keep her talking when she felt as sick as she obviously did.

"I'm going to check on the sails and make sure the horses are all right. It's also about time I relieved Jovin from his duty at the helm. Maybe the wind will pick up again as I steer the ship." Caz got up and winked at Rylla.

A slow blush crept up her face before he turned to leave. When he got to the horses, he remembered he hadn't gotten the piece of bark back from her. He'd have to get it later. Just another excuse to talk to her and win her trust. She still seemed a little guarded, but he could tell she was beginning to soften.

Regardless, he was heading to Isles, his new home. It was lucky this ship was unoccupied and fit for travel when they had found it, almost like it was waiting for them. There had been two other ships nearby—one docked in the water with a crack in its upper hull and the other beached ashore with torn sails on all its masts. Fixing either of them would have taken an entire day. Jovin had told him that Wyllund's throne paid to have these vessels serviced for their military, but with Grievon taking over with his own militant forces, these ships hadn't been used in years.

Caz hoped this string of luck bore good signs for him—that he was on the road to becoming a changed man. And if he had any say about it, he'd never go back to the mainland again. He'd never have any reason to.

⸙ ⸙ ⸙

Rylla watched Caz walk away, the blush on her cheeks overtaken by nausea. Their conversation had eased her somewhat but also realized her greater fear—she now knew Caz's message, but it wasn't one of comfort;

it had echoed Garth's story about Grievon. And she still had questions. Perhaps Moo had been right all along though: Caz had known from the beginning that she was an Earth-Treader, had known the risk of defying Grievon and his men, and yet…he did it anyway. He had kept her secret and had gone out of his way to find her. He said he wanted to break away from the mold and to help her. But why? There must be more he wasn't telling her.

As Rylla replayed their conversation over in her head and turned the golden piece of bark over in her fingers, she couldn't help but recall the way he had been looking at her, gently but intently. She'd never been looked at like that in her life, and when Moo made note that Caz's expression was a dead giveaway to his feelings though he himself was completely unaware of it, Rylla had blushed once more in embarrassment. Thank the heights Caz hadn't been able to understand. It was surely a jest anyway.

Rylla was surprised that when Caz left to resume his duties, she had felt the loss keenly. She chalked it up to the relief in finally having her questions answered. Or finally being able to talk more than five sentences after being trapped in Uwan's cave for weeks on end. At least their conversation had taken her mind off the blasted seasickness.

Speaking of which, she wanted to get off this ship. She wasn't sure how much longer she could last. Where was Moo? She looked out to the horizon once more, then twisted around at the sound of her name.

"Rylla, sorry it took me so long." Moo sauntered over to her. "You don't know how hard it is to get the information you need when you can't ask for it. Elowen finally asked Jovin how much longer 'til the Isles, and he said about two hours."

"Two hours?" Rylla swallowed the lump in her throat. "Perhaps I can summon a tempest or a gale strong enough to get us there in one."

"I think we'd all appreciate getting there sooner rather than later, especially the horses. I've just about had enough of those creatures and hope to never ride one again," Moo replied as he sat next to her.

"Not a fan, huh? I've actually never ridden before." Rylla sucked in a deep breath, bracing herself to conjure the wind, when her hand accidentally brushed against the Yellow Jaspers around her neck. She'd almost forgotten about them and their helpful reminder to keep going. If she fled the Heather Fields and humbled Uwan, surely she could handle a little seasickness.

"Well it's dreadful, and I hope you never have to." Moo began licking his paw.

"You know, there's something that's been worrying me…about the stones," Rylla changed the subject.

"And what's that?" Moo moved on to the other paw.

"I thought all the kings' stones were supposed to be good. If that's true, then why did the Obsidian seem to possess Uwan and corrupt him?"

"Ah yes, I wondered when you'd ask this. Do you remember what my grandfather said when he chose you for this mission? About your heart?" Moo inquired.

Rylla thought back and nodded. "He said it was pure, that I wouldn't use the stones for my own gain."

"Exactly. Uwan's soul was left wanting after he fled from his captivity, his spirit crushed and hopeless. The stone gave him his sight back but at a price, the power of prophecy and wisdom becoming a crutch rather than a gift. He reveled in its power, coveted it, and harbored it all for himself. It corrupted his very heart."

"Do you think the other stones could do that as well?" Rylla wondered.

And if my heart's so pure, then why do they tempt me?

"I think most stones, deemed good and useful, have the ability to corrupt the wielder if they are not careful. Realize that the Earth-Treader kings of old ruled together to create a harmonious reign throughout the provinces. They used their stones as a team even though they reigned apart. The five stones were never meant to work independently from one another, for therein lies the problem. Uwan is evidence of that. But there are some stones, like Lord Brennigan's, that are turned wicked and evil to their core—to tamper with them is like waltzing with death itself." Moo started to work out the kinks in his tail.

"Well, we have two stones so far. Do you think finding the rest will be difficult?"

"What's your definition of difficult?"

"I guess we'll have to find out." Rylla let out a short laugh, but quickly sank back into her swirling thoughts. "I've definitely gotten stronger, but I still don't know what I'm up against, Moo. All this talk of Lord Brennigan, and now Grievon…I don't know if I can do this." *I don't know if I can trust myself.* "I'm scared," she admitted.

"I'd be concerned if you weren't." Moo stopped his grooming to look her in the eyes. "But you were chosen for this, Rylla, and my grandfather doesn't make mistakes. He knew from when you were just a toddler in the Grove that you would be the one to do this." Moo looked at her carefully as if peering into her very soul. "You fear temptation, and rightly so, but why give power to something that only seeks to take away yours? When the time comes, you'll be able to rise above it."

Moo's words were like a balm to her heart, though she still felt unsettled. She'd have to wait and see, but the waiting felt like agony.

It amazed Rylla that only a few weeks ago she had been at home, working in her parent's orchard and helping her father with his maps. She hadn't known of her magic nor the task before her, and she hadn't known these people who were slowly becoming her friends. So much had happened in such a short amount of time. So much to process. If only she could find Finn and bring him home—and make it home herself.

"I sure hope you're right," Rylla whispered to Moo. She looked toward the upper deck and saw Elowen standing near the railing, watching her. Elowen quickly averted her gaze and resumed sharpening her arrow heads. Jovin had made his way to the captain's cabin and was now giving fresh water to the horses while Caz was busy steering the ship, his muscles taut and eyes decidedly focused on the distant horizon. She followed his gaze and her heart leapt at the sliver of greenish rock in the distance, shimmering in the sun. Was it the Isles finally? She looked back to Caz who was now consulting a compass, his eyes squinting against the sunlight. When Rylla resumed her view of the sea, the rock was gone. *Odd.* What had that been?

This whole mission and these friends—it was all so very random, but she was learning to accept it; she had no other choice.

"Thanks, Moo."

"It's always an honor to help you, Rylla." He seemed to smile as he got up and stretched his legs.

Rylla smiled in response and looked back at Caz, remembering his comment about the wind. Perhaps it was time to help him out. "Let's speed things up a bit, shall we?"

She closed her eyes and reached for the energy deep inside her, remembering the way Uwan told her to feel it. She summoned the wind with words and her mind, seeing it careen the ship on the wings of feathered birds across a golden lake as smooth as crystal glass. She was as light as a feather herself while the faces of her friends all flashed before her eyes. Now if only she were truly flying.

She peeked her eyes open for just a moment—long enough to see the smudge of color in the distance. The Isles loomed ahead through a light fog, the mountains and rocks creating both a menacing and beautiful welcome.

Chapter the Twenty-First

The Isles of Norviç's Throne

The sound of wood scraping against gravel and sand shook Rylla from her magic, her eyes opening to see Caz taking in the sails and Jovin making ready to drop anchor. Elowen was getting the horses while Moo was busy pouncing on a fish that had flopped on deck.

They must have been traveling at a quick pace for they had reached the Isles much sooner than Rylla had anticipated, and there was a substantial heap of golden dust piled around her now. She sneezed and a waft of gold puffed high into the air only to settle back to the ship's deck.

The ship swayed choppily in the shore-line serf. Her nausea lingered, and the ship's movements made it even worse since breaking from her Wind-spell. She felt like she was about to hurl.

Rylla picked up her satchel and ran to the edge of the ship. The drop was too far down to jump. Instead, she grabbed the oaken gangplank and haphazardly slid it down the side of the ship and into the shallow water below. Rylla wasted no time in making the descent, the water meeting her knees as she waded to shore. Once her shoes hit dry ground, she sat down, the nausea pooling in the pit of her stomach. It would pass, surely. She was now on steady ground, but she could feel her body rocking as if it were still on the ship. If there was one thing that rivaled Rylla's fear and distaste for the dark, it was the idea of vomiting.

"She's down there…" Elowen's voice could be heard over the breaking waves along the bank. When Rylla lifted her head, she scrutinized the ship once more. Despite it being a menace to her stomach, it really was quite beautiful. There *was* something freeing about gliding along a body of water, even if what lurked below was as mysterious as her nausea was inconvenient.

After a few moments, Elowen walked toward her with the two beautiful horses who seemed almost as relieved to be off the ship as she was, if not more so.

"Soo-hoo-hooo-hoo glad to escape that prison, Cinders," Rembrandt whinnied. His chestnut coat was dotted in seafoam.

"I hope we neeiiiighhhver have to get on it again," Cinders, a dusty gray horse replied. Rylla couldn't help but agree with them.

Wait. She could understand horses now? Since when had that happened? Her animal repertoire was growing like the owl had said! The nausea in her stomach was replaced with a jolt of excitement.

Caz followed close behind with the swords and the provisions while Moo clung desperately to his shoulders, avoiding the water as if it were death itself. Jovin came last, carrying two ropes attached to the ship which he took and staked into the sand a little way off.

"We didn't know where you'd gone to. When Caz asked, you weren't where I'd last seen you. I figured I might find you here." Elowen stopped just short of Rylla who was now sitting upright with her arms clasped around her knees. "You look like you've seen a ghoul. You okay?"

Rylla nodded and breathed deeply. "Feeling better. I guess I learned I don't care much for ships." She laughed a little. "Or they don't care much for me."

Rylla hadn't noted the beauty of her surroundings until now. The sand was crystal white and dotted with shells of various colors scattered throughout. She thought of Winnie back home and how she'd love one of these for her collection. Rylla pocketed a brilliant blue shell as dark as the waters of the basin. Close to the shore, but safe enough to avoid the tide, fishing boats were stacked three high. Tall, tropical trees grew near the water's edge while a forest of denser trees stood all around them in a half moon. In the distance to the left, somewhere through those trees, there was a pointed spire with a flag flapping in the wind. It must be the Isles' throne. To her right, she could see large mountain-like rocks jutting above the tree line. What was over there?

"Well, don't forget about the return journey home. You're going to have to board the ship again," Elowen said, always straight to the point.

"I'd rather not think about that right now." Rylla felt nauseous all over again.

The two men and Moo joined them and asked how Rylla was doing. She stood and brushed the sand from her pants, showing that she was fine.

"So where are yeh goin' next?" Jovin asked. "Where do yeh think this stone of yers is 'idin'?" He swept his blonde hair out of his eyes. The wind was extra blustery this side of the mainland, but he didn't seem to mind.

"It appears that the stones are most often buried, so perhaps I should find a spot to start digging," Rylla suggested.

"Your guess is as good as mine," Elowen responded. "I know stones, but I have no idea where this one could be."

"The Larimar has always been the most elusive of the five stones, according to the Earth-Lore," Moo chimed in. "Its light-blue and almost transparent color allows it to blend in and camouflage with its surroundings, making it almost impossible to identify. Though if you're in the dark, its blue light could fill an entire room."

"Very truuhoo, very truuhoo," Rembrandt gave his own two cents.

Rylla groaned.

"What's wrong?" Caz's eyebrows were drawn together.

"Something tells me this stone is going to take a little longer to find," Rylla replied as she looked at Moo. She reached to take out her map, but a horn blast went off in the expanse of the forest and she jumped in surprise. Rylla looked at the others, but they shared her same confused expression.

"Where did that come from?" Elowen scanned the woods.

"It sounds like it's coming from the direction of the throne. At least, that's my guess." Caz followed her gaze as he scanned the tree line.

The brassy sound reverberated all around them, growing louder and closer.

Then the horn stopped; it felt like it had ended as soon as it began, dying and blending into the currents of the wind. The five friends stood in silence, unsure of what just happened, or what was about to.

A rustling and snapping of twigs alerted them, but too late. Seven armed men the size of tree trunks emerged through the wood. They surrounded Rylla and the others before anyone had time to react.

Rylla stiffened, clutching her satchel to her side, ready to protect and use her magic if need be. The soldiers before her looked both determined and menacing, as if on some sort of errand. Dark blue and white paint smeared in streaks across their faces; their ears and parts of their flesh were pierced with many rings. Feathers were braided into their hair, and they smelt of pine and fish, a mixture of the earth and the sea.

What kind of soldiers were these?

"The throne requests your presence," one of the guards spoke. A painted white hand surrounded his left eye and hawk feathers were tied back in his hair.

"For what?" Elowen asked boldly.

"The throne will answer the questions you seek," another of the guards said, the ring piercing on his lip catching the sunlight as he spoke.

"If we go with you, we need to take care of the horses first." Caz looked at the restless creatures who weren't happy with the new additions to their group of five. "They need food and a good cleaning."

"Bring them," another replied.

"The throne has stables."

And with that, Rylla and the others were ushered through the forest to the Isle's throne whether they liked it or not. Rylla cast sideways glances at her friends, her fingers fidgeting with the Yellow Jaspers around her neck and her breath hitched in her throat. What awaited them in the throne? Rylla was about to utter an Earth-spell to help them escape when Caz gently pressed her hand and shook his head.

"Not now," he whispered. He held her hand only long enough to give it a slight squeeze before letting go.

It had done its job though, and the whirring magic coursing through her veins dulled. Instead, she felt cold, missing the warmth of his hand in hers.

What fate awaited them, one could only wonder. If this was some sort of trap like Uwan's cave, she wanted to be prepared, she wanted to be able to escape and not lose more time. Already she had lost weeks, and who knew what Lord Brennigan was up to now. If Rylla was feeling the urgency of the mission and the heavy weight of the kingdoms' fates, then surely Fang would be frustrated with the pace of her progress as well. She only had so much time.

⸙ ⸙ ⸙

Caz had only ever been in one of the Earthen-Crest thrones back when he was seven and forced to join Grievon's army in Ostglenden. He had been young and afraid, the towering castle a monolith of stone and rock which had made him feel small and insignificant. Now that he was older, walking toward the Isles of Norviç's throne left him feeling similarly. Would the Isles' throne be as cold, uninviting, and dripping in wealth like Ostglenden's back on the mainland?

As they approached the castle, they walked through the gates and the surrounding wattle and daub village with its reed and wood houses; it paled in comparison to the striking stone of the castle itself. Caz thought that he had never seen more of a contrast between wealth and poverty, though not unlike Ostglenden. The thought made him feel sick. It was as if this small island village had undergone years of neglect, and both the landscape and the people living amongst it were lacking in color and devoid of joy. Would he and Jovin live comfortably here? Were they willing to?

The guards led them out of the village and around the backside of the throne where a large stable was waiting for them. It was empty save for one lonely horse as Caz and Jovin led Rembrandt and Cinders inside the stalls closest to the stable's entrance. The horses calmed with the four walls surrounding them, relaxing their ears and slurping up the freshwater Rylla and Elowen had poured for them.

As everyone exited the stables, they were stopped short by the soldiers again.

"Leave your weapons," the one with the white handprint over his eye commanded. "And leave the cat." He cast a glance at Rylla and Moo, who bristled.

Caz and Jovin reluctantly removed their swords, but Elowen bristled even more than the cat.

Her eyes narrowed and her hands went to her hips. "Absolutely not. You dare strip a woman of her protection?"

The guard stepped forward, towering over Elowen, sneering. "You dare undermine my orders? Many a head ends up detached from the shoulders for such impertinence. Would you like that to be your fate?"

Elowen shrunk back slightly, her lips set in a thin line. Reluctantly, she handed over her quiver and then her bow, the guard having to pry her fingers free of the weapon.

Another guard bent to pick up Moo, but Rylla blocked his way.

Caz stared in shock. What was she doing? Had Elowen's behavior not been warning enough?

"He stays with me," she pleaded. "He's just a cat and can't do any harm. Please. He stays."

The guards exchanged glances but only shrugged in response.

Caz sighed in relief. He figured they didn't think a cat was much of a threat, but Rylla needed Moo like one needs a shield. Despite the look of fear in her eyes, she was bold to stand up for what she wanted. He admired that.

They left the stables lighter than when they had arrived and began circling back toward the front of the castle.

The towering archways and walls of the throne looked like they'd been washed and weathered by strong ocean currents, leaving it smooth and soft to the touch. But this was a place of power, no matter how smooth or soft it looked.

Once they were free of the throne, Caz and Jovin would have a talk about where to go next or what part of the island they could inhabit. Perhaps they could live close to the shore or string up a hut in the woods somewhere; it probably would be homier than the village they had just walked through. Surely Rylla didn't want them tagging along for much longer; she hadn't actually agreed to accept his help, but she hadn't refused him either. For some reason the thought sent an unexpected pang to his chest.

Caz and the others were escorted through the giant doors of the castle, a familiar horn announcing their arrival.

They entered a wide, dim hallway which had many doors leading off it. The walls were lined with picture frames depicting what he guessed were the past rulers of the Isles as wall sconces with glofish—bright yellow and red fish that radiated warm light—lit their path forward. Caz looked to Rylla who was holding her chin up but also seemed on high alert as if ready for the slightest thing to go wrong. She was obviously worried, and he could understand why.

If anything, Caz wanted Rylla to keep her magic a secret. If the king found out, he'd surely want to hold her hostage or use her skills for his benefit, like Grievon. She'd be trapped here forever, never to complete her mission, never to see her parents again. And he couldn't help but feel that it would be partly his fault. He couldn't bear that burden, too. No, he'd have to protect her from her magic, if not for her sake, at least for his own peace of mind.

"Through this door." One of the painted guards motioned them through a large opening at the end of the hallway.

Caz entered first, keeping a close eye on the others. If anything dangerous lurked beyond the door, then he wanted to be the one to take the brunt. It seemed Jovin got the hint because he remained in the rear in case anyone decided to attack them from behind.

They crossed the threshold into a large, empty room—one that might be used to host balls—without incident. All was well, for now.

Caz continued ahead of the others with Rylla and Moo following close behind. Those two were inseparable, and he often wondered what they talked about, or quite simply, what it was like to talk to an animal at all. Though he could only guess, he felt the cat was beginning to trust him, and perhaps Rylla was doing the same.

The guards led them to a set of large double doors and paused. One of them knocked and pressed his ear against the wood, waiting for a signal. After a few moments, the guards each took a door and opened them wide for the visitors to pass through.

Caz had to steady his reaction as he entered the vast chamber of the throne room. Though the wealth of the throne was like Ostglenden's, the warmth and color of the Isles painted a stark contrast. Everything was covered in turquoise, dark blue, brilliant orange, and coral silks and draperies, the floors made of smooth sea glass and the windows depicting stained glass images of mermaids and underwater worlds. Chandeliers of raw crystals hung from the ceilings while the same glofish sconces hung along the walls. Flower pots of seaweed and coral lined the walls and bubbles floated above them toward the ceiling. This place looked like it had popped straight out of *Neptucadis,* the lost underwater kingdom.

Caz recalled the conversation he'd had with Jovin about children's stories a few weeks past. As a child, the story of *Neptucadis* often left him imagining what it would be like to live underwater. Now he no longer had to.

He glanced at the others who looked similarly impressed. Jovin had his mouth wide open and Elowen pretended not to care a little too obviously. Rylla's eyes were huge, and all the hairs on Moo's back stood up straight.

But the man on the throne completely arrested their attention.

"Welcome," a booming voice echoed, "to my domain!" Upon the throne sat a middle-aged man with golden-yellow hair and a scepter in his hand that looked strangely like a trident. He pronounced his words with emphasis on the first syllables and his gaze scanned their group.

They all bowed, unsure of what to say.

"I am King Malik, and you are…?" His piercing blue eyes shined brightly like the sea glass and crystals all around him.

"I am Caz, and these are my friends Rylla, Elowen, and Jovin," Caz replied, hoping the others didn't mind being introduced.

"Welcome! I believe you're here for your reward!" King Malik clapped his hands together, face masked in relief. His smile was wide, though his large, white teeth were almost invisible behind an overgrown beard.

"Excuse me, Your Majesty, but what reward?" Caz questioned. He glanced at Rylla who went a shade paler, her fists clenched tight.

"What reward? What reward? Bah! You think me a fool?" The king laughed heartily. He finally stopped once he noticed that the others weren't. "Surely you jest!"

"My apologies, Your Majesty, but we don't know what you're talking about," Caz replied with a crease in his brow. Reward? Dread clenched in Caz's stomach. Was this about Rylla's Earth-Treading? Had he unknowingly brought her to her doom?

"Why, for slaying the Balagrix of course!" the king exclaimed, stretching out his hands. "The great and terrifying sea serpent!" He watched them with hope in his eyes.

Caz breathed a sigh of relief, but now he had a new problem. He exchanged looks with his friends, a funny feeling entering his gut. *Balagrix?* Was this why they were here? To receive an award for something they hadn't done?

"Don't tell me that blasted snake's still alive?" The king's relief wavered toward irritation, a crazed expression on his face, almost as if he were imploring them to lie. His blue eyes narrowed as they darted from person to person, challenging them to say otherwise.

"It seems we had no idea about this serpent until now," Caz replied. "We wish we could say otherwise seeing how much grief our news brings."

"But how did you make it across the basin? It's been uncrossable for years, forever it seems. The Balagrix tears hulls and masts apart limb by limb, feasting on passengers and their treasure!" The king looked seriously grieved and confused as he started yanking on his hair and ruffling his long beard.

"Luck was on our side, it appears. An' 'ave yeh no one 'ere ta combat the creature for yeh?" Jovin interjected.

"You don't think I've tried?" King Malik raised his voice. "I've lost about half my men in trying to fight this blasted beast! It's torn the Isles apart and has set all the villagers on edge. No provisions can come by sea, and our stores are dangerously low! We don't know how much longer we'll be able to survive!" The king tugged at his yellow hair more vigorously than before, and though he wasn't extremely old, the wrinkles and worry lines on his face suggested many years of stress. His blue eyes were wan and distant as if searching for something.

"Your Majesty." Caz searched for words that would buy them some time to think. "I ask that you allow my friends and I to talk in private. Perhaps we can come up with a plan."

King Malik came out of his stupor long enough to acknowledge that he still had visitors. "Oh, yes, of course!" He ran a hand over his face and rubbed his eyes. He pointed to the door behind them. "The ballroom should suit you fine—just come back when you're done."

Caz and the others bowed and thanked the king. As they exited the throne room, four of his guards followed them into the ballroom and took their positions near the two sets of doors.

Caz twisted his lips into a grimace—he had hoped to be alone.

Rylla moved to the center of the room and sat down, Moo beside her. Elowen and Jovin followed suit, so Caz was the last to join them. The five of them sat quietly in a circle, but Caz didn't know where to start.

"I saw something in the water," Rylla volunteered the first words. "Initially I thought it was just a rock, but it must have been the creature the king was talking about."

"Then why didn't it attack us?" Jovin questioned.

"I think Rylla's magic protected us and sped us along too quickly for the serpent to catch us," Caz responded, glancing sideways at her. "Thanks for that." He gave her a quick smile. "But now we have a problem on our hands."

"Are you suggesting we stay here and kill this Batamix—" Elowen began.

"Balagrix," Jovin interrupted.

"Yeah whatever—you want us to kill it?" Elowen asked.

"I don't know. These people are trapped here, and apparently only an Earth-Treader can get across unharmed, unless we were uncommonly lucky," Caz replied. He wanted to help, and if he and Jovin were going to live here, then all the more reason to defeat this beast. If Rylla were to leave the island without them, they'd be stranded for sure. Not to mention, if she wasn't as fortunate the second time…What if the beast attacked her?

Caz felt desperate. He wanted to do it quickly—to turn over the new leaf and wipe away the horror from his past. Being a poacher meant a life of hunting and taking, never giving. The women's screams and tears, the fear in children's eyes, the fire—the nightmares never stopped. He needed to clear his memory from those dark mistakes, of all the pain he had caused over the years. He had a lot of ground to cover, but he was beginning to see the light. If only it would come flooding in.

However, Rylla had a mission of her own, and he didn't feel right leading everyone into this battle with a mysterious serpent without their consent, especially hers. But she didn't even have to join if she didn't want to.

"What say you all? We fight the beast?" Caz looked around the small group.

Elowen and Jovin nodded in approval, and Caz purposefully turned to Rylla, searching her face to see if he could read her thoughts. Though Rylla wasn't one to volunteer a lot of information, he was learning to read her subtle expressions. She was a terrible liar.

"You don't have to join us. We know you are pressed for time," he said.

The others were silent for some time before Rylla opened her mouth to speak. "It's true, I've already lost so much time, and I don't know how much more I can afford to lose. Besides, who knows how long it will take for me to find this stone." She grew quiet for a moment and Caz could see her weighing the options and combating the fear of the unknown in her mind. Her jaw set firmly and she met his gaze. "I'd like to save these villagers and restore the peace. I want to help you all. The stone can wait a little longer. Though I don't much like the sound of this Balagrix."

"I'm itching to move. After being trapped in that cave for so long, my bow wants to see some real action!" Elowen agreed with enthusiasm.

"I'm with yeh, brothur. We can slay this beast," Jovin joined.

Caz released a silent sigh, letting a subtle thrill of excitement run through him. They would be helping this threatened kingdom and bringing back some semblance of peace—if they were successful, that is. And for reasons he couldn't quite place, the thought of spending more time with Rylla quelled the aching in his chest. She would return to the mainland after finding the Larimar, but with this added mission, she wouldn't be leaving him just yet.

The safety of his friends came first, and he vowed to himself that if the monster were to attack, he would be the only one risking his life.

Chapter the Twenty-Second

Moonlit Deception

That night Rylla tossed and turned in a restless sleep. Ever since embarking on this journey, she'd been having strange dreams, and they'd only become stranger since obtaining the Obsidian.

She was dreaming of the Balagrix snaking its way beneath the depths of the Ocean Basin, writhing in and out of shipwrecks and feasting on the remains of those lost at sea. There was one ship, however, untouched and gently plowing its way on the surface of moonlit blue, churning through the waves toward the Isles. The crew aboard were few, maybe only five, and they continued on their journey seemingly unaware of what lurked below.

A heavy thud slammed against the hull, throwing the ship off course as it swayed drastically from side to side. Large waves sloshed on deck and thoroughly drenched all on board. The crew looked around nervously, peering over the edges to see if perhaps they had run into a rock or coral, but nothing could be seen. Then, a flash of scaly green and gold, a baring of pointed fang, a razor back, a rancid odor; a giant sea serpent lunged upwards and towered over the small vessel.

The men fell on the deck in surprise, huddling together with weapons drawn. Surely their daggers and swords would prove a paltry defense when the giant sea snake scarfed them down one after the other. But one man unsheathed his dagger with a fierce determination, hoping to take out its one good eye.

But the serpent's tail snaked around him from behind and knocked the weapon from his hand. He was yanked skyward, and as his hood slipped back, a pair of familiar dark eyes showed beneath. But he was whisked away so fast the rest of the face was encased in shadow.

Another of the crew threw a dagger, and the hooded man fell. Instead, the serpent charged for the new attacker.

The men screamed as the large serpent began its descent upon their vessel. Their cries and Rylla's own jerked her awake. She sat up quickly, panting slightly as her eyes adjusted to the dim light of her surroundings. She didn't want to wake anyone but seeing that Elowen's bed was already empty and Moo's post abandoned, it left little worry for that. *Where are they?* There was a small chance Rylla would be able to fall back asleep at this rate, so perhaps a brief walk would calm her mind and ease her racing heart.

As she got up from her bed, she scanned the floor for her satchel; it wasn't next to her cot where she had left it. So much for easing her racing heart. A wave of anxiety hit her full force in the stomach; the stones were in the satchel, and now they were lost!

Had she left the bag in the courtyard and forgot to bring it in her room?

No, she always made sure to keep it with her. Someone had stolen it, and she was going to find out who.

Rylla gingerly tiptoed out the door and into a short corridor. She replayed the conversation from yesterday in her head—their group agreeing to fight the sea serpent and the king all too pleased to hear it, saying that these "miraculous warriors" from the mainland would mean their liberty as an island. They had been ushered into the finest guest chambers of the castle which abutted a small courtyard and provided a view of the western side of the basin. Everything was immaculate and too overwhelming to digest.

Now they were to fight this *Balagrix* creature, and if it looked anything like the monster in her dream, they were up for a rude awakening. But it would have to die if it meant the safety of the Isles. *And so does Lord Brennigan.* Rylla swallowed hard. She hadn't thought much about how she'd have to defeat him since the time Fang mentioned it to her in the Grove. And now there was King Grievon on her tail as well. When the moment arrived, would she be able to do it? Defeat them all? The pounding of her heart transitioned into a pounding within her head.

Another thought came to mind. The last time she had dreamt or had a vision of sorts was before she fell into the black abyss of Uwan's cave—the Obsidian had prompted her and shown her the future, foreshadowing what was to come. Would that also be true of her sea serpent dream? If so, who was on that ship? And whose dark eyes had she seen that looked so familiar?

The thought troubled her as she walked through a doorway studded with sea glass and shells and stepped into the moonlit courtyard. The night was still young as the stars twinkled like dancing fairy maidens above her. Did the stars ever fear their destiny? Did they even think of it?

She looked around then pulled back into the shadows at the sight of two figures with their backs facing her. Who was it? She was careful not to make any sounds as she crept closer. They stood by the balustrade overlooking the basin, and as she approached them, she recognized the profiles of Elowen and Caz deep in conversation.

Rylla knelt behind a large pot of coral and strained to listen, her heart beating wildly out of her chest. What were they doing out here? And all alone?

"I'm telling you, it's the best way!" Elowen raised her voice above a whisper.

"That's not my choice to make," Caz replied, not meeting her gaze.

"But you're the leader here, everyone can see that," she countered, reaching behind her to pick something off the ground and shoving it into his arms. *Rylla's satchel.* "And you know it too." She looked serious, but Caz seemed taken by surprise. "Come on, open it."

Rylla leaned forward, her forehead brushing against the coral and making a slight grating noise. Elowen glanced her way but didn't seem to notice her. Rylla watched as Caz lifted the flap and peered into the bag, his brow furrowed.

His eyes went wide and he reached in and pulled out two stones, one a blue-green opaque gemstone while the other as black as a moonless sky. He held them in his palm, time seeming to freeze as Rylla stared at him, motionless. Caz blinked and shook his head, obviously trying to remain focused, but the stones must have been befuddling his brain already. The pull was so great that Elowen stepped nearer, entranced. Rylla tried everything in her power not to jump out and give away her hiding spot.

"Can't you see, they would be perfect to use! You and I, utilizing their power to defeat this beast!" Elowen was practically drooling as she reached out to grab the Hawk's Eye. "I've been eying these stones for a while now."

Rylla could see Caz was struggling, too overcome to respond. She couldn't blame him, yet words of caution splayed across her mind. These stones were not theirs to use, these were no one's to use. Clarity entered Rylla's mind like a clear dawn breaking through a clouded sky. She couldn't watch this much longer.

"She won't dare to use them—she thinks she's above them, with her *magic*. But we could wear them around *our* necks, keep them hidden beneath the folds of our garments. It will be our little secret," Elowen said with bated breath, looking deeply into Caz's eyes while stroking the greenish stone. She was moving closer to him, seemingly transfixed.

Caz seemed frozen, yet more out of deep thought rather than the same hunger Elowen possessed. But still, he held onto the stone and his eyes didn't waver.

A pang of jealousy stabbed Rylla's heart and hurt shot through her. *So this is what betrayal feels like.* She needed to get out of here. She needed to breathe.

As she rose, she tripped on some floor cushions and low-lying shrubs, her cloak snagging around her ankles. Unwarranted tears stung her eyes, her breath hitching in her throat.

Caz broke the spell between him and Elowen and spun to see Rylla stumbling out of the room, slamming into Jovin standing motionless in the doorway with the cat at his feet.

Elowen blanched, her gaze toward the door. "I—I can explain." Her words came out hoarse and disjointed as she stood inches away from Caz, just moments away from kissing him.

"Rylla, wait!" Caz shouted, pleading for her to stay, but she and Jovin were already leaving the room, the hurt and confusion displayed clearly across their faces. Moo followed close at their heels.

Caz faced Elowen again, anger welling in his gut. He snatched the stone from her grasp and shoved both of them into the satchel, taking a step back.

"What was that about? Have you gone mad?" Caz ran a hand over his face to steady his thrumming head. Too much magic, too much power.

"I don't know what came over me," Elowen replied. "I only wanted to take a look at the stones. I just wanted to see them." She looked wild and frantic, as if touching the stone had branded its power into her memory.

He could still feel the thrumming magic of the stone tingling his own fingers. He stretched his palm wide then curled his fingers into a fist.

"And you wanted to tempt me in the process." Caz backed away further. This conversation was already over. He wouldn't linger a moment longer in this temptation. "You've made a grave mistake. Clearly Jovin and Rylla think so too. Was your goal to throw everyone off? If so, you succeeded."

"I…I had no idea what I was doing," Elowen choked, tears glinting in the corners of her eyes.

"Maybe next time you should stop and think before you drive a wedge between our company." Caz clutched Rylla's satchel, grabbed his book, and headed for the door. He needed to make things right with Rylla. He needed to fix this.

"I'm sorry," Elowen whispered but the words weighed as heavy as iron.

“Goodnight, Elowen.” The words were curt and firm as Caz fled the room.

He fumed silently as he left that conniving wench behind. Perhaps his words were too harsh, but she had no right to do what she’d done, not when it was Rylla’s mission to find the stones, not when she was just beginning to trust him. So many things were on the line, hearts included. The idea of losing her trust now was like a knife wound to his heart, but why did that matter so?

He knew he admired her character, cared for her even, but was there something more? The last thing he was looking for was love—women were vixens seeking to lead men astray. Elowen had just proven that to be true. But was Rylla the same?

No, she was different. He had already determined that.

But what now? How would the group fight the evil Balagrix with hearts so divided? He had seen Jovin’s face as he left the courtyard; it mimicked Rylla’s own creased brow and wounded eyes. They needed to come together. They needed to win and free these trapped people, and they needed to do it some way that didn’t involve using the stones; he had to make sure Rylla knew that.

Get it together. This can be fixed. He resisted the urge to tug furiously at his hair.

Caz paused outside her door, bracing himself. He knocked gently and waited. No response. He tried again.

“Rylla, can you open the door? I need to talk to you.” Caz tried the handle and found it locked. He knocked once more. “Please, let me talk.”

Nothing.

He slid Rylla's satchel underneath her door and walked away. At least now the stones would be back where they belonged. He'd have to try smoothing things over tomorrow.

Tonight, he'd fix things with Jovin.

Back in their room, Jovin was lying on his bed, staring up at the ceiling. Caz only made it two steps over the threshold before Jovin spoke.

"Why didn't yeh tell me, brothur? At least then I coulda seen it comin'," Jovin said to the tapestried ceiling.

"There's nothing to tell, Jovin. She came onto me." Caz sat on his own bed and steadied his anger with a slow exhale. "I have no feelings for that woman whatsoever."

"'er feelin's might say otherwise," Jovin continued.

"No—she wasn't fully herself. The power of those blasted stones took control. It was foolish and a lie, all of it." Caz stared at his hands, chest tight under the weight of awkwardness and anger.

"Real mystery that one is. She drives me mad." Jovin let out a small laugh, but continued to stare at the ceiling. He was quiet for some time.

Caz shifted in the silence. "So, are we good?"

The silence lingered between them a little longer before Jovin answered, "Yeh, we're good."

Caz heaved a sigh. If only talking to women was this easy. But he'd leave Elowen to pick up her pieces and settle things when she had the chance. For now, they had better all get some rest before defeating the Balagrix.

Who knew what they were all up against? Tomorrow would either be a day of victory or an escapade into the dark.

⸙ ⸙ ⸙

Rylla awoke the next morning, determined not to talk to anyone. She contemplated backing out on the mission to defeat the Balagrix, but she'd already given her word. Besides, they might need her magic. But the sooner they defeated this blasted snake, the sooner she could find the missing stone and get on the return voyage home and finish her quest. The journey across the basin couldn't come soon enough.

The pang in her heart surprised her. Was it more of jealousy or betrayal? If Rylla were honest with herself, everything about Elowen caused her envy: her confidence, her skill, sharing her brother, and now Caz—but the fact that they were planning to use her stones together, the sting was almost unbearable.

"Bah! It's all so foolish!" Rylla fitted her cloak around her shoulders and stopped at the sight of her satchel on the ground. Caz must have returned it after he knocked on her door last night. She bent down to look inside. The stones were both there. She fought the surge of hope that sought to pool in her stomach. No, she couldn't trust anyone.

"I know you're upset, but perhaps it's all a misunderstanding," Moo suggested as he got up from his own bed.

Moo had told Rylla last night he had been restless and decided to do rounds, checking in on everyone. He had found Jovin wide awake and decided to go for a walk with him around the courtyard. He meowed and motioned for Jovin to follow him, but what they had found upon arriving astounded them both. But Moo figured there was more to the story.

"You might be right, but I don't want to think about that right now. I just want to find the stone and end this mission once and for all. I'm ready to go home, Moo. I'm tired of all this." Rylla slung her satchel over her shoulders and trudged into the courtyard once more.

The scene of the crime.

Everyone was already gathered there and ready to embark. Rylla felt Caz's gaze on her, but she kept her head down.

King Malik and his men stepped into the courtyard shortly after her arrival.

"How are my serpent slayers this fair morning?" the king bellowed. He looked at the group and frowned. "You all look like you haven't seen sleep in days! Positively dead! Not second-guessing things, I hope, not after all I have given you!" He stretched his arms wide and gestured all around him.

"No, Your Majesty, we are ready," Rylla said. The words were short and curt, but she didn't even regret them; the quicker they got this done, the quicker she could leave.

"Great! I knew you wouldn't let me down!" The king now looked to his soldiers. "Men, fetch the Sanddoons and prepare for the drop off!" The painted soldiers bowed and immediately left the room through a side panel hidden in the wall.

Rylla shuddered. "Drop off" sounded more like abandonment than anything. Would there be a way back?

"Follow me, if you will." King Malik ushered everyone out the courtyard into the adjoining hallway and back into the throne room. From there, they left the same way they had first entered the castle and circled up around the stables.

"You may retrieve your weapons, slayers!" the king shouted in joy. "Unless you'd like some of my artillery, which is just as well—" He looked at each of them and stopped short at Rylla, noticing she hadn't grabbed anything. "What about you, miss? Where's your weapon? Surely you don't mean the cat! Bah!" he laughed heartily.

"I, um…" Rylla faltered, caught off guard. Her magic wasn't something one visibly wielded, nor was it something she was about to share.

"She'll use my dagger." Caz bent and slid out a small-looking knife from his boot.

"You sneak! Taking that into the presence of *my* throne? What cheek!" Instead of being mad, the king began to laugh harder, apparently thinking it was the funniest joke. "What do you hope to accomplish with that? Spear a krill?" This time he was leaning heavily on one of the stall doors, almost falling over.

"Never underestimate the power of small things; I find their unassuming ability can do more damage than a full-fledged sword," Caz countered, handing the dagger to Rylla.

She grabbed it reluctantly.

"Fine, fine! You amuse me, the lot of you! Just go kill that beast and don't die trying," he boomed again, his voice loud and audacious as he corralled everyone out of the stables and to an open patch of land. "They should be here any moment now!" the king exclaimed.

Sure enough, the painted soldiers rode up on three, strange cart-like contraptions that rivaled the sizes of exceptionally large heifers. Rylla stared in amazement at these bizarre vehicles. The wheels on which they rode were the strangest part—made of clear looking material; inside the wheels looked to be filled with water and striking orange fish.

"These, serpent slayers, are the illustrious Sanddoons of the Isles! As you can see, our native Catapari power the wheels; as they swim, the wheels rotate and move the cart forward. My tinker's latest invention." The king beamed from ear to ear, clearly forgetting about *why* they even needed these in the first place.

"Now the way to the cave is treacherous and rocky, a dangerous feat for, well, your feet!" King Malik lost himself in a hearty laugh. He recovered quickly, though, when he realized no one else was laughing. "Here." He gave Rylla a golden object. "My soldiers will drive you to the location and then retreat to the throne for safety. All you have to do is give this little whistle a blow to alert us to come get you. But you mustn't sound the note until the serpent is dead, do you understand? I've risked too many men as it is. To even send them as far as the cave is lunacy!"

Rylla and the others nodded and gave him their word. And with that, they were off.

Each Sanddoon was driven by a painted soldier, and since there were only three carts between the five of them, that meant doubling up. Elowen had quickly chosen her own cart and without so much as a backwards glance was off in the direction of the cave. Now there were only two left—Jovin had taken another while Caz took the last.

Rylla jumped behind Jovin as their cart sped away, leaving Caz and Moo to follow behind.

After a few moments, Jovin spoke over his shoulder. "She's a riddle, that one."

"Who?" Rylla was busy watching the trees as their Sanddoon sped through the forest, the Catapari swimming fiendishly.

"Elowen—I can't seem ta figure 'er out," Jovin said again.

"Me neither." Rylla pursed her lips, replaying the conversation she had overheard last night: Elowen grabbing the stone, causing Caz to lose his wits, and nearly *kissing* him of all things! Could she really fault them both for falling prey to the stones' enchantment? Regardless, the pain still went deep.

"'as she said anythin' 'bout me?" Jovin questioned, and Rylla's heart jolted.

The events from last night had affected him more deeply than she'd realized at first. Rylla shook her head; Elowen hardly spoke to anyone, let alone anyone about her feelings.

"She keeps things most precious under lock and key, Jovin. I think you know that." Rylla paused. "But after last night, perhaps something will soften." She didn't know what compelled her to say such things, but for some reason she wanted to give Jovin hope. He was a decent man, and if he truly cared for Elowen, then he was a special man indeed. And if she were being honest, part of her still wanted to hope that Caz was one of the few not entranced by Elowen's beauty.

As for herself, Rylla wasn't looking for a reason to trust Elowen again. If it wasn't for her brother's unfortunate marriage, then she wouldn't have to know Elowen at all. But some things were not in her power to control; she'd have to learn to make a red currant loaf out of moldy dough.

If anything, last night reminded her of the true power of the stones and their disastrous temptation—Uwan, and then Elowen. If she had stayed long enough, surely Caz would have fallen too.

Rylla had felt the pull, but then it vanished. Could it have overtaken her as well?

"Aye, we shall see," Jovin finally said. He seemed tense and eager for action, his sword swinging slightly by his hip with every tree stump and rock they rode over.

In the distance, looming rocks drew nearer. The salty air mixed with a stale odor of decay and wafted in their direction. Rylla caught her cloak as bile rose to her throat. She hadn't thrown up in years and already the Isles were testing that resolve for the second time.

As they drew closer to the large rock-like structure, the Sanddoons stopped and the painted soldiers hastily instructed the five of them to get off.

"Walk around the large rock, and the cave is over the next set of boulders," a soldier said.

"Best of luck," came another.

"Don't get eaten," was the last instruction.

Once the last foot had hit the ground, the Sanddoons were off in the direction they had come, the Catapari swimming so fast they blended into one unending string of orange. Rylla clutched the golden whistle tighter. Hopefully they'd see those strange carts again and go home to safety.

The five stood watching as the carts abandoned them at the base of the large rock, the air reeking even fouler now than on their ride in. There was no other option but to press onwards and see what they were up against.

⸙ ⸙ ⸙

"If these 'uge rocks are considered mere bouldurs, I'm curious ta know what those guards think of real mountains," Jovin said amidst ragged breaths.

Rylla couldn't help but agree, though she was thankful for the rigorous hike. It reminded her of home and being up high helped to set her heart at ease, if only a little. She again found herself wishing for wings, ones that would take her far away from the pain in her chest.

They crested the final boulder, this one exceptionally larger than the others. Now standing at the top, they could see part of the cave down below, steam and ocean spray coiling in wafts from its entrance. Everything was eerily still, and a subtle sheen of darkness seemed to cover their surroundings like a light mist. Was this the same Darkness as in the Heather Fields?

"It's not so bad." Elowen shifted to walk ahead of everyone. "As long as one treads carefully." She bounded down the boulder like a gazelle and disappeared behind a cluster of trees and rock, leaving Rylla and the others to follow after.

As they descended, stepping carefully over loose stones and weaving through spindly oaks and elms, they came upon a much slower Elowen whose small form was limping in the distance.

"That confounded woman," Jovin mumbled under his breath as he picked up his pace to meet her.

As Jovin left, Rylla and Caz were forced to descend the boulder on their own, with Moo at their heels. The silence lingering between them seemed denser than the fog swirling about them.

"Rylla, I…" Caz seemed to search for words.

Rylla kept walking and clutched her satchel tighter to her body. She didn't trust her heart.

"Rylla…"

"It's fine," she called over her shoulder.

"Would you stop it for once and listen to me?" Caz's voice grew stiff with impatience.

Something about this conversation sent images of Garth in her mind, of him walking away from her at the edge of the Heather Fields while she desperately tried to get his attention. But now Caz was in her shoes and she was being her brother.

She stopped and faced him, not meeting his gaze. She blinked several times, though he'd still be able to see the tiny beads that pooled in the corners of her eyes.

"I'm sorry, Caz, I just don't know if I can do this," Rylla croaked, seeming to break the tension and her resolve all at once. She clung even tighter to her satchel and tried to back away. She wasn't sure she could handle the truth, nor did she know what she could believe even if it were said.

Something in Caz softened. "No." He walked over to her and gently took her by the shoulders so she could face him. His touch warmed. "*I'm* sorry." He scanned her face. "What happened last night shouldn't have happened at all. I was out there reading when Elowen found me…I had no idea what had taken hold of her, and it was too late by the time I…"

By the time you became entranced by the power of the stones.

"I understand…" Rylla whispered.

"Do you?" He searched her face a little deeper, brow creased. "I don't fancy her, Rylla. And I never will." Caz dropped his hands from her shoulders and took a step back as the weight of his words settled in. "I told her no about the stones, by the way. I don't want to use them." He held Rylla's gaze steadily, his eyes begging her to trust him, to believe he was capable of keeping his word.

A warm flame kindled in Rylla's middle, almost like a fluttering, but at the same time cold dread knocked at the door. Perhaps Caz didn't like

Elowen, but would he be able to resist the temptation of the stones a second time? Their power was enticing and strong, leading even the most valiant of men astray—would Caz be one of them? She hoped they wouldn't have to find out, but Rylla felt she couldn't fully trust Caz until she knew for sure.

But still, he had said he didn't like Elowen, and for some reason, that felt like a balm to her aching heart.

Rylla and Caz continued down the boulder and met Elowen and Jovin waiting for them at the bottom. Elowen was sitting on a small rock, while Jovin had his arms crossed before him. They were feet away from the mouth of the cave.

"I'm fine—" Elowen protested.

"She twisted 'er ankle on a rock an' she insists she's fine—can 'ardly walk an' she thinks she's gonna fight the Balagrix." Jovin chuckled but his brow furrowed seriously.

"I *will* fight that monster, and it will take shackles to make me do otherwise," she countered. "I'm not scared of anything!"

"Not even Kabog-waiths?" Rylla teased, remembering Elowen's fear in the tunnel to the mines. She couldn't blame her for being afraid, those creatures were terrifying.

Elowen's eyes widened briefly, but she quickly turned it into a glare. "That doesn't count! I don't like things with wings—so what?" she retaliated.

"Looks like you two have your hands full," Caz said as he walked around them and stood at the mouth of the cave.

Rylla shook her head and chuckled silently as she walked after Caz, a lightness in her step that hadn't been there before.

The cave was dark and dank, the outer stone covered in lichen and moss. An odor of something rotting wafted from the cave's mouth, its breath repulsive. Rylla moved to Caz's side and peered into the cave's depths, holding the edge of her cloak over her mouth and nose.

Moo followed close behind.

"Smells like death and fish. But mostly death," Moo suggested.

"I think you're right." Rylla drew her cloak tighter around her face. If the creature didn't kill them, the fumes certainly would.

All five stood at the cave's entrance, Elowen leaning on a stick with a very swollen and purple foot.

"It's not as bad as it looks," she defended, but then she laughed at Jovin shaking his head.

Rylla thought Elowen lived to spite others, but perhaps Jovin was the one person who didn't seem to mind; rather, he seemed to like it. If Rylla could but take some lessons from him, perhaps she'd learn to get along better with her sister-in-law.

"All right, be on your guard, everyone. I'd rather not make this foul place our last, if you know what I mean," Caz said as he drew his sword.

Everyone else lifted their weapons, and Rylla remembered the dagger Caz had given her. She fished it out of her satchel and handed it back to him.

"Thanks for this, but I don't think I'll be needing it in here."

Rylla was thankful Caz had spared her the embarrassment around Malik and his men. It wasn't the first time either—like when he'd spared her from talking with her mouth full in Uwan's cave. It seemed Caz was always looking out for her, and when his hand gently brushed against hers to retrieve the weapon, her cheeks flushed with warmth. *Thank the high heavens it is too dark for him to see it.*

Caz nodded and returned the dagger to his boot. When he stood, he gave her a smile.

"Ready?" he asked.

"I…I guess so," Rylla replied nervously, trying to steady her beating heart as she readied her magic like the others readied their weapons. *Is it just the fear of the Balagrix making my heart beat like this or is there something else?*

Before she could contemplate further, all five stepped into the shadow of the cave.

Chapter the Twenty-Third

The Balagrix

The Sunstone shone brightly along the cave walls, swaying gently in the lantern Jovin carried. Elowen had insisted on carrying it herself, but with her injured foot, Jovin had argued all her energy should be put into avoiding falling. She begrudgingly agreed.

Rylla and Caz followed close behind in the wake of the light, peering into crevices along the rocky walls and taking heed not to twist their own ankles in the various dips and fissures in the ground. The air reeked of decay, growing stronger and fouler as they pressed on.

All was quiet, save for the occasional dripping of water from the pinnacles above and the footsteps of their company. Rylla kept her breaths shallow to avoid ingesting more of the fumes than necessary.

Slowly, gradually, a vague shape formed out of the darkness ahead.

"What's that?" Rylla whispered.

At the sound of her question, the object shifted and writhed.

"It's the sea-beast!" Elowen whispered loudly, dropping her walking stick and drawing her bow from her shoulder; she fixed an arrow to the string.

The men drew their weapons and made ready for battle, and Elowen let loose the arrow, aimed for the creature's heart.

The arrow sliced through the skin like paper and ricocheted off the wall like it hadn't hit anything at all. A disturbed seaghoul stepped out from behind the skin, charcoal wings outstretched and brilliant blue bill squawking in protest. It was a large bird with crimson talons and its eyes of piercing cobalt.

Elowen shrunk back and stifled a scream.

"Not afraid of anything, huh?" Rylla directed toward Elowen, teasing. Maybe she was being harsh, but she knew Elowen could handle it. Besides, something needed to knock her down a few pegs.

"Oh hush, you'd hate birds too if one attacked you as a child." Elowen lowered her bow and picked up her walking stick as she glowered at Rylla.

"Braaaaak, you dare disturb my hatchlings?" the seaghoul shouted, flapping its large wings to warn them not to come any closer.

The company let loose a collective sigh of relief at seeing it was only a shore bird. What they thought was the serpent was actually an enormous old skin the monster must have shed—the perfect place for a bird to build their nest underneath.

"We're sorry," Rylla replied. "We thought you were the sea-serpent."

The men re-sheathed their swords and Moo let his guard down as they watched Rylla.

"Braaaaaak, sea-serpent! Braaaaak. More like Sea-Queen," the bird screeched.

“Sea-Queen? What do you mean?” Rylla drew closer, careful not to startle the flustered bird.

“Braaaak, the Sea-Queen rules this cave, and by her leave, I may live here.”

“In exchange for what?” Rylla couldn’t believe that the rumored monster would be that hospitable.

“Braaaaak, in exchange for one of my eggs every new hatch. She’s promised me freedom as long as I do her bidding. I pay homage to my queen. Braaaaak.”

“It sounds like you’re a pawn in her savagery,” Rylla remarked.

“Nay, braaaaaak. In her shadow I am safe.” The seaghoul squawked some more and resumed sitting on her eggs.

“Rylla, can you ask if it’s seen the beast? Where we might find it?” Caz whispered behind her.

She nodded slightly and faced the bird once more. “Um, excuse me, can you tell me where the sea-ser…um, your Sea-Queen is? Is she nearby?”

“Braaaaaak, oh yes, her eyes are all about us. She is both near and far, though she doesn’t much like visitors, unless you give something in exchange…” the seaghoul screeched. “Press onwards and you may pay homage as well. Braaaak.”

Rylla nodded and stepped away from the bird to face her friends.

“We press on, though this bird doesn’t give us good tidings. She’s enslaved but finds it a mere blessing. If we find this serpent, I expect we may have to reason with it,” Rylla suggested, not much liking the idea.

“Reason with it?” Elowen countered, her eyes narrowing.

“‘ow are we suppose ta reason with a beast if we can’t even talk ta it?” Jovin spoke at the same time.

"Rylla, I have to agree with them. Why not simply kill it? There's no use reasoning when reasoning isn't to be had." Caz's voice was gentle, but a frown creased his brow.

Rylla wanted to agree with them, but something told her defeating the beast wouldn't be as simple as slitting its throat. It was powerful and cunning, that she had determined from her dream. Though was it all true?

She settled into thoughtful silence, nervousness tightening her throat as the group continued deeper into the cave. They came upon a cavernous room, streaming with beams of sunlight filtering in from openings in the ceiling. A quarter of the room was a stone floor while the other part held a pool which fed into the basin outside. It was quiet, like Rylla had walked into an old chapel, the eerie stillness sending shivers up her spine. The iridescent walls reflected the sunlight, too beautiful to touch—the weight of unspoken secrets, a sacred hole of mystery.

If the Balagrix is anywhere, it's here.

The group filed into the room, hands on their weapons. Nothing stirred, save for the sunlight dancing off some pointed stalactites, sending glistening patterns sparkling among their feet. If not for the horrible odor which still clung about the air, one could argue that the room felt strangely peaceful.

A thrill stirred Rylla's heart. If the Larimar was hidden anywhere on the island, why not with the very creature that sought to bring the Isles peril? She'd have to be on the lookout, but she hadn't a clue on where to begin nor if her hunch was right. But this place could be the start.

Rylla stepped farther into the room, and one of the stalactites reflected the sun's rays directly into her eyes. She winced and lifted a hand to shield her eyes as she pressed on. Her foot skidded on some rocks and someone grabbed her arm.

“It’s probably best to stop walking when you can’t see where you’re going. You nearly fell in.” Caz pulled her back.

Rylla regained her footing, accidentally scattering some pebbles into the water that she’d almost fallen headlong into while she wasn’t looking. A ring of ripples spread across the blue liquid, sending a rippling chill down her spine.

Rylla berated herself mentally; this wasn’t the first time she’d almost done something stupid. Her brothers had often told her she moved too fast for her own good and needed to slow down. The time she stubbed her toe while carrying food to the dinner table and spilled their mother’s roasted pork sauce on the floor, or when she was running to the orchard to retrieve lemons and ran into the clothesline. And now this—just more evidence of that fact.

“Thanks.” Rylla flushed as she stepped away from the edge. Caz had saved her yet again. She’d have to be more careful.

A low growling sound interrupted any further conversation, murmuring up from somewhere deep beneath them, but steadily growing louder. The ground trembled as the pool of water began to churn like the beginnings of a storm. Something was coming, and it was coming fast.

Rylla stumbled back, a cry stuck halfway up her throat.

First came the razor-back spine which drew zig zags through the water. Then scales, a translucent green as if they were mirrors. And then it disappeared.

Caz and Jovin, swords drawn, scanned the water for the beast, while Elowen had her bow bent at the ready. Moo scrambled onto some jutted portions of the rock wall behind them and peered downwards, back arched and ready to spring.

Rylla steadied her breathing and risked another glance at Caz. Beads of sweat dotted his hairline and his eyes were focused on his purpose. The water broke with a roar and a monolith of green scales raced skyward, its giant frame snaking through the filtering light above. Shadows danced around the cave as the Sunstone by Jovin's foot began to waver. The creature loomed above them, staring down with fangs bared and menacing.

No one dared to breath or move, too stunned by the towering monster before them.

This was definitely the creature from her dream.

Rylla stared at the snakelike body. Shafts of broken arrows and deep wounds barely scabbed over littered its hide; there were holes and slashes and missing scales interspersed throughout the serpent's frame. When Rylla looked at the creature's eyes, she saw pain, as deep and plentiful as the wounds it bore, but there was something else too—anger, and that too went deep and bore no signs of relenting.

A terrible growl rent the air, shaking the very foundations of the rocks, and the weaker stalactites trembled. Jovin pushed Elowen out of harm's way as a few of the pointed mineral clusters came crashing down near her while the rest fell in the water. Danger crackled through the air like an electric current, but Rylla couldn't take her eyes off the creature.

It hissed and growled and bared its teeth, challenging them to flee, warning them not to come any closer, and suggesting they lower their weapons all in one sound. But Rylla took a step forward despite the trepidation in her heart.

"Rylla!" Caz whisper-shouted. "What on earth are you doing?"

"Hold on," she whispered back as she continued to stare at the serpent, "It's in pain. I want to help it."

"I'd be in pain with that many arrows having gone through my flesh too, but the difference is, I'd be dead," Elowen hissed. "Rylla, don't."

"There's no reasonin' with a beast such as this," Jovin said, his eyes darting from Rylla to the monster.

The creature hissed more violently the closer Rylla approached, but it didn't move. Yet.

You can understand me. It seemed to speak from some place inside her, a voice dark, deep, and gravelly but as loud and clear as an audible voice.

"What?" Rylla spoke aloud.

I'm in your mind, your wordssss are usssselessssss. The creature hissed once more. *I know why you're here, why all of you are here—to kill me.*

Rylla swallowed, a metallic taste in her mouth. She realized she'd bitten her lip rather hard. She reached a hand to her mouth and pulled away to find blood. At the same time, she noticed the caked blood on the wounds of the serpent.

Like the resssst of them, buried deep beneath the wavesssss with bonesssss washed out to sssssssea. The creature hissed again, this time swaying, its eyes filled with greater rage. *To try and kill me meanssssss death, but not for me...*

Rylla saw the bloody wounds and broken arrow shafts, and her heart softened with compassion. She wanted to heal this creature.

Heal me? I don't need your pity. I am already whole. The serpent cried out louder than before and hissed a foul stench in her direction. *I am ruler of thisssss basssssin and have been for yearssssss. I am fine on my own!*

Already whole? Rylla narrowed her eyes. Maybe the monster was only vicious because of its wounds. It was stubborn, but it needed help, and she wanted to heal it. She felt she needed to. If she did, perhaps her actions would save them all.

The creature began to descend, its head drawing closer to her. Rylla whispered under her breath and stretched her hands before her. A gust of golden wind went forward and wrapped itself around the serpent's frame, around an arrow shaft, pushing away the flesh and drawing the broken wood out. Again and again, this happened until all broken shafts were out of the body. The serpent's wounds closed up with golden scales.

The monster roared loudly, anger flaring brilliantly behind its fiery eyes as it groaned afresh in wounded pride.

What have you done? Fool! The monster spat, baring its teeth. It had been healed, its body made new, but it had been unwanted.

Rylla stumbled back a pace, eyes wide. Her heart hammered against her ribs. Why was it mad at her? Hadn't she just helped it? Took away some of its burden?

You've only made my job of finishing you off easssssier. It lunged, mouth open, as Elowen let loose an arrow.

Rylla swallowed a scream. Yes, she'd made a horrible mistake.

The sharpened head hit just below the monster's jaw and it roared again. Caz ran forward with his sword, a fire of his own burning in his eyes. As the monster's head came down, Caz jumped in front of Rylla, his sword clanging against fangs—steel against rotten, calcified bone. The serpent growled but didn't flinch, pressing Caz back step by step beneath its immense strength.

Jovin ran, aiming a swing at part of the serpent's tail as it eased onto dry ground. But the serpent was quicker, side sweeping Jovin and sending him careening backwards against the wall. Rylla saw just in time and sent a buffet of wind to soften his fall. Jovin charged forward again but not before the serpent snaked its tail in Rylla's direction.

It came at her so fast that she was taken off guard. She summoned a wall of rock, but it didn't have time to grow to its full height. The tail whipped her across the face, leaving a long, red gash. Rylla stumbled, catching herself on hands and knees. Tears stung her eyes as her cheek burned with pain.

Elowen let loose another arrow that hit one of the Balagrix's eyes and Caz took advantage of the opportunity to hack away at one of the fangs, breaking off the decaying tip and sending it flying. Jovin caught it in his hand and lobbed it in the air; he swung his sword like one would a bat and smacked the broken fang in the direction of the serpent's mouth.

The monster choked as the tooth hit the back of its throat. The Balagrix howled in anger and disappeared below the surface of the pool. Ripples surged through the water, but the serpent had vanished from view save for a few green scales it had left behind. The cavern was swallowed in an eerie silence.

"Is that it?" Jovin mocked. "Is that the inf'mous beast of the Isles? We 'ave beaten it in five minutes!"

They all stared at the water. It couldn't have been that easy, surely.

Moo peered at the pool skeptically. "Trouble still brews," he spoke aloud.

Rylla felt the warning settle in her core.

"What do we tell the king?" Elowen asked.

Tell him a life for a life. The words hissed in Rylla's mind. The chipped fang shot out of the water and landed at Jovin's feet as the Balagrix's tail snaked out from the water as fast as a whip, slicing the strap of Rylla's satchel and grabbing her around the waist, dragging her over the edge.

"Caz!" she screamed, fingers clawing to find anything to grab onto. Her satchel lay on the ground just inches from her.

He was there in an instant, Jovin and Elowen close behind, as he grabbed one of her hands and pitted his strength against the Balagrix, but her fingers were slick with water and blood. Rylla was wrenched from his grasp. Water plunged over her head, muffling the shouts and cries above as she was dragged into the cold, dark depths below.

⸙ ⸙ ⸙

Thissss isss what it feelssssss like to die, to be ripped to shredssss in your heart and ssssscared of sssssuffocation. Tell me, Earth-Treader, are you afraid of death? The creature dragged Rylla deeper, and her lungs begged for mercy.

Was she afraid? Very. Is this how it felt to die?

Rylla groped for the Yellow Jaspers around her neck, and their power surged into her. She had to keep going, had to hold on and fight a little longer. She couldn't die, not here—not when the stones were above ground and free for the taking. Could her friends find the last three? Would they even be reliable for the task?

Images of Caz and Elowen's entrancement danced across her mind, of their almost kiss…her lungs screamed.

She needed oxygen. Now.

Rylla silently thanked Uwan for teaching her a Water-spell of harnessing oxygen from underwater plants to form a sort of mask about her face. She swept her right hand out in front of her and a clump of seaweed shot up from the bottom of the ocean and into her hands. She broke off some pieces and rotated her hands around the plants, gathering the golden oxygen into her palms and placing it around her nose and mouth.

Rylla gasped in her first breath and nearly blacked out from dizziness. Never would she take this simple gift for granted again.

Yes, Rylla was very scared, but she wouldn't die. She wouldn't allow it.

Hmmm, I find that hard to believe. I shall challenge that resssssssolve. The Balagrix pulled Rylla down and then came to a stop, throwing her roughly against a nest of some sort. Glofish that scuttled nearby and bioluminescent jellies gave off an eerie warm and green glow. From that light she glimpsed eggs beside her, too small to come from the Balagrix. Were these the seaghoul's penance?

Another light caught her attention, this one blue. It illuminated a portion of the serpent's domain—gems, golden trinkets, armor, and bones scattered on the ocean floor—and appeared to be on a pedestal as if on display.

What was that light? Could it be…? Rylla squinted her eyes to make out its shape but stopped short.

The huge serpent coiled its scaly green body around her, tightening its hold. In its movement the snake slammed its body into the cave's walls, sending currents through the water.

It was getting harder to breath, the serpent pressing in on her lungs. But she couldn't shake her gaze from the blue light.

What are you looking at? The snake hissed, turning toward the source of the light. *Ah...my precioussss ssssstone.* The creature weaved its head at the glowing gem, entranced. It turned to face Rylla once more. *Eyessss off—It'ssssss mine!*

Was it the Larimar? Rylla's heart sped at the thought. Had she actually found it?

Larimar? That'sssss right. I had forgotten itssssss name. The monster hissed and glowered at her. It watched her carefully. *I found it yearssss ago—sssssstole it for keepssssss.*

It *was* the stone! Now if only the serpent would loosen its hold. What had caused so much pain to this creature? It went deeper than mere flesh wounds.

If you mussssst know. They killed her, my only daughter. My hussssband died trying to ssssssave her. This was yearssssssss passsst, at the beginning of precioussss King Malik'ssss rule. I've been sssssseeking vengeance ever sssssssince, and the queen'ssssss death wassssssn't enough to satisssssfy me...now you mussssssst die.

This creature killed Malik's wife? Rylla shuddered in fear. The roiling anger and hatred of this creature reminded her of her own jealousies and frustrations toward Elowen, of her own anger and irritation. Was it hate? Could she end up down this same path?

You assssssk what I cannot ansssswer. But one mussssst take what isssss rightfully theirsssss. A life for a life. Sssssometimessssss more.

Rylla couldn't agree; no matter the scenario, nothing warranted such retaliation. Such bloodshed. Perhaps jealousy was just another branch of what it meant to hate—the thought sent a spike of guilt through her middle. She wanted nothing in common with this creature.

Despite the warring fear that tried to render her immobile and the snake's coils tightening their hold, Rylla's determination to stay alive grew all the more urgent. She had to escape and soon; her oxygen couldn't last forever, and she was already starting to feel the supply dwindling.

But the blue light! She had to get the Larimar.

Suddenly the beast howled viciously and dark blood wafted into the water around them. Rylla felt the coils loosen and her hands freed, and she twisted to see what was happening. Caz and Jovin swam out from behind the Balagrix, swords held before them. Though their movements were awkward in the water, they fought the creature as best they could, the serpent howling in rage.

She was free! Taking the opportunity, Rylla escaped the snake's clutches and swam to the shining blue light and paused. She turned—Caz and Jovin would run out of breath any second.

They were risking their lives to save hers. Though she was grateful to be freed, they'd die from lack of oxygen before defeating the beast. Rylla reached her palms outward and grabbed hold of more seaweed. She used the same Water-spell to capture the oxygen and sent the pockets of air toward Caz and Jovin's faces. The bubbles sped through the water and latched themselves over their noses and mouths, the relief on the men's faces apparent as they began to breathe freely.

Rylla turned once more to the pedestal and saw the Larimar's shape come into view. It was transparent and smaller than the other stones but no less brilliant as it gleamed up at her.

As quick as a lark, she snatched the stone and gripped it in her fist. An odd peace tingled into her fingertips and settled around her middle. Rylla thought she wouldn't mind holding onto it a little longer, maybe even indefinitely, for the peril of the Earthen-Crest kingdoms seemed to slip away into a calm.

She turned the stone over in her hands, and she was reminded that nothing lasts forever. Though the stone was powerful, it wasn't hers.

Another cry rent from the Balagrix, shaking the rocks and churning the waters. She needed to get out of here. Fast.

Rylla kicked for the surface, watching Caz and Jovin do the same. They were struggling to keep up with the beast snapping at their heels and their swords in their hands. They'd surely die. Rylla took a deep breath and broke her Water-spell. She put the stone in her mouth to free her hands and beckoned the seaweed to do her will for the third time; with her hands outstretched, she commanded the plants to take hold. The long, slimy tendrils snaked out and caught Caz and Jovin around the wrists and yanked them skyward. Rylla swam for the surface and once she broke through the top, Elowen and Moo were there to help her. She spat the stone into her hand and gasped for air.

"Where's Jovin? Caz?" Elowen cried, but she'd barely spoken before the seaweed plucked their bodies from the water and tossed them heavily on the ground.

As they came out, Jovin's foot knocked Rylla and she dropped the stone. It rolled and landed beside Caz's feet as he struggled free of the seaweed. The two men were panting and sputtering out water.

"Well that's convenient." Elowen rushed to check on the men.

The Balagrix broke through the surface with a roar of rage louder than before. Its good eye blazed with anger and the other bore marks of Elowen's arrow, its jagged fangs making it appear even more menacing. The monster scoured the ground until it settled on Rylla, snarling.

Rylla chanced a glance behind her. Caz was now holding the Larimar in his left hand, his face filled with the same curiosity and calm she'd felt earlier. He was studying it carefully as if he were unaware of what was around him. Fear gripped Rylla's chest as visions of the night before flashed before her eyes.

"Caz!" Rylla shouted.

He looked up slowly as if he hadn't quite heard his name. He blinked and refocused, shaking his head slightly. He looked at the Larimar and then back to Rylla, and finally at the beast.

"Toss me the stone!" Rylla yelled.

And now you will die. The Balagrix lunged once more, but Caz was faster. He threw the stone to Rylla, scrambling to reclaim his fallen sword.

Rylla caught the stone, but the serpent dove, mouth open wide as if it would swallow her whole. Everything seemed to slow down for a moment, as Rylla stared up at the beast.

"Rylla!" Caz shouted. "Move out of the way!" He ran toward her.

Elowen released arrows at the beast with incredible speed, but to no avail.

Rylla turned to face the monster, heaving in a deep breath and bracing herself. She did the only thing she could think of: she swung her hand back and threw the Larimar into the gullet of the serpent who was just a mere breath away. The beautiful blue stone hit the back of its throat and was swallowed as easily as a gulp of water.

The Balagrix hissed and reared back. It growled in anger as Rylla fell to the ground, Caz jumping in front of her with his sword shielding them both.

What have you done? The snake-like body shimmered with blue light as the stone gleamed through its green and gold scales. The creature convulsed in pain as its body swayed closer to them. Another cry rent the air, but this time for mercy. The creature tumbled. Rylla scrambled to her feet with Caz's help and they fled to the far side of the cave. The Balagrix crashed onto the stone ground like a felled tree before them.

Unmoving. Silent. Dead.

All was quiet in the cavernous room and no one dared move. Rylla's heart pounded wildly. Surely it was so loud everyone else could hear it too.

After a few moments, Caz braved the walk to the beast and nudged it with his foot, sword ready to strike if necessary. It didn't stir.

"Now that's 'bout 'ow long I thought it'd take." Jovin laughed as he wiped his sword on his clothes and sheathed it in its scabbard. Caz did the same. Elowen was surprisingly quiet. She sank to the ground beside Rylla, her bow on her lap.

"I thought you weren't coming back," Elowen spoke quietly beside her. "I admit the thought scared me a little."

"It scared me too," Rylla replied. The two girls looked at each other and hugged for the first time. Tears stung Rylla's eyes, mirrored in Elowen's own, but Rylla lost the battle against them and some slipped down her cheek. "I'm sorry, Elowen," she said and she really meant it.

"I'm sorry, too."

Rylla held on a little longer and let the silence between them do the rest of the talking. This was the beginning of healing and acceptance, and it had taken a blood-thirsty beast to make her want it.

Moo sidled up next to her and placed his paw on her forearm. "I'm glad you're safe, Rylla. If Elowen hadn't held me back, I would have jumped in myself."

"I know, Moo, and I know how much you hate water."

"But the stone, Rylla? Even I could tell that was the Larimar..." Moo trailed off.

"I did the only thing I could think of." Rylla looked at the Balagrix behind her. Her gut twisted inside. "Do you think we should cut the creature open and get it back?"

Moo looked at the beast and bristled. "No. Killing to defend and eat is one thing, but to mar a corpse, is another. It goes against the Earth-Treader code. Leave the dead to die in peace—to die whole. There's good reason for it." Moo turned to face Rylla. "We have to trust and hold to courage that your mission can still be completed without the Larimar."

Rylla swallowed and felt her mouth go dry. So there was no way of getting it back. She had given up the stone for good.

She shifted and found her friends' questioning glances, stopping when her gaze landed on Caz.

He had held the stone himself, had felt its power too, but he had surrendered it and that's why she was still alive. He had also tried to protect her—again.

Caz and Jovin looked exhausted—shoulders slumped and shirts soaked through with water and blood. There were cuts on their arms and dried blood was caked in their hair, the majority of which was plastered to their heads with some dry strands beginning to curl at the ends. Rylla could only imagine the state of her own. But that was the least of her worries. Elowen's foot was still swollen, but she didn't appear to be marked by the Balagrix.

Aside from a few scrapes here and there, no one looked to be any worse for the wear. Rylla reached a hand to her cheek and winced as her fingers brushed the still-stinging slash. She must have received the brunt of the Balagrix's wrath.

"I'm glad that creature is finally finished," Elowen said, staring down at the body.

"I guess we should tell the king the good news. Rylla, do you have the whistle?" Caz asked. When his gaze met her face, his brows creased. "Your cheek's bleeding."

Rylla blushed. "I'll be fine." She felt in her pockets and went to her broken satchel on the ground. There, the tiny, golden instrument gleamed up at her, settled snugly between the two stones and her map.

The five of them left the foreboding den of the Balagrix, the Sunstone guiding them through with its fading light as Jovin carried the broken remains of the Balagrix tooth in his hand.

"Proof of its defeat," he had said, tossing it and catching it in the air like a ball.

Once outside, a wave of fresh air smacked them in the face, reminding them how foul the air had been prior. Rylla glanced upwards at the boulders they would have to climb once again, the idea daunting as her legs ached and her shoulders drooped with exhaustion. But on the other side, the Sanddoons would pick them up and bring them back to the castle. She must press on.

"'ey, Caz, go long," Jovin shouted as he swung his arm back and threw the tooth.

Caz ran to the place, catching it and throwing it back. They proceeded in this game for some time, Elowen leaning on her walking stick as she watched. Rylla didn't pay much heed, she was busy replaying the scenes from the cave over in her head.

Moo's words kept haunting her. *"Leave the dead to die in peace—to die whole. There's good reason for it."*

There would be no getting the stone back. She had been rash—unthinking. Now she could only hope that her mission could still be completed with one less stone.

Chapter the Twenty-Fourth

Bitter Celebration

The prisoner and the small host of guards were working on mending the ship's hull as Gryfinn paced impatiently amongst them, the sound of leather boots against wood mingling with the tune of the sea. He was restless and tired of all these obstacles in his way, but shortly the ship would be ready to cross the water. If this girl was on the Isles, then she would soon be in his grasp and groveling at the feet of his master before the sun had a chance to set again.

Yes, and then all the stones she had found would be in his possession as well, and his master would be pleased. All that remained was Aylati's. The search party he dispatched weeks ago hadn't had any luck, but they were bound to bring reports of their findings soon. The cursed stone couldn't hide forever.

Gryfinn looked up to the darkening sky, the daylight retreating behind a sheen of stars. At this rate, they'd be crossing the Ocean Basin in pure moonlight.

"Faster!" Gryfinn barked at the workers as he continued to pace.

The prisoner and guards gave him scowls as he passed, but proceeded to work harder.

They had made it to the North Mountains late last night and camped there before continuing on their journey to the wharfs. If only Gryfinn had foreseen this small setback, they would have fixed the ship last night.

No matter, he was certain the girl was on the Isles—he could feel it. And she couldn't very well escape a small island without being caught.

Gryfinn paused his pacing as his ears picked up on a sound.

Drums could be heard in the distance, thrumming louder than before. They were more frequent as of late, and rumors of Lord Brennigan's schemes were beginning to unfurl into something more substantial than murmurings in the dark. He was making something, Gryfinn knew that much, but what?

When he returned with the girl, he would find out for certain.

⸙ ⸙ ⸙

Caz brushed itchy leaves off his forehead, scratching furiously at his skin. The sun beat heavily upon his shoulders and he silently berated himself for choosing to wear black instead of something lighter. How much longer would they have to do this? At least he was clean, but the blasted itching wouldn't stop.

King Malik had given them laurel wreaths upon their return which now rested atop all their heads like crowns. A tiny one was even made for Moo. After being ushered back to the castle to get cleaned up, Caz and the others were quickly made presentable, handed their crowns, and thrust into an eager throng of villagers.

They'd been parading through town like heroes for the past half hour as countless children danced about them, cheering and tossing flowers before their feet. But not everyone was dancing. The men, along with a sizable group of women, stood off to the side with arms crossed and scowling—either out of annoyance or shame that they hadn't been the ones to defeat the beast themselves, it was hard to tell. It was all rather uncomfortable to receive this much attention under mixed joy and scrutiny.

During the ceremony, the king made a scene with sweeping gestures, taking everyone by surprise. He waved his new scepter, the Balagrix's fang fashioned securely to the top, and showcased its triumph to all who looked upon it. He proclaimed that any of "his valiant serpent-slayers" could live on his Isles free of charge—to be revered and memorialized, though not to rival him as king.

"For that, my dear, dear friends, would be treason!" he bellowed, and broke into a hearty laugh, his scepter nearly hitting those closest to him in the crowd. "As long as you understand that, you are granted this gift. I would be honored should you accept." The king inclined his head to the five of them.

The already skeptical crowds frowned deeper, eyes narrowed and murmurs rippling through their midst.

It all seemed too easy. Caz came to the Isles specifically for this reason, to run away and start anew; this was his opportunity, and it had fallen seamlessly into his lap. All he had to do, perhaps, was say yes. *Perhaps?* When had he started doubting his plans?

As the parade wound down, the five champions were escorted out of the waning sunlight and back to the throne to feast on King Malik's hoarded preserves.

"Don't you worry, now that the blasted Balagrix is dead, there'll be plenty for all!" He chomped hungrily on a leg of ham, juice dribbling down his beard and onto his cufflinks. He grabbed a goblet of mulled wine and chased down the partially chewed food, belching as his chalice hit the table with a loud *thunk*.

"Please, eat!" He encouraged everyone to feast as he went in for another bite of ham, this time the juice squirting across the table and landing a few inches away from Caz's fork.

Jovin and Caz only hesitated a moment before digging in, and Elowen and Rylla followed suit, hunger overtaking them all. Moo was given a place of honor next to Rylla, lapping up the ham grease and chewing the fat.

The meal was a long ordeal with seven filling courses, three of which were different meat dishes—ham, turkey, and boar; two being soups—a thistle and nutmeg sprinkled with rosemary and sage and the other a hearty egg drop with noodles and thyme; and the last two being desserts of cocoa pudding and hazelnut tarts with a blackberry compote. It was all very extravagant and overwhelming.

Caz couldn't remember eating this well in a long time. Grievon had never been one to share his wealth nor his provisions. Most of Caz's meals came from hunting, which meant some days he went hungry.

But even Caz and Jovin were only able to finish about four courses, and Rylla and Elowen hardly finished two while King Malik demanded for seconds from the frantic servants as he downed yet another glass of wine. Caz hid a grimace but was forced to make merry as the conversation geared toward their valiant battle. Caz and Rylla exchanged glances, her face a mixture of feigned delight and something else he couldn't quite decipher.

Jovin and Elowen word jousted back and forth. It was quite the spectacle and King Malik found it all very entertaining.

But Caz couldn't stop thinking about what was next, and the unhappy faces of the villagers haunted in the back of his mind.

After dinner, they were invited—more like *expected*—to sleep in the king's wing: an elegant set of rooms with more silk draperies than air to breathe and a courtyard with a floor of more glistening sea glass than pebbles of sand on the shore, all overlooking a crystal pond even more brilliant and spectacular than the guest chambers had been. And on the morrow, they were told they must decide whether they would stay or leave the island—that way the royal builders could begin construction on their new homes.

The king left them all in the royal courtyard to make their decisions and get some sleep. "Warriors must get their rest too, hmm?" Malik boomed and clapped his hands loudly. He seemed even more full of spirit now that he was full of drink. "Each of you has your own room for the night, so enjoy the supremist luxury of the king!" he laughed heartily again and then bade them good night.

Elowen yawned and slumped onto a nearby couch, rubbing her swollen foot tenderly. The parade must have made it worse, but of course she wouldn't have wanted to show any signs of weakness in front of the king, nor in front of anyone for that matter. It seemed to have taken a lot out of her though, for in a matter of moments, she fell asleep.

"The king's a bit of a whack job, ain't 'e?" Jovin chuckled, and the others agreed. He yawned as he looked at Elowen asleep on the couch. "I think I'm ta 'ead ta bed myself. I'll carry 'er to 'er room an' then be on my way." He picked her up gently in his arms and paused once more. "It was an 'onor ta fight next ta both o'ye teday. 'Til the morrow." Jovin nodded to Caz and Rylla, then slipped into Elowen's room. After a few minutes, he entered his own and shut the door behind him, leaving Rylla and Caz alone.

Rylla looked tired and a little uncomfortable in the silence, but Caz shifted his position, releasing a long breath to break through the tension.

"Another night in this place." He looked around the courtyard and settled his gaze on Rylla's profile. Her curls fell beyond her shoulders and her lashes were long. She was beautiful in the candlelight.

"At least this courtyard has windows that open. The fresh air feels nice." Rylla gazed outside, watching the waves break against the shoreline.

"How's your face?" Caz asked, reaching toward the cut on her cheek, but dropping his hand away quickly as he realized what he was doing.

"My face?" Rylla turned to him, one of her brows quirked up in confusion.

"The cut." Caz gestured to his own face to mirror where it was on hers.

"Oh! Yes, that—the Balagrix's tail," Rylla replied, ducking her head slightly.

Caz stepped nearer, emboldened by something in her voice. He reached out and gently touched her cheek, making sure not to touch the freshly scabbed wound. "It doesn't look deep, though it might leave a scar."

He couldn't help but think back to the cave in Thrushwoode where he had tended the wound on Rylla's arm. How long ago had that been? So much had changed since then, their circumstances bringing them closer and now apart again. Tomorrow, Rylla would be leaving the Isles, bent upon finishing her mission, and he would be staying behind—he knew that much, but did *she*? It seemed like now was the perfect time to tell her, but he couldn't bring himself to say anything.

Caz's chest wrenched painfully as if something were trying to break out of it. Wasn't this what he had wanted all along though? To start a new life?

"What's bravery without something to show for it?" Rylla met his gaze.

"You were very brave, maddeningly so." Caz laughed, but grew serious as he looked at her a little closer, his hand not straying from her face. "I don't understand how it works, or what it must feel like to have the power you have." Caz paused to think. "Does it scare you? It's like everything you touch turns to gold."

Rylla looked a little surprised but answered willingly, "It scares me a lot. I didn't choose this, nor is it something I would have ever asked for. The gold part I can't explain either." She seemed to pause and contemplate her next words. "But I think I'm most scared for what's ahead, for what's to come."

Caz's own heart echoed her fear. He didn't want this night to end.

"By tomorrow's light, let that be when you confront those fears. For now, it's probably best you get some good rest and put those fears aside—in the shadows where they belong." Caz stroked her cheek gently with his calloused thumb. Rylla leaned her head into his hand. It took everything in his power not to kiss her then and there.

But another thought hit him: he had his own shadows, ones marked with a dark past. Did she have any idea of all the wrongs he had done, how many lives he had ruined by his carelessness? This wasn't a conversation he wanted to have, to resurface old wounds, but when Rylla leaned into his hand and looked at him with those trusting eyes, it tore him in two. She had the right to know—she needed to know everything.

"Rylla," Caz began, but stopped, not quite sure how to proceed.

"Yes?" Rylla looked like a doe in the wavering candlelight, eyes wide and curious.

"I'm not, I'm…" Caz tried again.

"You're not what?" She didn't pull away, her faith stronger than whatever doubts his words might bring.

"I'm not who you think I am," Caz said, his voice taut with pain. "The things I've done…" He steadied himself against the images that flooded his mind. The looks of betrayal in the eyes of women and children.

"We all have our pasts, Caz." Rylla held his gaze. "I believe it's how we choose to think and who we choose to be, despite our shadows, which ultimately defines us. That takes courage of the strongest kind."

What of courage? If she only knew. His past felt so dark and the shadows so large—they constantly hounded him like bloodthirsty beasts.

There was still more he had to tell.

"I've decided to stay here…" Caz forced it out, as difficult as swallowing dry bread without water. The words felt foreign on his tongue, almost as if he wasn't the one speaking—simply a bystander wanting to see what she thought. Almost like a silent plea for her to change his mind if she wanted him to. But he had spoken, and the words felt as if an instant barrier came between them.

Something changed in Rylla's demeanor as if she suddenly realized the hand lingering upon her cheek. She swallowed hard and backed away, her expression hardening and softening all at once. The air around them grew thick with tension.

She cleared her throat. "By tomorrow's light." She stepped back again and there was something in her eyes that he couldn't read, the same look he noticed at dinner. Far off and distant.

"Is something wrong?" Caz questioned, hope and grief mingling together. He hadn't wanted to cause her any pain, but he also didn't want secrets between them. And it wasn't his place to keep tagging along unless otherwise asked. He longed to protect her, but only if she wanted it, only if she wouldn't push him away after knowing his mistakes. The thought of rejection stung his heart.

A silence lingered between them, but this time it was filled with the heavy weight of unspoken things. Caz tried to say something but felt he didn't have the words. He stepped forward, but Rylla only stepped further away.

"It's been a long day; I should get some rest." She looked torn, like she wanted to say more. Her eyes glinted with water.

"Rylla—"

"I…I should go." Rylla turned away and grabbed her satchel.

"By tomorrow's light," Caz said to her back.

She turned around and looked at him one last time before nodding and disappearing into her room. Moo followed close behind.

Caz was left alone with his thoughts. His fingers felt cold without Rylla's warm cheek to caress. Maybe tomorrow she'd ask him to accompany her, maybe tomorrow he wouldn't have to say goodbye.

Chapter the Twenty-Fifth

Larimar

Rylla rested her head on her pillow, staring up at the intricate painting of a mermaid giving her voice away to a sea witch on the ceiling. The mermaid looked anguished and had her hands outstretched as if trying to capture what was once hers, only to find it gone and unreturnable. The sea witch was smiling wickedly as if she knew what it had cost the fin-maiden.

To lose something so precious as one's voice was one thing, but what about one's heart?

Rylla had planned to leave the Isles first thing in the morning, accompanied by her friends and Moo, but now things were different. At dinner she hadn't let the thought of separation dull her merriment, not actually considering that her friends might *want* to stay behind. But why wouldn't they? They were practically heroes on this island, and their lives were basically set with kingly riches and acclaim. She couldn't blame them, truly, but it didn't change the way she felt. The way it stung.

Is this how her parents would feel, if they couldn't be together? Even the question startled her. Uwan had mentioned the face of her "lover" back in the cave, but at the time she thought he was mad for even mentioning it. Now, she wasn't so sure. But did it count if it wasn't returned? Finding love had never been on the forefront of her mind, she just expected to fall into it should the time come, if it ever did. And now? It seemed she had little control over who her heart chose. As hard as she tried to avoid it or guard against it, Caz always seemed to fill that spot. No matter how dark his past, he had proven himself loyal, changed. He was trustworthy.

And she was beginning to love him. The thought scared her more than she could admit. And he was choosing to stay here.

"We're leaving tonight, Moo." Rylla sat up and flung her legs over the edge of the bed. She was determined and nothing would change her mind now. The last thing she wanted to be was a burden, and she didn't want anyone's pity.

But the thought of being on her own again sent a flurry of anxiety through her middle. At the onset of her journey, she had been anxious, the weight of her mission weighing her down with impossibilities. But now? Things were only getting more intense, and she knew that defeating Lord Brennigan and possibly King Grievon were next to impossible.

She had lied to Caz. She wasn't just scared, she was terrified.

If Rylla was honest with herself, she wanted to go home and pretend none of this ever happened. She wanted to be an ordinary girl with an ordinary, boring life. She had no dark past of her own but knew of the shadows in her own mind, enough to rival any of Caz's past mistakes. Fear had been her constant companion since she was young, and that clenching fear she knew too well was beginning to take hold once more—the fear she had felt on the day Garth and Finn left and never returned.

If only she'd never left home herself, then perhaps her parents would have been spared the hurt and her heart would still be in one piece. She felt weak. Her fear of loss and separation, deeply rooted in the disappearance of her brothers, and now knowing Finn was missing, made the thought of leaving her friends, especially Caz, unbearable. She grieved the loss, for what was and what could be. She felt utterly alone.

Rylla had to leave the Isles. Her heart couldn't bear to say goodbye for good, nor could she simply sit here and wait for the sun to shine once more. And she wasn't sure if she could complete this mission anymore, especially on her own.

"Tonight? But why?" Moo lifted his head and looked at her questioningly.

"I can't risk their lives, and I want…I want to go." Rylla felt she had no other words to say, the truth bubbling up like an overflowing pot of tea.

"No one's meant to do anything alone, Rylla, and you're not responsible for the lives of those who wish to help you." Moo looked at her seriously. "But if you want the mainland so badly, we can leave soon."

"Thank you." Rylla swallowed the lump in her throat as she checked the clasp on her locket. She made sure it was still tight and fingered the yellow stones. She needed to find the rest of the crests before Lord Brennigan did. Rylla had two so far and would've had three had she not fed it to the Balagrix. But she didn't want to listen to the Jasper's encouragement.

As if reading her thoughts, Moo spoke again. "Rylla, why did you *really* throw the Larimar into the sea-beast?"

"It was all I could think of at the time, but…I saw Caz with the stone and I got afraid." She paused as if she were searching for a memory. "While

I was in the water with the Balagrix, I felt the pull myself, to just hang onto it and remain as I was. I feared Caz would feel the same. I wanted to know he could resist its power. So I told him to toss it to me. He did."

"I'm not sure anyone else who held that stone would have been as willing to give it up," Moo said, searching her face. "I think you can stop worrying about him; you have too much on your mind as it is."

Yes, like the pain in her heart and the twists in her gut. Amongst other things.

"Ever the wise one, Moo. Do you have no fears yourself?"

"I have fears as much as anyone, I suppose. I just try to outrun them and best them before they best me," Moo said, cleaning his tail. "But now we're down a stone."

"I know…I'm still hoping I don't come to regret that," Rylla replied, trying to steady her breathing.

"Well, let's hope it doesn't make a costly difference. Best not to mention the beast at all. If I know Lord Brennigan, he'd probably cut the carcass open himself. He wouldn't follow the code of the Earth-Treaders," Moo continued.

"What are you saying?"

"I'm saying that he better not find out what happened to the Larimar. Best let him believe that it's still hidden." Moo got up to stretch.

That was an easy hope. No one from her company would willingly prostrate themselves before the cruel lord just to tell him about the Larimar's fate. Though the thought did little to comfort her.

What if they were caught and tortured into telling the truth?

"I think we should head out now, before it becomes light." Rylla checked her surroundings for any items she'd forgotten, fixing her freshly washed cloak over her shoulders and sliding her arms through the openings, exposing only portions of her forearms. She pulled her hair back in a low, braided knot and grabbed her broken satchel off the floor. The strap had been slashed in half, but Rylla tied the two ends together like it had never been broken. She opened it up and saw three stones gleaming up at her; she had put Garth's Sunstone in there after leaving the Balagrix's cave so she could deliver it back to her brother when the time came. Maybe it would be sooner rather than later.

Rylla went to her door and slowly turned the knob; she peered out through the small gap between the door and the doorframe. Only the flickering glow of starlight and Moonstones shifted in the courtyard beyond. She pulled the door open wider and cautiously stepped over the threshold.

"I hope we're not followed," Moo suggested.

"I'd rather not think about that." Rylla looked about her and silently ran to the door at the end of the courtyard. She twisted the knob and they both peered around the wooden frame and into an adjoining hallway with many doors. They had only just last night been escorted through this wing, and Rylla tried her best to remember which door would lead to the exit. The hairs on the back of her neck prickled as she looked about her. She couldn't help but feel that at any moment the king or one of his servants would pop out of nowhere.

They tried for the door on the far end of the hall, the one closest to where she thought the entrance to the castle was. Moo peered his head around carefully.

"All clear," he said and they both entered a large room which Rylla recognized as the banqueting hall. It was now more ominous in its vacancy and lowlight than it had been during the grandeur of dinner. All that remained of their feast was an untouched place setting which King Malik had said was for his late wife, taken too soon by the bloodlust of a beast. The amount of dust on the plate and silverware indicated that it had been sitting there for months, maybe even years. It was a plate filled with the fullness of invisible grief.

Rylla looked away from it quickly, feeling like her own griefs were heaped upon the same plate for all that she was leaving behind.

From here it was easier: another set of hallways and then out to freedom. They proceeded with caution, blending into the shadows in case anyone should try to stop them. But all was quiet and still, unaware of two passing beings—one girl, one cat—as they escaped into the night.

Oddly, there were no guards on duty, but then again, now that the Balagrix was dead and the villagers freed, what other threat did the Isles have? Perhaps everyone had the night off. Regardless, it was pure luck that Rylla and Moo could waltz out of the castle without being questioned. They ran under the starlit sky, through the sleeping village, passed the gates, and into the forest, following a path that would lead them back to the eastern shore.

They made quick work of it, memories of running through Thrushwoode flashing through Rylla's mind. Except here there were no poachers tracking her down; here there was no Caz chasing after her. Though she had the sneaking suspicion that she was being watched. But she heard nothing. It must all be in her imagination.

As Rylla and Moo emerged from the trees, they found themselves back where they arrived when they first landed on the Isles. The moonlight glistened off of every surface, and when the wind blew grains of sand into the air, it looked like a million star-lit fairies dancing along to the song of the sea. It stole Rylla's breath away.

She treasured the moment in her heart. She'd never forget this, nor her friends who she might never see again. Rylla bent down on the sand, her knees hitting the soft, tiny grains as she gathered the shells closest to her. She arranged five blue shells into a circle, one for each of their company. If they all couldn't be together, at least these shells could—like a memory of what once was. Rylla unclasped her necklace and pulled off one of the Yellow Jaspers; she carefully placed it inside the circle of shells and stood back, droplets of tears escaping her eyes.

It looked like a star belonging both to the blue of night and the yellow of day—it was all she could think of to leave them with. She only hoped that they'd see it.

"Rylla, we can't take the ship." Moo interrupted her thoughts. "You don't know how to steer one, and besides, how would the others return to the mainland?"

"I had thought of that, and I think I know the solution." Rylla got up and walked toward the shore. "Speaking of the others, Moo, I'm not even sure if they *will* return. Caz told me himself he's staying here," Rylla said over her shoulder, her voice hitching over the last words.

"He did? That doesn't sound like him." Moo followed after her.

"No, it doesn't." Rylla hadn't thought to ask him *why* he was remaining on the island, but she was afraid of the answer. Better to let a piece of her heart remain intact.

She paused in front of a stack of fishing boats, eyeing them carefully. She had noticed them when they first landed on the Isles but hadn't paid them much attention. Now? It seemed she had no other choice. She hoped one would be sturdy enough to bring them to the mainland, though the idea of getting back on the water made her stomach churn already. She stuffed down another wave of anxiety. She'd only just recovered her land legs and now she had to get back on the water.

"What do you think, Moo? Traveling by fishing boat." Rylla turned to face him.

"Good idea. No rudder necessary—just your Earth-Treader magic and a clear shot home!" Moo walked closer to the small vessels.

Home. If only. She'd forgotten how much she missed Aylati until she heard that word.

"Okay, let's see how heavy these things are." She took hold of the topmost boat and lifted it high enough over the lip of the one underneath and slid it down. Its weight challenged her muscles, pressing her strength to her limit. It hit the ground, sand crunching beneath it, and she dragged it over to the shoreline and peered inside. It was a small, hollowed-out vessel, big enough for two people, three if they were small. The perfect size for Moo and her.

Moo jumped in as Rylla pushed it into the water. With one last glance behind her, she scrambled into the small vessel. Her stomach churned in anticipation as the boat rocked beneath her movement and she clutched the sides to steady herself. The crossing would only take four hours with her Earth-spell, and if the wind was extra gracious, maybe even less than that.

Rylla grasped a battered paddle from the bottom of the boat and scooped it into the water, slowly pushing them farther out. She would spare no magic on this voyage; she didn't want to be out here for longer than absolutely necessary.

Before she had finished her thoughts, a deafening cry roared from the depths as if in agony. It sounded like a creature being slain or suffering something too violent to comprehend. The noise shook their little boat, sending it rocking back and forth. Waves lapped over the edges and splashed on Rylla's feet and Moo's fur. Rylla choked on a cry and Moo hissed in protest.

"What on the good-tilled earth was that?" Rylla's eyes were as large as saucers as she scanned the water around them. Her heart pounded like a drum. They were no longer close to the shore, but perhaps she should turn back around.

"That's not the sound any normal creature makes." Moo was alert, scanning the horizon and listening to the distant sounds of the ocean. His ears twitched in the breeze. "It's almost as if…"

"As if what?" The hair on back of Rylla's neck stuck up, goosebumps prickling her skin.

The gut-wrenching cry came a second time, louder but less out of agony and more of confusion. Their boat rocked again, this time larger waves splashing over the lip and around their ankles.

"It can't be—I suggest we press on, Rylla, and make for the distant shore." Moo leapt onto a low bench seat to avoid the water in the bow of the boat. "Let's make haste!"

"There's nothing I'd like more than to get off this blasted contraption," Rylla gulped, fear gripping her heart. But the quicker they travelled along the surface, the faster they'd once again touch shore, the promise of land a welcome relief. They just had to avoid whatever was potentially out there.

The Balagrix was dead, there was nothing else to fear.

What was once turbulent waters settled into a glassy surface, as flat and untouched as a patch of fresh snow. Rylla refocused her energy and asked the wind to speed their vessel like a hummingbird in the moonlight. It came upon them as gentle as a whisper but as quick as lightning, their small boat careening across the murky blue and leaving a trail of gold in its wake.

They would be on land soon, and that thought kept Rylla sane. But what had caused that earth-shattering sound? And where would she go when she touched the far shore?

⸙ ⸙ ⸙

"I think that's good for now." Rylla was out of breath as the boat came to a slow and steady stop, gliding gently across the water.

They had been travelling fast for the past two hours and were about halfway to the mainland. The moon shone brightly above them as the stars danced in and out of the clouds. In a few short hours, daylight would peel back the shadows with its golden hand and dance upon them like the stars once had. Until then, Rylla hugged her cloak tighter about her shoulders, Moo curled up in the folds by her feet.

"You've done well, Rylla. Only a little bit more now until we're home," Moo said, resting his head on her foot.

There it was again—home.

What if she didn't go to Rélynda?

The thought had been in the back of her mind this whole time, but she finally let it surface. Moo would be disappointed, but hopefully he'd come to understand. And the more Rylla thought about it, the more she realized that perhaps she never planned to go to Rélynda at all. But to abandon her mission entirely? Would her conscience allow it? So much depended on her success.

Rylla calmed her thoughts, taking a moment to steady her breathing. Something stirred in the water ahead, enshrouded in fog, and she narrowed her eyes, trying to focus on the object. It was large and seemed to glide with ease as it came nearer. She squinted and made out the remains of a tattered flag blowing in the breeze. A ragged bow and masts came into view.

A ship sailing at this time of night?

"Moo," Rylla said as she watched the ship draw nearer. She was close enough to see the vessel in its entirety now—any closer and she'd be counting the grains of wood on each plank. It was one of the neglected ships from the mainland, similar to the one she and her friends had used to get to the Isles. Except this one had a weathered and beaten red stripe running horizontally along its side instead of yellow.

Moo poked his head up from the cloak and stared at the large vessel before them. And then that same deafening cry roared forth from the depths and seemed to split the sea in half, a cacophony of sound so intense, a giant swell of water broke over their small boat and capsized them into the water.

The world spun in a dizzying swirl of darkness. Rylla screamed and clutched tighter to her satchel as she plummeted into the sea. Piercing cold water stole her breath away, muffling her screams. She was hurled underneath the waves so deep that the moonlit surface felt but a distant memory; Moo's small legs were kicking feverishly above her, trying to reach the top.

Rylla grabbed Moo around the middle and swam for the surface, her limbs growing numb and her movements slowed. Her head burst free and she gasped in a breath, spitting out water. She placed Moo securely on her shoulders as she treaded water, scanning the ocean in the dimness. Another deafening cry and a giant wave sent them under again. She clung to Moo and struggled to swim upwards, the weight of her sodden cloak pulling her down and tangling in her legs.

The ship loomed above them like a dark shadow, and something jumped from the deck into the water, something solid and moving fast. It swam toward her, and before she had a chance to register what it was, it grabbed her around the waist and brought her toward the surface.

Rylla gasped for oxygen, choking as another wave broke against them, filling her mouth with the salty taste of the ocean. Their rescuer grabbed a rope dangling from the side of the ship and they were dragged upward, then sprawled onto the deck. Rylla coughed out water, pushing up to her hands and knees as water pooled around her on the deck.

"Hold your ground!" one of the men shouted.

Rylla drew her wet hood over her face and quickly shoved Moo deeper into the folds of her cloak—better to be safe than sorry.

"What are you doing?" Moo protested.

"Trust me," was all Rylla had the chance to say, her fears driving her to caution.

She looked up into the profiles of five men: three were wearing dark livery, one in a tattered white shirt with ropes attached to his wrists, and finally the last in a dark green cloak with a crimson stone hanging about his neck. They all stared at the churning waters before them, swords drawn. What was going on? Who were these men?

Rylla panted to catch her breath, fear clenching in her chest. She couldn't see their full faces.

And which one of them was crazy enough to risk his life to save hers?

"Steady, men! Something's out there!" one said.

Rylla studied their profiles closer and noticed one of the livery-clad men was soaked and scowling as he pushed the man in ropes in front of him. He must have rescued her, though he didn't appear too thrilled. It must have been an order.

Another monstrous cry of anguish split through the air as a monolith of scaly green and gold shot out from the depths.

The Balagrix!

The men fell back toward the center of the deck, cowering in fear. But the man with the crimson stone stood up and faced the beast, a gleaming dagger in his hand drawn and ready. Just as he was about to strike, the Balagrix's tail snaked out behind him, splintering the integrity of the mainmast and snatching him around the waist. He yelled as his dagger fell from his hands and his body yanked skyward.

And underneath his hood Rylla glimpsed a pair of dark eyes. The rest of his face was in shadow, keeping his identity a mystery.

She gasped.

The dream.

This was the vision she'd had the night before facing the terrible sea-beast. She had seen this, but she had awoken before the final outcome. What was going to happen? Who was this man?

The splintered beam screeched in warning, threatening to fall on top of the deck and inflict serious damage. Rylla watched it bend with the movements of the ship, her heart racing.

One of the other men stood and threw a dagger at the beast, and the Balagrix dropped the cloaked man with the familiar eyes. He fell to the deck with a thud and the Balagrix hissed furiously at them as if in warning, but then it started sniffing the air.

Rylla shifted her gaze between the men and the monster who seemed to radiate a bluish light. Part of its tooth was missing and one of its eyes was badly wounded—both signs of the battle in the cave. But how was this beast not dead? Surely the power of the stone had finished it off. That's what they had all seen!

Moo's words thrummed in her ears. "*Killing to defend and eat is one thing, but to mar a corpse, is another.*" It hadn't been a corpse at all!

The man with the crimson stone and dark eyes faced the monster once more as he rose. He cautiously picked up his dagger as he watched the sea-serpent rear its head back and forth in confusion, sniffing the air like it had caught a scent in the wind. The Balagrix looked like it was searching for something, but why had it stopped attacking them? It hissed once more and Rylla felt its gaze on her. Clearly her hood did nothing to shield her from its knowing glances.

Yesssssss, I thought sssssso. You again, Earth-Treader! What have you done to me? The Balagrix hissed and swayed as it moved closer to her. *I've been sssearching for you. I don't know what I am, or what I've become...* The creature looked restless and weary. It leant precariously close to her, scanning her with its good eye.

Rylla looked at the men who were now all staring at her. They were frightened stiff and looked confused themselves. They had no idea that Rylla had seen this monster before, that she had fed it the Larimar which had apparently only knocked it unconscious.

The Larimar? You put my precioussss ssssstone in me? The creature hissed. *I want to attack you, but I feel sssstrange. Almossst calm.*

Rylla could argue that this beast was in fact not calm, but she didn't want to take her chances. Feeding the beast the Larimar had been an impulse, not something she had thought would result in much of anything, just buy her more time to stay alive.

You've taken my vengeance—I am plagued by your sssssacrifice—it hauntssss me! I only attack now if threatened, no longer for ssssssport. Sssssstrange, really, for I grow hungry. The creature growled a gruesome call. *But I feel as if I mussst owe you.* It hissed, clearly dissatisfied but unwavering.

What did the creature mean? There was nothing to owe. Then out of nowhere, as if he had grown anxious by the waiting, another of the men threw a dagger into the flesh of the Balagrix. The hilt stuck out somewhere below its heart.

The creature screamed as it reared upwards and lunged after the man, grabbing him in its jaws and swinging him high in the air. Its tail came out of the sea and sent a spray of water splattering across the deck. Rylla ducked her head and shielded her face as Moo burrowed deeper within the cloak.

The other men, now dripping from head to toe, had the decency to look afraid for their lives.

It'sssss time I left—thissssss one'ssss my parting gift it sssssseems. The Balagrix shifted the squirming man in her jaws. *Mmmmmm, extra wriggly.* It moved away from the ship, rising higher than ever. *Until next time, Rylla of Aylati—for we shall meet again.* The Balagrix plunged under the depths with its meal in tow, leaving Rylla in a greater state of perplexity than before.

The men stared out at the empty sea, silent and drenched. The once turbulent waters were now as calm as a sheen of glass.

"What in the blasted depths was that?" one of the dark-clad guards spoke.

"It must be *her*, who else could send a beast like that away without even a word?" Rylla's rescuer spoke.

"She's the witch! Maybe her cat drowned in the sea," the roped man replied, his fetters tearing into his skin. Was he some sort of prisoner?

The man with the dark eyes and hood drawn over his face held up his hand and their voices quieted instantly. "We can't take any chances," he said as he squatted in front of Rylla and snatched her satchel from over her head. He peered inside and took out three stones. Rylla could tell he felt their power; his frame stiffened and straightened at the same time, as if overwhelmed by the magic.

"It appears we hit the jackpot, boys, and we didn't even need to touch land. My master will be pleased," the man spoke. "Looks like the prisoner was right after all." He laughed, and the others joined.

Rylla trembled all over and she couldn't tell if it was from the cold or the dread in her heart. She suspected it was both. Who were these men? What were they doing with her stones? Her whole mission was crumbling beneath her feet, thoughts of returning home along with it. If they took the stones, she'd lose everything.

"Please, give those back," Rylla pleaded, her voice small.

"You hear that, boys? The little girl wants the stones back!" The cloaked man laughed harder as he squatted before her again. His hood blocked his face, but his voice, the way he talked, it all felt familiar. Around his neck hung a peculiar stone as red as blood and as beautiful as a rose.

"Who are you? Who are you working for?" Rylla croaked. She was shaking now more than ever, Moo huddled beneath her cloak, trying to stay warm. She kept her head down, hiding beneath her own hood for fear of being seen. They knew she was an Earth-Treader, but they didn't know who *she* was.

"My, my, she likes to ask the questions. My master doesn't like nosy people, I'm afraid, so you best get them over with now." He laughed again. "As for me, you don't know who I am—no one does." He reached his right hand up and snapped his fingers. "Bind her."

Rylla's heart dropped to her stomach, beating wildly like a wounded bird trapped in a cage. Bind her? She had to think fast. She couldn't be trapped.

She lifted her hands and uttered some words. The wind began to howl as waves sloshed against the sides of the ship. The vessel rocked back and forth, causing the men to stumble in their places.

"Stop her! She's using her spells against us!" the cloaked man yelled.

Rylla uttered another Earth-spell and a wave flecked with gold came crashing onto the deck, knocking the men off their feet. One of the livery-clad man got up faster than the others and wobbled in her direction, his eyes crazed. He held ropes. What was he planning on doing with them?

A splintering crash echoed in the gale and part of the broken mast came toppling toward the deck. Rylla looked up, her eyes wide. A split beam of wood wacked her across the head, blackening her vision as she fell over, the Earth-spell broken.

"That's enough of your black magic—witch." A guard knelt beside Rylla, his wet hands gripping her wrists. "Sit up!"

She blinked slowly and lifted her spinning head. As she sat up, it took everything in her power not to topple over again. Gold dust danced in and out of her sight before settling on the deck around her, the impact from the log still blurring her vision.

Moo shifted beneath the folds of the cloak, his presence giving her some comfort. Was he still okay?

The man roughly bound her hands and mouth, the rope biting into her skin. Another man placed a brown sack over her head that covered her eyes. Her stomach dropped; what was going on? She struggled against the calloused hands holding her, but without more of her magic, how could one woman fight off four large men? She was pinned in their arms, claustrophobic, her cage of darkness smelling of dust and burlap. The cold dread escalated into a gut-wrenching knot; she felt she would throw up.

"She's wily—dangerous, Gryfinn." One of the guard's said, his voice muffled through her burlap.

"Don't fret, yet. Though we have some ground to cover, she'll soon meet her doom. Until then, we can't have her seeing where we're going," the cloaked man spoke again, his voice muffled through the sack and distant as though he was walking away. "Gorvo, turn this ship around, now! We can't afford to be stranded out here when the wind finishes off the rest of the mast." He commanded.

Where were they taking her? Was this some sort of pirate gang? Who was their master?

Lord Brennigan? Grievon? Someone else? And who was Gryfinn?

Any hopes of returning home, let alone completing her mission, were dashed like waves upon a rocky shore. Her breath came in choked, silent sobs, dizziness making even the darkness around her whirl. If she didn't steady her mind, she'd surely pass out.

"Rylla," Moo's small voice called through her darkness. "They don't know I'm here. I'll get you out of this." He burrowed deeper into the cloak, making himself as small as possible.

"Pretty soon, Earth-Treader, you'll meet your end," came Gryfinn's distant voice somewhere behind her, his words trailing on the wind.

The wind swung around until it had changed direction completely—or perhaps the whole ship had turned and was heading back to the mainland. Rylla huddled against the side of the ship, helpless except to await a fate she could only guess at. She was a captive, a hostage, and under the fearsome grip of a group of faceless men.

If only she had never left home. If only she'd stayed on the Isles. If only her friends knew where she was: that she was off floating to her doom while they all dreamt of peaceful seas and their heroic deeds.

Part Four:

Stone

Chapter the Twenty-Sixth

Captive

Caz had hardly slept at all. Restless and disturbed, he had gotten up at first light to run laps around the courtyard and push the images out of his mind. The horrible, gut-twisting images that had danced in his head all night.

Visions of women and children cowering on the trodden earth, covered in dust and tears, their huts being ransacked before their very eyes. Soldiers running in and out of the villagers' tar and straw homes, even setting some ablaze if the men refused to comply with their orders.

And all the while, the heavy footsteps of Grievon striding amongst the ruins with pleasure.

Caz had seen himself, a younger and more eager version, busy tying a man's arms behind his back, pushing him into a prison on wheels, away from his wife and children who were screaming and crying. He had seen himself go back to them, taking the young boy away from his mother and sister and forcing him into a different cart to join the ranks.

Rembrandt nudged him, whinnying, and it had felt to Caz now like a cry of disapproval and anguish. The anguish went deep, for it echoed in Caz's own heart as he threw off the covers to face the waking world. Whether in dreams or in reality, the memories still haunted him.

He'd done much to improve Grievon's army, being young and naive, but at what cost? He had sacrificed his own happiness, his own morality, for the sake of servitude to a man who loathed anyone but himself.

Caz had been a slave to the shadows long enough, and he was a changed man now, even if his past said otherwise. He had to forgive himself.

"That takes courage of the strongest kind." Rylla's words still played over and over in his head.

Caz needed to believe there was still some good left in him, that helping Rylla was only the start to a new life. The Isles had seemed so compelling in the beginning, but was running from his problems truly the road to forgiveness?

As Caz jogged off these thoughts, he thought about knocking on Rylla's door to talk to her and clear things up, but it was still so early. He knew she was an early riser, but what if she wasn't yet awake? The sun was just beginning its slow ascent into the heavens.

Her hurt and distant look amidst the flickering candlelight and the pain in his own heart haunted across his vision. Last night could've gone so much smoother. The more he tried to fight it, the more he realized he didn't want to leave Rylla. The very plan he had constructed these past few months seemed lunacy now. He couldn't leave her.

After many turns about the room, Caz finally stopped and caught his breath, wiping sweat from his forehead. He'd been such a dunce. He needed to talk to her—now.

He wanted to offer his service and protection back to the mainland—perhaps he should have done that outright all along. But the selfish part of him was afraid she'd say no.

"Wounded pride bears a heavy weight, but it builds character depending upon how it is carried." Somewhere amongst the gruesome ranks of Grievon's army, he had gleaned this little bit of wisdom from his superiors and those gone before him.

Part of Caz wondered if there were others like him, either past or present who were reshaping their identities like he was now. Perhaps wounded pride would do him some good.

Caz caught his breath and knocked lightly on Rylla's door. No sound came from within, so he tried again, harder.

"Rylla?" He felt like he'd done this countless times before, calling out without getting a response. Would his role forever be to shout Markief without an answering Poslo? Markief had been the first king of the Isles and Poslo the first king of Rélynda. Their friendship forged strong despite the distance between them; when one called, the other responded. Over the years, children turned their communication into a silly game, and Caz had played it enough as a child in the orphanage to know silence like it was his friend. "Can you please open up?"

Nothing.

No matter how dark his past, he'd always known to respect women and their privacy, so the idea of barging in didn't sit right. But what if something happened to her? Even if she wasn't awake yet, Rylla was a light sleeper. She should be opening the door, or at least calling out to tell him to wait a minute.

Caz slowly twisted the knob and pushed the door in slightly. Still no sound. He pushed the door open farther and kept his eyes down, scanning the ground for any sign of her bag or the cat. Still nothing. He raised his gaze and his eyes froze upon the empty bed. A weight of silence lingered more heavily than the extravagant draperies.

Caz now understood—his pride had cost him more than he'd realized. She was gone.

He left the room and knocked on Jovin's and then Elowen's doors, pounding loud enough to wake them both.

Jovin came to his door first, opened it wide and peered out in confusion while rubbing his eyes. "What's goin' on?" he questioned.

Within a few moments, Elowen opened hers and poked her head out, the light brown mop of hair a tangled mess atop her head. A deep crease of irritation marked the space between her brows. "What?"

"Rylla's gone," Caz blurted so quickly he wasn't sure if they had heard him.

Their faces went blank, still dazed from sleep.

"Wait, what? Yeh can't be serious." Jovin frowned.

"She wasn't in her room this morning—she didn't answer when I knocked, so I went in only to find it empty." Caz wished they'd wake up quick. The urgency he felt would do little good amongst such slow action.

"Maybe she went for a walk. It seems like something she'd do," Elowen suggested, yawning slightly and adjusting her bed head. She didn't appear too concerned, but then again, reading women wasn't one of Caz's specialties.

Unless it was Rylla. But even so, he had butchered that countless times too.

"I don't think so. Something in her demeanor last night leads me to believe otherwise. You two were already asleep, but while we were talking—"

"What did you say to her?" Elowen demanded, suddenly serious as she stepped forward with arms crossed.

Caz quailed back internally, even though she was substantially smaller than himself.

"What do you mean?" he responded, the prickles of guilt burning deeper.

"You know what I mean. The thing about women is, even though we appear stubborn, deep down, the slightest remark can send us off course. Rylla, more than anyone, is like this. I've seen it myself. She hates to be a burden, and if she had the slightest idea that she wasn't wanted, then I'd expect her to act irrationally," Elowen said with firm confidence.

Caz should have seen this coming; he should have known.

He swallowed the lump in his throat and told them both the truth. It wouldn't bring Rylla back, but as soon as this conversation was over, he'd be on that ship.

"I tried to tell her about my past and that I'd be staying here on the Isles…I know now that it wasn't the smartest move. I was going to tell her this morning that I changed my mind, but she was gone already. I didn't think she'd leave…" Caz ran a hand through his hair and let the guilt he was feeling swallow him whole. "I've been a blithering idiot!" It was the least of what he deserved.

"Well you got one thing right," Elowen scoffed.

"Did yeh mention anythin' 'bout me stayin' behind too?" Jovin questioned.

"No, I didn't get around to that," Caz responded, irritation building in his throat. If he couldn't get a move on to remedy his mistake, he felt he'd lose his mind.

"You too? Don't tell me you both planned to abandon us for this wealthy scum-hole. I can't take it with you men!" Elowen threw her hands in the air and grabbed her quiver and bow. She scoured the floor for anything she might have missed and crossed the threshold from her room into the courtyard, slamming the door behind her. "Now if you don't mind, I think I'd like to save my sister-in-law before anyone else changes their minds and makes a stupid decision."

"You don't have to ask me twice; I've been ready to leave well before dawn." Caz ran to gather his belongings from his chamber. He laced his boots, donned his cloak, attached his scabbard, and hid his dagger—a pleading conversation muffled in the background.

It was Jovin's accented voice trying to smooth things over with Elowen, about his plans and how "they too have changed" since coming to the Isles. When Caz returned to the courtyard, he glanced at Elowen, but she pretended not to care or notice, though the slight smirk on her lips proved otherwise. It seemed Elowen and Jovin were a good match of wits, but it only drove the sting in Caz's heart deeper. What if he never had the chance to get it right with Rylla?

What was it that he even wanted? At first it was to find a new start and to run away from his mistakes, to find a new path. But perhaps this new path was leading him to her. It was unavoidable—no matter how wrecked he felt inside, no matter the scars of his past and how he longed to run, his heart was healing, softening, and telling him to stay. It was more than just a mere fondness.

Blithering dolt! He loved her. And he was going after her no matter what it took.

The group of three gathered all their belongings, exited the courtyard, and made their way out of the castle. A few turns here and there led them outside to the stables where they retrieved their horses. No guards were around, so no one stopped them as they began walking through the village and back toward the ship. Caz didn't want to stay and chat with the king; he didn't even want to tell him their decision. He just wanted to leave. Now.

A booming voice stopped them all in their tracks before they had made much progress. King Malik's guards held open the vast wooden doors of the castle as the blonde-haired ruler, hellfire burning in his eyes, came barging through. He stopped before the three travelers only to glare at each of them individually, almost like he was challenging them to explain themselves.

"Do you dare make a mockery of me? Of my hospitality? That you would use me so ill?" he shouted so loudly that the villagers stirred, opening their windows and stepping outside to see all the commotion.

"Your Majesty, we were only just leaving. We're sorry not to have informed you sooner," Caz said, glancing sideways at Jovin and Elowen who looked equally as confused.

"Leaving? More like sneaking away in secret after how you've treated me! The lies and false hope you've fed my kingdom, all the while feasting on my generosity! Barbarians!" he roared again.

Caz winced, but resisted the urge to stop his ears. "Your Majesty, what is it that we've done, exactly?" He was growing tired of Malik's outbursts—if it wasn't out of extreme pleasure, it was out of extreme loathing.

"You hear that? He has the gumption to ask what they've done!" the king directed this to the growing crowd, his fury burning menacingly like smoldering ash. "Bah! Like you don't know! That writhing beast of yours was seen early this morning in the basin, its calls echoing far and wide. The Balagrix still lives! And you stand before me today, a mere mirage of the heroes you once were." He spat and threw the scepter with the serpent's tooth at their feet.

Jovin bent down to pick it up, but Caz just stared.

The beast was still alive? Surely it couldn't be; they'd all seen it fall. "I assure you, Your Majesty, that we had no idea of this until now," Caz said, keeping his voice calm and level though he didn't feel it.

"You expect me to believe that? Where's the other girl, hmm? Slinking off during the night, guilt-ridden by her lies," King Malik snarled. "That's right, I have eyes everywhere. Hannock here saw her leave." He pointed to one of the guards with a huge ring in his nose. "And he followed her out into the basin only to see some large vessel being assaulted by the Balagrix itself. That writhing beast of hell! That fortunate ship somehow made it out alive, but *my* fishing boat was found destroyed, its pieces of wood lapping against my shores. She ran away and left my boat broken in the process! She is guilty twofold!" The bloodlust on his face proved a stark contrast to his extravagant and brightly colored robes. "Do I make myself clear?"

The words dulled in Caz's ears, his thoughts whirling. The Balagrix was indeed still alive, there had been another ship in the ocean, and the boat Rylla had been on was found broken. What happened to her? Was she even alive? His heart plummeted and sped up at once.

"Your Majesty, was Rylla taken on that ship?" His question came out breathless and desperate. He was already off this blasted island in his mind, now if only he could get his body off it too.

"You dare ask a question of the king?" Malik boomed, anger in his eyes.

"I do." Caz locked gazes with him, any worry or fear of disrespect gone. He glared at the king until one of them had to buckle, and he could feel the king growing slightly disconcerted.

As much as Malik seemed to throw around words, his bark was worse than his bite, and his anger rapidly dissolved into discomfort.

"If you must know, Hannock thought he saw something being hoisted out of the water, but he turned around and came back to land as soon as he laid eyes on that beast. No thanks to you, one of my best guards could have been killed!" The king seethed, though much quieter.

Caz hardly noticed, scrambling to put the pieces together. If Rylla had been rescued, who had done it? The twist in his stomach unknotted slightly, but if he didn't get a move on, he'd never forgive himself. He had to find her; he had to make sure she was still alive.

"Your Majesty, we must be on our way," Caz spoke curtly and began to turn toward the gates. Elowen and Jovin moved to follow after him.

"You either finish what you started and defeat the beast, or you never step foot on this island again," King Malik's commanding voice reached their backs, but no one turned around.

Caz was tired of this island and silently berated himself for even considering living on it. Maybe the Isles were once an enjoyable place to live, and perhaps there was hope for it in the future, but as far as he was concerned, there would be no freedom while Malik reigned on the throne.

"I see how it is. Fine, be gone, the lot of you! And never return!" he belted angrily. "If you so much as step one foot…"

That was fine with Caz because he never planned to. He walked away, the others by his side, not caring to listen to anymore of Malik's speech.

⸙ ⸙ ⸙

Caz turned a smooth, yellow stone over in his hand and felt Rylla's loss anew. He stared down at the circle of blue shells and knew Rylla had purposely arranged them with the hope of someone finding them. And she had left behind one of her Yellow Jaspers in the middle—something he would hold onto as a promise of seeing her again. He had to believe she was still alive. Or else, what would he do? As he held the stone, it sent a coursing desire through his veins to press on. But just staring at the shells and holding the stone wouldn't bring her back.

The group had left the furious king, made it past the scoffing leers from villagers, and were now staring at the large ship in front of them. It seemed foolish to Caz for all of them to have come to the Isles in the first place: Rylla had lost the stone she was looking for and now he had lost her. But if anything, the mistakes here had settled his resolve. He would do anything for that woman, no matter how often she would run away. He'd always be the one to go after her.

Chapter the Twenty-Seventh

The Edge of Rélynda

Deep in the bowels of the stone tower, fumes wafted high in the air and escaped through vents to the upper floors. Prisoners beat and bent metal, heating and cooling it into clasps and then placing stones within them. The stones were then hung on metal chains and tossed into a pile which was accumulating by the hundreds. Lord Brennigan had hordes of prisoners, but there were only a handful who were useful to him: those who weren't Earth-Treaders. These prisoners had been unfortunate enough to come too close to the tower and were captured, though Lord Brennigan counted it toward his fortune. With them, his plans were carried out much faster with more hands.

The other prisoners, those blasted Earth-Treaders, could rot in their cells for all he cared! And there was rotting aplenty even now, for the air tasted metallic and stale, infused with flakes of decaying flesh.

Growls and cries of agony accompanied the hammering of metal against iron, wailings so intense they competed with the howling winds outside the tower.

"Quit your pleas!" Lord Brennigan scoffed as he looked down into a dimly lit pit. "Your time is drawing near! Pretty soon you'll be thanking me, once you've come fully into form."

The pit writhed and wriggled like a mass of shadow. Eyes the color of blood peered back at him, hundreds, thousands in number. Within the shadows there appeared the shapes of animals, if one could even consider them as such—pointed ears like a fox's, long tails like a cat's, claws like a hawk's, arched backs like a wolf's, and fangs too large to belong to any sort of creature. They were grotesque, smelling as death itself, but Lord Brennigan felt only triumph instead of revulsion.

The beasts could not speak; their words were tears and agony. But if one listened close enough, one might detect an underlying "please" hidden beneath their cries and howls. Their pain was Lord Brennigan's pleasure. Upon hearing their cries, he was transported to another memory.

They were older now, Brenn in his late teens and Odinel approaching his mid-twenties. Despite their age and supposed maturity, the teasing and humiliation never seemed to stop.

The three of them were outside, Talih the peacemaker and middle child joining her two headstrong brothers for a hike up Mount Egret. They were nearing the top when Odinel decided to play a joke. He gave a low whistle and clasped his hands in front of him. Vines and leafy plants responded to the call as they crawled over the ground and stretched ahead to reach Brenn. A poke on a shoulder, a tap on the foot, Brenn swatted at the plants thinking they were pesky bugs. But then a vine ensnared his ankle and he tripped.

"Odinel, let me go," Brenn growled through his teeth.

"What? Little Brenn can't handle a joke?" Odinel scoffed.

"It's Brennigan." Brennigan reached for his small knife to cut through the vines, not wanting to wait for his brother. "How many times do I have to tell you that?"

"At least a dozen more. Come on you two, where's your humor?" Odinel protested as he looked from his glaring brother to his silent sister.

"Just leave him alone, Odie," Talih said.

"Fine," Odinel agreed with a scowl. "You two are no fun."

The three continued up the mountain, Brennigan trying to forget his brother's taunts and just enjoy the view. He reached into his pocket and felt the smoothness of the chestnut-sized stone, letting its familiarity clear his mind. Over the past few months, he had started carrying it in his pocket, the cramped confines of a musty shoebox no longer seeming an appropriate place to hide it. The stone was safer with him, he reasoned.

As the siblings finally reached the top, Odinel gave a large sigh.

"Well, that was boring," he said.

"We've climbed this mountain many times, maybe you should try a different one," Talih suggested, hands on her hips.

"Or perhaps you're too caught up with yourself to appreciate anything else," Brennigan muttered under his breath. He loved this mountain and its views.

"What was that?" Odinel glared at his brother.

Normally Brennigan would back down and pretend like nothing happened, but touching the stone seemed to empower him with boldness.

"I said, you're an addle-brained jerk and you need to grow up," he spoke louder this time, irritation in his voice.

"You're so stupid, Brenn, you can't even handle a joke," Odinel snapped back.

"Oh yeah? I can handle a joke just fine, it's just your Earth-Treader business I can't stand." Brennigan clenched his free hand into a fist, glaring at Odinel.

"You're just jealous, you've always been jealous of me," Odinel countered. "Always living in the shadow of your brother."

Brennigan gripped the stone even tighter, anger and loathing filling him so much that his chest burned. But he could see clearly what he had to do, what must be done.

"You're no brother of mine," Brennigan uttered. He lunged at Odinel but too slow.

Odinel countered with his magic, a gust of wind sending Brennigan backwards.

He tripped and fell against a rock. His dark hair fell over his face, but he glared at his brother beneath the lank strands. Red tinged the edges of his vision.

Odinel just laughed, thinking they were wrestling like old times, unaware of the Darkness brewing beneath the surface. Brennigan lunged again, stone clutched in one hand and knife unsheathed in the other. Talih screamed.

Odinel realized what was happening and he jumped upwards. He grabbed hold of a tree branch above him, the wind aiding in his attempts as he swung up. Brennigan nicked him in the ankle with his blade before he could retreat out of reach.

Odinel winced but swung his legs up over the branch before more damage could be done.

"Relax, Brenn, it's over. I can clearly see you're upset." Odinel seemed to finally acknowledge for the first time that perhaps he had pushed his brother a little too far. "I'll stop." He crouched on the branch, knees to his chest as he held onto a branch above him.

"It's too late, it's far too late," Brennigan roared. "I've detested you for years—since the moment you first used your *magic* against me. I hate Earth-Treaders, and I hate you!" Fury and malice glowed in his eyes and the hand clutching the dagger shook.

"We can settle this, Brenn, like two grown men. Just put down your blade and I'll stop," Odinel tried to reason.

Brennigan shifted his hand on the stone, momentarily loosening his hold. His face softened a moment as he paused. Did he want to stop this? He looked at his brother, hope and fear in the other man's expression.

All the torment and all the humiliation Odinel had caused flashed before Brennigan's eyes.

No. Brennigan wanted his brother to pay. He clasped the stone even tighter and burned with renewed rage. And he threw his blade, watching as it sliced through the air with an inhuman speed.

Odinel tried to react with one of his Earth-spells, but his wind wasn't thick or solid enough to use as a shield. It all happened so fast: the blade plunged through the air and found its mark, hilt-deep. Everything slowed as Odinel's limp form slipped backward from the tree.

"No! What have you done?" Talih screamed as she ran to catch him.

He landed partly on her and partly in a thicket bush. Talih tried to prop his head up in her arms as tears streamed down her face. Blood seeped into his shirt around the knife's blade protruding from his chest. "Odie, Odie, speak to me…Odie!"

"…Just a joke…only a joke…" he croaked before succumbing to the hand of death.

Talih sobbed, holding her brother to her chest. She raised her gaze to Brennigan, eyes wide and red-rimmed.

"Go…I never want to see you again!" she screamed, tears rolling down her face.

Brennigan finally dropped the stone, and his stomach heaved. Odinel's blood stained his vision, his blade, his heart. What had he done? "Talih, I…"

"I said go!" she screamed again, as if she couldn't bear to make eye contact any longer.

Brennigan backed away, tripping over stones and his own feet. He couldn't take back what was done, he could only run away from it.

As he fled down the mountain, a pool of water made him pause. Should he toss the stone into its depths? It had caused this. It had made him destroy his brother. But wasn't that what he always wanted?

"RrrrUGAAHHH." He gripped handfuls of his hair, tears already leaking from his eyes. He was torn. And in that moment, the words of the letter came back to him. "*Its power is too strong. Only the greatest Earth-Treader or a man more powerful than I might withstand it.*"

He wanted to be that man more than anything, and there was no turning back now. He knew what he must do.

He bent down to remove the leather lace from his shoe and fitted the stone onto it. He would wear it proudly now, where it could be kept closest to his heart.

Lord Brennigan shook himself from the memory. The killing had been too easy. Too natural. Pretty soon he'd wipe out the Earth-Treader race with his growing army, and this time, he wouldn't even need to lift a blade.

"We are to march on the kingdoms at the dawn of the second sun. And then the world shall know true power—my unyielding power!" Lord Brennigan shouted over the brooding pit.

The shadows squirmed in both hatred and fear. They both detested and revered their master.

Lord Brennigan left them to their miseries and decaying flesh as he spun on his heels to address the prisoners.

"The second sun, my lord?" the prisoner closest to him asked.

"It's an expression, you numbskull. It means very soon! Now quit your questions and give me updates. What of your progress?" He turned to address another prisoner.

The wide-eyed man cowered before him. "The…you—your…armor is a-al—"

"Out with it, you imbecile!" Lord Brennigan snapped at the poor man.

"Al…almost most finished, my lord," the man stuttered, and he held up a smooth and shining breastplate. He bowed with difficulty as Lord Brennigan snatched the armor from his hand to scrutinize the handiwork.

It looked to be sturdy and well made, but the reflection in the metal caught his attention. It was his face; though now much stronger, what made him pause were the eyes staring back at him. Around his eyes, darkened veins the color of a midnight sky snaked up to his temples and forehead, and then down into his beard and chin. It was as if a spider had spun its web upon his skin.

Instinctively his hand went to the stone around his neck, his Bloodstone. It whispered to him, "*The more you crave of my power, the more I leave my mark on you. Don't back down, don't grow afraid, for you and I are one.*"

Ever since Lord Brennigan put the Bloodstone back around his neck, he'd felt its power like a familiar force humming through his veins. But there had been a different note to it now. Strong yes, but almost as if it wanted to do the controlling rather than yield its power to the one who possessed it.

But that was only a passing thought—surely stones held no such abilities. He was the one with all the power, and pretty soon the world would know.

He'd march on the kingdoms soon.

❦ ❦ ❦

The sun warmed Rylla's burlap cocoon to the point of suffocation. With the gag in her mouth and the stale heat about her head, she was beginning to find herself rather lightheaded. She couldn't remember the taste of water—did it even have a taste? If only she could have some to coat her throat and parched lips.

Were they now walking up a hill? The ground seemed to be coming up to meet her, perhaps if she bent her knees and leaned back then she'd be okay. She felt the guard tighten his grip on her bonds. Were they going downhill? She leaned the other way and almost tripped.

"What are you about, woman?" Her captor yanked her forward, but the dizziness became too much and Rylla's knees collapsed. The guard, not prepared for the sudden jerk in motion, let her slip from his grasp.

Rylla's world dimmed and blurred. Where had Moo gone? She fell asleep before she even hit the ground.

⸙ ⸙ ⸙

"Gryfinn, how much longer are we to remain here? I thought this was an urgent mission," one of the guards asked him.

Gryfinn had his back toward everyone. No one could see his face, but it was tilted down, focused on what lay in his hands. He turned the smooth stones over with his fingers, feeling their power course through him, though the sand-colored one with orange flecks was strangely silent, a dud. Perhaps it took time to activate its power. Still, he felt stronger. He could do anything, become anyone. And…perhaps his master didn't deserve them.

"Soon, but there is no great rush now that we've found the girl." *And the stones.* "Besides, you seedy lot can't both carry her deadweight much longer *and* watch the prisoner. We're at the border of the North Mountains, so I suggest we get some rest, then cross over after."

Gryfinn turned to see surprised looks on their faces. Apparently, they thought he was being considerate—truthfully, he just wanted an excuse to hold the stones a little longer. But they just continued to stare at him.

"Get a grip, you fools. Choose who'll take first watch over the prisoners. I'm going to scan our perimeter and make sure we weren't followed." Gryfinn slunk away into the shadows of the mountains, disappearing from sight of the others. In his hands he still clung fast to the stones as a snide grin spread about his face.

He was finally feeling worthy.

⸙ ⸙ ⸙

Somewhere in Rylla's dreams she heard snoring, the deep and throaty kind that often leaves the mouth open and saliva dripping in pools. It felt both distant and near. Was it coming from her? Something tugged at the bonds around her wrists, and she cracked her eyes open to muted light. Her heart plummeted; no, she wasn't the one snoring, and she was still trapped in this blasted burlap sack. She tried to move but a voice stilled her.

"Rylla, I'm trying to get you out of here, just give me a few minutes." Moo! But where had he come from? She remembered that before being pulled off the ship, Moo had said he'd come up with a plan—one that involved barrels and a good amount of sneaking. Once the ship docked on land, Moo had escaped the folds of her cloak to assume his new position behind these supposed barrels. Rylla had trusted his plan, but it was terrifying being alone and hauled away by a faceless group of men, especially while not being able to see. Thankfully burlap was a porous material so enough light glowed through that she could tell what time of day it was.

Still, what she wouldn't give for some fresh air. She hated feeling like a caged bird when all she'd ever wanted was to spread her wings and fly. She wished more than anything that she could talk, but this gag in her mouth made it nearly impossible.

"The guards fell asleep and their leader doesn't seem to be around. But we need to hurry." Moo was eagerly attacking her bonds and had even gotten one of them slightly loose when he suddenly paused. "Wait, I have to hide. The prisoner is stirring. I'll be back," Moo whispered, then scampered away.

Rylla was left on the ground, blind to her surroundings but straining for any sound of movement. There was a rough sawing sound like someone was cutting through rope, quietly so as not to wake anyone. Moo had mentioned the prisoner, was this him making his escape?

As Rylla lay motionless, steadying her breathing and attuning her ears, she counted the seconds. After about twenty, the sawing stopped and footsteps were headed in her direction. They were quiet, yet determined, and they didn't stop once they passed her. In fact, she could hear them slowly turning into a run as they picked up their pace and disappeared altogether.

Moo returned in another moment and told her what he'd seen. The prisoner had filed through his bonds with a knife. How he came to possess such a weapon, Moo had no clue. Either it was already hidden on his person, or he had somehow gotten his hands on it during the fray of the ship. Regardless, he was free and Rylla most certainly was not. The thought did little to comfort her. Without the prisoner, all their attention would be on her.

But before Moo could try loosening her bonds more, the sound of approaching footsteps stopped him. These footsteps crunched on the ground, growing louder as whoever it was approached.

"I'm sorry, Rylla, I have to go once more. I think it's Gryfinn."

The leader. Rylla had learned his name on the ship. The guards didn't seem to like him, judging by the whispers behind his back, yet they feared him all the same.

Moo ran away as quickly as he had come and the footsteps suddenly stopped close to her head. All was silent until she heard the thud of a booted foot making contact with something solid. A curse followed and Rylla could only guess that someone had just been kicked in the stomach. The same sequence of events happened again.

"You blasted idiots!" The voice belonged to an infuriated Gryfinn. "I leave you for half an hour and you fall asleep on the job! Thanks to your idiocy, our prisoner has escaped! How could you let this happen?"

The guards muttered supplications and apologies, their voices filled with fear for their lives. Surely this mistake would cost them greatly.

"Gorvo was supposed to keep watch—he told me so himself!"

"No, you said you'd keep watch, you blasted liar!"

"That's not true, you know it ain't!"

"You measly scum…!"

"Shut up!" Gryfinn's voice rose above the bickering. "Gorvo, Henrick, you're both idiots. If I didn't need you, I'd kill you right now!" Gryfinn fumed with barely repressed rage. "Go, split up and fix your blunder. You will find him! He knows too much to fall into the wrong hands, do you understand? Your mistake could very well cost me *my* life! And we all know which of ours is most important."

Rylla couldn't help but shudder in fear at the tone of Gryfinn's voice. It sounded oddly familiar, but she'd never known anyone with this much anger or this much power. And without even realizing it, she suddenly began to miss her friends, terribly. If Elowen were with her, she'd be as infuriated as a clawless cat. If Jovin were here, he'd be cracking jokes and making light of the situation. And if Caz were here, well, Rylla was certain that he'd be right beside her and telling her everything was going to be okay.

Leaving them all behind was the stupidest thing she could have done, and no matter how much Gryfinn fumed at his guards for being idiots, Rylla was the truest idiot out of them all.

By now the guards had left the scene; she was sure of it because she no longer heard their bickering or their footsteps. Moo had to be close by, but it still didn't shake her fear that she and the angry Gryfinn were the only two left in the clearing.

"Now *I* have the unpleasant task of delivering you to the tower myself. Surely, you're awake now," he complained as he bent down to pull Rylla to her feet. As he hoisted her up, he mumbled something softly under his breath, "If those fools don't find the prisoner, my master will make sure I lose everything…"

The tower? Rylla swayed on her feet for a moment before she found her balance, relieved to finally be able to go somewhere, but she was even more relieved to hear something else in Gryfinn's tone. She hadn't detected it before, but behind his anger, she was certain there was an underlying fear. For all Gryfinn's commanding authority, he actually seemed to be afraid of the authority above him. It seemed that no matter how tough one's outer façade, there was always someone more powerful lurking above and pulling the strings. If not for her gag, she could talk to him, to relate to him on some level and escape. She knew fear, and perhaps that's what was making him so cruel.

But there would be no time for that, seeing as she was still gagged and being led up some sort of path. Gryfinn had mentioned the North Mountains, and if she heard him correctly, he was planning on crossing over them soon.

Rylla's heart began to pound. He was taking her to Rélynda. She knew it was on the other side of this mountain range—she'd studied it countless times on her maps. But why was he taking her there? What hidden secrets lay beyond these ridges? And where was this supposed tower? It was rather convenient, or ironic, or frustrating rather, that the location she was contemplating on both going to and running away from was the very place she was being taken to in spite of her own free will. She had considered abandoning her mission altogether and returning home, but that seemed the least likely of options now.

But how would she get Rélynda's stone if she remained a prisoner? Perhaps Moo had another plan up his sleeve, one which involved her freedom and the kingdoms' restoration. She could only dream. And then another thought struck her—if her friends ever found out she was captured, would they come after her? Would she ever live to see them again?

Rylla knew her mission was a dangerous one and that it was her burden to bear, but when she had left the Isles, she had been running away from her heart and the fear left quaking in its wake. And now that she was faced with an uncertain path before her, one that very well could lead to her doom, she was left wishing to run back to her heart and claim it once more. But would her heart be strong enough to face Caz again?

"Pick up the pace, will you? I want to make it back before nightfall." Gryfinn's voice was gruff.

Rylla struggled onward, not complaining. She hated the dark and wanted this bag off her head as soon as possible.

Wherever they were going, hopefully there was light enough to properly illuminate her surroundings, unlike the filtering burlap. The thought of sunshine sent a pang of longing through her middle, and she felt like she was transported back to the darkness of Uwan's cave. But surely she wouldn't be trapped in this bag for months on end. Now if only her racing heart and nerves could calm down enough so she could preserve her energy. She didn't want to pass out again.

They continued their journey, Rylla tripping along the path littered with holes and loose stones. She was sure Moo would follow; she clung to the thread of hope like it was her last. There was no reason for him to go anywhere else, and he was her only friend now. Where would he run to? No one else was coming to rescue her. In Rylla's mind, there were only two scenarios that would ensure her escape. Either Moo clung to the shadows long enough to set her free or once she was free of her gag, she would unleash an Earth-spell unlike anything this world had ever seen.

She secretly wished for the second.

Chapter the Twenty-Eighth

The Stone Tower

They had made it across the Ocean Basin without any issues, no shining scales or pointed fang in their path. The Balagrix had left them alone, and Caz was left wondering why. If it was truly alive, why would it let them pass so easily?

He scanned the shoreline, pausing. The other two ships were still there, but something looked different. The one that had the broken hull bobbed heavily beside one of the wharfs, its hull now fixed but its mainmast split in two and its sails torn. His heart sped up. Only the Balagrix could have caused that much damage. Was this the vessel that had rescued Rylla?

Caz brought their ship's starboard side up against the empty mainland wharf and Jovin slid the gangplank down, scrambling to secure the vessel with ropes. The tide was high and the winds blustering. Caz leaned into the gusts, finding his balance so the gale wouldn't send him sideways.

Elowen prepared the horses and led them down the gangplank onto the wharf, and then toward the sandy shore. Caz and Jovin finished securing the ship, then Caz ran toward the other vessel, his sword bumping against his leg with each stride. Maybe there were signs Rylla had been on it. He needed to know.

His boots hit the sand before stepping onto the second wharf. He slowed to a jog, his footsteps echoing the crashing waves as his boots pounded against the wooden boards. Caz eyed the ship and grabbed a coarse rope hanging over its edge, hauling himself up. His muscles strained in his arms, his hands on fire. Reaching the top, he gripped the ship's ledge and pulled himself up the rest of the way, heaving a sigh as he planted his feet on the deck.

Overturned barrels and splintered wood littered its surface. The broken mast lay like a felled tree, having damaged the port side of the ship with its impact. Caz walked the length of the vessel, stepping over the wreckage and scanning the ground. Rope cuttings and strands of burlap blew across the deck, but aside from these few things, there were no signs of Rylla. Had she been on here?

Caz shifted and a shimmer of something caught his eye. Could it be? He bent down and wiped his finger along the deck, lifting his hand to reveal golden dust on his skin. He'd seen this gold before—the tree bark in Aylati, Rylla's wind magic on their way to the Isles. Hope surged in his chest.

Rylla had been here. She was still alive. If only he knew where she was now.

Caz took one last look at the deck before climbing over its side and down the rope. When his feet found the wharf, he jogged toward his friends who were waiting on the sand.

"Find anythin'?" Jovin's brow creased.

"Rylla's been on that ship. I found traces of her magic. She's still alive, but there are no further clues as to where she is." Caz scanned the horizon, running his hand through his hair, damp with ocean spray.

Now that they had finally arrived on the mainland, Caz looked at the land stretching before him and felt his hope turn to despair. Rylla had planned to go to Rélynda, he knew that much. But King Malik had said her boat was torn apart and she was potentially rescued by a strange ship. He knew that to be the truth now, but where had she gone? And what if her rescuers were captors in disguise? What then? Regardless, Caz had to move and make a decision. Staying put and worrying over the details would get him nowhere. He didn't know where Rylla was, but Rélynda seemed the likeliest of places. He would just have to go with that.

"It's now late afternoon, and we should make for Rélynda before dark. Jovin, do you know the fastest route?" Caz questioned, all determination and eagerness.

"It be fastest ta go through the north pass in the mountains, though goin' 'round them is much easier an'—"

"I'm not looking for easier," Caz cut him off.

Jovin crossed his arms over his chest and leaned against his horse. "Well, we 'ave our 'orses, an' then there's Elowen's foot…I think it'd be best if we walk 'round them an' go through the forest instead." Somehow he was both nonchalant and concerned.

"Oh, be quiet, I can handle it," Elowen protested. If she hadn't been holding the horses' bridles, Caz was sure she would have crossed her arms in her defiance.

"I've 'iked these mountains in my youth, El, you'd best believe they'd eat yeh alive in the state yer in," Jovin responded, a frown on his brow though he upheld is carefree demeanor.

As much as Caz wanted speed, he felt he must heed Jovin's advice. The horses weren't fit for mountain travel nor was Elowen's still healing ankle. He cursed under his breath at the idea of a set-back.

"How much will it delay us?" he asked.

"'bout an 'our or so. But if we ride our 'orses, we can cut that time in 'alf." Jovin grinned.

"All right, let's get a move on then." Caz took his bridle from Elowen and mounted Rembrandt. His feet slid naturally into the stirrups and his body felt right at home in the saddle. Strange how he hadn't realized how much he missed riding until now. He was only too grateful that Rembrandt and Cinders hadn't run away while he was trapped in Uwan's cave, though he still wondered what had kept them fed and alive.

Jovin helped Elowen onto his horse and climbed on behind her. "I'll ride with yeh for a few miles an' then get off ta lighten the load. Cinders is made of 'earty stock, but she'll need a break eventually." His grin broadened as he laughed.

No matter the circumstance, whether dire or dreary, Jovin was always smiling. That was something Caz could appreciate, for he had a penchant for often being too serious himself, as Rylla had pointed out. The thought of that conversation brought a laugh to his lips.

Elowen, despite her prior protestations, complied willingly as she sat atop Jovin's horse. Perhaps her ankle was hurting her worse than she let on.

They all took one last glance at the raging sea, the wind whipping about their hair and faces. Caz had enjoyed the ocean more than he had thought, but he was eager to be near the mountains. And most of all, he just wanted to find Rylla—he'd be content to never see the crashing waves again as long as he knew she was alive.

⸙ ⸙ ⸙

They had been riding through the trees for some time and Jovin was now walking alongside his horse, Elowen still sitting atop it and swaying in time with the motion of its hips. Caz still rode Rembrandt, but they were all moving at a much slower pace than before. To their left, the mountains loomed like dusty giants piercing the sky; the very tops were covered with snow, but the bottoms were dry and scattered with various plant life.

For miles, they'd been walking through a small forest which continued and stretched to their right, a canopy of trees above shadowing their path below. Countless speckled deer had dashed through the trees and a family of rabbits had disappeared into the mountains. Even a few snakes had slithered across their path and the horses reared to avoid them.

Their route around the base of the mountains wasn't all bad, but Caz wished he could have experienced the mountains in their fullest splendor by going through them. Staring at them wasn't enough. A low sort of muttering carried on the wind down the peaks, so soft he could be imagining it. Were the mountains calling out to him? Was it Rylla?

He slowed to a halt and focused his attention on the sound, Jovin and Elowen stopping just ahead of him. They gave him a look, but he held up his hand for silence. The murmurings grew louder and were turning into actual words.

“That blasted Henrick…find the prisoner…what’ll happen,” the voice drifted in and out of earshot, curt and quick. “Searched and…nothing!”

The voice was definitely a man’s and most assuredly not Rylla’s. And he seemed to be getting closer, for his sentences were now clearer.

“At least Gryff’s finally got the girl and the stones, that’s what the boss truly wanted anyway…” The voice trailed off again, but Caz realized that it was no longer coming from the mountains. It seemed to be coming from the forest path directly behind them.

The girl? The stones? He must be talking about Rylla. Caz’s mind spun like the wheels of a Sanddoon. He had to know for certain.

By this time, Jovin and Elowen had heard the voice as well. Caz wheeled Rembrandt and hurried him into the shadows of the trees, the other two right behind him. They stationed themselves a little way off but still close enough to the path to hear and see. Elowen crouched low on Cinders to peer through the dense trees.

The voice continued in its muttered monologue as a man walked along the path. He was clad in dark livery, had a sword hanging from his waist, and he was walking with a hesitant stride. He looked to be some sort of guard and somewhere in his early thirties.

“I’m going to talk to him.” Caz dismounted Rembrandt before his friends had a chance to stop him; he steadily approached the path, making sure to keep hidden amongst the tree trunks. The man was so close now.

“Yes, the girl will have to be enough…” the man muttered once more, but his speech was cut short. Caz burst confidently through the woods only paces away. The man’s eyes grew wide, as he drew his sword and faltered in his steps.

Caz drew his own sword in response, his jaw set. He'd unearth this man's secrets. Now.

"What do you want?" the guard bared a menacing scowl, but Caz was unmoved. He'd seen worse.

"I want to know who you've been talking about—this girl, who is she?" Caz wasted no time.

"Wouldn't you like to know…you some lovelorn halfwit?" The guard scoffed.

"Answer my question." Caz shifted his sword nearer the guard, narrowing his eyes. He wasn't actually planning on hurting the man, but if the man didn't realize that, it would be all the easier.

"I don't have to answer to you," the guard jeered back and slashed the air with his sword as if in warning, clearly thinking he had the upper hand. "Step any closer and I'll have your head."

"Tha' won't be necessary," Jovin said as he and Elowen emerged from the trees, his sword drawn and her bow at the ready.

The guard's eyes went wide and then he swallowed hard. He took a few steps back as he looked between the three of them, and then he was off running in the direction which he first came.

Jovin was after him in a second, catching him by his armor and tossing him backwards. His sword was knocked out of his hand and he landed sprawled on his back.

Caz walked over and pointed his own sword at, but not touching, the guard's throat.

"I'm not here to hurt you, I'm just here for some information," Caz said, his hand twitching on the hilt of his sword.

For all the guard's scowls and threatening words, he now had the humility to look frightened. He raised his hands by his head in surrender as he looked cross-eyed at the sword hovering above him.

"Wh-what information do you seek?"

"We heard you mumbling about a girl. Who is she?" Caz drew nearer, eager to hear his answer.

"I don't know who she is," he replied.

Caz brought the sword point even closer to the man's throat, challenging him to change his answer. "Try that again."

"No, honest! She never said her name," pleaded the guard, eyes wide.

"Where did you find her?" Caz inquired, heartbeat quickening.

"In the Ocean Basin. She'd capsized, and I was forced to retrieve her body from the water before this beast-thing tried to attack us! But she somehow made it go away—that's how we knew she was the one we were looking for," the guard spoke fast now, recalling every detail.

Caz's hunch was confirmed. "We? You speak of others when you're all alone," he challenged. The man had obviously found Rylla, but where had she been taken? And where was everyone else? As for *why* they took her, he could only guess it had something to do with her magic.

"There were five of us, including myself. But that monster ate Boufer, our prisoner ran away—never caught his name either, but Henrick is out looking for him."

"That still leaves one man unaccounted for." Caz narrowed his eyes. "Are you to tell me he has Rylla? Where is she?"

"Rylla, huh? A pretty name for a pretty—" The point of Caz's blade touched the man's skin and silenced him.

"I wouldn't finish that sentence if I were you." Caz didn't like the tone in the guard's voice. How dare he make sport of her beauty. He was half convinced he'd cut out the man's tongue if he tried that again.

"Okay, okay, just remove your sword," the guard croaked, trying not to move his head.

"Where is he taking her?" Caz asked again.

"I'm not supposed to say…"

Caz pressed the sword tip nearer, just enough to pinch the skin. He needed answers and any time wasted only lengthened the gap between him and Rylla.

"Okay, fine! He's taking her to the East Tower, but it's an arduous journey—you'll never find it yourself." The guard smirked at this.

"But that's why we have you," Caz responded.

The smirk dropped into a scowl.

Caz then turned to Jovin. "Do you have any rope in that saddle bag of yours? We need to ensure his captivity if he's to come with us."

In a matter of moments, Jovin had found some rope and bound the guard's wrists while Elowen had retrieved his fallen sword. He couldn't attack them even if he wanted to. Feeling the threat substantially minimized, Caz re-sheathed his sword and picked the guard up off the ground.

"Lead on, and if you dare lead us in the wrong direction, you and my sword will become better acquainted," Caz threatened. He didn't want to hurt the man, but Rylla's life was at stake. He'd do anything it took to protect her, and they had already wasted too much time.

They followed the guard through the forest, continuing on their path. The sun was beginning its descent, and in a couple of hours, it'd be nightfall.

⸙ ⸙ ⸙

Rylla was practically being hoisted up what she thought were rocks, but she couldn't see to be sure. Her ears were working twice as hard though, and she could tell they were somewhere near the coast from the crashing of waves echoing all about them. Where were they? She tried to envision her map and the various locations in Rélynda, but nothing was coming to mind.

Gryfinn continued to lead her forward; his hold on her arm was firm, though for all his verbal gruffness, he was no rougher than necessary. She was thankful for that at least.

"We're almost there," he said, a weird hitch in his voice. Was that some sort of remorse? Was he finally feeling bad for capturing her? Somehow that seemed the least likely of answers.

Rylla felt the ground level out below her feet as she was led forward at a slower pace than before. Was he reluctant to bring her here? Her toe hit a stone and she tripped, pitching forward, but Gryfinn's grip on her arm jerked her up so she couldn't fall on her face.

"That's the threshold. We're here," he spoke quietly. "Just a few more stairs."

Every step she took was a step closer to something bad, very bad indeed. She counted the steps, the minutes until she met her fate. Eventually they stopped their ascent and Gryfinn pounded on something—probably the door. Rusted hinges creaked and Gryfinn shuffled her onwards.

Where was she now? Rylla tried to steady her breathing. The back of her neck tingled like something sinister was lurking just beyond the burlap. Something was different about where she was; some dark magic coursed through the air. It made her skin prickle. She wanted more than anything to be able to see and assure herself all was well.

"Is this the girl?" a voice broke through the silence. It was unlike anything Rylla had ever heard before. Deep, dark, and gravelly, as if the rocks themselves were speaking.

Instantly her mind went to Lord Brennigan—was this him? Or was it Grievon? Someone else? Her heart pounded against her ribs and she felt it would plummet into her stomach.

"Ye-yes, my lord," Gryfinn replied, though Rylla could tell he was nervous.

"And the stones?" the dark voice spoke again.

"Here, my lord."

"Well, what are you waiting for, you blithering imbecile? Give them to me!" the voice raised in impatience.

Gryfinn finally loosened his hold and left her side. He must be approaching whoever was speaking and giving him the stones she had worked so hard to collect. Her stomach clenched into a knot at the thought.

Gryfinn returned to her side once more, holding her upper arm as an eerie silence filled the room. Tension crackled almost audibly, and the air was a thick fog in her lungs.

"There's only two—you were supposed to get three," the voice came out cool and flat.

"My lord? But I did bring you three…you have them there in your hand."

"There's only two and you were supposed to get three!" the voice roared.

"I don't understand, my lord," Gryfinn croaked, seeming to cower beside Rylla.

"Don't understand? You've given me a blasted Sunstone instead of the Larimar!" the man yelled and Rylla heard something shatter on the ground. Was that Garth's Sunstone?

"Per-perhaps she never found the Larimar, my lord," Gryfinn suggested nervously.

Rylla silently thanked him for that.

"You dare suggest I'm a blind fool? What do you make of this?" the man yelled again, obviously gesturing to something Rylla couldn't see.

Gryfinn's hold on her arm tightened, and Rylla was left to wonder how this man knew the stone was missing.

"I…have no idea how that can be true, my lord. She only had these stones when we found her in the water," Gryfinn replied.

"Either you're too idiotic to see that she's lying to you or someone else found the stone. My guess is the first one!" His anger was as palpable as a knife, but even more deadly. "And speaking of 'we', where are the rest of my men? And the prisoner? Did you fail to bring them back too?"

Gryfinn's silence spoke louder than words.

"I see. You have failed me, Gryfinn. You showed loyalty, but you've botched it for good. You've toed a fine line with me, and your utter stupidity and folly have now sent you to the dungeons where you'll rot for the remainder of your days. You don't deserve to wear that stone upon your neck!" the man yelled. Movement rustled and Gryfinn gasped next to her. Was his stone just taken?

"Guards!" the man bellowed loudly as he reclaimed his seat and Rylla felt men move in around her to take hold of Gryfinn.

"My lord, please—I can try again. Give me another chance!" Gryfinn pleaded.

"Take him away," the command came much quieter now, but Gryfinn's pleas echoed all along the corridor.

Finally they faded, and in the silence that remained, Rylla felt that the angry man was studying her.

"Guards, remove her mask, but leave her bonds. I'd like to know what I'm dealing with here."

Movement shuffled again and the suffocating cage of burlap was pulled free. Sudden exposure to the light sent Rylla's eyes screaming as she gasped in a breath of air through the rope covering her mouth. The guard before her pushed back her hood, but left her hands bound and her mouth gagged.

Her eyes adjusted. She could see! Rylla felt strangely light as she looked about the room, but when her eyes found the man before her, her breath was snatched away like she was being suffocated all over again.

Dark veins snaked out from his eyes, tracing spider webs across his skin. His eyes were practically black holes, a Darkness so deep and bottomless that when Rylla looked into them, she felt as if she were falling in the ores all over again.

"Ah, a pretty one, if not a bit on the scrawny side. I am Lord Brennigan—welcome to my fortress." Lord Brennigan forced a smile, but it looked more like a scowl.

So, this *was* him. This was the man she was sent to defeat.

Rylla stared at Lord Brennigan on his throne, silent. He reeked of pompous pride and a power unmatched. His long fingers clutched around the stones like he would never let them go again.

"Enough with formalities. You're the supposed Earth-Treader who's been stealing *my* stones." Lord Brennigan leaned back in his seat, studying her disapprovingly.

Rylla shifted her feet and tried looking away but found that it was rather difficult. When she finally pulled her gaze away, her eyes rested on gilded picture frames which hung along one wall. They were all empty save for one—where a blurry photo of a green stone was displayed. *Curious*.

"My magicked mirrors. Yes, they are one of a kind. They help me keep track of my stones," Lord Brennigan boasted. "You see, once a stone has been found and touched by human hands, it disappears from the frame—I am thus lost to it. But I know it means it'll soon be in my possession, like Rélynda's and now these two here."

Rylla blanched, her heart dropping. Had he found Rélynda's stone?

"Ah, you didn't know." Lord Brennigan smirked. "Yes, Gryfinn found it a few weeks ago. The only good he *has* done." He fingered the stones in his grasp. "All that's left, it appears, is Aylati's Jade and the Larimar from the Isles…" At this, Lord Brennigan leaned forward in his seat, his eyes searching Rylla's. "But you've seen the Larimar, haven't you? I can see it in your eyes. It was your hands which filched it from my frame."

Rylla simply stared back, fear wreaking havoc on all her nerves. He'd already found Rélynda's stone. And so much for Moo's advice on pretending the Larimar was still on the Isles. This cruel overlord knew the truth. The more Rylla tried to figure out some sort of solution, the more she wished Moo was nearby to give her comfort and council. Where was he?

"I can see Gryfinn was telling the truth about one thing—you don't have the Larimar on you. But you *have* touched it. Gryfinn's folly lies in not searching the island himself!" Lord Brennigan spat on the ground. "I'll send another recruit to the Isles tonight and soon those searching Aylati will find the Jade and bring it to me. Then I'll have all five stones in my possession. By the time the sun sets tomorrow and rises the next, this earth shall finally know true power." Lord Brennigan seethed in euphoric fury.

"Guards, throw her in the dungeons with Gryfinn! She can rot alongside the other Earth-Treaders. If she gives you any trouble, kill her!" Lord Brennigan commanded.

Two guards came and grabbed Rylla by the arms before she could even think to struggle. No, this couldn't be happening. Not when she'd come so far and gotten so close.

She was to receive the same fate as Gryfinn. She was going to die. She had once thought Gryfinn was cruel, but he was nothing compared to Lord Brennigan.

As she was marched down the narrow steps, leading into the dimly lit bowels of the tower, all Rylla could think about were her family and friends. Would she ever see her parents again? Would she ever have a chance to find Finn? What about Caz? And where *was* Moo? She didn't want to believe it, but perhaps he had abandoned her long ago.

Finally, the guards led her deep enough and stopped in front of a large iron door. There was another set of stairs on her left which seemed to go down further, and she wondered where to. Weren't the dungeons usually on the bottom floor?

One of the guards fumbled with some keys, and fitted one into the lock. He opened the door, a waft of something unpleasant and most assuredly human reaching Rylla's nose. She tried to focus her breathing into shallow breaths, but bile rose in her throat despite her efforts. A recurring theme as of late.

The guards seemed unfazed by the stench as they led her through a dim hallway lined with many cells, their booted feet tapping against the stone floor. Rylla could see young and old alike within the cells, bound and gagged like her, groveling on their knees and withering away in their own waste and filth, their eyes pleading for food or something to drink. Rylla felt sicker than any odor could make her, silently vowing to free these people if she ever got the chance.

Eventually the guards stopped at an empty cell and threw her in. She was thrust against a stone wall, her legs buckling beneath her as her own weight became too much to carry. She fell to her knees as the lock clicked back into place audibly. The guards were out of the dungeons as quickly as they had arrived.

Rylla's head spun with the awful fumes and the weight upon her heart. Why were Earth-Treaders so feared? Lord Brennigan was imprisoning them unjustly, and though Fang had told her as such, she didn't know the harsh reality until she experienced it herself. This must be stopped.

And then out of nowhere, a sharp gasp caught her attention. A cry of disbelief came from the cell next to hers—a familiar voice.

"No, it can't be!"

Chapter the Twenty-Ninth

Aid From the Enemy

Full darkness had blotted out the blue of the sky, and the guard, Gorvo, was tripping on the ground in front of him. Whether he actually couldn't see or was trying to buy himself time, Caz was beginning to see the reason in stopping for some rest. Even the horses were moving slower, and Elowen was growing irritable. They could begin again at first light. As much as he hated stopping, it would be wise if they'd found a place to sleep.

"Quit your tripping, Gorvo, we should all rest for the night," Caz said to the guard, a few paces ahead of him.

Jovin was holding onto the rope tied to Gorvo's wrists, so despite this mock freedom, he couldn't go far.

"I'll find a spot where we ca' make camp," Jovin volunteered, and he gave the rope to Caz and disappeared in the woods.

Gorvo seemed both relieved and smug that his plan had worked, but Caz wasn't so ready to make him believe he had the upper hand.

"Make sure you find a sturdy tree for our prisoner!" Caz hollered in Jovin's direction, his eyes still on Gorvo.

The man's snide smile faltered.

Jovin returned in a few minutes and led them off the path and through the dense foliage of the surrounding trees. By the time everyone was settled, the horses secured, and Gorvo securely tied to the base of a hearty pine, Elowen had a fire going.

"You know, I've grown up in these lands, but I haven't the slightest clue where the East Tower is," she said amidst the dancing flames. "If I did, we wouldn't need to answer to him." She gestured to the tree where Gorvo was tied, obviously not liking the fact that he was watching them all very closely. "I wonder if Rylla's being taken to Kytchidell, my home village."

Caz, Jovin, and Elowen were grouped around the fire in a half moon, sitting on their backsides with their feet and hands stretched toward the warmth.

"Is there an East Tower in Kytchidell?" Caz questioned.

"Not that I know of," Elowen replied.

"'ow can we be sure 'e's even takin' us ta the right place? What if the East Tower doesn't exist?" Jovin chimed in, voicing Caz's fear.

Caz had been racking his brain over that thought for the last few hours. He believed Gorvo was telling the truth about a tower, but maybe its name was just unknown.

"What lies in the east of Rélynda?" he asked Elowen.

She paused to think, the firelight flickering off her hair. Caz wished he could see it dancing in Rylla's dark curls and along her freckled cheeks. He wanted more than anything to touch those cheeks and feel the soft skin beneath his fingertips, if she would have him that is.

"Just the cliffs," Elowen replied.

"Cliffs?" Caz questioned, trying to refocus his thoughts.

"The Cliffs of Cavalcade—they say that when the waves crash against the rocks, it sounds like a stampede of horses. I've been a few times as a young girl, but I can't seem to remember much. Only that it was quite the hike when my legs were half the size they are now. They're just mounds of rock overlooking the Great Blue."

"Was there any sort of tower there by chance?"

"My parents never let Mari and I venture too far for fear of falling over the edge, so I never got the chance to explore." Elowen's brows furrowed and she seemed to be searching her memory.

Caz grew silent, watching Jovin poke a stick in the fire as Elowen stared into its flames. No one knew what to say; all their hopes rested on the success and loyalty of their guard. Would Gorvo lead them astray?

Caz shifted restlessly. He needed some time to think. He got up and stretched his legs before speaking, "I'll take the first watch. You two get some sleep, I'm going to keep our prisoner company."

The two nodded and Jovin patted him on the back, then Caz parted from his friends.

Hopefully they could rest; his mind was racing with too many thoughts to get any sleep himself, though he was sure it would catch up to him by morning. In the meantime, he had a few more questions for Gorvo that couldn't wait.

The guard was snoring faintly as Caz approached. The man had been awake only moments before, so the fact that he was now asleep seemed rather unlikely. Caz nudged him with his foot and the man's eyes opened instantly.

“Can’t a man get some rest?” Gorvo spoke up in the darkness, his eyes alert.

“We both know you weren’t resting,” Caz replied as he sat down next to the guard.

Gorvo’s hands were still tied and his torso was sufficiently strapped to the tree. There was no way he could escape.

“Worth a try anyway,” Gorvo sneered. “What do you want with me?”

“I want nothing to do with you,” Caz answered. “I want to know who took Rylla and where.”

“Ah, a man in love—how pitiful,” Gorvo scoffed, yet there was something in his tone that betrayed an element of pain.

“A man in love at least has a heart. You, I’m not so sure about.” Caz withdrew the knife from his boot and began turning it in his fingers. He watched as the flames from the fire reflected in the metal; Gorvo’s eyes were trained on it. “Though I wonder if your disdain of love has actually been wrought by a broken heart.” It was a shot in the dark, but something told Caz he was touching upon some truth.

“You know nothing.” Gorvo’s eyes widened for a moment, then narrowed again, shock and anger conflicted in his gaze. He seemed to be figuring out which emotion he wanted to hold onto.

“I’d wager you’ve lost someone you loved, though I don’t know how long ago. But someone you cared about…” Caz pressed on as he stared at his knife.

The guard was silent and the permanent sneer went away, his face growing somber instead. “Almost a year,” he whispered so softly in the dark, it was almost inaudible.

"What happened?" Caz asked. Finding Rylla might depend on him having this conversation, so he pressed on.

"I was promised a steady job, a way to make a living, and she rejected me." Gorvo sighed. "That's why love is pitiful and women are nothing but wolves in sheep's clothing."

"What job?" Caz ignored the rest.

Gorvo hesitated, the same hesitation Caz had witnessed earlier when Gorvo had been coming up the path in the woods hours before.

"He'd have my tongue if I uttered a word," Gorvo muttered, looking away.

"Surely he won't know about this conversation…"

"Well if I bring you to him, he will. He'll not only have my tongue, he'll have my head!"

Caz took in these words, the dagger stilling. "So, you weren't planning on bringing us to Rylla at all…I should have known." This was turning out to be more aggravating than he thought. Caz slumped back, leaning on the tree next to Gorvo's, feeling defeated. How was he to get to Rylla? It could take days to scour all of Rélynda, and it might not even amount to anything.

"Look, I know you want to save the girl, but it's not wise. You're walking into an early grave. Trust me, if one isn't absolutely loyal, Lord Bre—blast." Gorvo's face flushed, and he clamped his lips shut.

"Lord Brennigan?" Caz ran a hand over his face. Rylla had been right, not like he had doubted her. "He hired you?"

Gorvo, obviously realizing he had nothing else to hide, nodded. "He promised me freedom and wealth and was the first one to warn me from the dangers of devotion. He said it would only lead to heartache, that any kind of love would always stab you in the back—seems he was right."

Caz's head spun. He was still getting over the fact that Lord Brennigan was alive. He thought back to the conversation he'd had with Rylla on the ship, about the stones and how she was being hunted by two power-hungry men. It was all happening too fast.

And now he was talking with this guard who had been with Lord Brennigan face to face.

"No, he's not," Caz rebutted.

"Excuse me?"

"Love can lead to heartache, yes, but not always. Lord Brennigan's been feeding you only half truths."

"What makes you the expert on love? *You* can't even keep the girl you love from running away," Gorvo countered.

Caz's mouth opened but no words came out.

The guard saw the look of shock on Caz's face and some of his original sneer returned. "That's right, I heard that Elowen girl mention that this girl of yours left you in the dust after you'd butchered everything. You're a fool."

The words affected Caz more than he wanted to let on. It was true, he hadn't been able to stop Rylla from running away, but then again, he hadn't really tried.

"You're right, I am a fool. I made a mistake, but I'm determined to never make it again. That's why I'm going after her," Caz responded. "And if you truly loved this girl who left you, you'd go after her too. And if she doesn't want you anyway, then at least you tried."

Gorvo had the decency to look ashamed.

"What if she doesn't want to see me again?" he questioned, doubt warring with hope. "I'm not even sure if she lives in the same place anymore."

"If you don't try, I think you'll always wonder. Besides, you don't know why she ran away in the first place," Caz replied.

"You have a point."

"Why don't we make a deal—you take us to Rylla safely, and I promise to help you find your lady once all this madness is over." Caz continued to rotate the small blade in his fingers.

Gorvo seemed to consider this. He was silent for a few moments before he spoke. "Lord Brennigan will have my skin if I lead you to him. He'll throw me in the dungeon or kill me on the spot…" He paused, and finally a bold smile spread across his face. "But I'd like to see him try."

"Does this mean you're in agreement?" Caz asked, his heart filled with anticipation.

"I guess it does," Gorvo replied.

Caz was both shocked and relieved that his plan had worked. But if Gorvo and him were to be in agreement over this deal, Gorvo had to be treated like an equal. It was only fair. Caz bent down and used his dagger to file away at his bonds.

As the ropes dropped to the ground, Gorvo looked up in astonishment, clearly not having expected this.

"But I haven't even brought you to her yet," Gorvo said.

"I know. But we're on the same side now." Caz sheathed his dagger and placed it back in his boot. "Setting you free now shows promise that I'll keep my word. And if you haven't left by morning, then I know I can trust you to uphold your end of the bargain as well."

Caz walked away, weariness tugging at him finally. The conversation had drained him. Either he was a blithering lunatic for setting Gorvo free, or he was a hopeful fool for trusting in the enemy, but he knew what it was like being a puppet in a place of power, of working against one's will for someone that neither respected people nor themselves. Perhaps he had just given Gorvo a chance to hope again, a chance to change his life around if he wanted to.

Caz lay down near the dying flames, and he felt himself drifting off to sleep. Try as he might, he couldn't keep his heavy eyes open much longer.

He could only hope Gorvo would still be there in the morning.

⸙ ⸙ ⸙

The sun filtered through the trees in patches of light, covering the ground like a spotted blanket. Birds tweeted their morning songs overhead, flying from branch to branch while the bunnies and squirrels were out scavenging for food on the ground. It was a peaceful morning; the earth was awake while its human inhabitants were still slumbering.

A loud whinny from Rembrandt shook Caz from his sleep; it had been dreamless and calm, unlike most nights. As Caz registered his surroundings, he quickly shot up from the ground. He accidentally knocked Jovin who rolled over and accidentally kicked Elowen. They both woke, groaning loudly, and didn't look too thrilled.

"We overslept!" Caz was on his feet and tightening the girth on Rembrandt's saddle. He double checked the stirrups and pulled on the saddle bags to make sure they were secure. "We need to get going now."

Elowen let out a cry, and Caz stopped, turning quickly. She was pointing in the direction of the tree Gorvo had been tied to.

Caz's heart plummeted; he'd almost forgotten what he'd done last night.

"That horrible guard escaped!" Elowen fumed.

"'ow's that possible? I took 'is sword…unless—" Jovin strode over beside her.

"Unless what?" Elowen tugged her bow closer to her body and made sure her quiver was securely on her back.

"Per'aps 'e was 'idin' another weapon," Jovin suggested.

"I knew having him around was only trouble. He could have stolen *our* weapons or slit our throats in our sleep!" Elowen walked over to the discarded rope and frowned. "These cuts look too clean though. His hands were bound pretty tight, so how could he have done this?"

"I did it," Caz spoke up.

Elowen spun to face him, eyes wide.

"You set that imbecile free?" She walked over to him, jabbing her finger at his chest.

Jovin held her back by her shoulders.

"I'm not accusin' yeh, brothur, unlike this one 'ere, but why'd yeh do it?" Jovin asked. "I thought 'e was our ticket ta Rylla."

"I am," another voice spoke from behind them. "I hope you don't mind my showing up late, I was just relieving myself."

Caz breathed a sigh of relief. So he hadn't made a huge mistake after all.

Elowen turned to Gorvo. "Showing up? You were supposed to be with us this whole time! Caz, why is he free?" She looked back and forth between Gorvo and Caz.

"We made a deal. He promised to get us safely to Rylla and I offered to help him in return. I freed him because he's no longer our enemy," Caz returned. He wouldn't feel guilty about this; it was the right choice to make. If his friends didn't understand now, he only hoped they would in time.

"Fine, whatever. But I don't want him anywhere near me." Elowen threw her hands in the air in exasperation and moved to Cinders' side.

"She'll get over it soon, she always does." Jovin smirked, then leaned closer to Caz and spoke more quietly, "What 'bout 'is sword? Surely yeh want me to 'old onta it."

"As our ally, he is to be treated fairly. The sword belongs to him," Caz responded.

Jovin shrugged. "All right, brothur." He took the extra sword from his waist and walked over to Gorvo. He paused in front of the guard and held it out to him. "I believe this belongs ta yeh." He stopped as Gorvo grabbed onto the hilt. "I trust yeh'll use it right."

"You have my word," Gorvo replied.

"Great, looks like we're all on the same side. Gorvo, how much farther?" Caz asked.

"We should arrive in a couple of hours, I'd wager."

"Let's head out then." Caz gripped Rembrandt's bridle while Jovin grabbed Cinders' who was already carrying Elowen.

"All right, follow my lead," Gorvo instructed as he fitted his sword about his waist and moved in front of everyone.

Finally, something on this awful journey was going right. Only a few more hours and they'd reach Rylla, then Caz would never leave her again if she would forgive him.

Chapter the Thirtieth

Gryfinn

Rylla's cell was dimly lit, but the one next to hers was encased in shadow. She could tell the voice had come from that general direction, but she didn't know who had spoken.

"Is it truly you?" the voice asked again, and shuffling movements drew nearer. The voice sounded like Gryfinn's, but without a face, it felt strangely ominous. She knew he was down here, but why would he be so shocked to see her again?

She braced herself for the drawn hood, the featureless face like she had glimpsed on the ship, the angry tone with the injustice from being thrown in prison.

What she didn't expect was to see someone she knew staring back at her, dark eyes intense and lined with concern.

His fingers gripped the bars in front of him as he peered into her cell, face lined in shadows. "It's me, don't you remember?" His eyes searched hers. "What are you doing here?"

She couldn't forget this face even if she had tried. But how could this be? How did he end up here after all these years? And did he not realize he was the one to bring her here in the first place? Rylla wanted to scream and ask a million questions all at once, yet she was still gagged, and her hands were tied behind her back. All she could make were muffled noises that couldn't amount to anything.

"Come closer so I can remove your bonds," he said.

Rylla wasn't sure if she could trust him fully, but being able to move and speak again was a freedom she couldn't pass up. As she edged closer, his hands reached through the bars and undid both the gag and the rope around her wrists. She was free.

She breathed in deeply and instantly regretted it. The air was rancid and stale, and her stomach churned. But that was the least of her worries. What was *he* doing here?

She turned to face him. How could she have been so blind to not recognize him earlier? But she hadn't seen his face, nor had he seen hers, and the version on the ship had been so dark and mean, cruel and commanding—not the boy she knew as a child.

"Finn?" Rylla whispered.

"It's been a while since I've gone by that name," he responded with a short laugh, bitterness twisting the sound. It faded quickly and he grew serious again, his expression made of stone. "I've almost forgotten it…" He seemed to get lost in thought and then looked at her again. "What are you doing here, Rylla? This is no place for a girl such as yourself."

"What's that supposed to mean? If this is no place for 'a girl such as myself', then why did you bring me here at all?" Irritation swelled in her chest. She had finally found Finn, or he had found her, and he was proving to be just as difficult as Garth. Were her brothers always this troubling?

"Wait, how did I…no…" Finn's eyes widened. "The ship? The Earth-Treader girl? That was you?" He looked like he had just swallowed something cold and bitter. He reached for the space below his neck, but his fingers grasped at nothing, and his eyes grew wider in fear. Desperation.

"Yes, thank you very much." Sarcasm drenched Rylla's voice, confusion her heart. "Why did you do it?"

"My stone…it's gone!" Finn fumbled again for the stone that had hung around his neck, seeming to suddenly remember that Lord Brennigan had taken it. He appeared to be perspiring even in the coolness of the dungeon, his breaths ragged and shortened. His head pressed against the bars. "I feel as though…I'm suffocating. No oxygen—my power…"

"Finn, what's gotten ahold of you?" Rylla shook the bars of his cell, rattling him from his muttering. A look of rage passed across his face as fleeting as a swift sparrow and in its place was left a dejected and troubled expression.

"Finn?" Rylla backed away, a tremble shuddering through her.

"I need my stone back, I'm nothing without it," his voice was low and shallow. "Rylla, I…"

Rylla thought back to the crimson stone she had seen on the ship both in and outside of her dreams. Finn must have been wearing it for some time now and it had only recently been snatched off his neck by Lord Brennigan himself. That stone. And the more Finn complained about not having it, the more certain Rylla was that he should never touch it again.

"It's poisoned your mind, Finn. Whatever it's promised you, it's all lies laced in truth…a sort of binding magic." Rylla remembered what Fang had told her about these kinds of stones—the kind the Earth-Lore said were to be avoided at all costs, those dark in their intent. She only knew of Lord Brennigan's Bloodstone, but now she was convinced this crimson stone was cut from the same cloth. "It was a good thing he took it away!" Rylla said, though she had a feeling it was taken for other purposes than freeing Finn's mind.

Finn's head appeared to have cleared, if only for the moment, as his breathing began to steady. "Rylla, I never meant to harm you." He seemed too ashamed to look her in the eyes, staring at the floor before her.

"I think I know that now, but why did you leave Garth? He's been worried sick over you!"

Finn's head snapped up. At the mention of Garth, a new sharpness came into Finn's eyes, a look of jealousy mixed with pain. Again, he reached for the spot where his stone once rested. Empty. "I wasn't to be his burden, Rylla. I could handle being on my own fine enough."

"Yes, you've definitely proven that by getting yourself locked up in prison and by having your soul sucked clean from a blasted stone!" Rylla retaliated.

"You'll never understand. I've lived in his shadow long enough. I wanted to create my own path and find *my* purpose—something I was good at, not another one of Garth's understudies," Finn spoke quickly, as if recollecting his past all at once.

"Finn, you've fled your supposed shadows only to fly into deeper ones! You've been seeking a power you already possess, but at the hands of a cruel, cruel man. It's ludicrous!" Rylla felt like she was looking into the eyes of someone she no longer knew, just a distant memory of what once was. "And you've captured me in the process."

"It wasn't supposed to be this way—I didn't realize *you* were the one he was after…the one with…" Finn paused, and his eyes grew wide once more, but this time in sudden realization.

"With the Earth-Treader magic?" Rylla asked. "The race of people Lord Brennigan is wiping from this earth and has been for the past five-hundred years? No, I'm sure you didn't. You just went along with his nefarious schemes without any consideration for the truth." Rylla had always spoken her mind around her brothers, but usually about silly things. There was nothing funny about their situation now, and she wanted more than anything for Finn to get that through his head.

"What truth, Rylla? Earth-Treaders are dangerous and have been destroying the kingdoms for as long as can be remembered," Finn protested. "And you're one of them!"

Rylla stared at him, opened mouthed. Just how deep did Lord Brennigan's lies run? "Yes, I am one of them, but you've got it wrong. The Earth-Treader's purpose has and always will be to keep peace and protect the kingdoms. We aren't to be feared. Lord Brennigan's the one who needs to be stopped, not us!" Would he even listen to her defense, or was his heart too twisted already? Rylla felt that no matter how much she spoke, she wouldn't be able to get through to him. But she had to try.

"Grrrrughhh! This is too confusing!" Finn yelled in agony, gripping his shirt where the stone used to be. He disappeared back into the shadows, cries of exasperation escaping his lips.

There were several thuds and a flurry of dust danced in the air—he must have kicked the ground or walls in his helpless confusion. Finn groaned like a wounded animal, begging to be put out from its misery.

Was he okay? Had he hurt himself? "Finn?" Rylla drew nearer.

After some time, he returned to the light, his eyes were red and rimmed with tears. She'd never seen Finn this broken, but maybe he'd felt this broken for a long time but never showed it.

Rylla felt a place in her heart crack at seeing her brother like this. She couldn't fault him entirely—she knew the power the kingdoms' stone crests had over others, the power they had over her. Even though they were "good" stones, they were still dangerous. Perhaps there wasn't much difference between the good and bad stones after all—they all possessed a power, just of a different kind. It would take the strongest of men, a god-like strength, to overcome their pull. Perhaps she and her brother were more alike than she realized.

"I can't see straight—like I'm seeing through a cloud…" Finn whispered, rubbing his eyes. "So heavy…" He slumped to the ground, his head leaning against the iron bars and his chest heaving with ragged breaths.

A wave of nausea hit Rylla's middle. Yes, her brother had made a grave mistake, but how much was entirely his fault? Lord Brennigan had played on his weakness and had fed him lies that would fester his wounds. Finn was a product of manipulation, and seeing him so weak sent a shiver down her spine. Her heart plummeted in her stomach as she sat against the bars near him.

"Finn, if it helps, I've already forgiven you." She didn't know where this came from, but she knew in her heart she had.

"But what are we to do? I've brought you to him. He has the stones he needs, and he's bent on finding the other two. It's only a matter of time until he marches on all the kingdoms and destroys anything that stands in his way. I've heard murmurings, things in the dark—he's planning something, I just don't know what…" Finn shivered.

Rylla's heart raced. Is this what Lord Brennigan had meant when he said the kingdoms would finally know true power? Was he going to march on them with some hidden army? That meant her parents back in Aylati, Fang in the Grove, Garth and Mari and the kids in Wyllund, the suffering Uwan in his cave, her friends back on the Isles, Caz—the holder of her heart, and Moo, wherever he was. They and countless others were all going to perish because she had failed her mission. She had lost everything.

"We need to stop him." Rylla heard the words but was surprised to hear them coming from Finn instead of herself. He raised his head, and though his eyes narrowed in pain, there was a new determination in them.

"But how?" Rylla wanted to believe she could fix this, but like her dream of flying, it was near to impossible. Though Uwan told her Earth-Treaders could use the wind currents to fly, it was a skill only a few could master and required years of experience. She had a long way to go. And defeating Lord Brennigan would be even harder.

"You have your magic. I saw a glimpse of it on the ship, but show me how it's supposed to work—how it's used for good," Finn prodded.

"I don't know if I can…" Doubts warred in her mind.

"Please…" Finn whispered, the look of desperation in his eyes haunting her.

After a few moments, Rylla nodded.

She felt a fluttering against her ribs when she realized what she had to do. But it wouldn't be easy, and it would take some planning. She had acted irrationally before, had almost buried people alive, but not this time.

This time she would free herself and Finn. And she would free all the prisoners. She couldn't wait for Moo now, there was no time.

⸙ ⸙ ⸙

His short legs moved as fast as they could, dodging holes and rocks, bounding over streams and fallen logs. He was almost there, almost through the last remaining tendrils of the Heather Fields. He had made the mistake of crossing the fields too slowly once. Now, he wasn't taking any chances as he bolted faster than he'd ever run before. He could see the enchanted Darkness looming in the distance, but it seemed preoccupied with something else. He didn't stop running though—he only stopped once his feet were touching grass and he was standing in front of a very large elm.

He didn't even take time to catch his breath before addressing the tree. "My lord, my lord, are you currently inhabiting your abode?" Moo panted.

The Great Owl peered out from behind some leaves, its large silver eye observing the ground. Then he stepped out onto a branch and puffed up his feathers.

"Hoo, hoo, hoo, how delightful to be granted this pleasure, and so soon, young squire. But I must inquire, what it is you seek, for you appear in great haste! To have traversed through the formidable heather proves that resolve!" The owl brought its head lower as it waited for a response.

"Yes, my lord, you are astute. I am in dire need of assistance. Rylla has been captured and taken into Rélynda, bound and gagged," Moo spoke earnestly. "I fear I may not be able to rely solely on my skills to free her. Her captors mentioned word about a stone tower—I came to seek your guidance on this matter. Something Dark is brewing, though I know nothing of its strength." Moo bowed.

"Taw, taw, taw, do you know what inhabits that very stone tower in Rélynda?" The barred owl paused and waited, though for dramatic effect. "Lord Brennigan himself!" the owl hooted loudly and flapped his wings.

Other birds nearby fluttered off their branches, startled by the outburst.

"My lord, how did you come by this knowledge? Could we have been forewarned?" Moo inquired, feeling himself grow weak in the limbs. Poor Rylla. And he had left her to face the overlord alone.

"'Tis information I only recently acquired. You see, not too long before you traversed this way, a man, haggard and torn, came stumbling through my very forest and carried onwards toward Ostglenden. How he escaped the Heather Fields alive is beyond my knowledge, but his eyes beheld a hidden goal—one I determined to unearth," the owl hooted again and leaned forward.

"Thus, I followed him to Ostglenden's throne. He rattled the portcullis only to find King Grievon out of doors and astride his charger. I perched on a nearby ash, close enough to heed and far enough to remain hid, and I unearthed his goal.

"He spoke of his capture and of your Lady Rylla, though her name was unknown to him. He recalled his imprisonment in a stone tower, a location so dark and dank, and inhabited by none other than Lord Brennigan himself. Hoo-hoo-hoo, you can quite imagine the look on Grievon's countenance upon hearing such insight." The owl made noises which sounded like laughter.

"What did you do afterward? Pray tell," Moo beseeched, struggling to keep impatience from his voice. Worry for Rylla cramped in his stomach.

"Before I was homeward bound, I heard the haggard man, who I soon learned was named Bryant, tell Grievon he presumes Lord Brennigan is constructing an army, and that he plans on claiming sole power over our kingdoms. Roo, roo, roo! The nerve! Grievon became so disgruntled, he began gathering his men at once!" The owl puffed out his feathers.

"What might this mean?" Moo questioned.

"That all that's beautiful and green will turn to ash. That the sun will no longer shine upon a fruitful land, instead it will shine where there's but naught a sprout to grow. Humankind may cease to exist as it does presently, and all that remains will be a corruption darker than our lands have ever known. The Darkness will rise, perhaps in more ways than one."

"We must stop this at once, my lord!" Moo felt it as deeply as he knew he needed to rescue his friend. "But Rylla must be found first!"

"In time, young squire. My silver eye pierces through the darkest of shrouds—your Lady Rylla will be well. But our help she will still need, and others included. The sky is gathering its stars now, however. Stay for this night, and on the morrow we will fly to find them," the owl said.

"Fly? Them?" Moo didn't like what he was hearing, and he was more confused than ever.

"It appears you will be receiving your second ride in the air, young squire. Hoo-hoo-hoo, I suggest you get some slumber." The Great Owl laughed as he retreated into the shadows of the branches.

"Them? My lord?" Moo asked again, but the owl still hadn't answered his question and Moo had a feeling he never would. Instead, Moo sat at the base of the elm and contemplated his situation.

Had he done the right thing by coming here? He hoped Rylla wouldn't hate him for leaving, and that she would understand why he left. He didn't have a silver eye that could pierce through shrouds of Darkness like the owl, but he too felt like something big was going to happen. And it was beyond anything he or Rylla could handle on their own.

⸙ ⸙ ⸙

It was sometime in the night when Moo heard footsteps and hoofbeats. They were loud and many and thundered through the trees. Moo lifted his head to observe his surroundings, peeking through his warm covering of fallen leaves.

Hundreds, possibly thousands, of soldiers crept through the trees, moving north. They moved like shifting shadows against the backdrop of the moon, plowing through the heather both on horseback and on foot like a force to be reckoned with. How many troops would actually make it through those wicked fields alive? Moo had heard the Heather Fields were most active at night, searching for souls to feast upon. Some cries echoed in the distance and the cold presence of the Darkness reached even to the elm tree. But still, the soldiers pressed on.

Moo wanted to get up and go—these men were marching toward Rylla and he couldn't just stand by and watch. The last of the soldiers filtered through the trees, followed by a man in extravagant robes sitting atop a large white charger. He sat pompously on his horse, stroking his beard idly, like he wasn't embarking on some sinister mission of war.

Moo's insides recoiled, and he felt he very much wouldn't mind clawing at his robes and shortening his beard to a few hairs. Moo got up, about to act on his instincts, when a voice caught his attention.

"Not now, young squire. They are beginning a battle in which our time has not yet come. It would be folly to follow in haste. Wait out the night, for the dawn will make it all the clearer." The barred owl had alighted on a branch closest to Moo, stopping him in his tracks.

"You must understand, my lord, it takes everything in me to heed your instruction. It's against my very nature to remain stagnant and wait." Moo's tail twitched as he paced the base of the tree. Was Rylla okay? Where was she now?

"Understood, but you must if you wish your Lady Rylla to survive." The owl ruffled his feathers again, spreading his large wings wide. "Now, if you'll excuse me, I am off to hunt—it's against my very nature to remain hungry."

With that, the Great Owl flew into the night sky and Moo watched as the last glimpse of Grievon and his men disappeared through the heather.

If only waiting were easier. The dawn couldn't come soon enough.

Chapter the Thirty-First

Earth-Lore

How long had they been planning? It was a slow process with Finn relapsing into angry spurts, clutching at his neck, and saying that he was going blind. Each time Rylla tried to console him, reminding him of what happened and where he was. Would the stone's poison always be a part of her brother?

These were thoughts she'd have to confront later. Right now, they needed to get out and rescue as many people as they could, and to do that she needed Finn's knowledge of the tower.

Though she craved freedom, Rylla's stomach twisted into a knot at the thought of leaving the safety of her cell to go into the unknowns of the stone fortress. What if she was caught? Then she'd end up back where she started and so would everyone else. What other dangers lurked in the shadows and the gathering Darkness? Surely there was Lord Brennigan, but even he was still a mystery. So many things left to the unknown! At least if she stayed in her cell, there would be no surprises. But hadn't she felt the same way about leaving her house in the first place?

Back in the Grove, Fang had suggested that Rylla was holding herself back more than her parents were, and perhaps he'd been right. For the sake of keeping her family sane and together, she had silently vowed to stay home and fill the void of her missing brothers, her parent's fears of letting her go only driving that point further. But maybe it had been her fear all along that kept her from moving forward. Wasn't she feeling the same way now?

It wasn't until Caz had inadvertently forced her to flee her home that she had finally been able to break away and taste the freedom her soul craved. She could see now that though the journey had been a difficult one and was far from over, leaving had done some good, for she had found both her brothers, and perhaps she was learning to find herself.

Rylla felt now, more than ever, that she'd been spared an utter folly from having returned home prematurely. She was going to free the other Earth-Treaders, and she *would* complete her mission. She needed to go, wanted to, no matter what lay on the other side. Her freedom and the freedom of everyone else depended on her.

"Okay, I think we're ready," Rylla spoke amidst the wavering light.

Finn watched her carefully as she got up from the ground and faced her cell door. It didn't look much different than the walls: iron rods placed close enough to keep one in but far enough apart to give a false hope of escape, but there was a box-like contraption on the outside of the door which indicated where the key would go to open it. But Rylla had no key.

This required precision and care: forcing open iron bars wasn't something Uwan had really taught her. He stuck more to earth and wood, even venturing into water, but he only once mentioned metals. *"It all comes back to nature and what existed before man's touch: all the natural elements; they shall always bend to the wielder of our type of magic. Even the most stubborn materials such as metals 'ave natural roots. They just require a firm 'and and firm words to find them. Don't forget one without the other."*

As Rylla faced her doorway to freedom, she turned over in her mind what Uwan had said. "Even the most stubborn materials have natural roots," she spoke aloud as she planted her feet more firmly and lifted her hands forward. "Firm hand, firm words."

When Rylla and her friends had escaped Uwan's cave, there had been earth all around her. The vines had grown from within to help peel back the layers of glass. Now? She was surrounded by hard-packed stone with little trace of earth if at all. Escaping here would require additional focus.

Rylla closed her eyes, blocking out all around her as she searched deep for boldness, words that would hold enough power and sway to bend the iron's will. She had to get it right. She *had* to.

She tasted the breath of wind and it rapidly rose into a gale, one so intense that it ignited a fire in her middle. She was a bird, trapped in a cage and fluttering against the bars, trying to break them with her wings. And then the words came:

A bird trapped in iron
Desperate for freedom
The hunger for song
The need for flight
These iron bars
Stand tall like soldiers
Like faceless defenders

Filled with might
But the iron is not strong
It bends and it buckles
And its natural roots
Are merely wound too tight
The iron is weak
It buckles and twists
It will surrender its will
So the bird can take flight

As Rylla stretched her hands forward, she felt the effect of her words as the pressure on her hands became lighter; she no longer felt the heavy burden of peeling back metal. Instead, she heard a subtle squeaking like iron was being moved and reformed. When she opened her eyes, Rylla saw that the bars in front of her had turned a bronzy gold and were bent and coiled into the shapes of flowers and birds, delicate yet intricate. There was not a single bar in front of her which stood up straight, and there was a sizable gap for her to simply walk through without any difficulty.

She had done it! The iron bent to her will!

Rylla chanced a glance at Finn. He stared at her, eyes wide and mouth open like a trout. A small, secret thrill of pride tingled down her spine as she snuck through the opening and took the second set of keys hanging on the wall nearest the dungeon's exit. The air smelt stale, infused with iron and the metallic signs of stale blood. Two Earth-Treaders nearest the exit pressed their heads against the bars of their iron cages, hair greasy and eyes filled with unspoken pleas. Their mouths and hands were bound like Rylla's had once been, their frail forms showing signs of malnourishment.

"I'll be back for you. For all of you," Rylla said to the prisoners as she ran past all their cells back to Finn's. She fumbled with the keys, trying one after the other until she'd found one that fit. The levers clicked into place and the door swung open. Rylla didn't wait for Finn to follow before shuffling to free all the Earth-Treaders who were bound and gagged.

As young and old emerged from their cells, they looked at Rylla like she was some goddess come to rescue them from their demise, but Rylla ignored the stares and continued to free everyone while Finn loosened their bonds.

In a short time, everyone was free as they congregated in the middle of the dungeon between all the open cells and discarded ropes. Rylla looked across the huddled group. There were old men and women, weathered by life's storms, yet bearing a hidden strength in their eyes; many who were middle-aged, less fragile and with more energy; even children younger than her were there, the youngest not being much older than ten. In all, there were about fifty of them.

"How long have you all been here?" Rylla asked, meeting their gaunt eyes and far off gazes one by one. Her heart ached for them.

"A few months…"

"Coming upon a year…"

"Fifteen weeks…"

"About five-hundred years…"

At this last statement, everyone turned to look at a woman as old and frail as the youth were young and strong. She was short with sagging skin, and her eyes were sunken in and glossy. She hobbled toward the center of the circle and looked at Rylla before training her weak eyes on Finn. There she stopped and squinted up at him.

"You." She pointed a finger toward his face. "That look in your eyes. I've seen it before. You've held Darkness in your palms. Anger and now loss—all signs of dark magic." She squinted harder. "The effects are strong and permanent, I'm afraid. I would know…"

"What do you mean?" Finn asked.

Rylla stared in silence, too stunned to speak. How had this woman lived this long? And was she blind? Surely not if she noticed Finn's eyes.

"I once had a stone—I found it many years ago, or so I thought. Little did I know what power it possessed, but I have come now to believe that *it* found *me*. I roamed the realms for many years, distraught over having lost my brothers—one dead at the hand of the other. I thought, what would stop him from killing me next if he only knew the truth?" she asked this rhetorically, but everyone listening was looking from person to person as if searching for the right answer.

Rylla watched with rapt attention.

"I thought I found my answer. For many years, the stone offered me protection. It cloaked me in invisibility if I so desired, but it also had a dark side. It eased my burden. It was everything I needed, but I was afraid. No matter what I did, the stone had become a part of me. It had taken part of my soul, and in exchange, it gave me long-lasting life. Too long." She sighed and lifted her gaze toward the ceiling before settling it back on Finn.

"But it disappeared from my neck about the time Brennigan was awakened. When you found his Bloodstone, something happened to mine, as if its will was being bent to his instead. My stone left me—five-hundred years later—abandoned, half-blind, and delirious. And do you know where it ended up?" she asked another question, this time only directing it toward Finn.

Rylla found it odd that she had said Brennigan instead of Lord Brennigan, as if there was something between them.

"Around your neck! It fled my presence and ended up in yours. That crimson stone is bound to Brennigan's through a magic I only recently discovered, and it will leave all who possess it, or have possessed it, crawling around like soulless creatures until he and the Bloodstone are destroyed for good."

Rylla was at a loss for words. Surely this woman was mad and had made up at least half this story. But when she looked to Finn, he seemed hooked on her every word. Did he believe her? If she were telling the truth, what did it mean when Lord Brennigan and his stone were destroyed? Would Finn be gone too? Her brain spun with a hundred doubts and questions. So far escaping prison had not turned out the way she had anticipated.

"How did you end up here? How do we know your story is true?" Rylla asked only two of the questions swirling about in her mind.

"I had been invisible and hiding my Earth-Treader magic these past five-hundred years—afraid. I was like my oldest brother, you see. He was killed for his magic, and I knew I would be too if Brennigan ever guessed the truth. When my stone fled, I was found and imprisoned in this tower. In truth, I haven't been here long, but I've walked these kingdoms many years. I'm only a portion of the woman I once was, an old magicked being. My wits have returned, but my sight is weak." She turned to Finn. "I can still see, but it comes and goes, as I'm sure you're figuring out yourself."

Finn nodded, swallowing hard. "It's irksome, to say the least." He reached to rub his eyes.

Rylla tried to digest all this new information, urgency churning in her stomach; already they had spent too much time talking. It would be hard enough to exit the tower by herself, but with fifty others? She hoped this woman knew what she was talking about.

"And what about your story being true?" Rylla asked again. "How are we to know?"

"Oh, yes, yes. You see, my name is Talih. I am Brennigan's older sister."

⸙⸙⸙

"Older sister?" Finn asked. Why hadn't Lord Brennigan mentioned anything about his siblings? Then again, Finn hadn't tried remembering his either. After all these years away from home, seeing Rylla sent a pang to his heart. He'd missed her.

"Yes, quite a lot older now—too old, I'd say." Talih chuckled. "And if Brennigan weren't such a coward, he'd realize he locked his own sister away. But as it were, he rarely ventures down here. The fool."

"What about this magic? The kind you said you recently discovered?" Since losing his stone, his senses were clearer and yet somehow more muddled. He felt freer, yet there was still something tugging on the recesses of his mind. A sort of restlessness.

"Ah, how quickly I forget. It happens with age, you'll find." Talih straightened visibly as she collected her thoughts. "Yes, this magic…well, the Earth-Lore has it wrong. There aren't many stones with dark abilities, there is only one, and its power has the ability to consume all the rest. Brennigan's Bloodstone is that very stone of which I speak. Many stones have already been consumed by its power for years, from the beginning of time, even before Brennigan found it himself. This includes the crimson stone I wore around my neck which then ended up on yours. That is why the Earth-Lore states there are many dark stones, but in reality, there is only one. The Bloodstone controls all the others."

"How did you learn all this? If you knew Lord Brennigan was asleep all those years, could you do nothing to stop him?" Finn beseeched, his vision going blurry once more.

"I've roamed these kingdoms far longer than any human should. I've watched Brennigan's heart turn cold, and watched my eldest brother's death. I was hiding amongst the Heather Fields when Brennigan fought the Earth-Treader kings of old, and in his disappearance, I have felt the earth shift—like it had harvested stores of dark magic but was biding its time in unleashing it. Little by little, the Darkness snuck out and trickled into streams, roots, and stones. It seeped into people's minds, including those of the kings and their generations after.

"I have experienced freedom and imprisonment, and I've lived long enough to know that sometimes the worst type of captivity isn't solely physical. When I wore that stone, I was a slave—I didn't have the power to take it off nor the strength to stop Brennigan. I was finally free when the stone left me, though its curse of long-lasting life has rendered me a sharp-witted fool with eyes as dull as toadstools. I shan't know true rest and neither shall our realm until his stone is gone. And it's even more urgent now," Talih said.

"Why now?" Rylla frowned.

Talih cleared her throat. “Because he’s growing stronger and his power is spreading. His control is widening, I can feel it in my bosom, as I’m sure can you.” Talih looked in Finn’s direction.

He nodded. That tugging in the back of his mind grew more present for a moment. He knew the pull to Darkness even though the stone no longer hung about his neck. A lingering poison.

Talih brought her attention back to Rylla. “The very stones you’ve been seeking are the ones he hopes to control with his Bloodstone. And now that he has them, who knows how powerful he’ll become? It may only take days or hours, even minutes, for the Bloodstone to consume the Earth-Treader stones, so let’s hope it's the former.”

“I fear we may be lingering too long. We need to get those stones away from him now!” Rylla spoke, addressing it to everyone though she was looking at Talih and Finn.

Finn studied his sister and noticed how much she’d matured. Hard lines now creased her determined brow and she stood with a new confidence, replacing the smooth features and timidness he remembered as a child. She’d grown into a woman. When had that happened?

He wanted to help, but his mind was still reeling with the loss of his stone. How were they going to succeed? Lord Brennigan was a monster, heartless and determined. They’d have to be extra careful escaping or else Lord Brennigan would crush them before they stepped foot out of the tower.

He gave Rylla a nod, following her and the other Earth-Treaders through the door and onto a stone landing. A narrow set of steps led upstairs and flaming sconces sent flickering shadows to dance along the high walls which loomed like menacing guards. Finn stepped beside Rylla, glancing up the stairwell. He took a breath, then paused, listening.

Footsteps thudded somewhere above them, growing louder. Finn's heartbeat quickened. If everyone retreated to their cells, it would be all for naught. If they climbed the stairs, they were sure to be executed on the spot. And if Lord Brennigan or even his men found he was helping Rylla and the Earth-Treaders? They'd spare no mercy.

The original plan had been to escape in shifts up the stairs and out one of the ground entrances through the kitchen, but now it looked like they'd have to change tactics.

"Finn, what are we to do? Where should we go?" Rylla whispered through his clouded thinking. Her gaze darted about the narrow corridor, but there weren't enough crevices or shadows for all of them. Then her eyes rested on the stairwell to the left, the one that descended even deeper into the tower. "What's down there?"

"A dead end. It might buy us some time, but we'll still have to find our way out of here." Finn moved in front of his sister, Talih and the others close behind. "I'll lead us down slowly, but if you hear the footsteps coming nearer—run," he said with as much confidence as he could.

He was feeling all sorts of strange, like his heart and his mind were playing tug-of-war. His vision was murky like pond water, and he felt his lungs were short of breath. But if he wanted to survive, if he wanted to help, he needed to remain strong.

He stepped down the first couple of stairs, the others following behind. He hoped he wasn't bringing them to their doom.

⸙ ⸙ ⸙

It was strange having Finn back in her life and under these circumstances. Stranger still was the fact that she was partially in charge of a group of Earth-Treaders, one of them related to and as old as Lord Brennigan himself. Rylla felt highly underqualified, but here she was, slipping from beneath Brennigan's fingertips and fleeing for her life.

The footsteps behind them had passed on and there were no shouts of alarm. No one had found their empty cells—yet. But that could change at any time. Finn led everyone down the dark stairwell, only stopping when he reached a marbled floor.

"This is it," Finn said, slowly stepping out into the center of the room.

The space was small and lit by Moonstones. Intricate tapestries hung about the walls and barrels of ale and bottles of spirits rested in the center. It was only a wine room! Rylla's heart dropped at the dead end. Finn *had* warned her, but secretly she'd hoped for another way out. How long would they have to wait down here before trying the stairs once more?

"Something doesn't feel right in this room," Talih spoke from behind her. "This is not a dead end. There's more than meets the eye."

Rylla let go of her disappointment and tried to focus her attention on the room itself. She could feel it now too—something was definitely off. There was a draft and the air seemed to tingle with herbs and magic. But it was only a small room, what else could be down here?

"Someone check behind those tapestries. If I know my brother, he'd be hiding something right under our noses," Talih suggested.

Rylla and Finn moved to test Talih's theory. They worked their way around the room, moving tapestries aside to reveal anything they covered, but there was nothing. The wall behind was solid stone.

Rylla came upon the last tapestry and braced herself to see some sort of doorway. This was the one, surely. She pulled back the heavy folds of material and held her breath, but was met with another wall of stone. Nothing. How could there be nothing?

She started to turn away, the tapestry beginning to fall back over the wall, when something caught her eye. *Curious.* There were markings on the stones, and though this portion of the wall seemed solid, some of the stones weren't flush with one another. She peered closer. There were sizable spaces in the grout which stretched down to the floor. It was easy to miss at a glance, but if one looked with a keen eye, they would notice the outline of a hidden door.

"I found something!" Rylla called quietly.

The others gathered around her as she moved the tapestry away from the wall.

"It's a door, to be sure, but it's sealed by dark magic. Ancient words bind it together and keep it from falling apart. But to utter them is disastrous—" Talih spoke calmly, running her hand along the stones.

"Disastrous?" Rylla questioned. "Surely not!" How else would they get through?

"Oh yes, quite. To utter them darkens the soul beyond repair. A type of magic put on by the Bloodstone—I can feel it." Talih pressed her palm flat against the stones, her weary expression creased with the burden of understanding. "Move aside, everyone, if you will," Talih addressed those who were standing closest to her. She adjusted her hands on the wall and uttered strange words, so strange that Rylla felt they weren't words at all.

Rylla looked at Finn, who seemed less confused than he did shocked and fearful, and she was left wondering what had been said.

As Talih finished saying the words, she cried out in agony, her fingers blackening at the tips. Darkness spread down into her hands.

Rylla reached out to stabilize her, stomach lurching. *Blood, death, and payment.* These words echoed in her mind. *What's happening?* She clung to Talih until the old woman was safely on the ground. Finally, the voices stopped.

Rylla stared down at Talih. What was going on?

"Give me a moment." Talih breathed heavily. "Look—the way is now opened."

Sure enough, the rocks were moving and disappearing into one another, revealing a doorway which led into a long, dimly lit tunnel. Light from outside peered through tiny cracks in the stone, enough to illuminate the tunnel's surroundings. Hope surged in Rylla's chest—would this lead them to the outdoors?

The other Earth-Treaders seemed to think the same; they began to file into the tunnel, leaving Rylla, Finn, and Talih behind.

"Are you sure you're okay?" Rylla crouched next to the frail woman.

"Yes, but I don't have long now. It's only a matter of time before the Darkness reaches my heart." Talih refused help as she slowly got to her feet. "Let's just hope the Bloodstone is destroyed before then." She steadied herself against the wall of the tunnel as she shuffled after the other Earth-Treaders.

Rylla stared after her a moment, stomach knotting. What happens when the Darkness reaches someone's heart?

She turned to her brother. "Finn, you're connected to the Bloodstone too, though the connection be small. I've visibly seen your anguish. How is it that Talih bears no outward signs of her own save for her poor eye sight and now her marred skin?" *She doesn't pine after the stone like you still do.* The knot in Rylla's stomach wound tighter, her vision blurring.

Finn frowned. "She's marred and bruised more than she lets on, Rylla. Some wounds are too deep and too painful to bear outwardly. She's in agony. And now even more so," Finn spoke tightly, like he was living the horror himself.

Rylla had no words, she just embraced her brother as tears stung her eyes. This pain would surely pass. Once Lord Brennigan and his stone were defeated, the Darkness would flee for good and the corruption of the stones would end.

She'd see to it. This mission was becoming even more personal than it already was.

Now if they could just escape this tower…She only hoped there was an exit on the other end of this underpass.

Rylla and Finn followed Talih and the Earth-Treaders through the long and winding tunnel. It stretched and curved for what seemed like miles, the sunlight filtering through the cracks, until finally they entered a cavernous room. The walls were miles high and they revealed a dawn-filled sky shining through crevices in the stone above. It reminded Rylla of the ores and where Uwan lived, except here there was no ceiling. Even though the room wasn't sealed off, the entire place felt eerily heavy and riddled with foreign spices. The scents she had smelled earlier were barely wisps, but now they were as bold as a blazing fire. Rotten flesh mingled with the herbs, and she held her hand over her mouth to keep herself from gagging.

What was rotting down here? The thought sent a shiver up her spine. This was a dark, dark place. There had to be a way out.

Rylla searched her surroundings. Anvils, traces of weapon-mongery, and bones of what she hoped to only be an animal's were scattered about the cavern. Rylla could feel the Darkness of the magic here, and though she couldn't understand it like Finn and Talih, she knew it was dangerous. She began to follow the perimeter of the room, but pulled back sharply as her foot nearly slipped. She reeled back from a gaping pit in the floor, heart bruising her ribs. It was deep and dark and foul, and in it there were even more bones and varying types of flesh and fur littered throughout the bottom.

What had happened down there?

"Rylla, take a look at this! I can't make it out clearly, my eyes are giving me trouble again," Finn called her over to him, pointing at some papers and a large map which laid on top of an iron table.

She crossed to him, glancing at the other Earth-Treaders busy looking for an exit. Between the lot of them, someone might find a way out of here. Talih hobbled her way over to stand on the other side of Finn.

"I'm not an expert on our kingdoms, but why does this map look different?" Finn asked, frowning at the parchment spread before them.

"Because it is." Rylla bent to look more closely at the map, staring in disbelief. There off the coast of Aylati was a small island called *Abbredun*, simply floating in the Indigo Tide like it had belonged there all its life. But this couldn't be true, surely her father would have seen it and taught her its history. She would have learned the types of trees, the culture, the highest points of elevation. She would have put this on the map she'd made with her father.

But as she shifted on her feet, the light and shadows danced across the map, revealing something else she hadn't noticed before. Rylla looked closer and barely made out the subtle pencil scratches which read '*sunk*' right below the island.

What did it mean? A sunken island? Without thinking, Rylla found herself rummaging through the other papers on the table, poring over one after the other. Her hands only paused when her eyes rested on a letter, signed by some king from the Isle of Abbredun. There was mention of a Bloodstone. Was it the same as Lord Brennigan's?

She turned the letter over. A postscript was scrawled on the back, written in the same hand as on the front:

P.S. From this day forward, the Earth-Lore will count only five stone crests. But while my kingdom stood, strong and proud, there were six. There isn't time to recount all that happened, only to mourn the loss. Whoever finds this Bloodstone now holds the sixth stone. Let's hope a heart less corrupted can restore what once was.

"I can't believe it." Rylla felt like the floor was sinking beneath her feet. How did no one see this coming? She vaguely remembered hearing a children's story about a sunken island, but was it based off of Abbredun or somewhere else? What was myth and what was truth? She held the letter out to Talih who squinted hard at the paper.

"So, it is as I feared," Talih said. "That Bloodstone is too powerful to be anything less than what it actually is."

"But the corruption, the Darkness…surely the kingdoms have always been governed by light!" Rylla was at a loss for words. If the Bloodstone was one of the stone crests, how had it become so dark? Why weren't the others that way also? Amidst all her questioning, Rylla realized how much she missed Moo. Where was he? Surely he'd have an answer for this, wouldn't he?

"I'm afraid it's not so much the stone as it is the wielder. Like a seed, it only takes a single weed to choke out the good. Perhaps that's what happened with this one a long, long time ago…or the kings of ages past had simply chosen the wrong stone to begin with."

Rylla's head ached. There was so much to take in. First Finn, then the escape and Talih's story, now the stone.

"Then it definitely needs to be destroyed," Rylla said.

"Yes, but now we have an even trickier problem. A kingdom's stone can only be defeated by all the others. All five must work against the one, or else, it still stands. It can't merely be destroyed like the common stones. Do you *have* all five?" Talih asked.

Rylla's spine tingled with cold. She didn't have any now. How could they possibly defeat Lord Brennigan?

Talih read the worried expression on Rylla's face. "Then we must fight and do our part while our feet still stand up underneath us."

"Hey! Over here! We found an exit!" one of the Earth-Treaders shouted from the other end of the room, gesturing to a dark corner.

Closer inspection revealed a narrow set of stairs which hugged the wall tightly. It ascended upwards for what seemed like an eternity, and it blended into the wall so well, it was as if it didn't exist at first glance.

Before Rylla could follow the others up the stairwell, the sound of drums echoed down from somewhere overhead. It had been a while since she last heard them, but they were loud, their cries deafening and reverberating within the cavernous walls. Rylla's heart sped up, a pit of fear in her middle. What accompanied those drums was what she really feared.

What was Lord Brennigan planning? She quickly gathered his map off the table and folded it. She put it in her back pocket; this was something her father would want to see. And then she fled, joining the others making the long climb to escape.

Talih's words repeated in her head with every step she took closer to the drums. The fate of the Bloodstone depended on having all five stones, but that was next to impossible when only three had been found—and those were in Lord Brennigan's possession—and the others were either in the gut of the Balagrix or still hidden in Aylati's dirt. She'd have to steal the three from Lord Brennigan and hope that without Aylati's Jade and the Isles' Larimar, their strength would work all the same.

Chapter the Thirty-Second

March on the Kingdoms

"She's in there?" Caz asked Gorvo. The guard had led them through the remainder of the forest and up and around and through countless mounds of rocks. They had made it to the cliffs, but even so, no one knew where they were aside from Gorvo. Elowen had said only parts of it looked familiar to her, but she was soon rendered silent along with everyone else as they weaved their way up narrow paths and around winding bends. The taste of salt clung heavily in the air. Were they this close to the ocean?

They finally stopped walking and crouched low, hidden behind some low-lying shrubs and staring at the stone tower a little way off. To their right, a large wall of rock stretched between them and the tower, the perfect covering to shield them as they moved in closer. Caz wanted to charge in now; it pained him to have to wait, but when he tried to move, Gorvo held fast to his shoulder.

"Don't you hear that?" Gorvo asked.

Caz paused and listened. He heard a loud thrumming and crashing in the distance. It must be the waves breaking against the rocks—the cavalcade of the Cliffs. Or…no, perhaps not. The rhythm was too consistent to be just the waves. There was something else. It was a steady beating sound, like drums. Now that he was listening more intently, he was amazed that he hadn't detected it before. And they were growing louder.

"I've heard these drums before. Why should they stop me from rescuing Rylla?" Caz shrugged off Gorvo's hold and peered through the brush.

"Because this time, these drums mean war," Gorvo spoke calmly, but Caz could tell he was afraid by the twitch of a muscle tightening his jaw.

Caz looked to Elowen and Jovin who exchanged similar glances, uncertainty lining their faces.

"They've never been this determined, and even now the wind feels different. The tide is changing." Gorvo shuddered.

Caz paused and he too felt the change in the wind. It had grown both stale and infused with something he couldn't place. As he looked up to the tower, a black and red flag was being raised on the highest pinnacle, the banner unfurling with a snap and flapping violently in the breeze.

Then it happened. Animals, masses of them, came pouring out from the tall rocks on their right, from the crevices and shadows as if they had been waiting for a signal. Caz swallowed hard. Moments ago, he'd thought about using those rocks as shelter. His heart picked up speed as he looked more closely at the animals; they were unlike anything he'd ever seen. They were bent creatures, shadowy beasts, a mashup of countless animals all meshed into a single entity with fangs as long as javelins and eyes as red as a blood moon. And upon each of their necks hung a stone fashioned in an iron clasp. Hellfire burned in their eyes as they ran down the rocks on the left, bounding over them like fleet-footed fairies and disappearing from sight.

Several stayed back and paced amongst the rocks between Caz and the tower.

How would he ever get to Rylla now? Caz tried to count the creatures, to have some sort of gauge on their numbers, but they were moving too fast and there were too many.

"What are those things?" Elowen whispered, her eyes wide.

The shadow beasts sniffed the ground and scoured their surroundings; whatever they were, Caz was certain he didn't want them coming any closer than they already were. Had Rylla encountered one of these monsters? The thought made his heart race even faster.

"I just got here too, I'm as clueless as the lot of you," Gorvo whispered in response. "But it doesn't bode well. The march has begun. We're too late."

Too late? Before anyone else had time to respond, another of the devilish animals emerged from the rocky shadows, this time bearing a rider. The beast was an exceptionally large creature with flaming eyes, and on its back sat a man with three stones draped around his neck and one strapped to a crown atop his head. In the man's eyes burned another type of fire, a smoldering ashpit rimmed with blackened veins. Caz didn't take long to guess who the man was.

"That'd be Lord Brennigan," Gorvo said, his throat bobbing in a swallow.

"*That's* Lord Brennigan?" Elowen shuddered, her fingers twitching on her bow.

Lord Brennigan steered the beast forward and yanked hard on a handful of fur, his shadowy mount halting at the edge of the cliff only a few yards from Caz. Other nearby shadow beasts flanked Lord Brennigan's side, whining and scratching at the ground, sending a flurry of dust into the air.

Caz ducked lower and peered more closely through the brush. Though Lord Brennigan's muscles pulsed with life, his skin looked thin, black veins standing out like cracks across his face, back slightly hunched, and cheeks a bit sallow. But despite all this, Lord Brennigan was probably more powerful than he appeared. A lot more, especially with the stones hanging off his neck. The determination and hunger in his eyes were even more proof of that.

But above all, it was the dark rims around his eyes and throughout his face which rendered Caz speechless. Lord Brennigan was marked.

Behind him, foot soldiers emerged from the same rocks, not nearly as many in number as the creatures, and they quickly flanked Lord Brennigan, alongside the shadow beasts. On each of the soldiers' necks also hung a single stone. Then strangely enough, the shadow beasts vanished, as if they hadn't been there at all, though he could still hear their growls and cries.

What on the good-tilled earth was going on?

Caz wanted to charge through the bushes, find Rylla, and take her away from this place, but to do so would be lunacy, and he'd surely get himself killed if he tried. No, finding Rylla required patience, something he had very little of these days. He needed to bide his time.

As Caz continued to peer through the shrubs in front of him, Lord Brennigan stretched out his hand and uttered some sort of command. The animals stopped their cries, the guards stopped their chatter, and the drums died in the wind—all that could be heard were the waves, but if Lord Brennigan could control them, Caz was sure they would have been silenced too.

"My soldiers," Lord Brennigan spoke, turning from side to side to survey his troops. He stretched his hands outwards and continued, "Feast your eyes on this land before you. Once we march on all these kingdoms, this land shall know true power—an infinite and unyielding power that has no limitations."

Despite himself, Caz shuddered at the sound of Lord Brennigan's voice. He felt its deep baritone reverberate inside of him, the words themselves heavy with magic.

"Though I am missing two stones, I still have four," Lord Brennigan continued.

Four? If there were only five stones, then how could he be missing two? Caz looked to his friends and they shared the same expression—confusion and disbelief.

"But they shall soon be in my possession! The transfer is almost complete. My Bloodstone shall have full control over these stones before the battle is won, and with any luck, over all the stones before the end of this day. As we march on these kingdoms, you are to defeat anyone who stands against me and find the remaining stones. Once I have them all, then Abbredun will be raised! There I shall build my new throne, one fit for a true king to rule in glory over all the Earthen-Crest kingdoms!" Lord Brennigan shouted.

"We will be victorious today. I am counting on all of you to fight and hold your ground. Do not disappoint me! Do not be cowards in this fight, for we march on an unaware enemy. We shall take them by storm and by stone! We shall take…"

Lord Brennigan stopped shouting and turned his head in the direction of Rélynda's border, eyes squinted and jawline taut. What had caught his attention? Caz turned to look too, but he couldn't see past the crest of the rocks. He could make out the sounds of heavy hoofbeats on the ground, and as the hoofbeats drew nearer, he looked back to Lord Brennigan who now had a mischievous smile plastered on his face. It seemed he was pleased with whatever was going to happen.

"Ah, it appears we have company," Lord Brennigan spoke loud enough for whoever was in earshot to hear. "Come, come, the more the merrier. In fact, you'll only be making my job easier." His lips were turned up at the ends as he played with the stones around his neck. His gaze was fixed downwards on whoever rested at the base of the cliffs.

"Brennigan, I've come here to discuss a truce," came a reply from the ground. Caz could hear the voice loud and clear, so perhaps the cliffs weren't so high up as he had thought. The way the newcomer had said "Brennigan" showed little care or concern for his title and ferocity. Who had dared to approach him so nonchalantly?

"Ah, you must be this Grievon I've heard so much about. But a truce? Surely you have more gall than that," Lord Brennigan scoffed.

A wave of nausea hit Caz. The man he had run away from was here. Undoubtedly, he wouldn't come without his army either, so the very men Caz had once served with were somewhere just out of sight. But why? Grievon never left Ostglenden himself if he could help it. Had he come to fight Lord Brennigan?

It felt like Caz was about to end up right where he had begun. He glanced to Jovin who only nodded. Caz released a shaky breath. He was a changed man now, they both were. He needed to remember his courage.

"We both want the same thing, don't we? The Earth-Treaders," Grievon said.

"Yes, but the thing is I want them dead or to rot in prison, and you—you want them as your servants," Lord Brennigan spat.

"What's the difference, really, when they'll end up dying either way? You'd rather let their magic go to waste than use it for your own gain?" Grievon countered.

"The difference is that I'll be king, and your reign will end, and so will all the Earth-Treaders—so will all who come up against me. When you're dead, you'll have no use for them anyway," Lord Brennigan challenged Grievon coldly.

"I urge you to reconsider. We can both reign as kings and divide the stones—surely their power is too burdensome for one person alone…" Grievon offered.

Caz heard the bluff in Grievon's voice. The man was a covetous fool. He'd never settle for anything less than taking full control of the stones for himself.

"Reign as kings? Divide the stones? Bah! That's the very thing I've been trying to avoid. To even suggest otherwise shows what little you know. I want sole reign and for you to be my footstool!" Lord Brennigan yelled.

"Then I guess you leave me no choice but to take everything from you by force," Grievon replied, an answering challenge in his voice.

"It seems you've finally come to your senses." Lord Brennigan appeared almost gleeful.

"But I don't see your army. It's hardly a fight with just you and your few men against my thousands," Grievon stated. He scoffed slightly.

Lord Brennigan lifted his hand and snapped his fingers. Instantly, growls and cries could be heard from along the rocky cliffs as the creatures standing near Lord Brennigan came into view once more.

Had these beasts simply gone invisible? What kind of magic is this?

Cries of alarm broke out among Grievon's army below as the sound of metal scraping against scabbards and bows nocking arrows joined the noise.

"Do you see them now?" Lord Brennigan laughed. "Fight as hard as you can, for we have the higher ground." He whistled through his teeth and at his command the animals began to move.

Caz couldn't see what was going on down below, but he could already hear tearing flesh and screams of agony lifting high into the heavens. Growls and hissing accompanied yelps and a whooshing of arrows; the two sides were fighting one another as Lord Brennigan sat atop his beast and watched in silent approval.

"What do we do now? We can't simply stay here and watch, but we also can't fight," Elowen spoke the very thoughts Caz had running through his head. "We're outnumbered a million to one!"

"This doesn't bode well, but we need ta do somethin'," Jovin agreed.

"I can take us further up the rocks, closer to the tower, but there's a risk we'll be seen. Lord Brennigan has eyes everywhere." Gorvo shook his head.

"Let's just hope his eyes are trained on that battlefield. We need to find Rylla and get her away from this place." Caz turned to follow Gorvo's lead.

"It's dangerous, but at least it will be better than staying here. Come, stay close and don't make any noise." Gorvo led them back down the rocks a little way and up another passage, this one steeper and with less coverage.

Caz felt naked and exposed as they precariously climbed and ducked behind anything they could find. Eventually, they were up pretty high and could see the battlefield before them. The monstrous beasts were fighting against men clad in armor, the bodies of both man and beast lying dead all around them. Still, there were masses of fighters still alive, moving like a giant ant heap converging and separating only to converge once more.

Caz and the others were almost to the tower; they were moving closer when suddenly a giant apparition of shadowy fur rose up before them. A musty odor met their noses, and fangs the length of Elowen's bow came down on the rock beside Caz's foot.

Caz leapt back and drew his sword. Without a moment's hesitation, he swung his arm forward and stabbed the creature between the eyes. A wisp of shadow seeped out of the monster and disappeared before the unmoving beast slumped to the ground.

It was over so fast, he hadn't had time to think. "That was close." Caz's breath was tight, and he scanned the rocks ahead.

There were more. Fang and fur and smoky shadows. Caz, Jovin, and Gorvo found themselves with unsheathed swords and Elowen with a drawn bow, slashing and firing at the onslaught of beasts. They were surrounded, and no matter how many they felled, more kept coming.

"I'd really like it if someone told us what these things are," Elowen panted as she unleashed an arrow into the beast closest to her.

The arrow pierced its skull and it fell into another creature, pinning it to the ground. Another crept up behind her and slashed at her shoulder. She stumbled forward, gasping, then spun and sent an arrow into the beast's eye.

"I think it's best ta assume they aren't 'ouse-pets," Jovin responded as he brought his sword up and sliced through another creature. He wheeled around and brought the metal blade sharply against a new set of fangs. Gorvo was right beside him, slashing and stabbing anything that moved.

"Whatever they are, they die pretty easily." Caz stabbed a beast in the jaw and then slashed at another's side. No matter how many he killed, more kept coming. "But there's so many, it makes little difference."

Each time a beast was felled, wisps of shadows left them and disappeared, leaving the bodies sounder vessels than before. It seemed that when living, their bodies were made of shadows and once dead, the shadows left behind solid beings in their place. Caz already had cuts on his face, arms, and legs, and a nasty gash on his forearm. Even if the beasts themselves were merely wraiths and illusions, their bites and attacks certainly weren't.

If they continued like this, they'd surely be killed. It seemed more beasts were guarding the tower than the path they had just come from. If perhaps Caz and the others could double back, they'd have greater success.

"We need to get out of here! It won't do your woman any good if we show up dead trying to rescue her," Gorvo shouted as he continued to slash his sword against the shadow beasts.

"There's not enough o' us—we need reinforcements!" Jovin said.

Caz agreed. They needed more people on their side—those who weren't trying to overthrow the kingdoms in a ridiculous power struggle.

But more shadow beasts must have heard the scuffle, and they bounded up the path behind them. To turn back now would be folly. To think they could outrun these beasts would be idiotic at best.

"Then we fight until they come!" Caz shouted in response as he raised his sword at another beast. He only hoped he didn't live to regret those words.

⸙ ⸙ ⸙

Their exit was barely a sliver in size, but it showcased a strip of blue sky. They were almost to the top of the stairs, the warm sunshine beating down from above. The older Earth-Treaders found the climb difficult, but with the taste of the fresh air on the wind, they pressed on. How long had it been since they used their magic? Since an Earth-spell was uttered?

The first of their company who reached the top stair and crawled out of the small opening was the young child Rylla had seen earlier. But instead of walking onwards, he stopped as still as stone, staring off in the distance.

"Melchi, what's wrong?" Talih called after him, urging the others to keep moving.

But the child was too afraid to speak. Eventually someone pulled him aside and the steady flow of climbers resumed. It wasn't until Rylla almost crested the last few steps and slipped out the opening when she felt a change in both the wind and nature. She had already heard the drums, but now there were screams and cries of anguish. The rocks trembled underfoot while the wind tugged viciously on her hair. And the ocean—she could hear the waves crashing violently as if a storm were coming up through the water. Nature was in agony, but why?

As Rylla stepped onto the flat rock above, the world opened up before her like a vast wilderness of space. Except this wilderness was filled with bloodshed and teeth. She was no longer near the stone tower. The cliffs rounded like a horseshoe: she was on the far side while Lord Brennigan was on the other, the tower situated somewhere along the bend in the middle. He sat proudly on his beastly mount, watching. A grassy plain stretched across the land between them, a war raging between beast and man and the once-green grass pooling red with blood. The metallic stench wafted high over the rocks, circled about her nose, and then went out to sea. All that stood between Rylla and the kingdoms' stones were the gruesome battlefield and the element of surprise.

Rylla's heart cracked, her legs shaking. The horrors of war displayed before her—metal against flesh, bones against sword, cries of agony, blood—the noises echoed in her chest and the images stole her breath. It took every ounce of strength not to let the tears escape.

She knew Lord Brennigan was planning on taking over the kingdoms, but what were these beasts? And who was he fighting against? Was this Grievon's army that Caz had warned her about?

Even amongst all the questions and fears, Rylla knew she couldn't stand back and watch. Fang had given her a mission.

"I need to get those stones from Lord Brennigan before he puts an end to everything," Rylla spoke to the group.

Those nearest her stared at her like her head wasn't on straight, and their collective complaints only made matters worse:

"Do you see their numbers? They'd pick you clean before you even stepped foot into his presence," one protested.

"Besides, there's a second army out there. Do we fight with them or against them?"

"We fight with them, of course! Surely anyone against Lord Brennigan is an ally!"

"It's a hopeless battle. Our kingdoms are doomed!"

"Who is even foolish enough to challenge him?"

"What about the children?"

The group went back and forth, fear tightening every word. Rylla felt their fears echo in her own mind. All she wanted to do was run away and cower in fear. But turning back now would be pointless. She'd come this far.

Fang had given this mission to her, and Moo said he always knew what he was talking about. No matter how afraid she was, Rylla couldn't simply stand by and watch. Her conscience wouldn't allow her to. And the lives of those she loved depended on her.

She ran her hand over the Yellow Jaspers and felt the prompting: she needed to save these kingdoms, she wanted to. She then held onto the locket which usually only brought her comfort, but for a reason Rylla couldn't comprehend, she felt pure strength despite the hard truth. She might die, she almost certainly would get hurt, but at least she was holding true to her word. She wasn't the same girl she was when she left home, and that gave her courage.

"It's only doomed if those who seek justice and peace stand by and do nothing." Rylla stood boldly before the Earth-Treaders. "You call it foolish to fight a powerful opponent, but I'd consider it foolish not to. I'm tired of letting something else dictate what I can or cannot do, I'm tired of it holding me back. I've spent too long living in my own shadows. We have magic, a magic so strong that Lord Brennigan himself fears it. We have nature, the earth, and truth on our side—everything he detests. But we need those stones in order to defeat him!"

The Earth-Treaders were giving Rylla their full attention now, looking to her as their leader. Finn beamed at her with pride in his wounded eyes and Talih gave a slow, soft smile.

"And the children will stay behind. They'll be much safer here." Rylla said.

"But I want to fight!" Melchi chirped up, the other young ones echoing his enthusiasm.

"No, Melchi," Rylla crouched and looked him in the eyes. "Your job will be to look after the others, to keep them safe. I'm counting on you."

Melchi looked like he wanted to protest.

"You'll be a hero," Rylla pressed his hand and smiled.

He swallowed and nodded, standing a little taller.

Rylla stood and looked at the group once more.

"And the other army?" someone asked.

"I have reason to believe it's Grievon and his men, here to rage war and seek the same thing Brennigan wants: power," Talih responded. "To fight with them is folly, but to fight against them is death."

"What are you saying?" Rylla questioned.

"I think she means us to fight neutrally, but use their skill to our advantage," Finn filled in the gaps. "I'm no Earth-Treader but I can still wield a sword. I'll find a discarded one on the battlefield, but I'll need you to cover me." He looked to Rylla.

"You have my word." She met his gaze and then addressed the group. "We are small in number, but our power is great. Don't hold back, and try to get Lord Brennigan's army away from him. This very well could be the last march of the Earth-Treader race, so let's not fail our kingdoms now!"

The group of Earth-Treaders cheered loudly, and turned to face the fight. Anxiety and excitement coursed through Rylla's veins. She had friends, others like her, who were going to unleash their Earth-spells alongside her own. And if they were successful, perhaps she would get to see Caz again and the faces of her parents.

At the very least, she could know they would be safe when she was gone.

Chapter the Thirty-Third

The Cliffs of Cavalcade

Earth-spells sang through the air left and right as Earth-Treaders buffeted their powers on the wind's currents. Mounds of dirt and trees of varying sizes and kinds were raised high around the battlefield while a strong gale weaved in and out of the fighters, knocking the beasts to the ground, stripping the men of their weapons, and pushing them off course. Rylla had never seen this much magic all at once before, but even so, the enemy was advancing.

Rylla chanced a glance at Lord Brennigan who still sat atop his beast, a look of fierce determination on his face as he held fast to the stones around his neck. But was that fear in his gaze? Even he must realize that having so many Earth-Treaders loose on the battlefield could change the course of the war, but he kept issuing commands as more monstrous beasts came pouring out of the rocks. Would this onslaught never end? It seemed that once the beasts were killed, their shadow spirits left their slain bodies, only to enter into a new body, thus constantly replenishing Lord Brennigan's forces.

She needed to destroy that Bloodstone. But she needed the other stones first.

Even Grievon's men weren't sure who to fight. Some Earth-Treaders attacked the beastly animals with vines and dirt, only to inadvertently disarm Grievon's soldiers, who ended up being mauled by another set of creatures.

It was a disaster—three different armies warring against each other in the name of achieving their own versions of peace. Every side was receiving losses, but only Lord Brennigan's was acquiring reinforcements. At this rate, Grievon's army and the Earth-Treaders would merely water the land with their own blood.

Rylla whirled around and sent a gust of golden wind careening into a beast. She whistled between her teeth and clapped her hands together, summoning snaking vines from the earth to take hold of another's legs.

She saw Finn cross the field, searching for a sword. He ran and dodged soldiers and shadow beasts, eyes scanning the ground. Rylla sent an Earth-spell in his direction, pushing back a writhing creature before it had a chance to sink its teeth into her brother. Finn kicked a body with his foot and pulled something loose from its side. He'd found a sword.

"Finn! Over here!" Rylla shouted.

Finn came running and took his place beside her, fighting with his newly acquired weapon. He slashed at another shadow beast as Rylla shielded him with dirt walls and rocks. The other Earth-Treaders were moving about the battlefield like nimble leaves in the wind, but already Rylla saw some of their slain bodies mingled amongst the fallen. She was only too thankful to have left the little ones behind. They were too young to experience this horror.

She couldn't look at the dead now—she needed to keep fighting. She needed to get to the stone. The beasts charged at anything and everyone, gorging people with their fangs and breaking limbs with their hind legs. Grievon's men formed a line of defense, swords and bows at the ready, but Rylla knew their attempts would prove futile at the rate the beasts were charging. They'd all be dead within a few minutes.

Rylla uttered a few words and sent a violent gust of wind in the direction of the creatures, knocking them back. This allowed time for the soldiers to give the first attack.

She spun around again and did the same for another one of Grievon's groups and stepped a few paces closer in the direction of the stones.

Who knew she'd be trying to protect the very man and his army that Caz had sought to warn her about? But she had to get to the stones. She was trying, but the progress was slow.

Rylla blocked another attack and observed Talih floating in the middle of the battlefield and moving her darkened, shriveled hands in circular motions as bursts of sticky mud and quicksand pooled around her ankles. A sinking pit formed beneath her feet. Both men and beats fell victim to the sludge and found themselves sinking deeper and deeper the more they struggled.

Even the shadowy souls of the monsters were stuck in the mud, making it impossible to escape and go into new bodies. Perhaps this was the answer! But Talih's magic was ancient. How many other Earth-Treaders could create quicksand out of the dirt? She'd never tried it before, never knew it was possible. And the number of beasts getting trapped paled in comparison to those who weren't. Their shadows were still roaming freely and forming greater numbers.

It seemed all hope was lost.

Rylla spun and sent another golden wave of wind in the direction of two shadow creatures, their mouths frothing with foam as they scratched viciously at the ground. She took a few more steps closer to the stones.

Movement from beyond the battle caught Rylla's eye. Behind Lord Brennigan, almost hidden behind part of the stone tower, another skirmish was going on. Three fighters with swords and one with a bow were fighting off the same beasts that were on the battlefield.

But it was the way in which one of the swordsmen moved which caught her attention. The way the sun glinted off his brown hair and tanned skin. Her heart leapt. Caz was here, he had come after all! And she was going to have to watch him die.

⸙ ⸙ ⸙

Caz felled his enemies, swiping at fang and fur. Their limp bodies were scattered about his feet as wisps of shadows circled overhead and disappeared in the crevices of the rocks. It was no use, the beasts kept coming in droves. He turned to see his friends struggling to stay alive amidst the attacks, blood seeping from open wounds and mingling with sweat.

He'd been so focused on fighting that he hadn't looked at the battlefield in quite some time. He chanced a glance and was shocked at seeing different fighters on the field than before. Caz slashed at a beast that had snuck up behind him, cutting its neck and sending it sideways. He saw movement in the corner of his eye. He spun and decapitated another monster, and turned his gaze to the field once more. The new fighters weren't clad in uniforms or using weapons, instead, they wore tattered rags and were bending the will of nature.

Earth-Treaders! His heart leapt as a shadow beast leapt on him, pinning his shoulders down with its teeth, piercing his skin. A muted cry escaped his lips as he lifted his sword and pierced the creature through its heart. Caz bent his knees and pressed his boots to the creature's ribs as its body became deadweight. He kicked his legs out and sent the monster toppling with its last breath. Caz stood, his shoulders on fire, brandishing his sword once more. Where had all these Earth-Treaders come from? And then it hit him. Rylla must have something to do with it. She was out there on that field, he was sure of it.

He kept fighting off the beasts—stabbing, slicing, defending—as he searched the battlefield to find her. He needed to see she was alive. But it was no use, the monsters were pressing harder and circling around them again. At this rate, he didn't know how much strength he had left to keep fighting with no sign of deliverance.

And then a piercing cry rent the air. The screech echoed over the battlefield, then again, louder and closer, but this time accompanied by heavy wingbeats. The battle paused as men and beast alike looked skyward.

It was the barred owl! The huge bird flapped into view and circled the battlefield, silhouetted against the sky. From where Caz was standing, he felt its size rivaled that of a small dragon. Its piercing cries reverberated the heavens once more.

Behind, flew thousands of birds—rocks, tree branches long and short, and a mismatch of varying tools and weaponry all clutched in their talons. The owl descended and hovered briefly as something in an earthy cloak got off its back. Caz looked more closely and felt shock surge in his chest. It was Uwan! Why was he here? Was he looking for the Obsidian again? Another owl similar in size dropped off a different man who Caz didn't know but thought looked oddly familiar. Both men stood on the battlefield, as if waiting for the battle to continue at any moment. The birds circled high over their heads and seemed to blot out the sun with their numbers.

And when Caz thought it couldn't get any better, a black and white cat bounded onto the field, a group of bears, deer, leopards, mountain lions, hares, foxes, and more following close behind. It was Rylla's cat, Moo!

The animals charged into battle and the armies unfroze, the clang of swords and cries of pain resuming instantly. But this time Lord Brennigan's numbers began to dwindle.

Caz arched his arm in a wide circle and thrust his sword into another shadow beast. The breath hitched in his throat, his brow dripping sweat. The creatures continued to come, but now at a slower rate. A few hawks and ravens were beginning to help, sending debris and crushing objects onto the beasts below. Caz glanced toward the battlefield again as he sliced upwards and cut a creature in two.

Uwan had moved to float alongside Talih, a hawk on his shoulder guiding him around the field. He took up the same Earth-spell and began to make the puddle of mud and quicksand larger, widening the expanse so more creatures were falling into it. Was the hawk being his eyes?

Caz ducked as another beast lunged for him. He swerved to the right and brought his blade down sharply along its spine. The monster slumped to the ground. Already, the battleground was piled high with bodies, death ringing in the air. Caz had probably killed at least thirty creatures himself.

Over the battlefield, the massive aviary was sending a tumble of branches and heavy objects onto the monsters below, impaling their shadowy bodies into the earth. The birds helping Caz and his group increased in number enough that Caz finally felt the freedom to seek shelter and breathe.

"This has got to be the only time I've ever been relieved to see so many birds," Elowen said, blood dripping from a cut on her head as she bent to catch her breath.

Caz agreed. It was the perfect time to attack Lord Brennigan. He was only a few yards away. He made to move in the overlord's direction, but Jovin shouted at him.

"What in the blast do yeh think yeh doin'?"

"This may be the only chance I get!" Caz shouted behind him as he made a run for it. His friends tried to follow but an invisible force threw them backward.

Lord Brennigan clutched onto the stones, uttering an incantation of blackest magic, and Caz was snatched from his feet and sent high into the air. His breath choked in his throat and he lost his grip on his sword as the ground rushed up toward him again.

Something jerked his fall to a stop before he could hit the ground, and he was roughly lowered the last little way. Caz landed on his backside, and looked up in time to see a large red-tailed hawk swooping away.

"On second thought, maybe that wasn't the smartest decision," he gasped, staggering to his feet. Caz retrieved his sword and glared at Lord Brennigan still a stone's throw away.

"We can't get close enough ta 'im. We don't 'ave the magic." Jovin clambered up as well and helped Elowen to her feet. Gorvo was on guard, ready to attack any of the beasts, but the birds were taking them out one by one, talon against fang.

"I know you don't like it, Caz, but this is something only Rylla can do. Lord Brennigan is hers to defeat," Elowen's words pierced him sharply.

Caz grimaced. It wasn't that he didn't think Rylla could fight Brennigan, it's just that he wanted to protect her, to rescue her. But Caz was helpless.

"Then let's make it easier for her to do so." Caz clutched his sword harder and moved toward the battlefield. He was going to pave a clear path for the woman he loved. Even if it meant he'd die trying.

⸙ ⸙ ⸙

A beast charged toward Finn, breathing heavily and eyes blazing with hellfire. *Where is Rylla?* There was no way his sword would be able to take such a blow as this, let alone his body. Finn braced himself for the impact and the claws and teeth, but just before the beast could leap on him, a bear pounced from his right and rammed into the creature's side. The two tumbled over each other, growls and howls echoing from the heated battle.

A figure ran forward, past the battling creatures, and emerged from the haze of dust into view. Finn stared. Garth stood facing him, sword drawn and eyes filled with questions as they stared at each other in disbelief.

"Finn?" Garth began to walk toward him, then he was running. He met his brother in an embrace but let him go once he realized Finn wasn't hugging him back.

Finn could only stare. Now felt like the strangest time to catch up, but if not now, would there be a next time?

"I tried searching everywhere for you…" Garth began, pain in his eyes.

Seeing his brother again wasn't something Finn had anticipated, but the numb shock slipped away finally, igniting a fury in his already wounded heart. Garth was the reason he had run away in the first place, why Lord Brennigan's promises had sounded so appealing. Finn wanted to be his own man, someone who made his own path and didn't live in the shadow of his brother's glory. That's what he and Lord Brennigan had in common; they both couldn't bear to be viewed as inferior or weak. And without his stone, Finn felt that tension anew. He reached up to his neck to feel for the crimson stone once more, hoping that by some chance it might appear again. His fingers met only emptiness.

"Get away from me." Finn fell back and gripped his sword tighter, the sounds of battle raging on around him. His head felt fuzzy and his vision was blurring again. He was weak and pitiful. Part of him wanted to turn to Garth and mend what he had broken. That scared him even more.

"Finn, what happened to you?" Garth's brow furrowed in hurt, and Finn knew it was because of him.

He'd always had a knack for disappointing others, but that stone had made him feel worth something. He needed to get it back. It wasn't until he'd seen Garth that he felt the truth of his desire. He was weak without it. The stone completed him.

"I don't need you, I never have," Finn said flatly, his shoulders heavy with the weight of his words and the brokenness in his heart. If he just got his stone back, perhaps it would numb the guilt nagging his brain.

But Lord Brennigan wouldn't give it to him, he knew that much. He'd have to take matters into his own hands.

And before he knew what he was doing, he charged for his brother, sword raised. Just to prove he was worth something after all. Finn brought his sword down, and Garth met it with his own blade. They parried across the battlefield, brother against brother.

"Why are you doing this?" Garth frowned as he blocked Finn's attack.

"Because I need you to see that I'm more than just your little brother." Finn pressed forwards.

"What are you talking about? You'll always be my little brother, Finn." Garth brought his sword down hard on top of Finn's.

"But don't you see? I've hated living in your shadow! For once I want you to recognize me for who I am, not another bystander to your accomplishments." Finn countered Garth's attack and dislodged the sword from his hand. In the process, he sent a nasty cut along Garth's cheek.

Finn pressed on and raised his sword to strike, but something held him back. He couldn't do it.

In his moment of hesitation, Garth retrieved his sword and started pushing back, forcing Finn backward pace by pace, his eyes welling with intense pain that didn't seem to have anything to do with the blood dripping from his face.

⸙ ⸙ ⸙

Rylla broke away from her Earth-spells to check on Finn and see if he needed coverage. Where had he gone? She spotted him partway across the battlefield, locked in a duel with…Garth? Her heart broke at the sight of her brothers, but there was nothing she could do about it now. She had a battle to win; she had to trust that they would work it out in the end.

"I'll hurt them both if they end up dead because of one another," she mumbled under her breath.

In the center of the field, Uwan and Talih were working on making their mud pit larger. They'd done an impressive job and many shadow beasts were falling victim to it. Rylla scanned the field, her heart lifting. The number of beasts were finally decreasing hope was finally on their side. The birds above kept fighting as the true animals on the ground kept charging and tearing at the shadow beasts. Never had she seen so many four-footed creatures engaged in battle. Grievon's army was still holding up, though their numbers were significantly decreased.

"Press onwards!" Grievon yelled as his army advanced closer to where Lord Brennigan was stationed. But Lord Brennigan was unfazed. He simply mumbled a few words and he held fast to the stones as a giant beam of shadow, a pit so devoid of any light, poured forth from the Bloodstone on his crown. It snaked forward and seemed to swallow up the men, turning them into dust and ash before everyone's eyes.

"Fall back! Fall back now!" Grievon shouted again as his soldiers tried to turn around. There were only a few hundred left as Grievon led them out of Brennigan's range. A beast hiding behind a giant mound of earth pounced as the men passed and pulled some of the soldiers off their horses. The horses reared and kicked in fear. One of them caught Grievon in the chin with a hoof and sent him tumbling to the ground.

The king was on his knees but he unsheathed his sword and tried to stand up, his chin broken and hanging at an odd angle. Even from her distance, Rylla saw his eyes grow wide as a giant shadow creature came nearer, its fangs dripping with blood. Grievon held his sword up and the beast pounced, but it was speared through its middle. Struggling with the beast on his sword, Grievon didn't see the other monster sneaking up behind him.

Rylla sent a gust of golden wind, but by the time her magic reached him, the shadow beast had already taken a nasty bite. Her wind picked up rocks and collided with the creature, snaking vines exploding from the ground around it, knocking it to the earth and trapping its body in a cyclone. A bird flew overhead and dropped a large rock on top of the beast and ended it for good.

Would Grievon live? Rylla couldn't see him clearly anymore, and there was no time to check.

"Bow to my command. Yield to my power. None can stop me!" Lord Brennigan roared to everyone on the field.

Rylla needed to get those stones away from him, and fast. But how? There were still too many shadow beasts blocking her path.

"Moo!" She spotted him running alongside a jackal as it mauled one of the hideous creatures. When he saw Rylla, he bounded over to her as quickly as he could.

"Rylla, I'm sorry I left you, but I had to do something!" He panted.

"It's you I have to thank for bringing reinforcements and for giving us a fighting chance." Rylla wanted to hug him right then and there, but there was still so much that had to be done. "Moo, how can I get to Lord Brennigan and steal his stones? He's already growing too powerful!"

"Leave it to me!" Moo ran off and seemed to disappear.

Rylla fought off more beasts with her Earth-spells, dodging their attacks and countering back with her own. But something seemed different. Rylla felt herself being lifted high into the air and riding along the currents of the wind. Was this her magic? Had she learned so much already? It felt as if the wings on her cloak had sprung forth from their seams and materialized, holding her like a breath. She was doing it; she was actually flying!

Time seemed to slow as Rylla gazed downwards—so much bloodshed and pain as the war raged on. But as she gazed toward the horizon, the sparkling, turbulent waters of the Great Blue reflected the golden rays in the sky. This was what birds saw every day? The beauty took her breath away, but the contrast of the desolation below made her heart ache.

She had embarked on this journey unexperienced and afraid, never having tasted freedom but desiring it with all her might. And way up here in the sky, she felt that perhaps anything was possible. The fears and the shadows didn't appear so large in the presence of the sun.

As she lifted her gaze upwards, she finally noticed a large barred owl with a silver eye was staring down at her, huge wings pounding the air. She shifted her position and felt the talons at her shoulders. Of course, she was being carried. Disappointment lingered briefly, but it was replaced with hope. Even though this wasn't her magic, she knew her time would come—she'd fly on her own someday.

She looked to her left and to her right and noticed that other birds had picked up Garth and Finn as well. Perhaps Moo thought she needed reinforcements, and he wasn't wrong. Caz, Jovin, and Elowen were fighting on the rocks not too far away from Lord Brennigan himself, glancing upwards. Relief surged in her middle to see them all still alive.

Lord Brennigan was too focused on annihilating Grievon's army and the Earth-Treaders to look up. He didn't see when the birds dropped Rylla and her brothers on the rocks next to him since his vision was so ensnared by the stone's power. But the beasts guarding him saw, and they alerted him of their presence with a low growl.

The shadow beam ceased its destructive hunger and pulled back, swirling on the face of the Bloodstone. Lord Brennigan turned to see his new company, a wicked smile splayed across his face. Despite all the losses his army was taking, the beasts kept replenishing, proving that he was still the stronger. And they were circling in on Rylla and her brothers. Caz and the others fought their way closer, making their small group even larger. But would they be enough?

"Ah, it appears I have some guests." Lord Brennigan dismounted from his beast and gave it a slap on the rump. "Take the rest of the pack with you to the battlefield to finish off the others, these ones are mine." Lord Brennigan stepped closer to the group, his back toward the ocean. "Now let's see, seven against one—I'm afraid you'll need more men."

Rylla swallowed. He'd sent his beasts away? He had no protection now save for his sword. Surely his pride would be his downfall.

Before Rylla knew what was happening, Finn left her side and fell to his knees in front of Lord Brennigan. "My lord, please take me back. Give me my stone, I beseech you," he begged, hands pressed to his temples. His voice shook, hesitancy clouding each word.

What was her brother doing? He couldn't really mean it, could he?

"Oh get up." Lord Brennigan kicked Finn aside as he circled around the group, gaining higher ground. "You were never a threat, Gryfinn, and you'll always prove the imbecile you are. Surely you already know that." Lord Brennigan cackled, his slow movements drawing Rylla and the others away from the battle.

"Please, my lord, please…" Finn crawled forward and begged once more. Rylla couldn't help but see how similar her brother's actions were to

Uwan with the Obsidian. But Uwan had recovered—though his stone wasn't controlled by the Bloodstone like Finn's, at least not yet.

"You disappoint me. You were nothing when I found you and you're nothing to me now." Lord Brennigan kept moving until his back was toward the ocean again, giving him a vantage point to see the whole battle, and forcing Rylla to face away from any potential surprise attacks. "When I'm through with all of you, that villainous aviary won't be able to tell the difference between their food and your ashes." He sneered.

"You won't win, Brennigan," another voice joined their group, but this one much older and frailer.

Rylla turned around to see Talih floating on a cloud, moisture dripping from her ankles as she hovered above the ground. "You haven't won these past five-hundred years, not even when you killed our brother."

"Talih?" Lord Brennigan's smile faded and his skin went even paler. His face had a look of horror. "How are you here? An…an Earth-Treader?" His eyes were wide and filled with shock as he watched Talih hovering on the wind.

In that moment, Finn lurched up, sword in his hand, and he cut the stones loose from around Lord Brennigan's neck. The power was now in Finn's grasp, and he fell back, eyes wide beneath the rush of it.

"What have you done?" Lord Brennigan turned from Talih to Finn and gave a deafening cry, unsheathing his sword and preparing to thrust it into Finn's heart. But before he had the chance, both Talih and Rylla were there with their Earth-spells. Vines and wind and stone stopped the blade from going any further.

Lord Brennigan gave another exasperated cry. "You should be dead!" he yelled to his sister.

"And so should you, along with that stone of yours. Brennigan, it's time to end this!" Talih replied.

A fleeting glimpse of remorse crossed Lord Brennigan's features, but it was replaced with bitter malice so quickly Rylla wasn't sure she'd seen it at all. "You're right, it's time to end this." He began to utter the dark words of the Bloodstone as he placed his hand over the stone on his crown.

"Steady your swords, prepare for anything!" Caz shouted as he, Jovin, Gorvo, and Garth held their weapons in front of them. Rylla and Talih had their own magic ready while Elowen was close by with her bow, already letting loose an arrow.

The arrow lodged itself into Lord Brennigan's side. He hollered in more intense anger as a beam of Darkness poured out of the Bloodstone, eating up any life it touched.

"No!" Elowen screamed as the Darkness singed her shirt, but Talih was there with her magic, countering the Darkness by bending its beam into the wind and dousing it in water.

Still, Lord Brennigan pressed on. Caz, Jovin, and Garth tried to attack him, but the power of his stone formed an impenetrable shield around him.

Rylla watched as Talih fought off the dark magic, and then her eyes went to Finn. He was caressing the stones, his eyes wide and hungry for power. She needed to get them away from him. She needed to defeat Lord Brennigan.

"Finn, toss me the stones!" Rylla cried out amongst the chaos. There were only three, would it even work? She had to try even though Talih said it was impossible.

Finn looked up, eyes cold. Her heart sank. He was holding onto them, and it would take something a lot stronger than words to make him let go.

"Don't do this Finn!" It was no use.

Lord Brennigan kept pursuing the others with his dark magic, the Bloodstone eating up everything in its path that Talih wasn't able to protect, though its power seemed to be fading. This desecration of the earth and of anything living provided a clear and untouched path to Finn. Lord Brennigan approached him, sword raised and ready.

"Give me my stones," Lord Brennigan commanded. "Their power is too great for the likes of you. Join me, Gryfinn, and you can command my armies for generations to come. But you must give me the stones," he challenged, traces of half-truths in every word.

"No! You don't deserve them like I do. They're mine!" Finn yelled back, a crazed look in his eyes.

Lord Brennigan bared his teeth and raised his sword higher to strike, but before it could reach its mark, Garth jumped in front of his brother, taking the sword to his own stomach.

"No!" Rylla screamed, her heart stopping.

Garth fell backwards into Finn, knocking the stones from his brother's grasp. Lord Brennigan cursed in fiery anger.

Something seemed to break in Finn's stony expression. His eyes widened in disbelief and he clung to Garth's fallen body lying on top of him.

"Brother?" Tears streamed down Finn's face at the blood gushing from his brother's wound. "Why would you do something like this?" He held Garth steady, making sure not to move him for fear of causing more pain.

"It's…always been you…who I looked up to…" Garth spoke as he slumped lower to the ground.

Finn continued to hold him and tried to staunch the blood flow as best he could.

"I'm sorry…I…We'll get help, just hold on," Finn sobbed, the stones lying by his side untouched.

Caz snatched the stones from the ground and tossed them to Rylla before Lord Brennigan had a chance to get them himself.

Her heart broke over her brothers; she needed to know if Garth would be okay. But first, she had to try and end this once and for all, before Lord Brennigan caused more ruin. How much damage could three stones do? She hoped it would be enough.

She caught the stones and felt their power course through her like an old friend: the protection of the Hawk's Eye, the wisdom of the Obsidian, the courage of the Howlite, and strangely enough, the purity of Aylati's Jade. An aroma of peace seemed to waft on the air, as if it was drifting in from the ocean. As she glimpsed the raging waters behind Lord Brennigan, she thought she saw a glimmer of green, gold and blue.

It'sssssssss time. The words came from the sea as they echoed in her head, but she knew they were not her own. *I am here to pay back what I owe…* The voice was familiar and slithering, encouraging her to make her final move.

From out of the depths, a shiny object was flung high into the air, too far away to be discerned. But then it was caught up in the talons of the Great Owl circling above the shimmering waters. The bird now carried it over to the cliffs. Before Rylla knew what was happening, the Larimar dropped into her hands.

You mussssssst act now. The voice was nearer. Eager.

Rylla knew what she had to do:

You fight with shadows
I fight with gold
The Darkness you wield
Is all but foretold
To live and reign
No longer with you
But to disappear for good
In the depths of the Blue

The power of the stones enveloped Rylla like a burning, hot inferno, entrapping her body in a cage of sun as she radiated brilliant golden light from head to toe. Her locket gleamed, hot to the touch, and buzzed with magic. She could feel everything: protection, courage, wisdom, purity, and peace, as if she were the embodiment of them herself. What was happening? Was it working?

The rays were so bright and blinding, Lord Brennigan had to cover his eyes as he dropped his sword and stumbled backwards. A beam of golden light shot forth from Rylla and pushed Lord Brennigan closer to the edge of the cliff. He groveled on his hands and knees, clinging to cracks in the stones by his fingernails.

"Stop this madness, I beg of you!" he cried and tried to harness the black magic within his own stone, but it proved futile. Instead, the Bloodstone was cracking under the intense pressure of the light, the shadows escaping through the cracks and burning up instantly. "Please!" He was nearly weeping. Something in his voice sounded too much like Finn.

At the sound of his “please” Rylla let her guard down slightly. The wave of intense light retreated and hovered before him, waiting. In that space, Lord Brennigan struggled to stand, his skin sagging, revealing aged bones and ashy blood.

“I know you couldn’t do it, you’re too weak.” Lord Brennigan spat, and reached up to touch the Bloodstone.

Something green and gold burst forth from the sea, towering above him.

The Balagrix! Rylla smiled in spite of herself for the monster had been true to its word.

Lord Brennigan only looked up a moment to see what had covered him in shadow as Rylla sent forth the golden beam of light once more. It exploded against his body, pushing him closer to the edge and therefore closer to the Balagrix.

Lord Brennigan fixed his gaze back on Rylla, eyes wide in horror as the golden light splintered the Bloodstone on his crown, eventually choking out the shadows and disintegrating it altogether. Gone.

Thissssss onessss mine! The Balagrix hissed in delight.

The hungry sea-serpent descended upon him, her giant mouth open as she plucked Lord Brennigan’s withering and horror-struck body from the earth, swallowing him whole. The light from the stones, an array of brilliant hues all mingled together, formed a display of color and warmth unlike anything Rylla had ever seen.

The gathering shadows had been driven back by the golden light and the sounds of battle ceased behind them. When Rylla turned around, both the live shadow beasts and the dead had disappeared.

She glanced over at Talih. The old woman hovered on her cloud, a wistful smile lifting her lips, one filled with relief and peace as her body too began to dissipate in the wind.

"Thank you. At last, I am free." Her words became a whisper in the breeze.

The sky shone with radiant orange, red, blue, and gold, reflecting off the power still glowing from Rylla. And then a crack and an eruption of light like falling stars and raining gold descended upon the earth like gentle snow.

As quickly as it had begun, the power of the stones faded like a warm ember in a hearth. And as the light fell upon the earth so did Rylla, her knees crumbling beneath her.

Warm arms wrapped around her form, and she could hear people calling her name, but it felt like a hazy daydream, and she wasn't quite ready to wake up.

Chapter the Thirty-Fourth

Back to the Beginning

Rylla woke slowly to the motion of gentle swaying. She opened her heavy eyes and found herself sitting atop a horse with someone sitting behind her. This was her first time on horseback and her body felt both numb and exhausted; she was only too glad not to have to walk.

Rylla looked up over her shoulder and saw what looked to be Caz's chin. His strong arms around her kept her upright as he held onto the reins. She leaned closer to his chest, her head feeling as heavy as bricks. Prickling pain tingled through her with each movement, her hands burned, and a feverish headache pounded against her temples. She fell back into a fitful sleep once more.

Sometime later, maybe even days, she woke again, groaning in pain. She sat up in the saddle, gasping as Caz gently wrapped his arm around her and brought her close to his chest once more. He began rubbing her arm with his hand in gentle circles.

"You're okay. It's all over, Rylla. You did it. Try to get some sleep. We're almost there."

She thought she heard voices. Who else was with them? She remembered her brothers. Was Garth okay? What happened to Finn? Moo? There were so many people and so many questions, but nothing was making sense and her head felt like it was in a blazing oven.

When Rylla opened her eyes again, her head was far less foggy and the pain less intense. As she looked forward, she could see mountains coming into view. But not just any mountains, the Eastern Ridges. And if she squinted hard enough, she could see Mount Egret standing tall in the distance. Her mountain. She was going home.

There was so much to say, so much to talk about, but Rylla was too tired to speak. Her mouth felt parched and dry as though she had swallowed the sun. She peered around, but no one was in sight. Whose voices had she heard earlier? Perhaps she had been delirious and simply imagined them.

Another wave of exhaustion and dizziness hit Rylla again and she was soon dreaming of stones and sinister smiles from Lord Brennigan.

Rylla stretched and found herself lying flat, a pillow beneath her head and a warm blanket pulled up to her shoulders. She was clean, her curly hair slightly damp and smelling of mint. When she looked up, she found she was staring at a wood-paneled ceiling, the scent of lemons and springtime in the air. She tilted her head. In the corner she noticed the hearth and the kitchen. She looked to her left and spotted a ladder leading into a loft and a door leading to a basement. The scent of ink and dusty book pages wafted up from the doorway.

This was home. She was home at last. And she was sleeping on her family's cot in their living room. A slow smile crept onto her face. But where was everyone?

Rylla sat up slowly, pain coursing through her entire body. She winced when she put pressure on her hands. She turned them over to see deep burns scarring her skin. It reminded her of Garth's scar from his Sunstone. Speaking of Garth…

"Ma, Da?" Rylla tried her voice for the first time in what felt like weeks. "Caz? Where is everyone?"

The back door of the cottage was pushed open and her mother ran in, as beautiful and loving as she remembered. Her eyes glimmered with tears and a look of love unmatched by anything Rylla had ever seen. Her mother quickly moved to sit next to Rylla on the cot and she gently stroked her daughter's head.

"Oh, my Sweet, you're awake!" Rylla's mother blinked rapidly. "I've been so worried. I had no idea where you were." She gently stroked Rylla's cheek, wiping the stray tears. "Anders, quick! Rylla's awake!"

Next came her father, clunking up the stairs with his cane. He stopped in the doorway and smiled. "Blessed be. We thought the worst had happened. I thought I'd lost my little girl. Not only once, but when you returned, we weren't sure if you'd ever wake up again. You've been asleep for a couple of days." Rylla's father hurried over to the cot and sat on a nearby armchair.

He reached over to grab hold of her hand but stopped himself in time and instead stroked her head and brushed a loose curl behind her ear, tears in his eyes. "We searched for you everywhere, and when days led to weeks, we…" He ran a hand over his face, sighing deeply in obvious relief. "We can't tell you how happy and thankful we are to have you home again. We missed you so much."

"I'm sorry…so sorry. I never meant to cause you pain. I feared you'd both be heartbroken if I ever left, especially with Garth and Finn having disappeared…I wanted to come home and tell you, but I couldn't," Rylla croaked, her voice still raspy and dry as tears formed in her eyes.

"Oh, my Sweet. Their leaving was never your burden to carry, we don't blame you for anything. You know that, don't you?" her mother said, the look of understanding in her eyes a balm to Rylla's heart.

"I do now." Rylla smiled. But there was still so much to tell, and so much she needed to find out. "I don't even know where to begin with this whole thing."

"We know, and you don't have to," her father chimed in.

"Wait, you know?" Rylla was shocked they didn't have more questions.

"Yes, don't worry. Your friend explained everything to us," her father responded, his lips pulling into a knowing smile. "He suggested you'd be willing to share your side of the story when you were ready, but we're in no rush."

Her friend? Had that been Caz?

"But what about Garth? And Finn?" Rylla tried to get out of the cot, eager to know what happened to her brothers.

"Shhh, it's okay." Her mother steadied her gently, pushing her back on the cot. "You'll be happy to know that Garth is going to be okay and Finn is with him, helping to take care of his family. Your father and I plan to visit once you've sufficiently recovered. It's so relieving to know where they are after all these years. It does a mother's heart good."

The look of assurance in her parents' eyes was enough to make Rylla feel as though she was floating in a pool of relief. Her mission would have been worth it just for the smile on her mother's face.

"What about the others? Elowen? Jovin?" Did she dare mention Caz? For some reason the idea of speaking his name aloud to her parents sent a flurry of butterflies in her middle.

"Elowen is back with her sister. As for Jovin, I believe he's with your friend. Something about upholding their end of a bargain or something like that." At the mention of "your friend," Rylla's father gave another knowing smile, this time accompanied by a subtle wink. How much did they know? Her stomach somersaulted.

"Everyone's gone?" Rylla's eagerness sank a little.

"Not everyone." This time her mother winked as she stood up and went to the front door. She gave a high whistle and in a matter of minutes a black and white cat came running into the house.

"Moo! You're here!" Rylla's heart leapt as he jumped onto her cot and ran into her arms. Even though Rylla knew Moo didn't like being touched much, she was sure he didn't care about that now.

"Of course! I ran along Rembrandt's side the entire journey here. I never left." Moo sat beside her and began to lick his fur.

"But you hate horses! And the entire journey?" Rylla asked, then heat flushed to her cheeks and she looked up at her parents.

They exchanged a glance, knowing smiles on their faces.

"We always knew there was something special about you, Rylla. With or without your magic, we knew you'd find your wings. We'll leave you two to catch up. Dinner will be within the hour," her mother said sweetly and nudged her father to follow her.

Moo and Rylla were left alone.

"You have nice parents, Rylla. They care a lot about you," Moo spoke. "And so does Caz."

Rylla's heart sped up at the mention of Caz. She missed him so much already and there were still so many unsaid things between them. The fact that he *had* come to find her after all, and the way he comforted her on their journey here...surely it meant something. But where had he gone? When would he be back?

"Have you seen your grandfather yet?" Rylla asked, trying to distract her thoughts.

"I have, and I told him everything. Apparently, he wasn't surprised to learn of a sixth stone crest; he'd heard rumors of such things from his own father hundreds of years ago, of the legend of Abbredun. I only found out about these rumors recently—it's amazing how quickly news spreads on a battlefield."

"Speaking of the stones, what happened to them?" Rylla couldn't remember anything after the Balagrix had taken Brennigan.

"With the loss of the Bloodstone, the other stones didn't have the fortitude to retain their shapes. Thus, they shattered into pieces and rained down upon the cliffs like confetti. The cliffs which were once all gray are now a contrast of brilliant colors, and the ground feels strangely sacred. If you ask me, it's better this way. If one needs counsel, one need only to consult the cliffs rather than try to harness a magic too powerful to hold in one's hand. This hopefully means less wars or potential for wars in the future."

Rylla nodded, but a nudge of confusion still pricked at the back of her mind. “But how did I defeat the Bloodstone when I only had four stones? Talih told me I needed all five.”

“And you had them. By brilliant happenstance, the Larimar was returned to you by the Balagrix, as you well remember, but little did you know that Aylati’s Jade was hidden in your locket this entire time. When the stones shattered, it broke free from its chamber. All five stones were united in the end to destroy the shadow of the corrupted stone.”

“How can this be? It never disappeared from Lord Brennigan’s frames! And all along it was around my neck?” Rylla felt for her Jaspers and realized they were missing. Maybe her necklace had shattered along with the other stones.

“Yes, you’ve carried purity of heart and truth with you this entire journey, Rylla, but I believe the stone only enhanced what you already bore so well. And I believe it was this very stone which helped you withstand temptation and to think clearly. My grandfather knew as much when he sent you off. In fact, it was he who had put the stone inside the locket in the first place, knowing the magicked frames wouldn’t be affected by the touch of a cat. He told me so himself, only moments ago.”

“Wait! You’re telling me Fang knew I had Aylati’s Jade the entire time? That he planted it on me?” Rylla sat up straighter. She couldn’t tell if she was mad or confused.

“Yes, and he was wise not to mention it. If you had known, you would have protected it more closely, or you probably would have refused to wear it at all. It’s those who hunger for the stones and what power it gives them which leads to trouble. You were unaware that its power was willingly being granted to you. And like my grandfather prompting you to bring your map to the Grove, I believe he prompted Winnie to first find the locket and then place it on the necklace she gave you before your journey. You see, my grandfather knew you wouldn't have taken the stone had he given it to you himself, so he had to figure out a natural way for you to acquire it." Moo laughed and Rylla couldn't help but smile, though her head still spun.

"But I thought you had to be an Earth-Treader to be affected by an animal's magic. If Winnie was prompted by Fang, then that must mean…"

"She has many years ahead of her, but yes, in time she should come fully into her gifting like you have with yours." Moo smiled as he cleaned behind his ears.

Rylla felt that she owed Winnie a million beautiful seashells; one simply was not enough. She vowed that one day she'd take her to the Isles so she could pick as many as she liked. Perhaps she'd even help train her one day, when she was ready.

Rylla couldn't believe that this whole time Fang had deceived her, but for a good cause. He had been looking out for her since the beginning. What other things did she not know?

"Moo, my parents said that Finn is with Garth. I half feared he'd disappear along with Talih once Lord Brennigan's stone was defeated. Did you get to see him before he left?" *Does he look as broken as when I last saw him?*

"He didn't disappear like Talih, no, but when the shadows fled, so did parts of him. Though he is still alive, I can guarantee that the Bloodstone will haunt his memory for years to come. As to that end, only time will tell."

Again with only "time will tell." Rylla didn't like hearing it, though she knew Moo spoke wisdom.

"What happened to the others?" Rylla didn't know how many Earth-Treaders survived, the status of Grievon and his men, or the state of the animals after the battle. Had they all died before she had a chance to save them? The thought made her stomach ache along with the rest of her body.

"Grievon died on the battlefield, and his men have either mourned the loss or triumphed over their newfound freedom. Though there are more relieved than there are filled with sorrow. He was not a kind leader, Rylla. His death is not your fault." Moo looked her in the eyes firmly.

"Many Earth-Treaders died, but mostly the elderly. All the young and middle-aged have gone to their homes or what remains of them. I know you feel responsible, but you gave them a chance to fight one last time before death took them anyway. You gave them a gift, Rylla, and it was their choice to protect the young with their lives so they could raise up future generations of Earth-Treaders for years to come." Moo paused to scratch his ear. "As for the animals, we received plenty of casualties ourselves, but such is the course of nature. Their time just came a little sooner than they would have liked."

"Why is it that none of this makes me feel any better?" Rylla questioned.

"Because death is never comfortable, especially when you feel the burden of it riding on your shoulders. And particularly when it occurs due to an unnecessary evil. You're not weak, Rylla. You just feel deeply. That in itself is a gift," Moo spoke with certainty.

Rylla tried to process Moo's words. Though she still felt awful, his words brought some comfort. Still, what she wouldn't give to see everyone's faces. When she was feeling better, she'd take the long journey with her parents to visit her brothers and Elowen. But that still left Jovin and Caz. When would she see either of them again? She rubbed her temples, feeling the headache return.

"Rylla, I think you should get some more rest. I'm going to have dinner with my grandfather, but I'll tell him you said hello. If you're feeling better tomorrow, maybe we can walk to the Grove together so you can see him yourself." Moo hopped down from the cot and walked over to an open window. He hopped onto the sill and turned around one last time before leaving. "You're the greatest friend I've ever had, you know that?" And he was gone.

Dinner that night was filled with stories and catching up. Rylla had found enough strength to make it to the kitchen table to eat with her parents, only getting slightly dizzy when she stood. Perhaps after another good night's rest, she really could make it to the Grove tomorrow.

Her family sat around the table eating roasted potatoes, lemon-buttered chicken, and red-currant biscuits dipped in gravy.

Rylla was about to take another bite of potatoes when she almost dropped her fork, turning to her father with anguished eyes.

"Da, I just realized—I don't have our map…my satchel and everything…" Rylla felt the loss like a pang in her chest. "We had worked so hard on it."

"Don't worry, my girl, we'll make a new one," he said warmly without a trace of blame. "Besides, I found a strange looking map in your back pocket when you arrived. Now, what's this about Abbredun?"

Pretty soon Rylla was telling her parents about Lord Brennigan and the stones, filling them in on all the missed details. After weeks of being away, finally having them beside her was like a cool balm to her weary heart; it was everything Rylla had dreamed of and more. She realized anew just how much she had missed her parents while on her perilous mission. Knowing where her brothers were was like icing on a cherry cake.

But something was missing. Deep in her heart, Rylla knew that she'd never be the same after her adventure. A new restlessness began to stir inside her. How had she so often wanted to return to the comforts and safety of home when the journey got hard? Now that she was here, as much as she loved it, there was so much of the kingdoms left to explore.

She had always longed for adventure but had never really known what it was like to actually go on one. Now that she did, it was hard to go back. And with the Darkness put to rest, she wondered what the Heather Fields and the Cliffs of Cavalcade looked like during the different seasons or if Uwan's cave looked different now that he wasn't haunted by the Obsidian. Would the Earthen-Crest kings be less cruel and had the Bloodstone's destruction brought about any positive changes for them? She wondered what new king would grace Ostglenden's throne.

But most of all, she longed for a brown-eyed boy with tanned skin and a smile as bright as the moon—whenever he chose not to be serious, that is. If he were by her side, it didn't matter where she went. But would she ever see him again?

Rylla finished her meal quietly and went to bed early. Her parents kissed her goodnight and she soon drifted off to sleep with the promise of a new day around the corner. With any luck, she would be able to get out of the house tomorrow.

⸙ ⸙ ⸙

Rylla felt the pain in her muscles and joints with every step, but her parents had allowed her to go with Moo to the Grove as long as she walked slowly and came back before lunch. If not, her father was coming after her.

But every step became easier as her muscles grew used to the motion once more. She passed Winnie's house but the little girl wasn't outside. Rylla would be sure to stop by soon when she had more time, when she could properly sit her down and tell the whole story. Rylla kept following Moo and soon entered the forest path. She walked for a while longer and paused at a familiar tree, staring curiously at the golden patch of bark, a piece missing in the middle.

"The tree you touched the night you ran away," Moo said. "It feels so long ago now, hmm?"

Long ago indeed. Rylla still had the missing piece Caz had given her tucked carefully in her pocket. She took it out and fitted it in the space, the vacant spot receiving the broken bit like an offering as it molded back into the bark. The tree shimmered in reply as if thanking her.

The two kept walking and soon entered a clearing with signs of new growth and budding plants. The trees that had been bent were now straighter and the clematis, foxgloves, and snapdragons were sprouting new heads. Patches of dead grass were growing lush and green in new places and the trees were unfurling their leaves, stretching toward the sun. A slow trickle of water was filling the streambed while meadowlarks and wrens flitted about the skies. A family of rabbits scurried away upon their arrival, but Rylla felt as though she had entered into her past, seeing the Grove as it used to be as a child.

"It's a wonder what happened to this place, is it not?" Rylla spun around at the sound of the deep voice. Fang emerged from some leafy brush, looking a little grayer but none worse for the wear. "Well done, Earthie. You have made these kingdoms proud. I knew you had it in you, you only had to find that out for yourself." He bowed his head and gave what Rylla thought was his attempt at a smile.

She couldn't help but laugh.

"Now, if you'll excuse me, my grandson and I have something to discuss. But I trust you'll enjoy the company, nonetheless. You and I will catch up soon." Fang motioned for Moo to follow him.

"Company? What other company?" Rylla questioned, but the two cats vanished into the undergrowth and left her alone.

"I was hoping to surprise you at your house, but I think here works just as well," Caz spoke as he stepped out from behind a tree. A wide grin brightened his face as he slowly walked forward. "Seeing as this is where I saw you in the first place."

"Caz!" Rylla ran into his arms, hugging him as tightly as her sore limbs would allow. It wasn't until she realized what she was doing that she took a few steps back, too embarrassed to meet his gaze. "You came back," she tried to sound nonchalant.

"Believe me, I hadn't wanted to leave in the first place. But I got here as soon as I could. I had to see you again." Caz closed the space between them again and gently placed his hand under her chin. "Will you look at me, please? I haven't seen those eyes of yours in far too long."

She lifted her head as Caz's hand moved to caress her cheek.

Rylla's heart beat wildly at the closeness between them and the warmth of his hand on her face. Looking into his honeyed eyes, it took everything in her power not to run away, or worse, hug him again.

She tried to change the subject so her thoughts had a chance to calm down. "Where's Jovin? My parents said he was with you."

"He was, but he's going to check on his uncle, and he plans to stop by and collect Elowen along the way. Between you and me, I think he's lost his head for good over that woman." Caz laughed, his eyes bright and filled with mirth.

"I think so too." Rylla couldn't help but laugh with him, but she soon grew quiet, her heart not quite sure how to feel. It seemed that Jovin and Elowen were on the road to figuring everything out between them. Could she say the same of her and Caz?

"But he's not the only one who's lost his head." Caz's mirth turned into a tone of seriousness. "Rylla, I was a complete fool. An utter idiot. I never meant for you to go to Rélynda alone. I was too ashamed of my past to believe that perhaps there could be a future with you in it. I thought that if you knew the real me, the broken and mangled parts, then maybe you'd reject me," Caz began.

"You don't give me enough credit," Rylla said quietly.

"You're right. I didn't, and I'm sorry for it. You are the bravest woman I know. You speak the truth even when it hurts and aren't afraid to do so. Your heart is as pure as the golden sun, and there's not an ounce in you that condemns others for their mistakes."

"Now you give me too high of praise, Caz." Heat rose to her cheeks, his words warming her core.

"You also don't look where you're going, you move way too fast for your own good, and you can be as stubborn as a horse. There, is that better?" One side of his mouth lifted into a teasing grin and Rylla couldn't help but laugh in return.

“Much better.” Rylla was smiling now too.

“What I need you to know, Rylla, is that I love you. I’ve loved you for a long time, it just took me a while to realize it. And I want to spend the rest of my life loving you. If you’ll have me, that is.” Caz stepped away enough to drop down onto one knee, his eyes raw and earnest. “Will you marry me?”

Rylla hadn’t thought it possible for someone to want her as badly as she wanted him in return.

The birds chirped and danced overhead as golden beams of sunlight filtered in through the canopy of trees. The air was warm and a gentle breeze tugged playfully on Rylla’s curls. Her heart was filled to bursting. Here was this man who she once thought was an enemy but was now professing his love. It didn’t feel strange though, for she knew love blossomed and bloomed in the strangest of places, some quick and some slow. And as she looked down into Caz’s loving eyes, she realized all over again how very much she loved this man in front of her.

“I’ll have you for the rest of my days, Caz,” she said softly. “I’ll gladly marry you if you’ll accept me as I am, an Earth-Treader.”

“But that’s only part of who you are. You’re so much more. Rylla, you’re a woman who isn’t afraid to face her fears and has more strength and courage than most people possess in a lifetime. You’re confident and bold even when you don’t feel it. And your cheeks…don’t even get me started about those cheeks of yours.” Caz laughed as he peered up at her, eyes full of love and longing. “Will you accept me as I am? A man whose past is filled with shadows?”

Tears stung at the corners of Rylla's eyes, her smile reflecting the same joy as his. "You're more than your shadows, Caz, and you've proven that time and time again. And I love you too." Rylla felt as light as a feather.

Caz stood and peered into her eyes with a look of deep longing, and her stomach somersaulted.

"I'd very much like to kiss you now." Caz was staring at her mouth, a smile on his lips.

"I'd very much like that." Rylla smiled in return as his mouth found hers.

And for the second time, flying didn't seem so impossible.

The End.

Acknowledgments

I had no idea how lengthy and time consuming this whole writing process would be. Even though it's often a solo venture, there are *many* people in the background who deserve a huge "Thank you!" So here's mine:

I want to first thank my brothers. For Nick, the one who read this manuscript when it was just a fledgling and provided feedback and helpful critiques. I wouldn't have made it this far without your help. And for Josh who always inquired about my progress and encouraged me along the way. Thank you to my sisters-in-law Katie and Janelle for your support as well, for reading and for listening.

For my parents, my mom being my biggest cheerleader and my dad a voice of fortitude. You both have always encouraged my dreams, and for that, I don't have enough words to express my gratitude. Thank you so much.

For Jordan Yaworski, my fellow writing buddy, thank you for all your support. I'm so excited to have had you walk alongside me on this journey and for the ability to do the same for you as you write your own novel. For my beta readers Rachael Crisanti, Tiffany Brockmann, Elisabeth Brown, Havilah Wardell, and Lora Schultz, thank you for taking the time to read this book and for your encouragement and critiques. I took a lot of your advice which truly made the book ten times better.

For Jane Maree, thank you for editing my novel and for providing excellent feedback. Working with you has been so easy and encouraging. You really made The Earth-Treader shine!

For Kirk DouPonce, thank you for making a killer cover for my book. It's beautiful and I love it! You made The Earth-Treader come alive!

For Chaim Holtjer, thank you for taking my map and turning it into something that feels like a real place. It's stunning! The other artwork is incredible as well!

For Michelle M. Bruhn, thank you for formatting my book and for being so easy to work with! You've also been super gracious in answering all of my publishing questions when I felt that Google wasn't sufficient enough. Your patience rivals that of a saint!

For my cat, Moo, the true hero, thank you for being such a good boy.

For my amazing husband Zac, my Caz, your love and support has been huge. You've seen me both determined and crazy and have somehow loved me patiently through it all. Thank you and I love you!

To my other friends and extended family who have shown interest and support, thank you as well. It means the world!

And lastly, for Jesus, the true creator of creativity and imagination. I couldn't have come up with this story without Him.

I hope you enjoyed reading this novel, I know I enjoyed writing it!

www.ingramcontent.com/pod-product-compliance
Lightning Source LLC
Chambersburg PA
CBHW071730110726
47908CB00006B/1555

* 9 7 8 1 7 3 6 1 3 7 1 1 6 *